WARNER BROS. PICTURES & LEGENDARY PICTURES

PACIFIC RIM

TALES FROM
YEAR ZERO

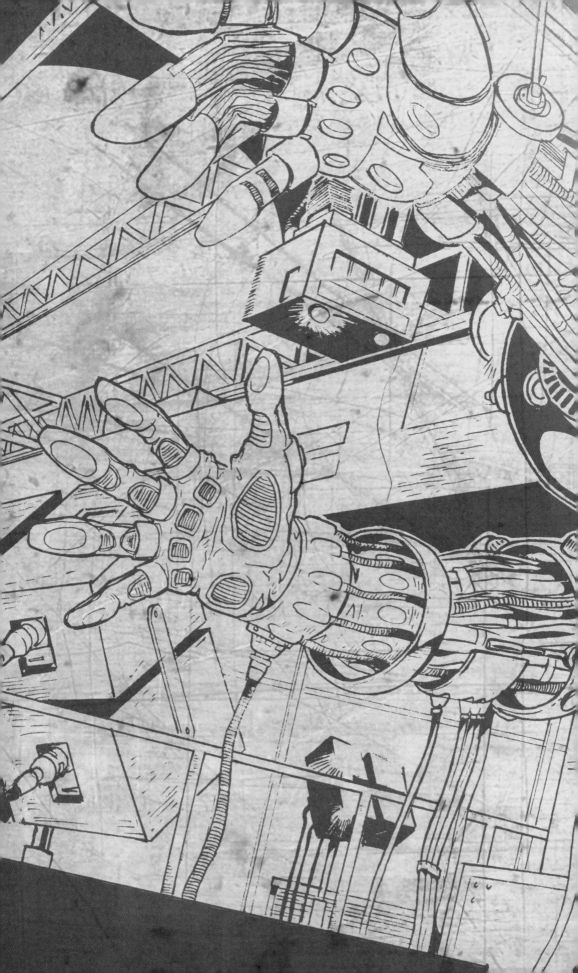

WARNER BROS. PICTURES & LEGENDARY PICTURES

PACIFIC RIM
TALES FROM
YEAR ZERO

WRITER
Travis Beacham

PENCILERS
Sean Chen
Yvel Guichet
Pericles Junior
Chris Batista
Geoff Shaw

INKERS
Mark McKenna
Steven Bird
Pericles Junior
Matt Banning

COLORISTS
Guy Major
Tom Chu
Dom Regan

LETTERER
Patrick Brosseau

PRE-PRESS & PRODUCTION
Nicolas Sienty

BOOK DESIGNER
John J. Hill

COVER ARTIST
Alex Ross

ASSISTANT EDITOR
Greg Tumbarello

EDITOR
Bob Schreck

SUPERVISING EDITOR
Guillermo del Toro

INTRODUCTION

The book in your hands is built on the notion that the world doesn't fit in its story; the story fits in its world – but we'll get to that a little later.

For my part, I came into PACIFIC RIM's world back around 2007. I was walking on the beach one foggy morning in Santa Monica, when I looked up and was struck by the shape of the pier with its empty amusement rides looming in the mist. The vista was so spooky and evocative that I couldn't help but picture a hulking mech standing in the slate-gray water behind the Ferris wheel, ready to do battle with some towering Lovecraftian thing rising from the depths. That was the germ of the idea.

For a long time, I knew that I (like any right-thinking human being) wanted to see giant robots fight giant monsters in a big, modern, summer movie, but there'd been something in the way of my making sense of it. I'd think about it now and again, jot down some notes, hit a dead end, and put it aside. Then, weeks or sometimes months later, I'd come back and do it all again.

Neither the monsters nor the mechs held me up from getting into it. I had been certifiably nuts about that stuff for the better chunk of my life. I was a fan of monsters and robots before I was anything. My earliest memory is watching a Godzilla movie. My toy trunk was full of Voltron parts and Inhumanoids. Ray Harryhausen was the first filmmaker I knew by name. From the Ymir to Gamera, from Ultraman to Big O, my imagination has always hungrily devoured any giant it came across. So I knew good and well that big, city-stomping monsters would be fun to write. I knew that rocket-punching mechs would be fun to write. That much was a given. But I just couldn't know I had any idea at all until I knew why all the parts in between would be fun to write. I had to know whose story it was.

And I should pause here to say that the very geekiest corner of my brain always has this knee-jerk urge to correct anybody who calls the Jaegers "robots" (though I'm as guilty of it as anyone). Technically, a "robot" acts on its own behalf. What I was picturing was more of a mech – an anthropomorphic vehicle with a pilot. That had always been part of what drew me to the whole sub-genre. Not just, "Oh, look at those giant things wrestling," but, "What if when an apocalyptic catastrophe struck, you could fight it – I mean really fight

it?" So if it was a mech, someone had to be driving, and there had to be some reason to care about that person that was every bit as big as the monster.

The realization that the Jaeger, in fact, needed not just one but two pilots changed everything. The whole thematic identity began to drift into focus and the story very briskly started pulling itself together. Suddenly, human beings mattered in those epic battles. Baggage mattered. Relationships mattered. Humanity quite literally drove the machines, and it was the difference between winning and losing. There was something worth fighting for. There was the threat of loss and the prospect of redemption. There was a knight in the suit of armor.

People, after all, are what makes the best mythology feel truly sprawling and alive. You'd think a bird's eye view paints the picture, but the truth is that the world tends to look smaller and toy-ish from thirty thousand feet. However, when you're on the ground, with the people, invested in their personal issues, their world feels all the bigger as a result. What all of my favorite science fiction and fantasy stories have had in common (from Star Wars to Blade Runner to Game of Thrones) is that basic character-centeric perspective, not so overly concerned with exposition that it isn't comfortable breezing past some tempting bit of texture without explaining what it means – like the "Kessel run" or "c-beams glittering in the dark near the Tannhäuser Gate." I absolutely love all those little odds and ends, because they are the frayed edges of a wider world, seductive in their brevity. It's evidence that these people did not simply pop into existence the moment you started paying attention, but have instead been around this interesting world of theirs and seen things – thereby leaving you with the impression that if you stepped through the fourth wall and peeked around the corner, you'd find that the universe kept right on going.

The prevailing impulse of the "Industry" at large is to try to explain the hell out of anything remotely intriguing, leaving no tantalizing scraps or ellipses behind. But PACIFIC RIM was fortunate enough to have a team as geekishly detail-inclined as Legendary. To that point, I will for the rest of my days remember how in one of my early meetings, Thomas Tull (head of Legendary and all around fan of awesomeness) asked if the connection between the pilots had anything to do with "quantum entanglement."...What Hollywood exec thinks of that? Well, the producer of this movie, that's who.

And Guillermo del Toro – my god, where do I even begin? To say he only lives and breathes this stuff is a glaringly insufficient understatement. There may not be anyone in the universe who loves monsters more sincerely or more deeply. It is not only his religion, but he may as well be its Pope. Beyond a bottomless enthusiasm, singular artistic vision, and impeccable eye for design, he has a rare creative knack for the details of world creation.

Because, like I said, the story is in the world; not the other way around. That is to say, a world is big and hopelessly uncontainable. It spills messily outside the edges of any one story. A world has books on its shelves and articles in its newspapers. It has ephemera and lore. It has slang and jargon. It has footnotes and obscure references to take for granted. It has a deep past and a far side. It has roads that fork away from the plot to some only hinted-at place. Just as "real world" stories set themselves on this Earth, with all her richness and complexity, the challenge of genres like science fiction and fantasy is to not only spin a good tale, but to invent for that tale an imagined backdrop that seems to stretch clear into the horizon.

Pathological haters of genre fare may derisively call it "escapism," but that's just never had the smack of truth to me. It's all wanderlust – a basic willingness to engage; the yearning for discovery. I climb a crooked set of stone stairs off a hiking trail for the exact same reason I like maps at the front of fantasy novels and sandbox-style video games. We're tantalized by the prospect of discovery. We are hardwired to explore, both inside and outside the imagination.

This was, and is, much of the lasting fun of working on PACIFIC RIM – not just inventing and falling in love with these characters or fantasizing about god-like battles between sky-scraping machines and hellish behemoths, but also imagining the world a decade of giant monster attacks would create. What that meant in practice was building volumes upon volumes of supplemental information. We all knew we probably wouldn't even use most of this narrative "dark matter" in the movie, not to any great length, but the process of creating it and our awareness of it would nevertheless inform the unseen weight of this universe. We've always known that the film was but one story in a whole world of possible stories. It opens in the twilight of a long (and mostly offscreen) war and finds a handful of people to tag along with. Essentially, we're joining history already in progress.

That's the trail this graphic novel follows back through time. It serves as a prelude, a partial history, an opportunity to delve into the world of PACIFIC RIM. As we move between the framing story (which takes place in a time gap after the movie's opening sequence) and different key points in the world's history, you'll witness some of the headline moments from ground level, you'll learn a little more about what makes some of the people in the film tick, and you'll meet a few brand new faces.

Candidly, I am proud as hell of it. It's my own first crack at a graphic novel, and I count myself surpassingly lucky to have had such an impressive and experienced team of artists working so hard to breathe life into it. So, without any further delay, I'm glad to welcome you into the world of PACIFIC RIM. And I hope very much that you feel every bit as at home in it as I do.

Travis Beacham

2/13/2013 Santa Monica, CA

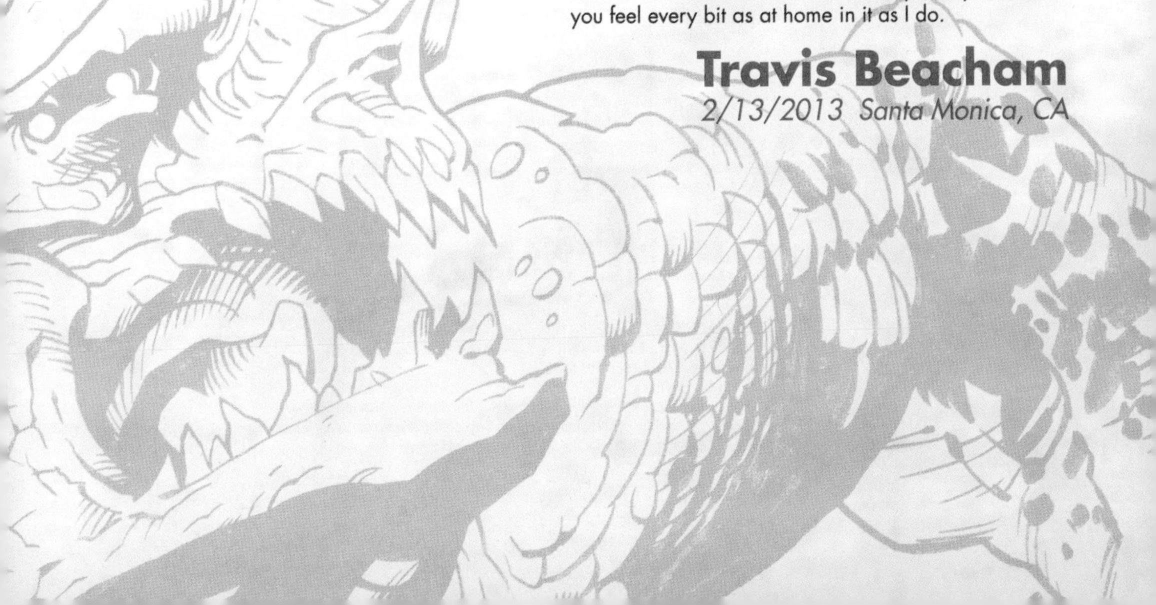

Thomas Tull - Chairman and Chief Executive Officer
Jon Jashni - President and Chief Creative Officer
Jillian Zaks - Vice President, Creative Affairs
Bob Schreck - Editor-in-Chief
Joel Chiodi - EVP, Marketing
Peter Stone - Director, Marketing
Jessica Kantor - Senior Counsel
Natalie LeVeck - Legal Counsel
Greg Tumbarello - Assistant Editor
David Sadove - Publishing Operations Coordinator
Ian Gibson - Assistant to Guillermo del Toro

LEGENDARY

Published by Legendary Comics, 4000 Warner Blvd. Bldg. 76, Burbank, CA 91522.
ISBN-10: 0-7851-5394-2, ISBN-13: 978-0-7851-5394-8. Printed in the United States.
Manufactured between 4/8/2013 & 5/20/2013 by R.R. DONNELLEY, INC., SALEM, VA, USA.
First Printing June 2013 10 9 8 7 6 5 4 3 2 1

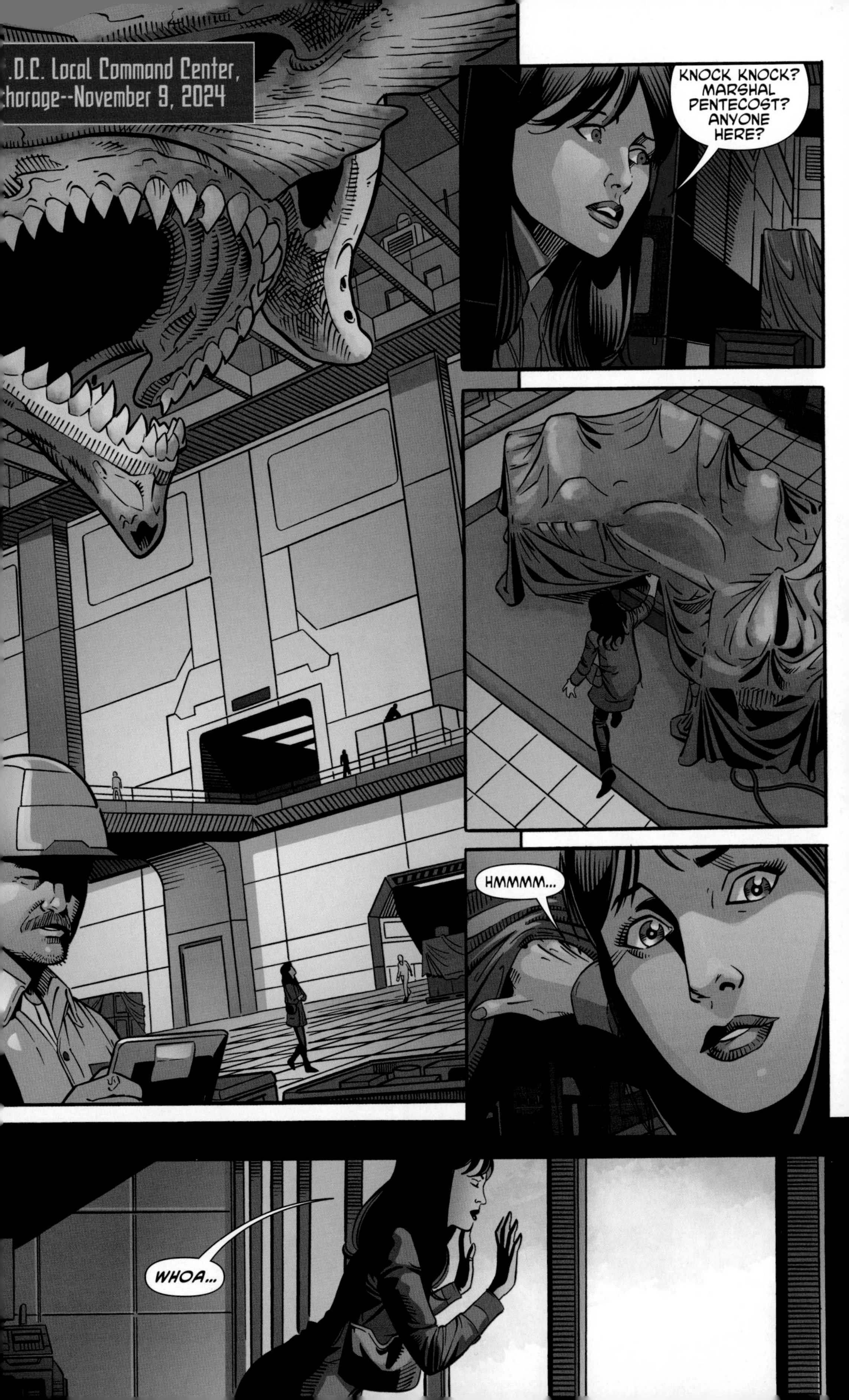
.D.C. Local Command Center,
chorage--November 9, 2024
KNOCK KNOCK? MARSHAL PENTECOST? ANYONE HERE?
HMMMM...
WHOA...

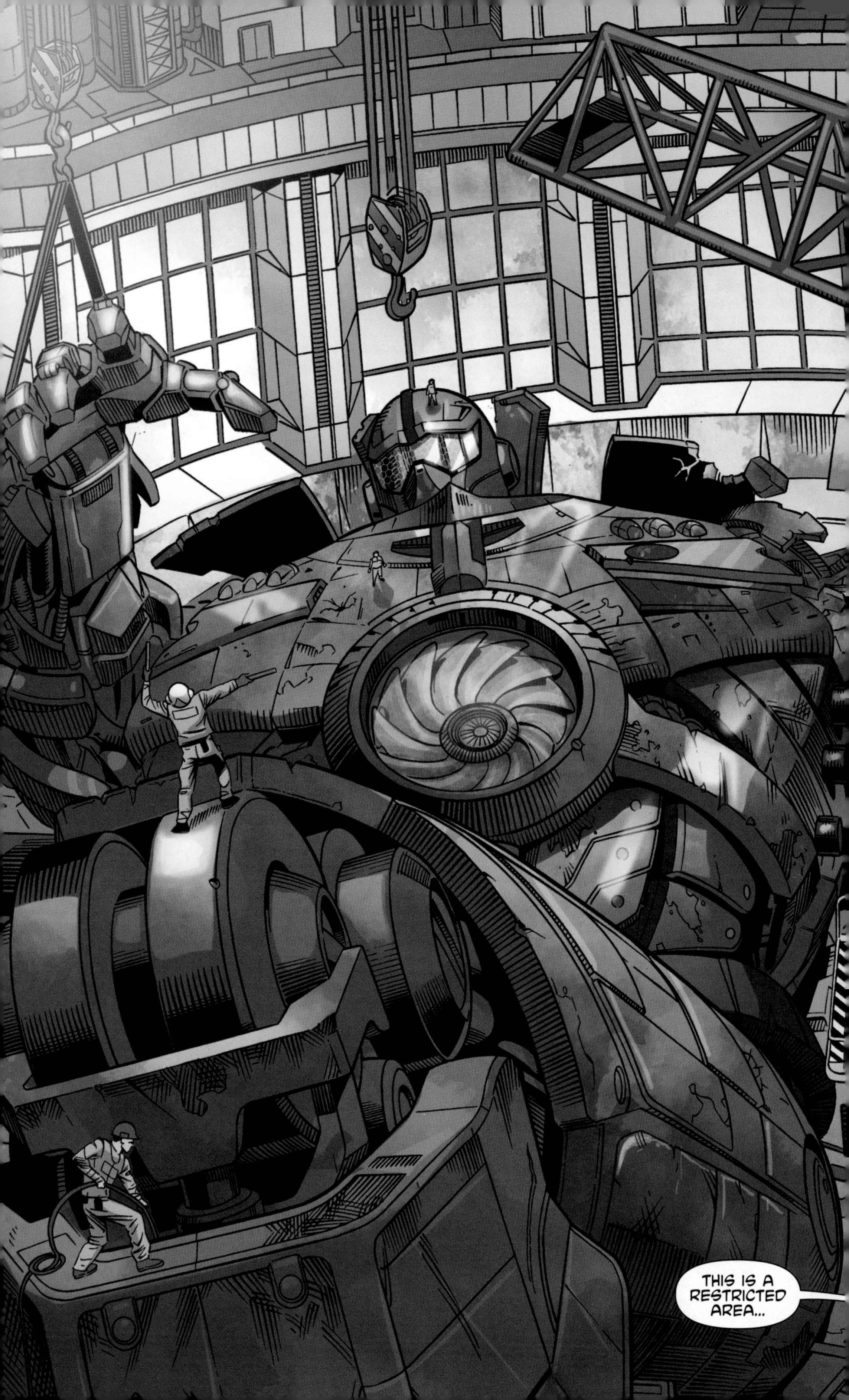
THIS IS A RESTRICTED AREA...

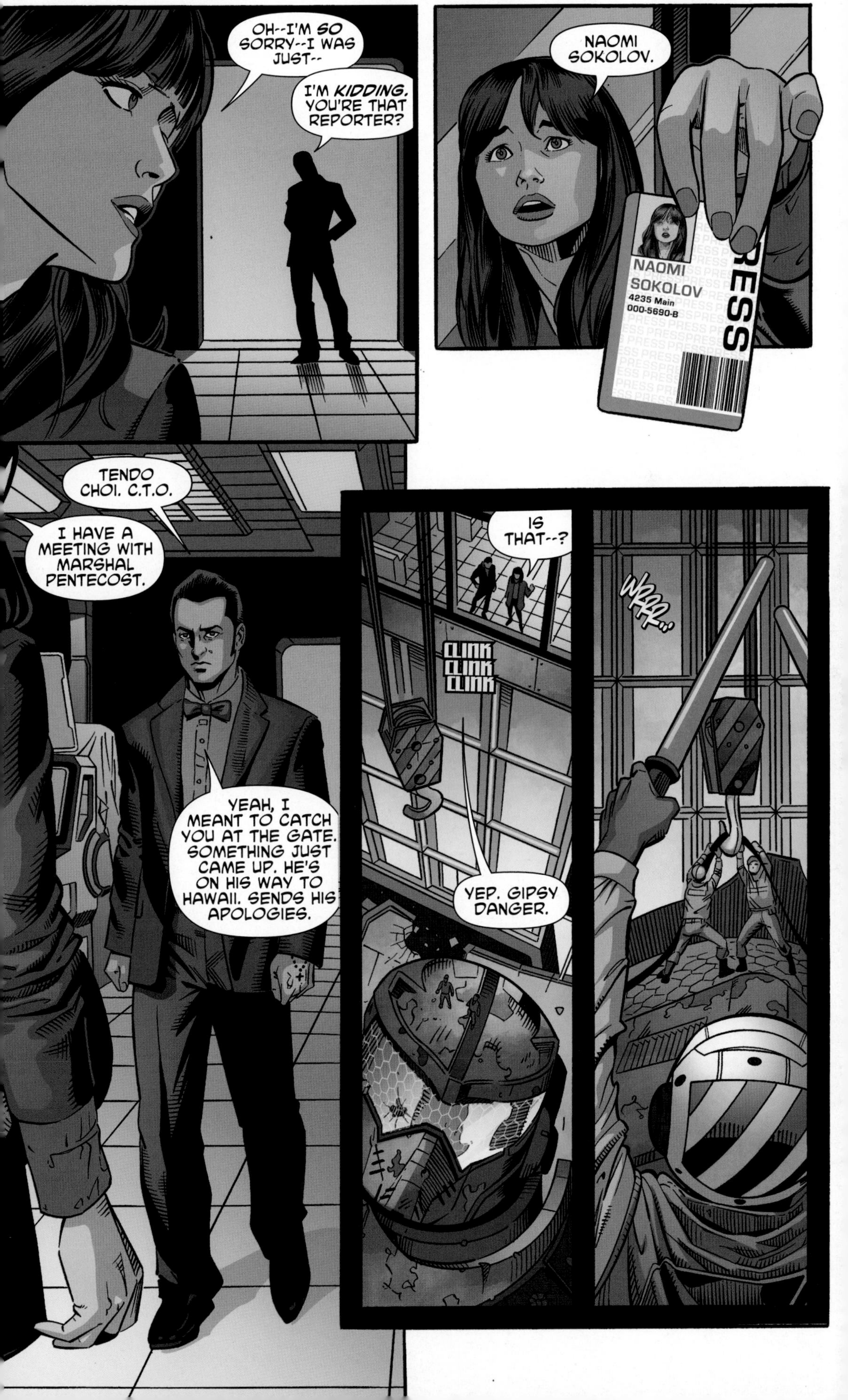
OH--I'M *SO* SORRY--I WAS JUST--
I'M *KIDDING.* YOU'RE THAT REPORTER?
NAOMI SOKOLOV.
NAOMI SOKOLOV
4235 Main
000-5690-B
PRESS
TENDO CHOI. C.T.O.
I HAVE A MEETING WITH MARSHAL PENTECOST.
YEAH, I MEANT TO CATCH YOU AT THE GATE. SOMETHING JUST CAME UP. HE'S ON HIS WAY TO HAWAII. SENDS HIS APOLOGIES.
IS THAT--?
CLINK CLINK CLINK
YEP. GIPSY DANGER.
WRRR...

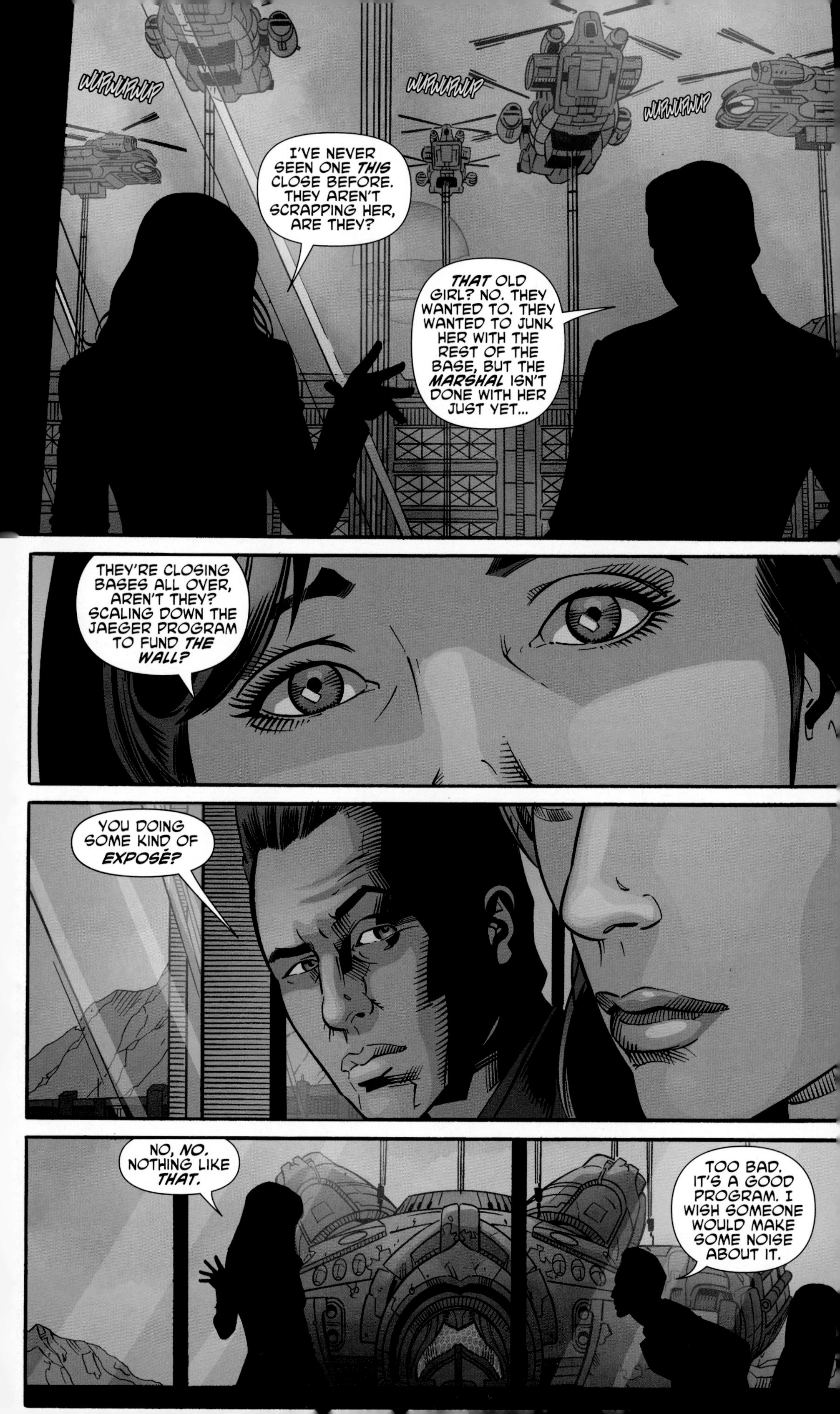
WUPWUPWUP
WUPWUPWUP
WUPWUPWUP
I'VE NEVER SEEN ONE THIS CLOSE BEFORE. THEY AREN'T SCRAPPING HER, ARE THEY?
THAT OLD GIRL? NO. THEY WANTED TO. THEY WANTED TO JUNK HER WITH THE REST OF THE BASE, BUT THE MARSHAL ISN'T DONE WITH HER JUST YET...
THEY'RE CLOSING BASES ALL OVER, AREN'T THEY? SCALING DOWN THE JAEGER PROGRAM TO FUND THE WALL?
YOU DOING SOME KIND OF EXPOSÉ?
NO, NO. NOTHING LIKE THAT.
TOO BAD. IT'S A GOOD PROGRAM. I WISH SOMEONE WOULD MAKE SOME NOISE ABOUT IT.

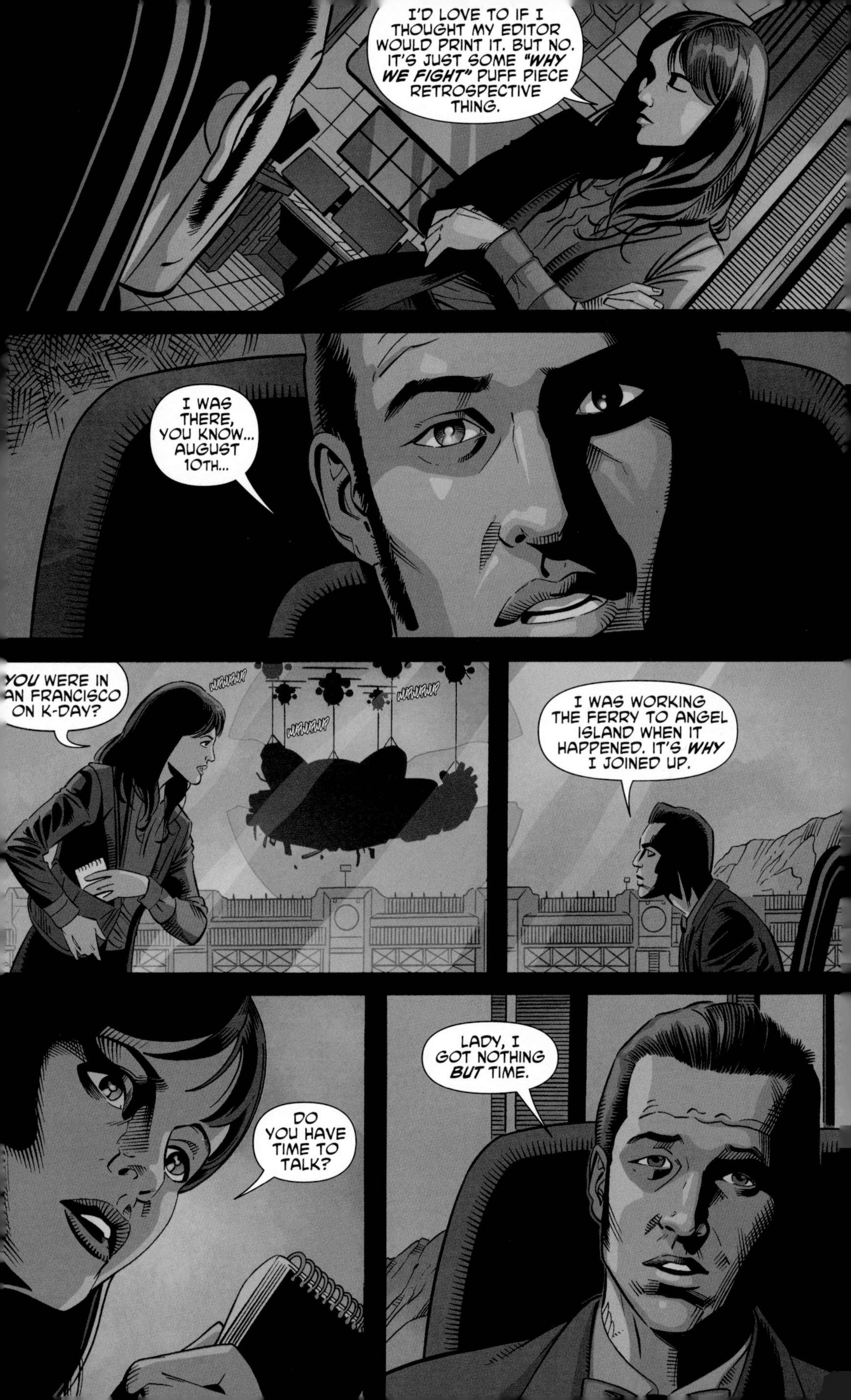
I'D LOVE TO IF I THOUGHT MY EDITOR WOULD PRINT IT. BUT NO. IT'S JUST SOME *"WHY WE FIGHT"* PUFF PIECE RETROSPECTIVE THING.
I WAS THERE, YOU KNOW... AUGUST 10TH...
YOU WERE IN SAN FRANCISCO ON K-DAY?
I WAS WORKING THE FERRY TO ANGEL ISLAND WHEN IT HAPPENED. IT'S *WHY* I JOINED UP.
DO YOU HAVE TIME TO TALK?
LADY, I GOT NOTHING *BUT* TIME.

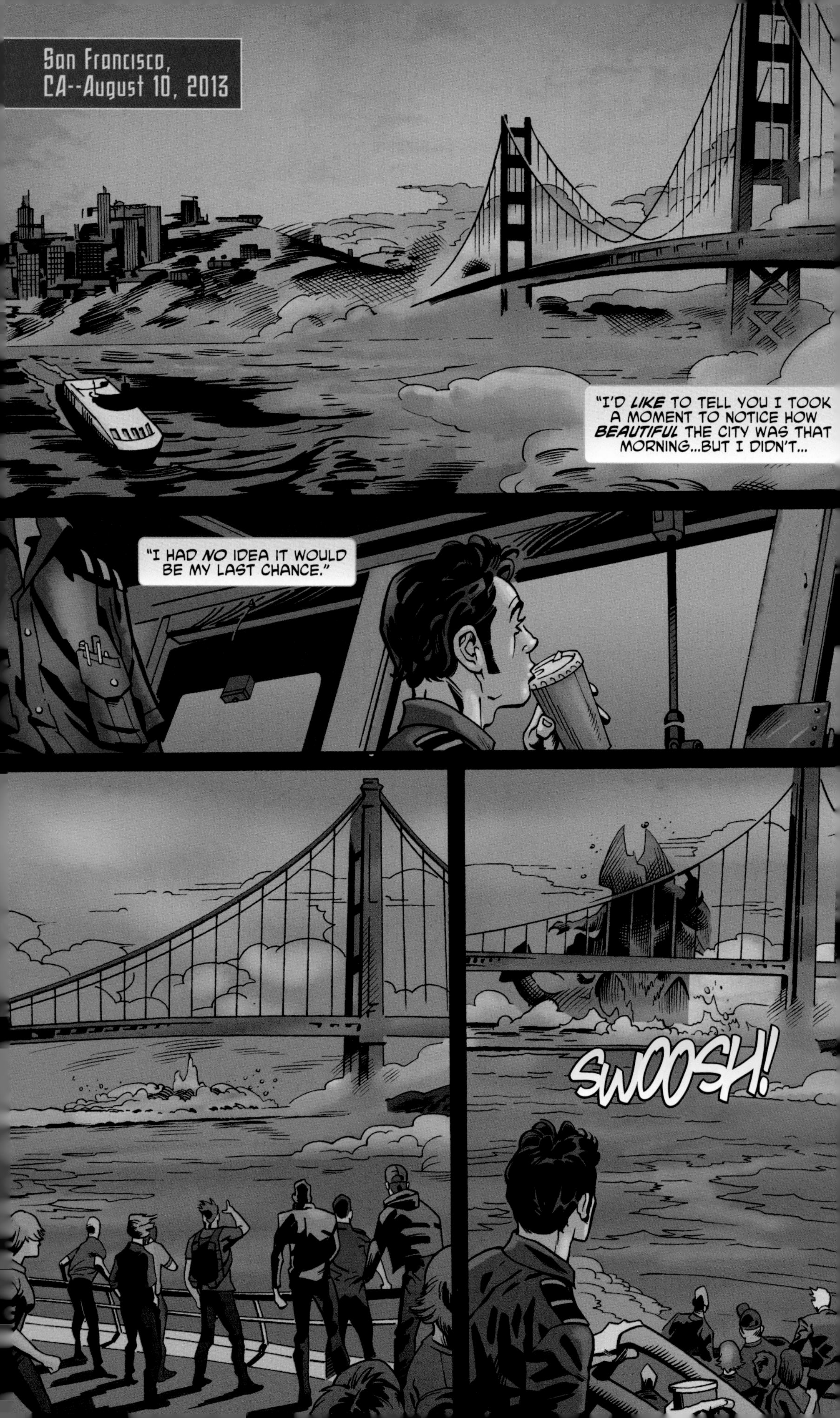
San Francisco, CA--August 10, 2013
"I'D LIKE TO TELL YOU I TOOK A MOMENT TO NOTICE HOW BEAUTIFUL THE CITY WAS THAT MORNING...BUT I DIDN'T...
"I HAD NO IDEA IT WOULD BE MY LAST CHANCE."
SWOOSH!

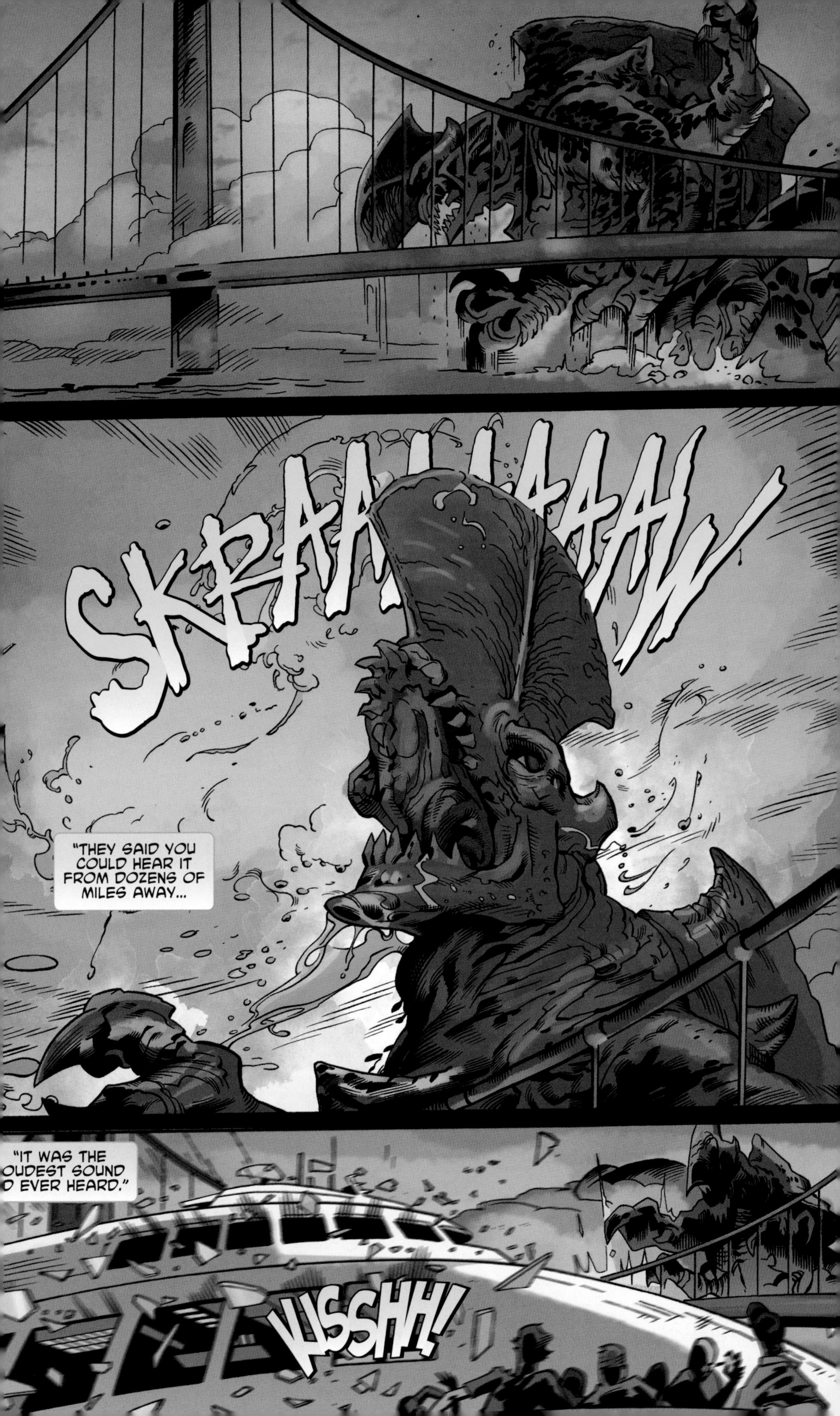
SKRAAAAAAAW
"THEY SAID YOU COULD HEAR IT FROM DOZENS OF MILES AWAY...
"IT WAS THE OUDEST SOUND D EVER HEARD."
KISSHH!

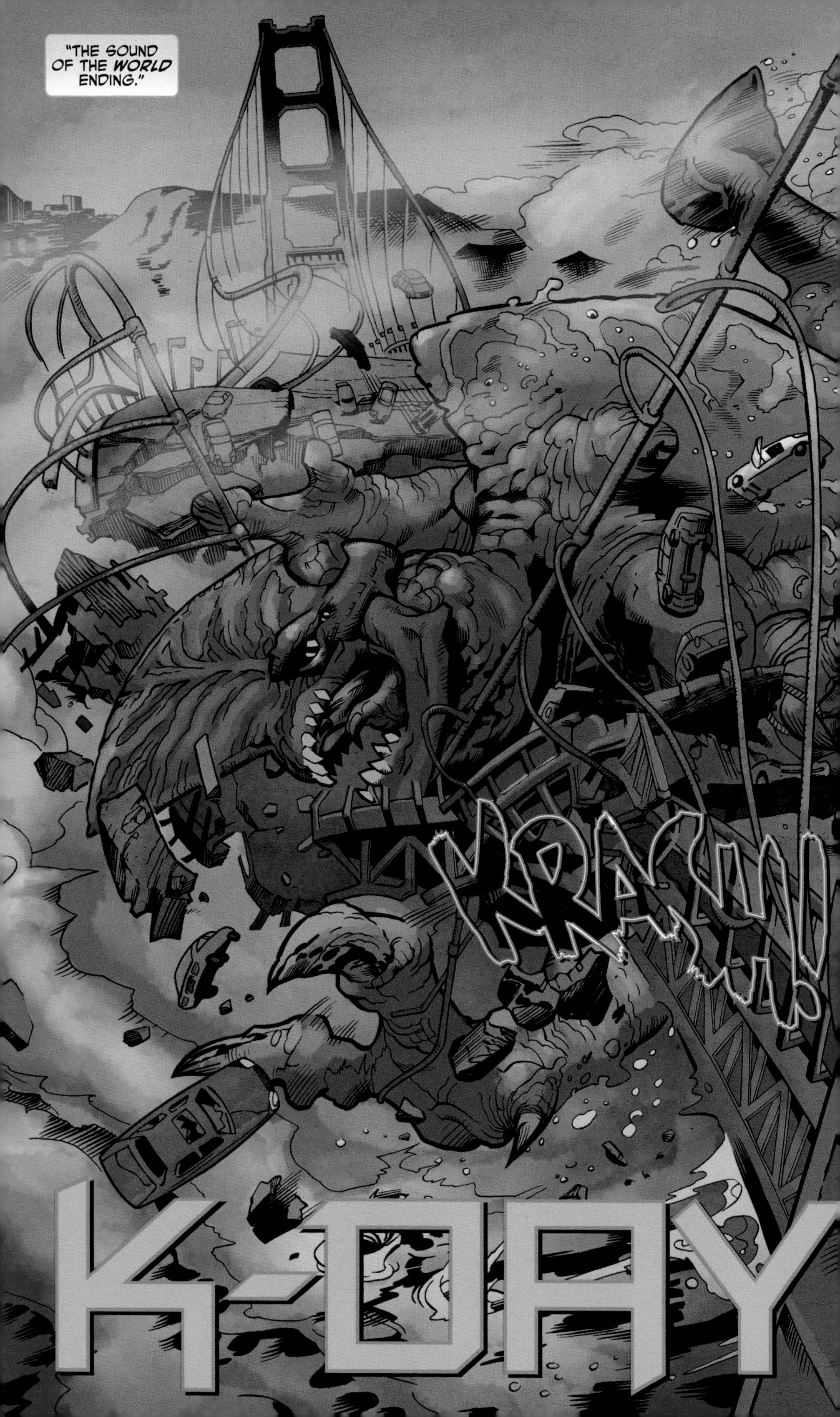
"THE SOUND OF THE WORLD ENDING."
KRAASH!!
K-DAY

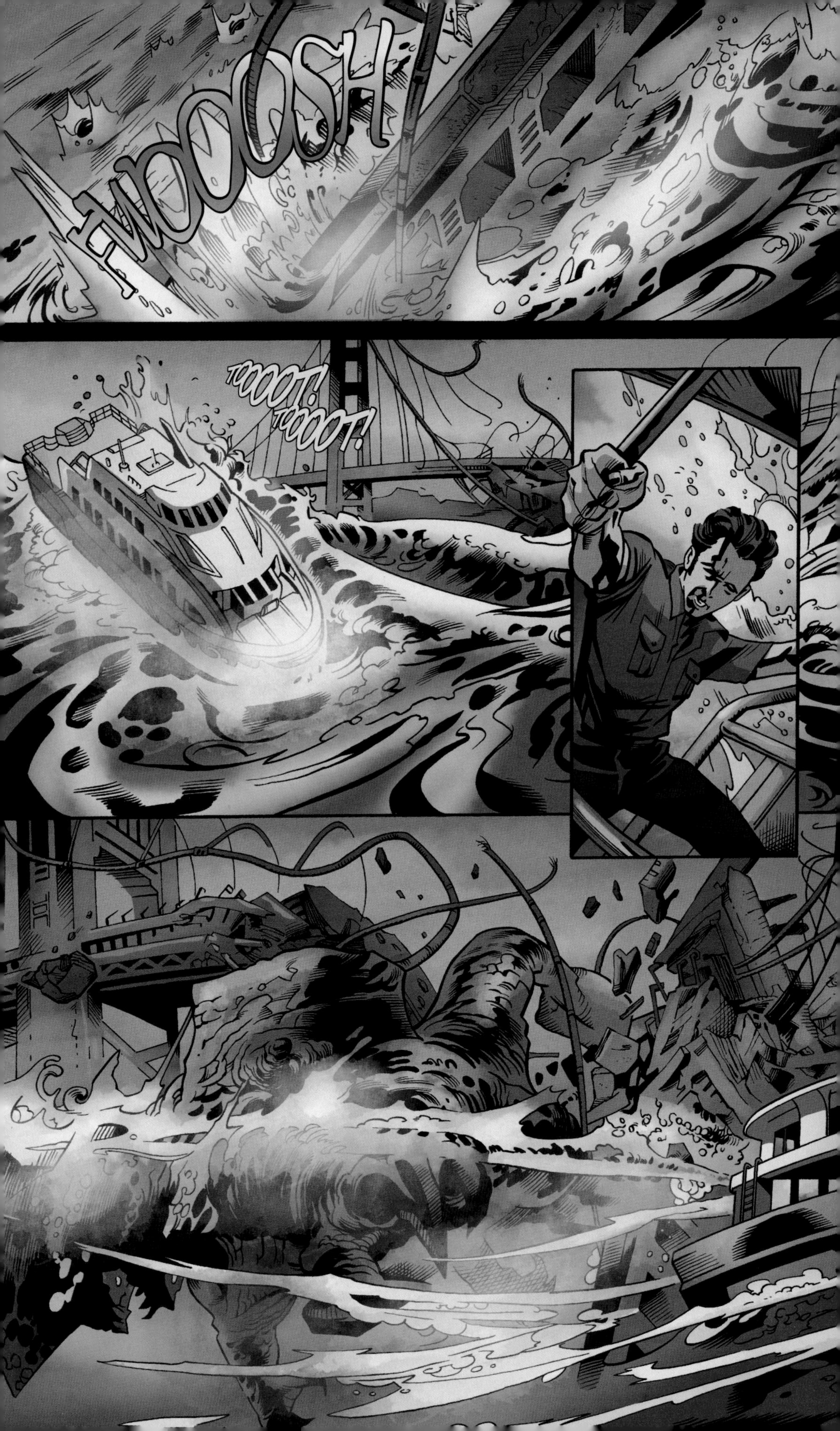
WHOOOSH
TOOOOT!
TOOOOT!

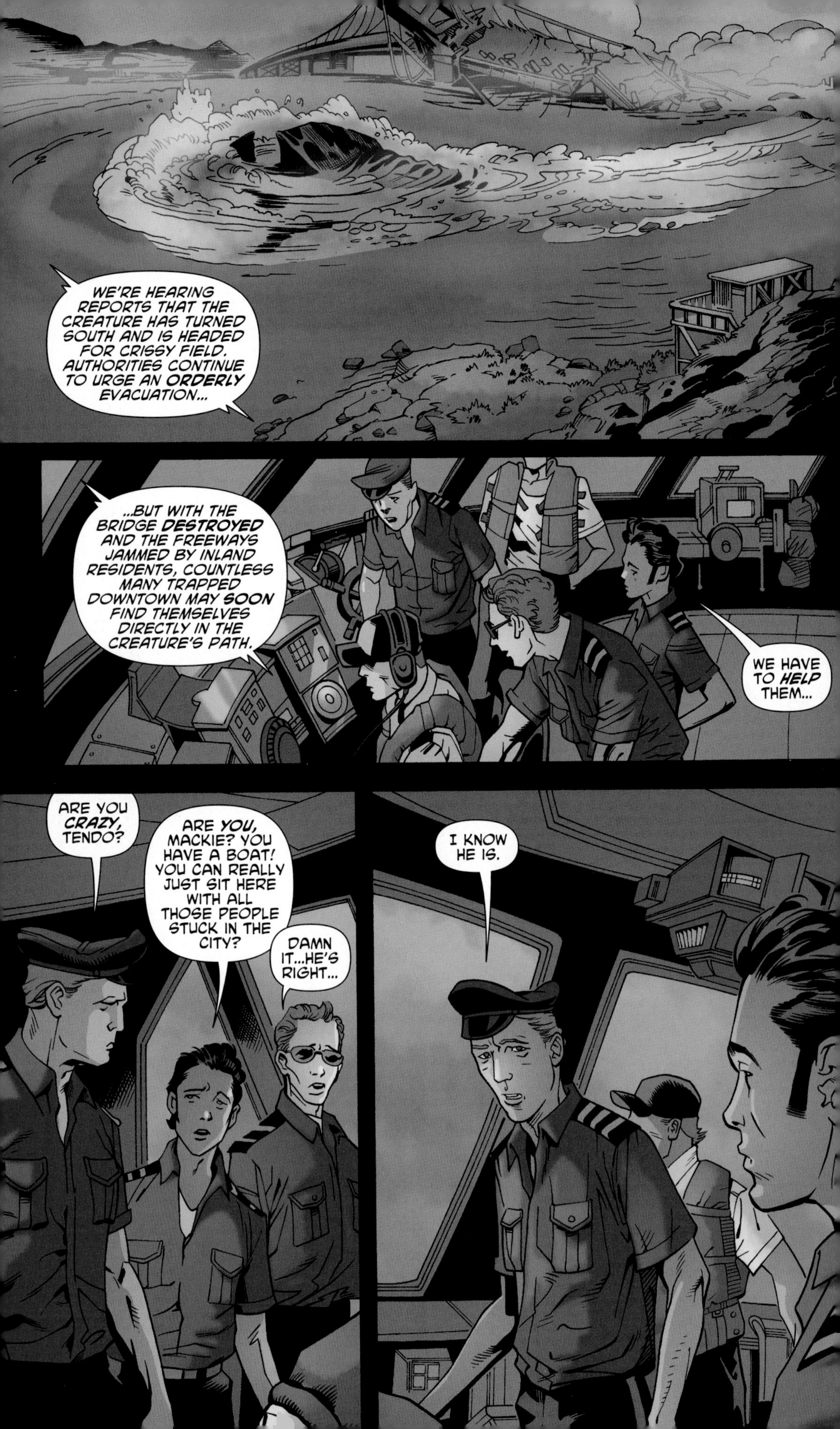
WE'RE HEARING REPORTS THAT THE CREATURE HAS TURNED SOUTH AND IS HEADED FOR CRISSY FIELD. AUTHORITIES CONTINUE TO URGE AN ORDERLY EVACUATION...
...BUT WITH THE BRIDGE DESTROYED AND THE FREEWAYS JAMMED BY INLAND RESIDENTS, COUNTLESS MANY TRAPPED DOWNTOWN MAY SOON FIND THEMSELVES DIRECTLY IN THE CREATURE'S PATH.
WE HAVE TO HELP THEM...
ARE YOU CRAZY, TENDO?
ARE YOU, MACKIE? YOU HAVE A BOAT! YOU CAN REALLY JUST SIT HERE WITH ALL THOSE PEOPLE STUCK IN THE CITY?
DAMN IT...HE'S RIGHT...
I KNOW HE IS.

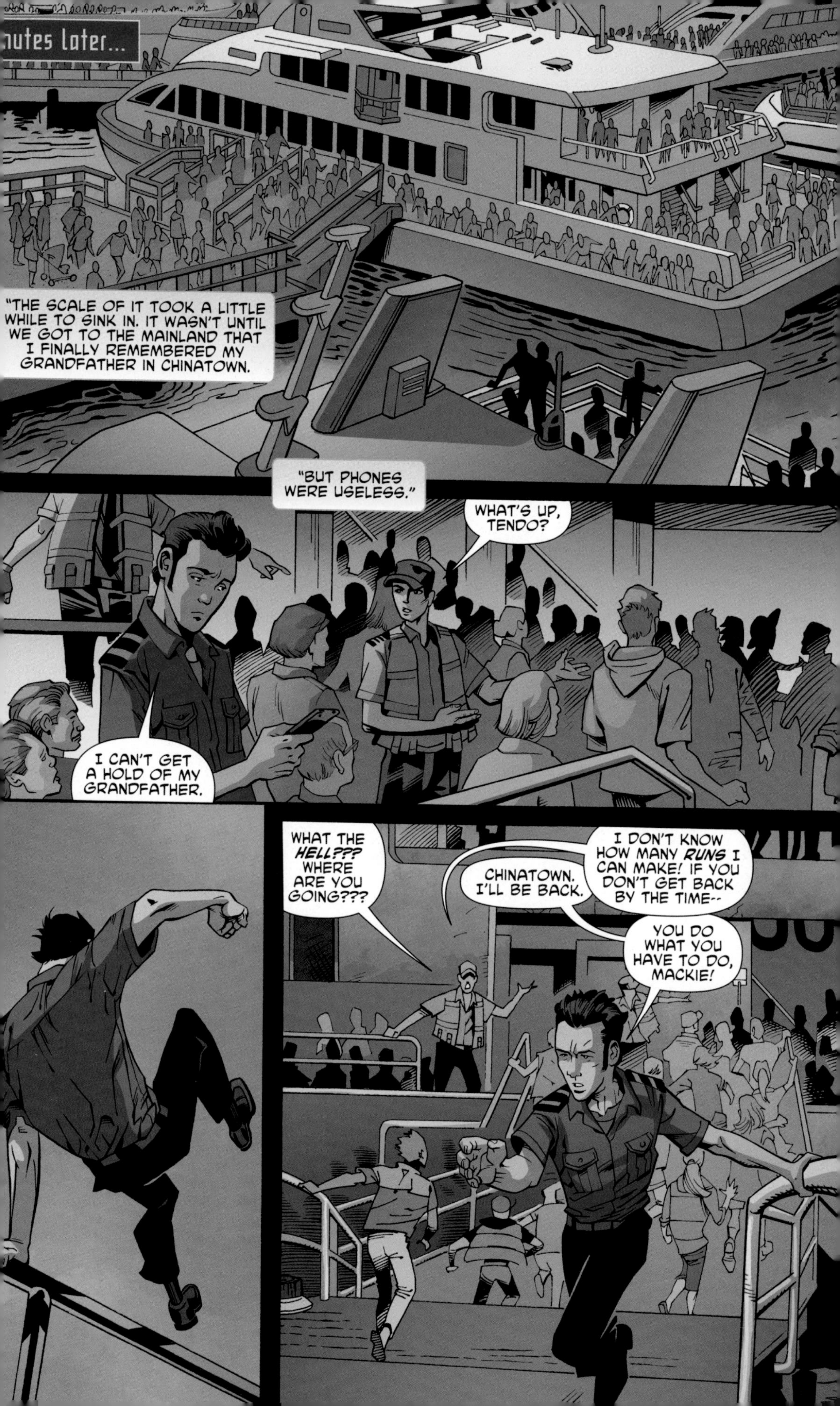

...nutes later...
"THE SCALE OF IT TOOK A LITTLE WHILE TO SINK IN. IT WASN'T UNTIL WE GOT TO THE MAINLAND THAT I FINALLY REMEMBERED MY GRANDFATHER IN CHINATOWN.
"BUT PHONES WERE USELESS."
WHAT'S UP, TENDO?
I CAN'T GET A HOLD OF MY GRANDFATHER.
WHAT THE HELL??? WHERE ARE YOU GOING???
CHINATOWN. I'LL BE BACK.
I DON'T KNOW HOW MANY RUNS I CAN MAKE! IF YOU DON'T GET BACK BY THE TIME--
YOU DO WHAT YOU HAVE TO DO, MACKIE!

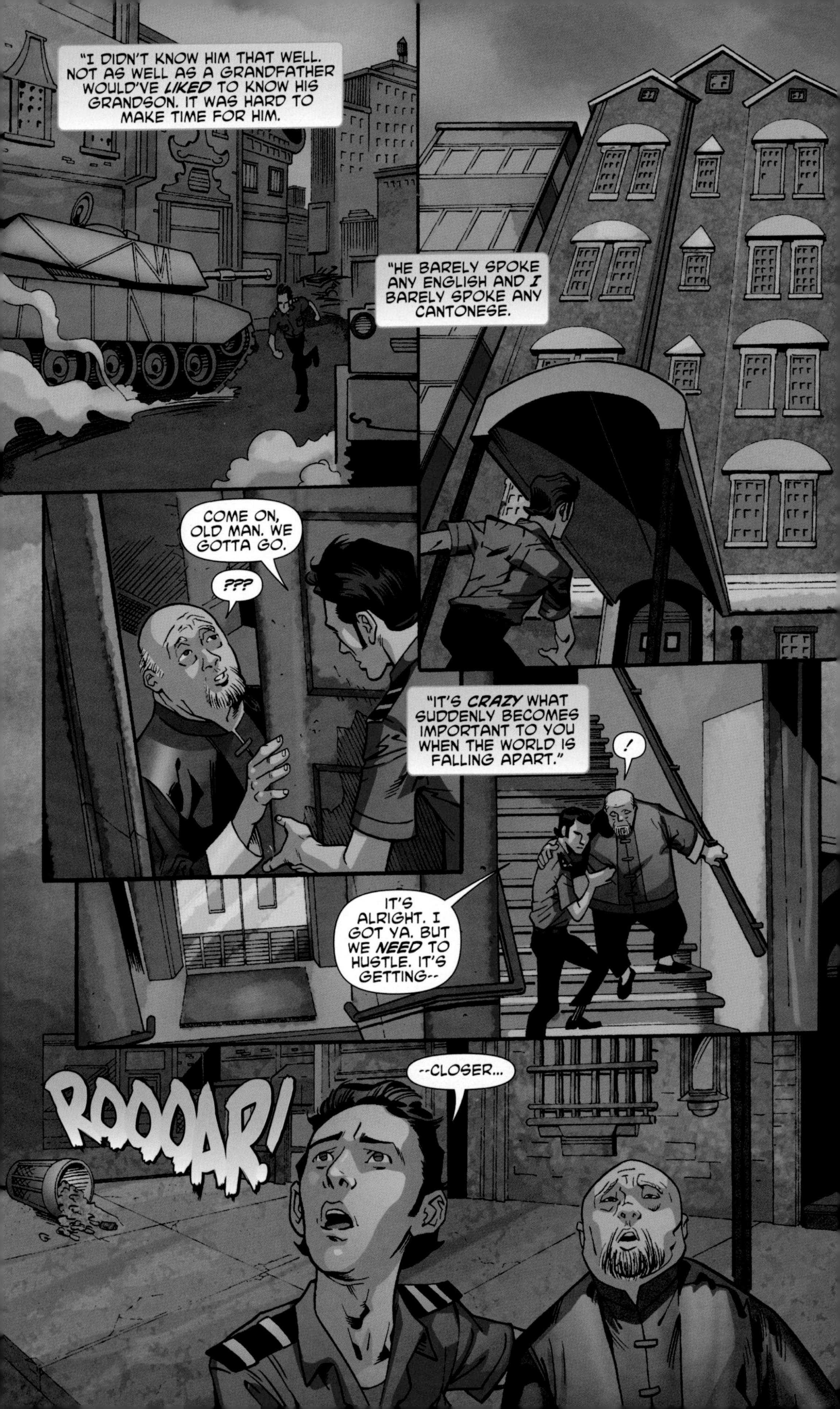
"I DIDN'T KNOW HIM THAT WELL. NOT AS WELL AS A GRANDFATHER WOULD'VE *LIKED* TO KNOW HIS GRANDSON. IT WAS HARD TO MAKE TIME FOR HIM.
"HE BARELY SPOKE ANY ENGLISH AND *I* BARELY SPOKE ANY CANTONESE.
COME ON, OLD MAN. WE GOTTA GO.
???
"IT'S *CRAZY* WHAT SUDDENLY BECOMES IMPORTANT TO YOU WHEN THE WORLD IS FALLING APART."
!
IT'S ALRIGHT. I GOT YA. BUT WE *NEED* TO HUSTLE. IT'S GETTING--
--CLOSER...
ROOOAR!

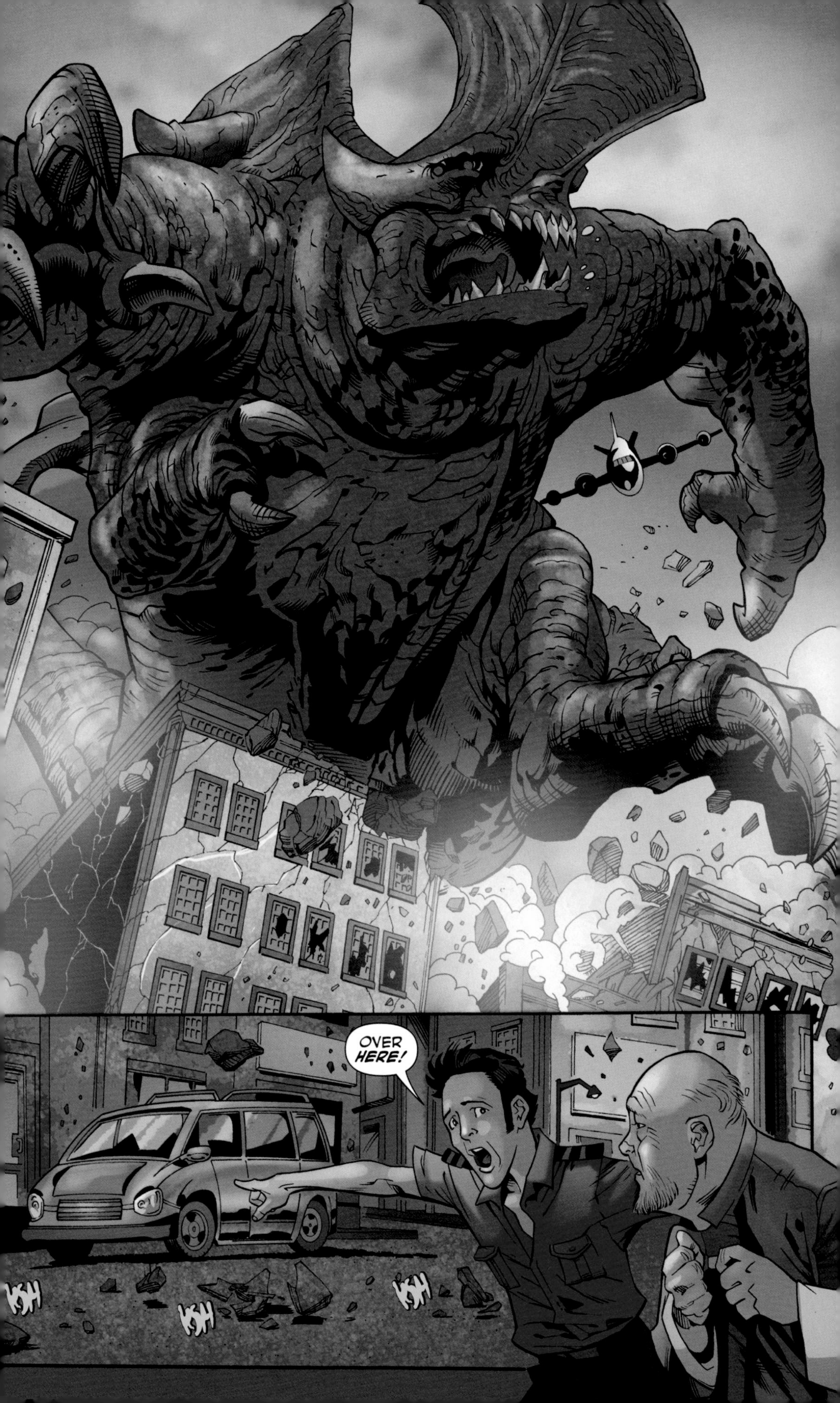

OVER HERE!
KSH
KSH
KSH

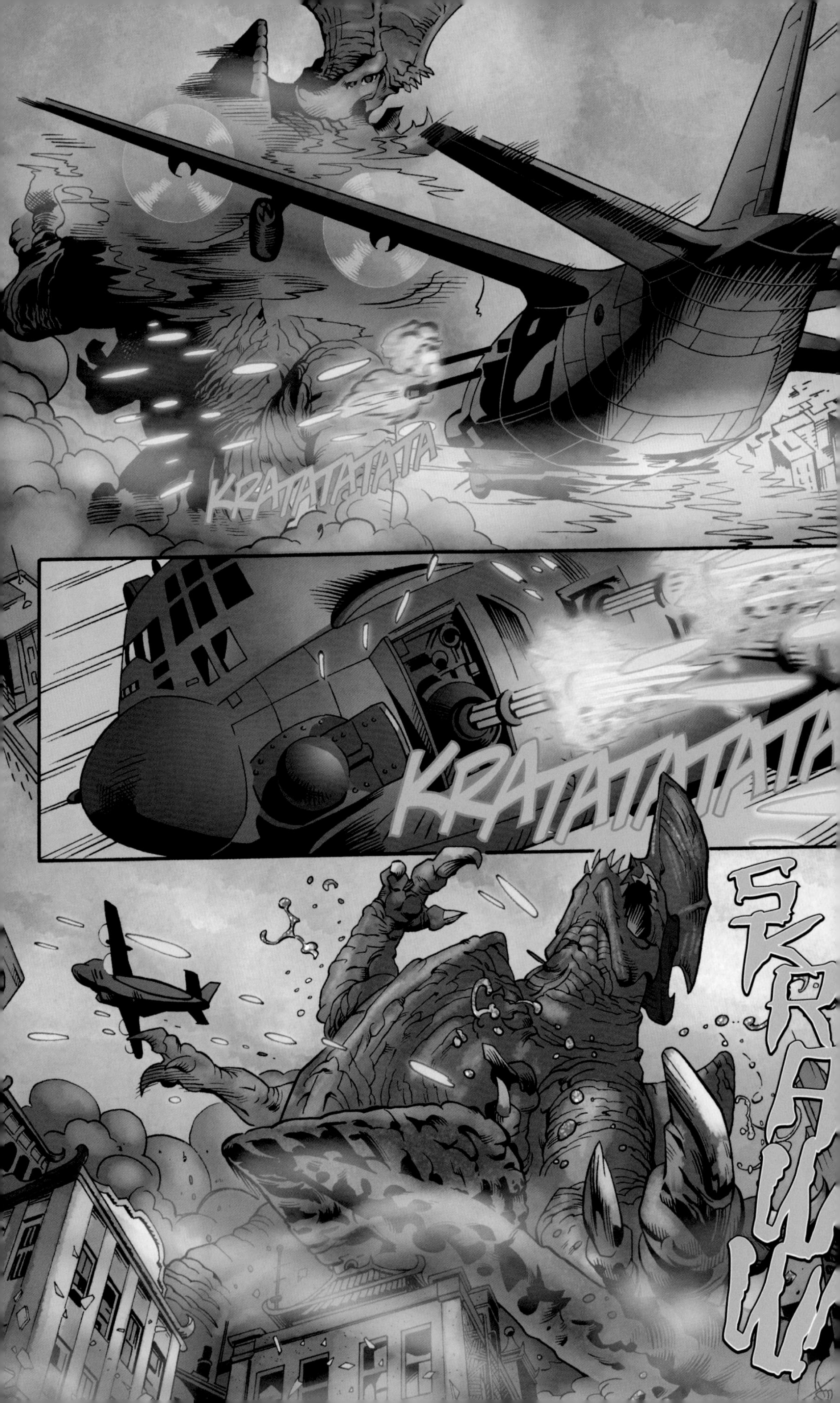
KRATATATATA
KRATATATATA
SKRAW

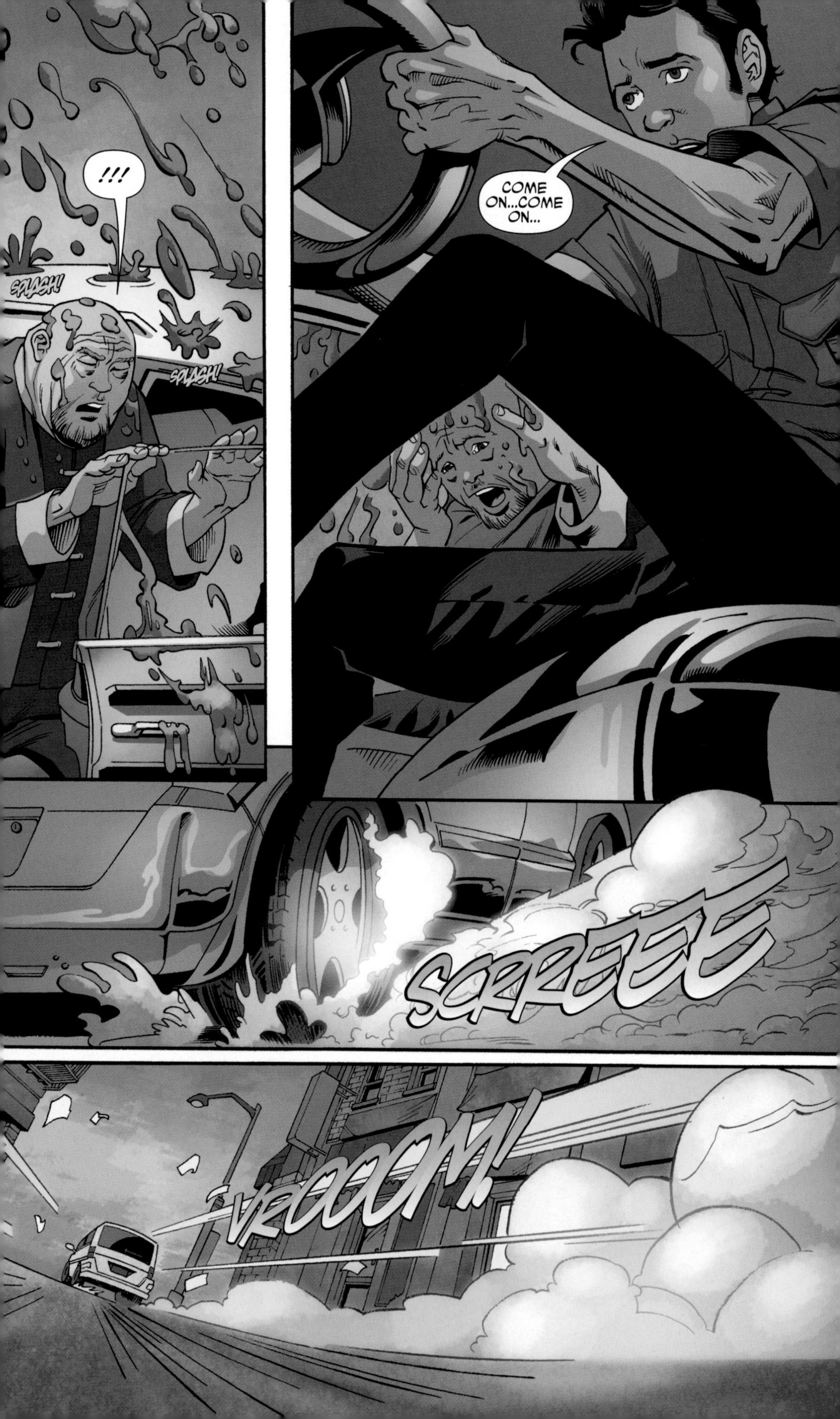
!!!
SPLASH!
SPLASH!
COME ON...COME ON...
SCREEEE
VROOOOM!

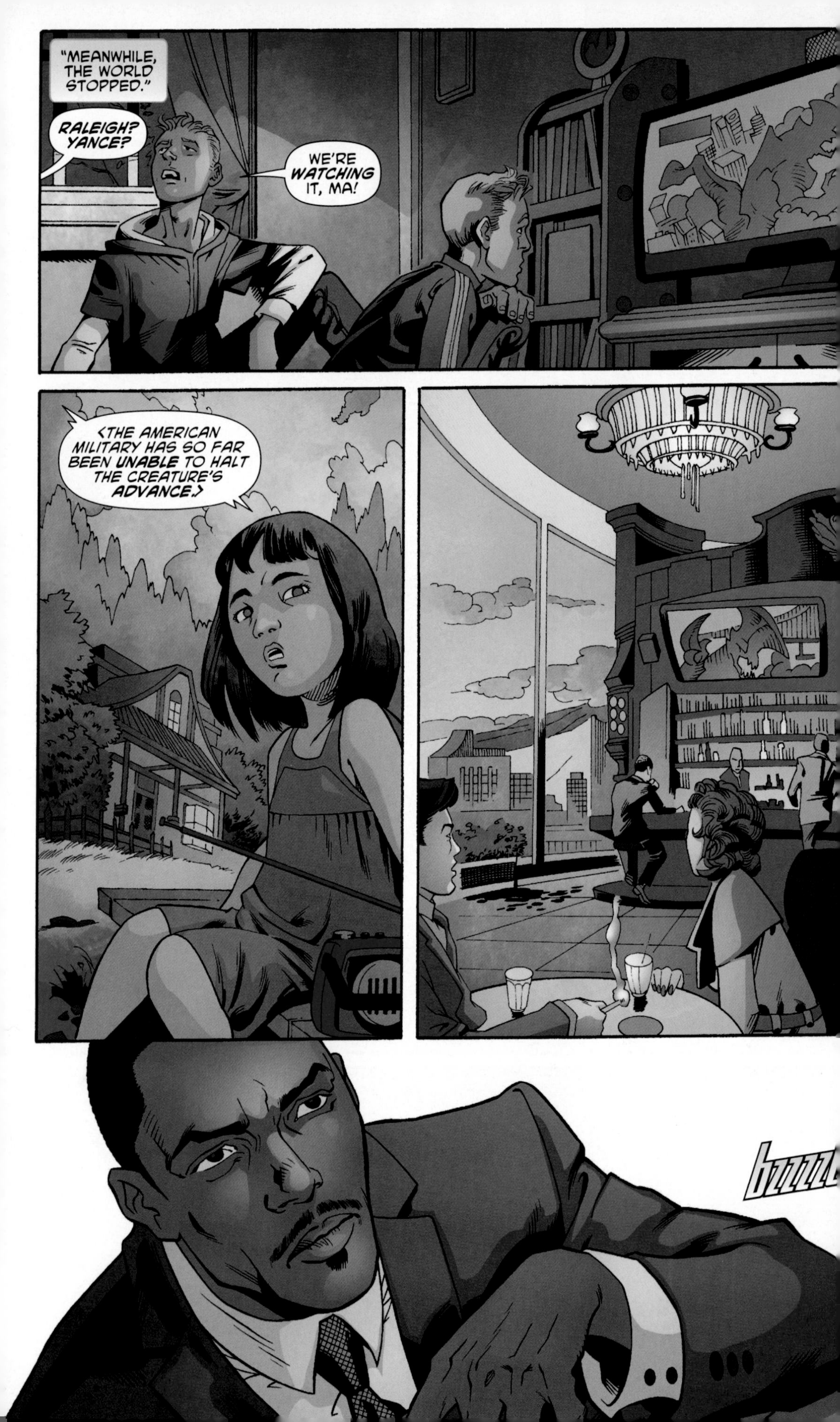
"MEANWHILE, THE WORLD STOPPED."
RALEIGH? YANCE?
WE'RE WATCHING IT, MA!
<THE AMERICAN MILITARY HAS SO FAR BEEN UNABLE TO HALT THE CREATURE'S ADVANCE.>
bzzzz

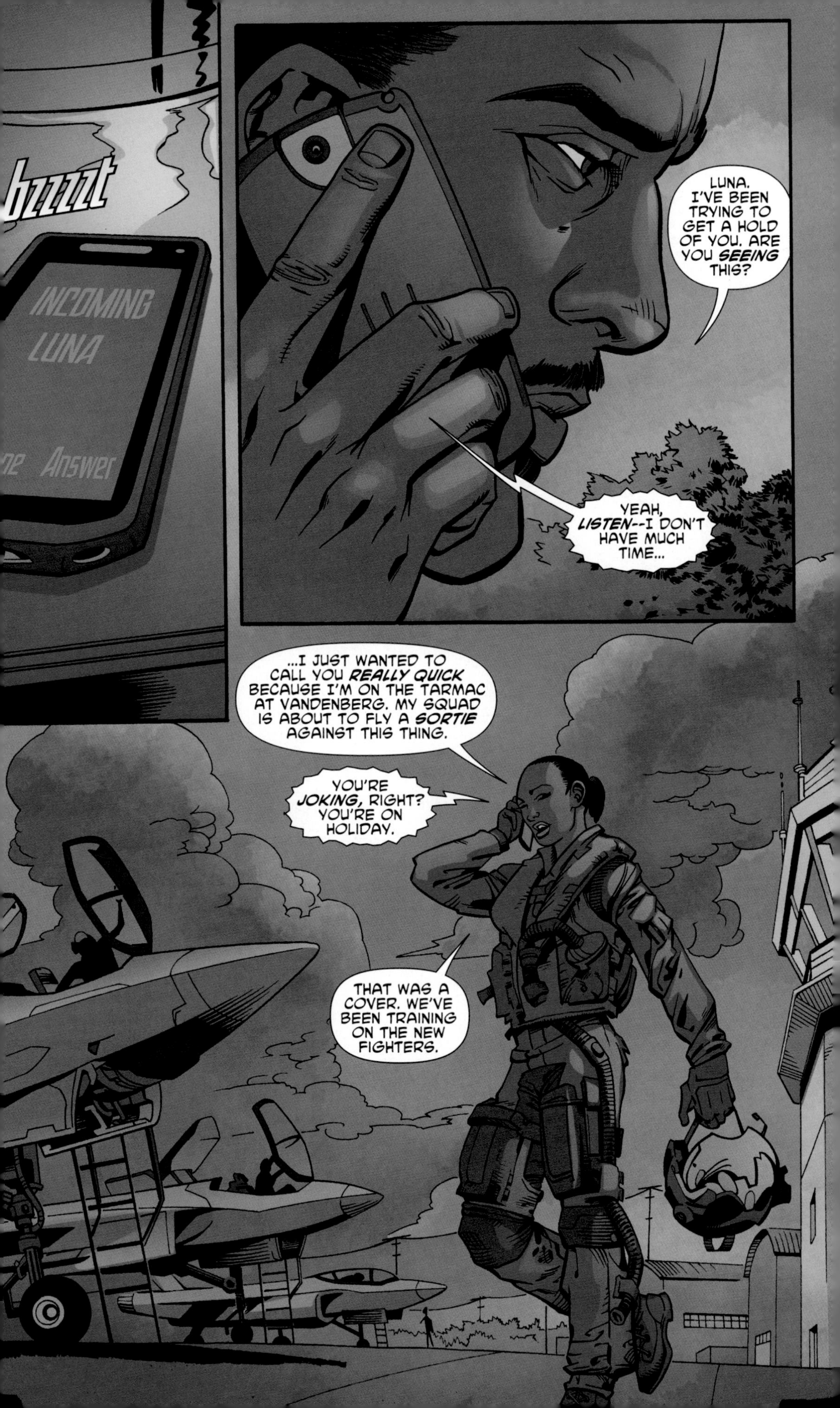
bzzzzt
INCOMING
LUNA
Answer
LUNA. I'VE BEEN TRYING TO GET A HOLD OF YOU. ARE YOU *SEEING* THIS?
YEAH, *LISTEN*--I DON'T HAVE MUCH TIME...
...I JUST WANTED TO CALL YOU *REALLY QUICK* BECAUSE I'M ON THE TARMAC AT VANDENBERG. MY SQUAD IS ABOUT TO FLY A *SORTIE* AGAINST THIS THING.
YOU'RE *JOKING,* RIGHT? YOU'RE ON HOLIDAY.
THAT WAS A COVER. WE'VE BEEN TRAINING ON THE NEW FIGHTERS.

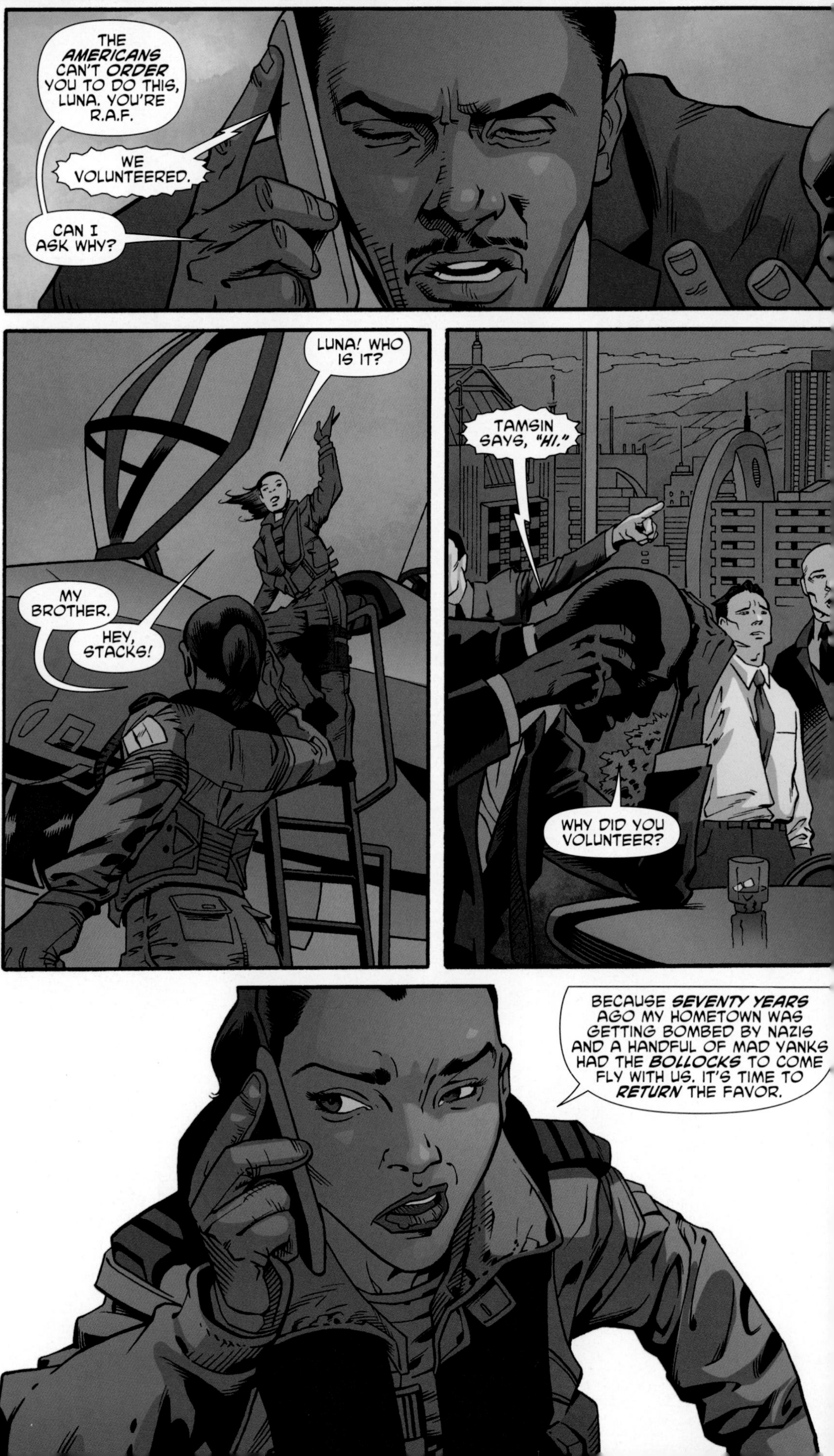
THE AMERICANS CAN'T ORDER YOU TO DO THIS, LUNA. YOU'RE R.A.F.
WE VOLUNTEERED.
CAN I ASK WHY?
LUNA! WHO IS IT?
MY BROTHER.
HEY, STACKS!
TAMSIN SAYS, "HI."
WHY DID YOU VOLUNTEER?
BECAUSE SEVENTY YEARS AGO MY HOMETOWN WAS GETTING BOMBED BY NAZIS AND A HANDFUL OF MAD YANKS HAD THE BOLLOCKS TO COME FLY WITH US. IT'S TIME TO RETURN THE FAVOR.

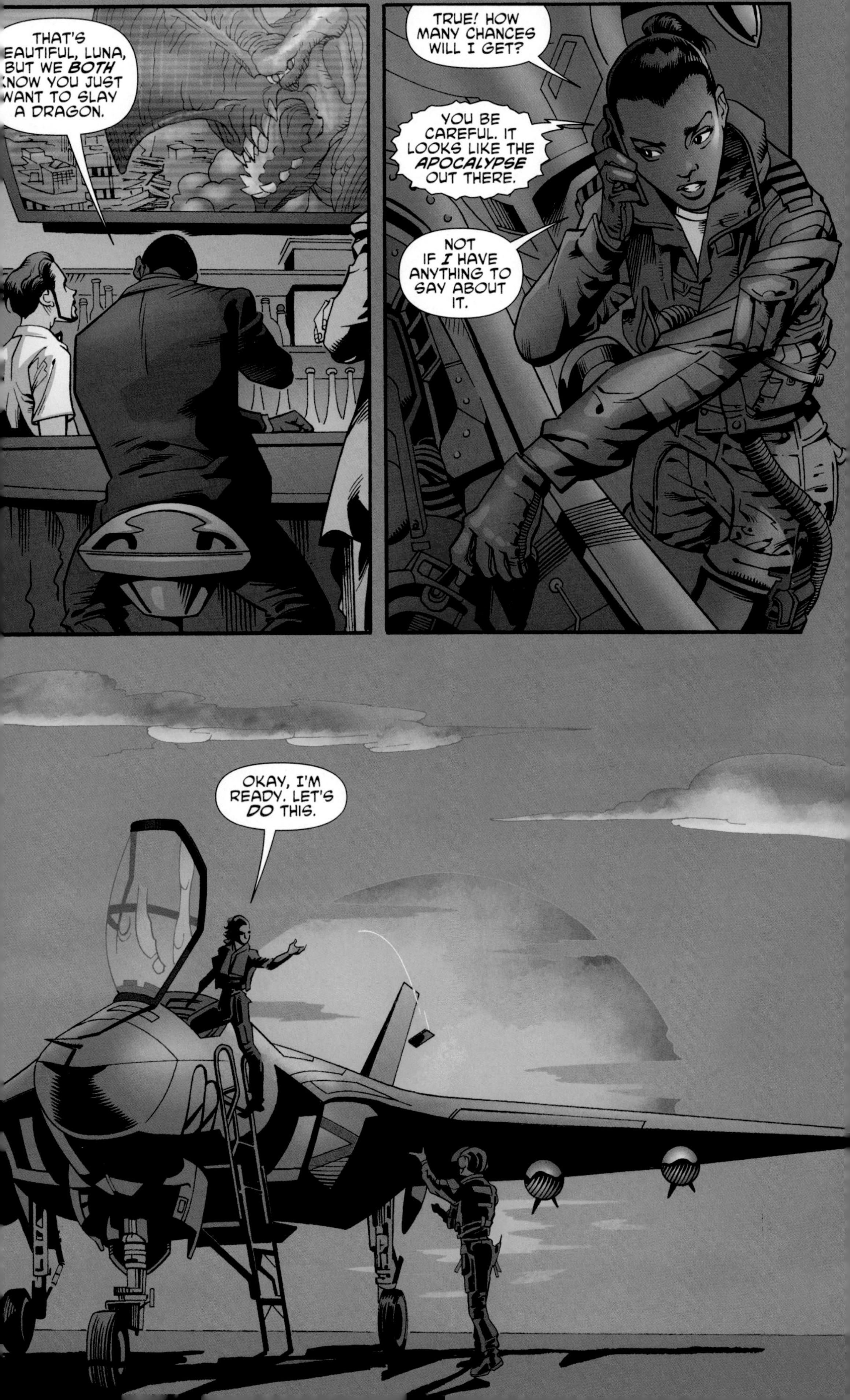
THAT'S BEAUTIFUL, LUNA, BUT WE *BOTH* KNOW YOU JUST WANT TO SLAY A DRAGON.
TRUE! HOW MANY CHANCES WILL I GET?
YOU BE CAREFUL. IT LOOKS LIKE THE *APOCALYPSE* OUT THERE.
NOT IF *I* HAVE ANYTHING TO SAY ABOUT IT.
OKAY, I'M READY. LET'S *DO* THIS.

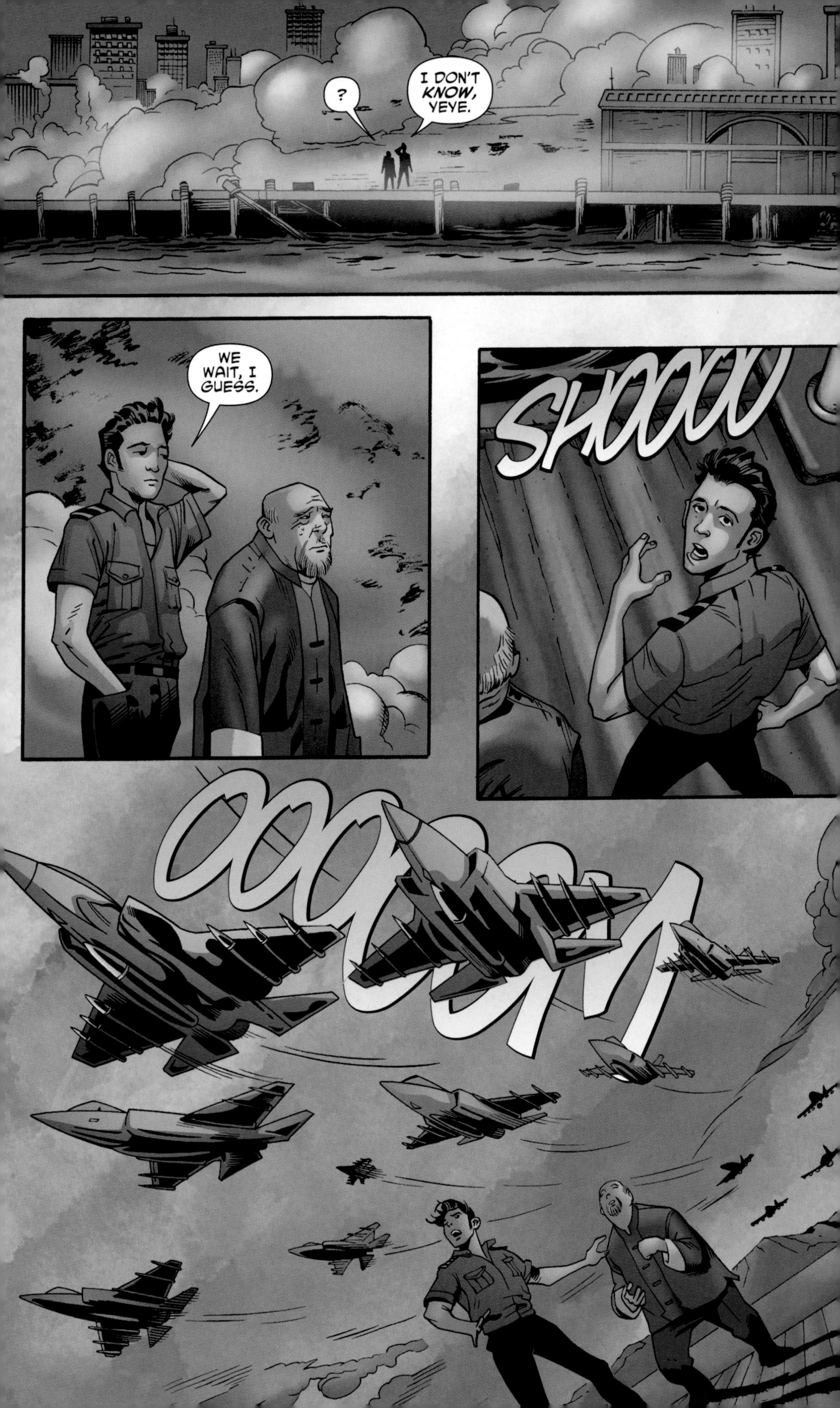

?
I DON'T KNOW, YEYE.
WE WAIT, I GUESS.
SHOOOO
OOOOOM

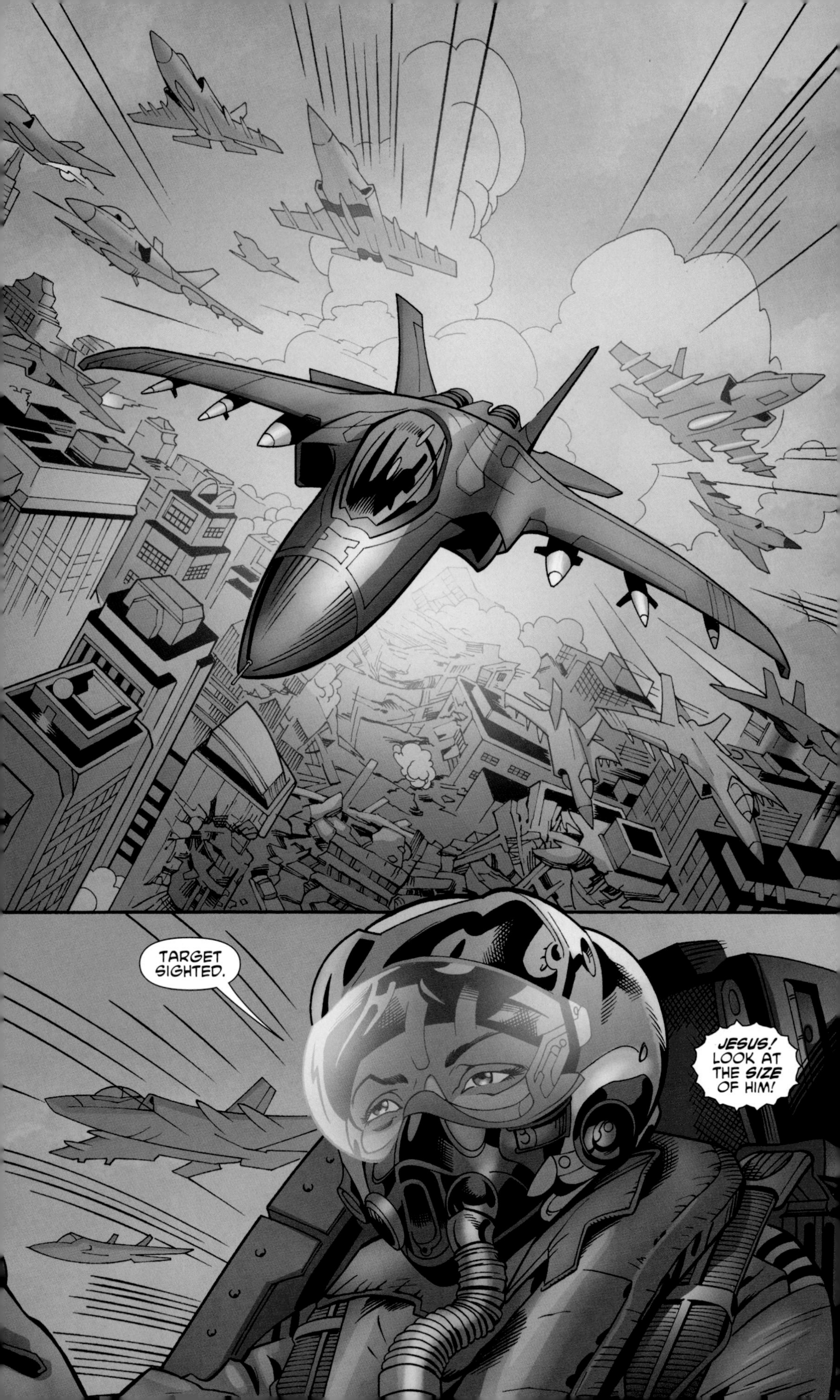
TARGET SIGHTED.
JESUS! LOOK AT THE SIZE OF HIM!

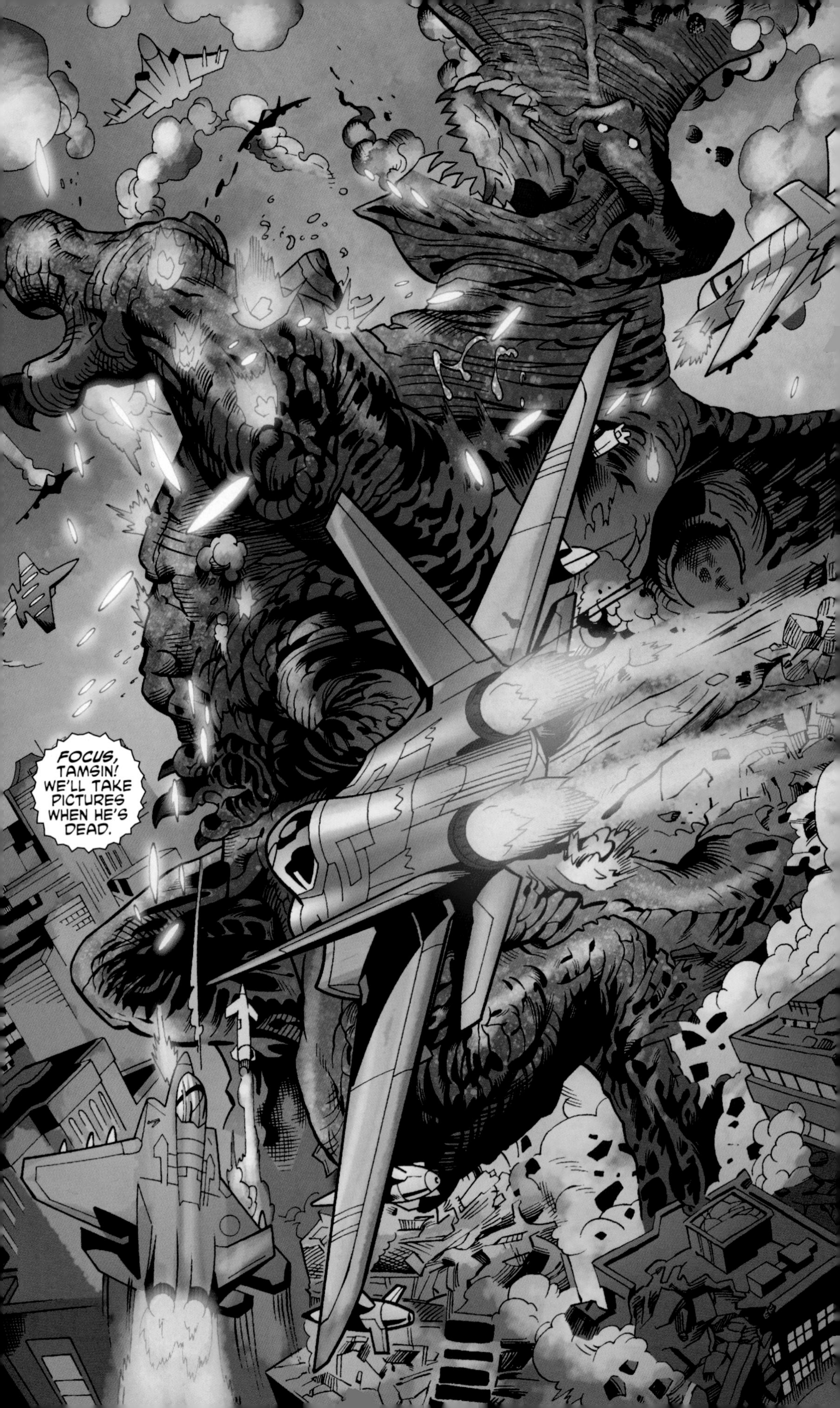
FOCUS, TAMSIN! WE'LL TAKE PICTURES WHEN HE'S DEAD.

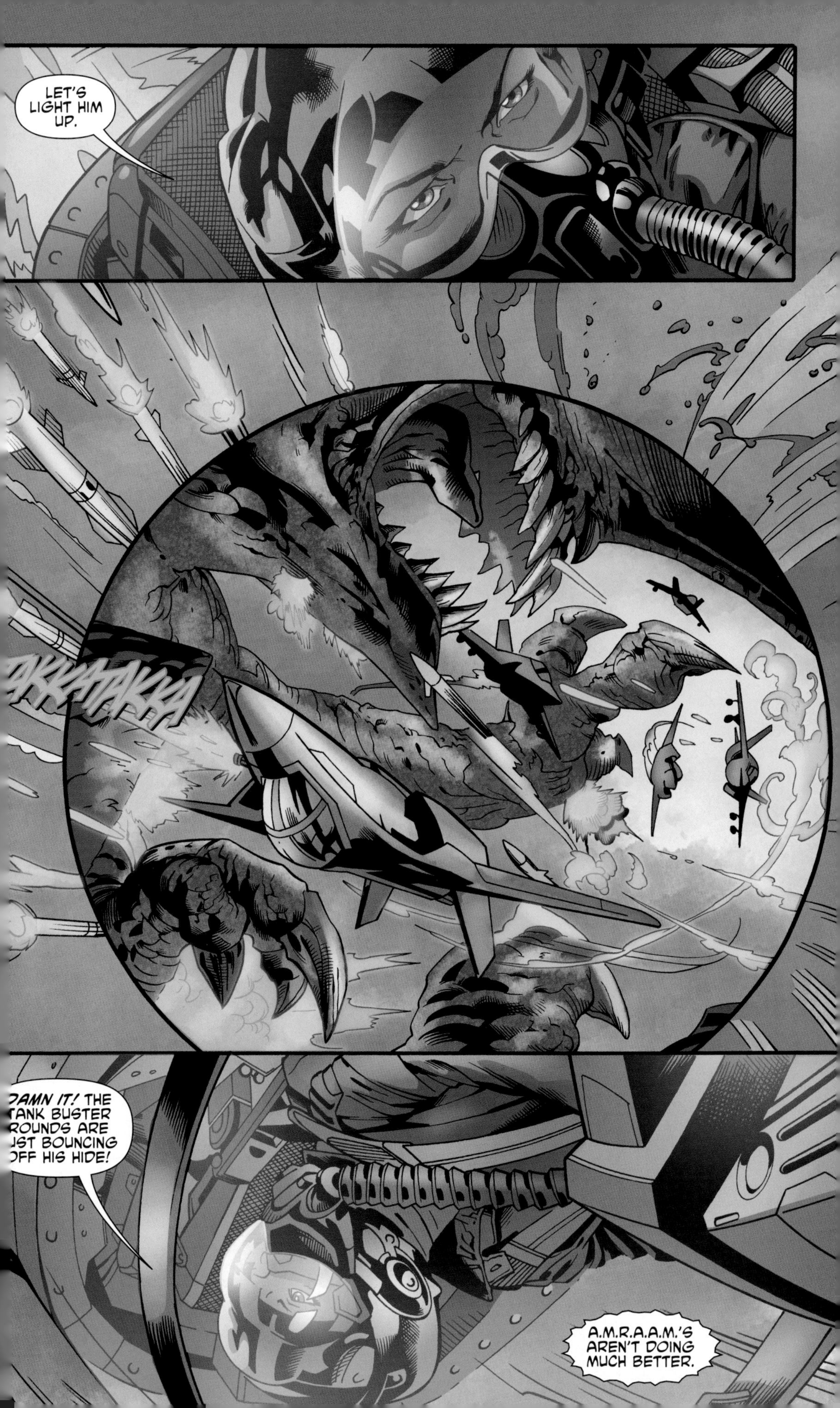
LET'S LIGHT HIM UP.
TAKKATAKKA
DAMN IT! THE TANK BUSTER ROUNDS ARE JUST BOUNCING OFF HIS HIDE!
A.M.R.A.A.M.'S AREN'T DOING MUCH BETTER.

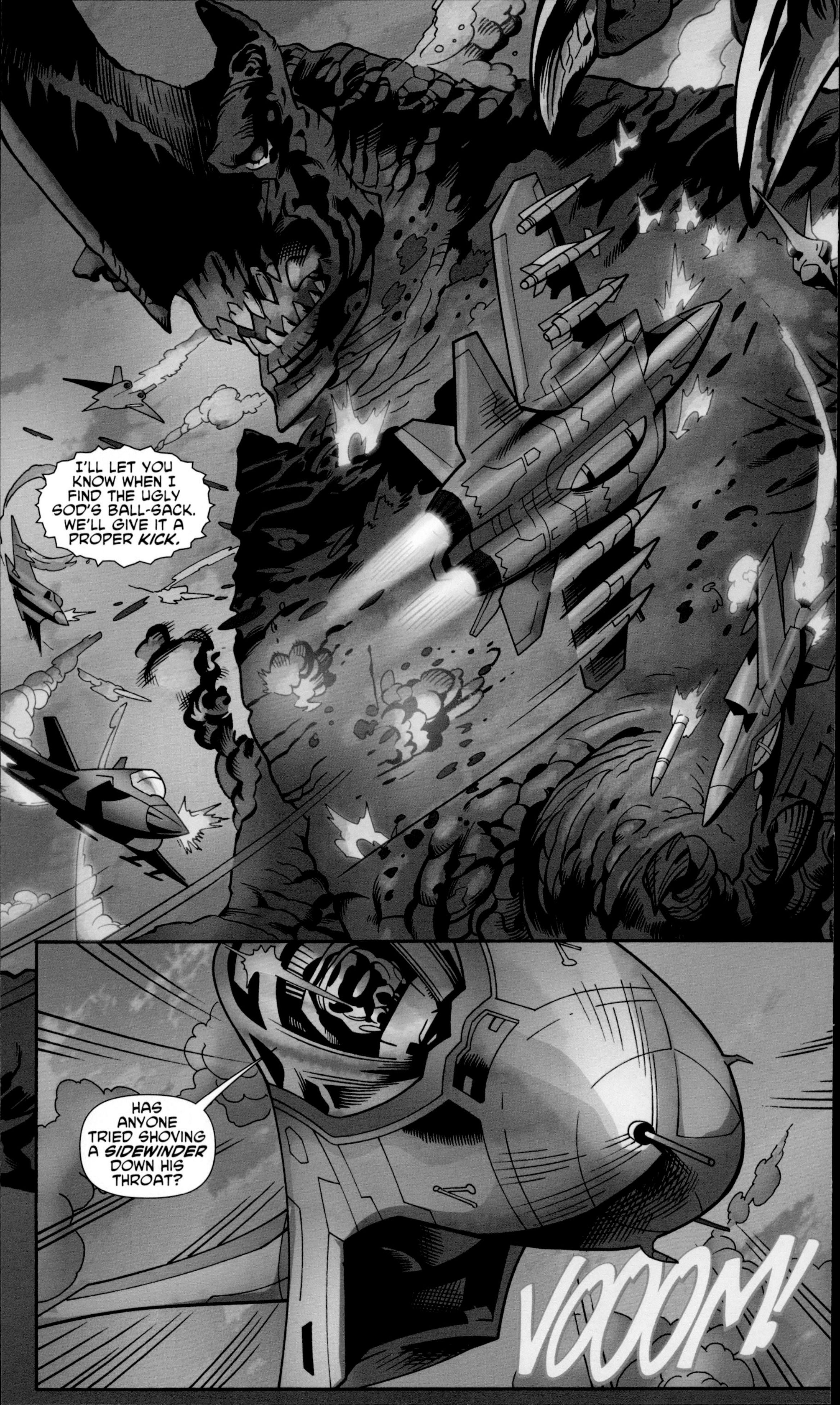
I'LL LET YOU KNOW WHEN I FIND THE UGLY SOD'S BALL-SACK. WE'LL GIVE IT A PROPER *KICK.*
HAS ANYONE TRIED SHOVING A *SIDEWINDER* DOWN HIS THROAT?
VOOOM!

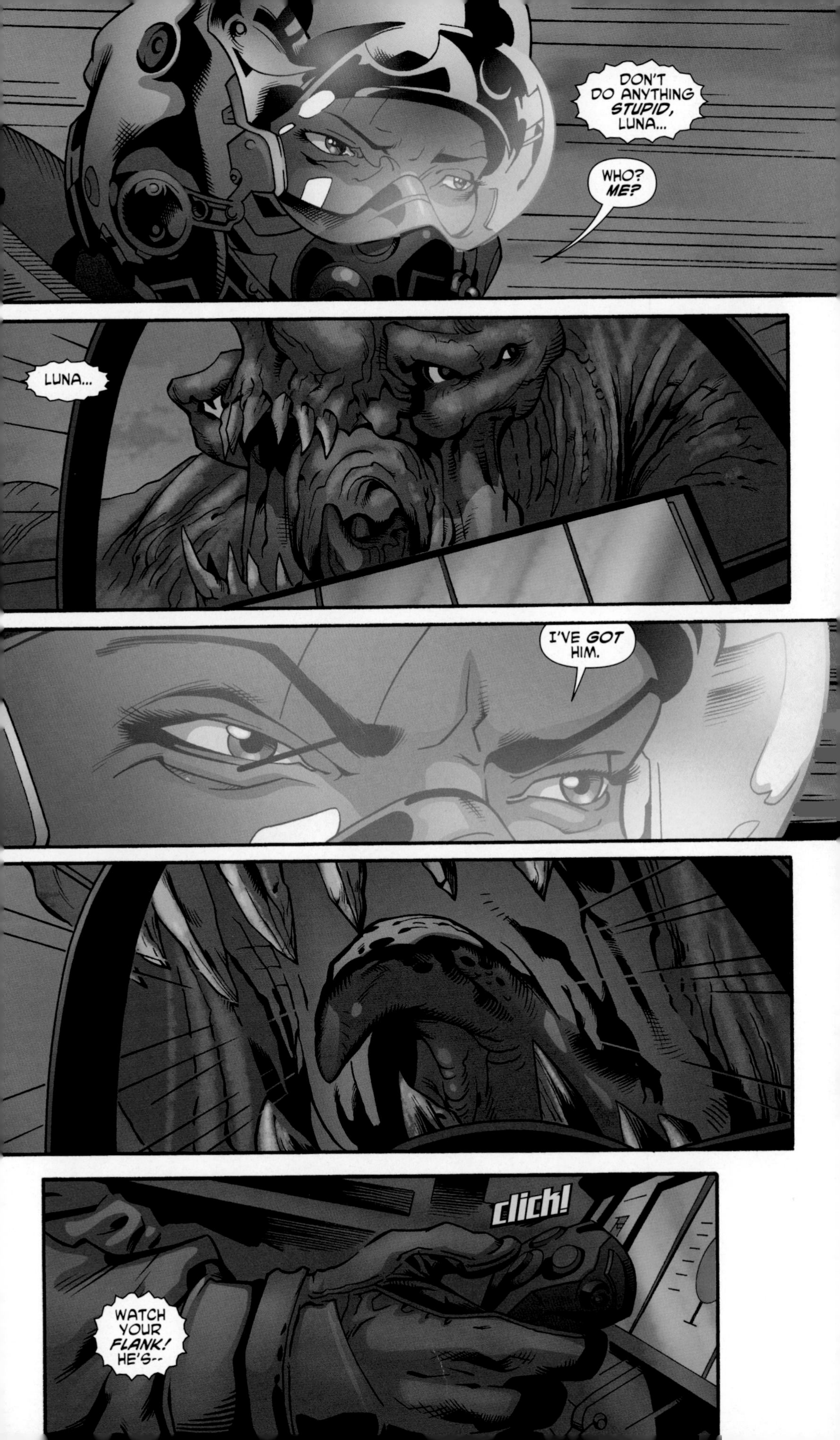

DON'T DO ANYTHING *STUPID*, LUNA...
WHO? *ME?*
LUNA...
I'VE *GOT* HIM.
CLICK!
WATCH YOUR *FLANK!* HE'S--

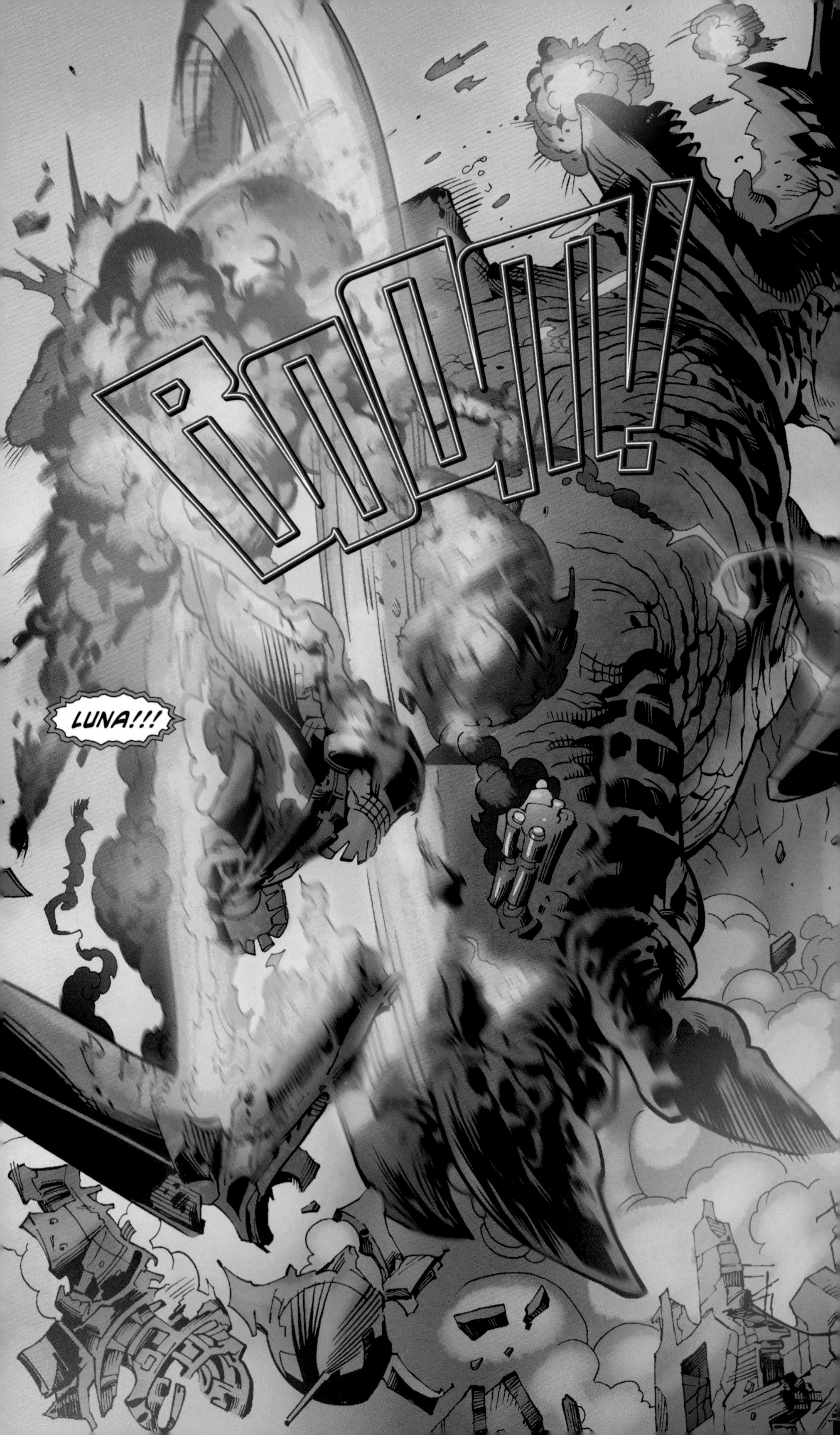
LUNA!!!

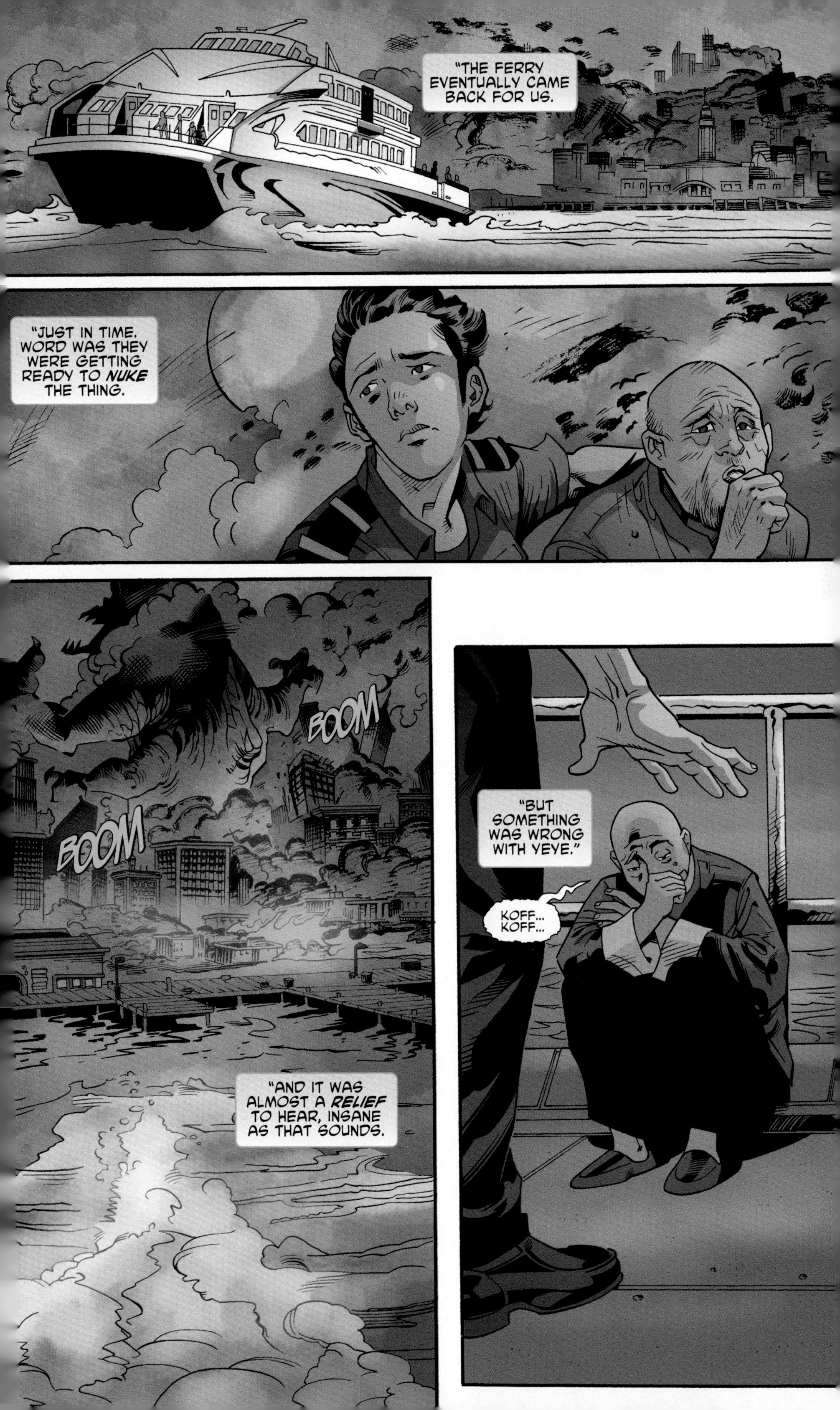

"THE FERRY EVENTUALLY CAME BACK FOR US.
"JUST IN TIME. WORD WAS THEY WERE GETTING READY TO NUKE THE THING.
BOOM
BOOM
"AND IT WAS ALMOST A RELIEF TO HEAR, INSANE AS THAT SOUNDS.
"BUT SOMETHING WAS WRONG WITH YEYE."
KOFF... KOFF...

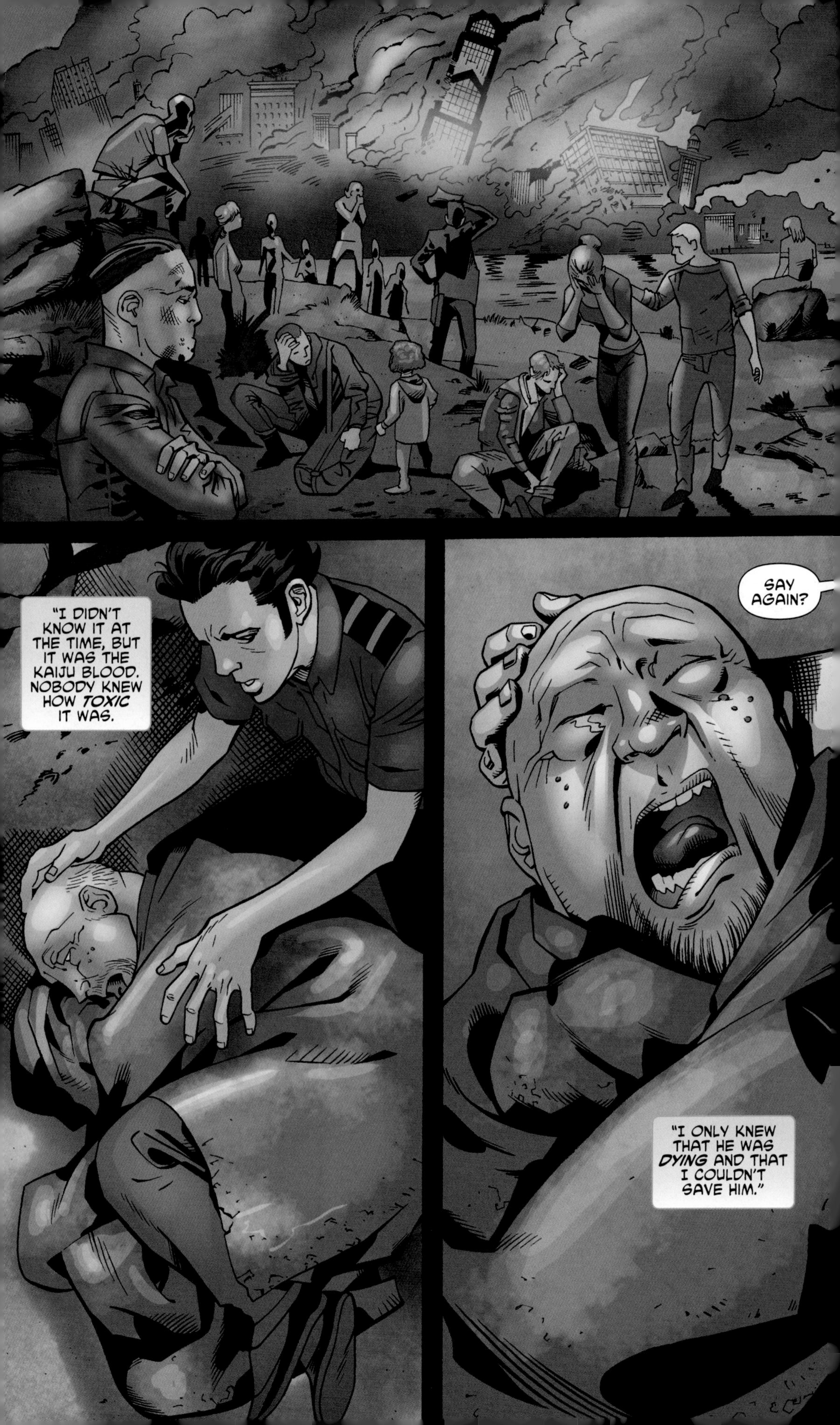
"I DIDN'T KNOW IT AT THE TIME, BUT IT WAS THE KAIJU BLOOD. NOBODY KNEW HOW *TOXIC* IT WAS.
SAY AGAIN?
"I ONLY KNEW THAT HE WAS *DYING* AND THAT I COULDN'T SAVE HIM."

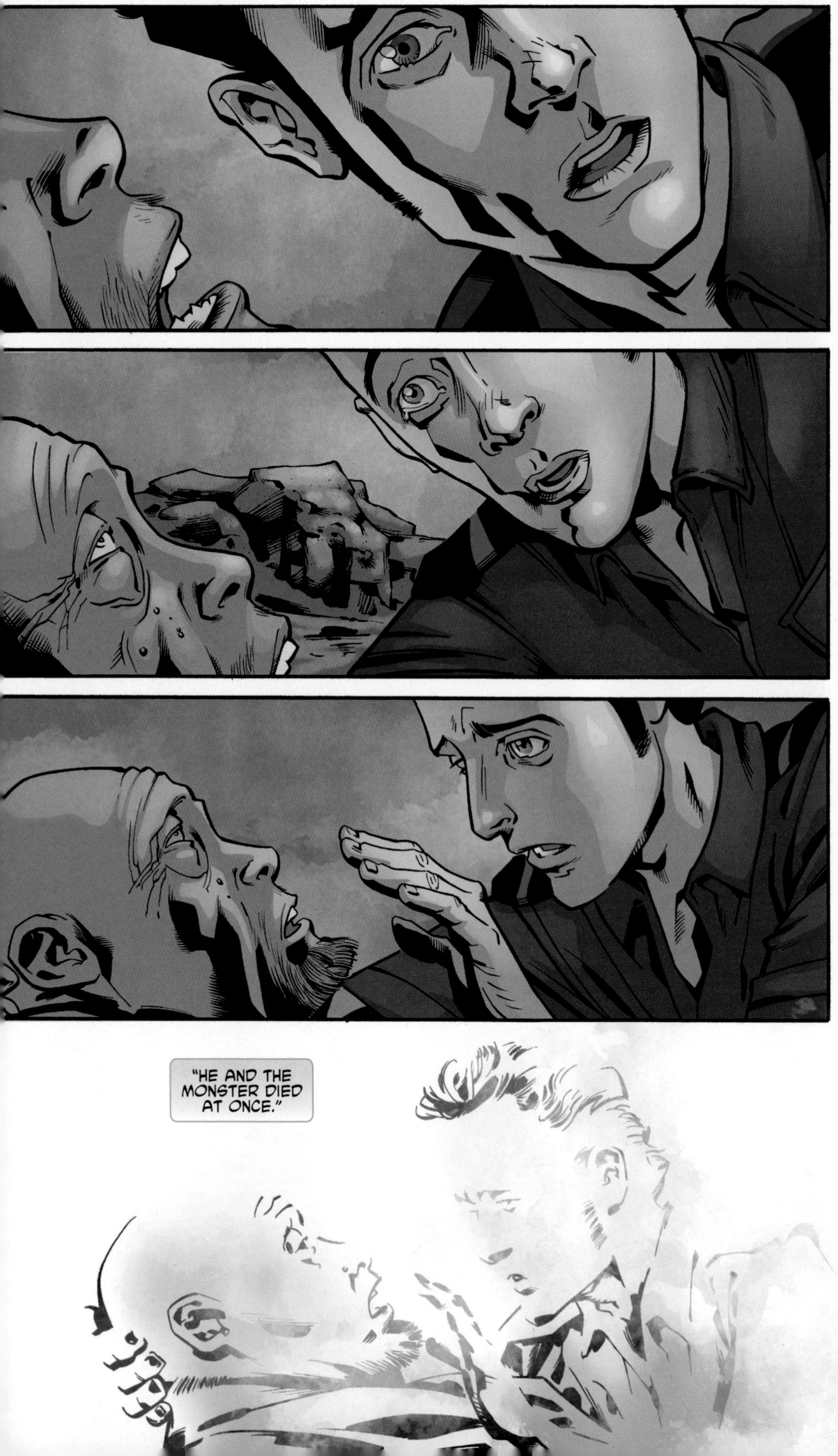
"HE AND THE MONSTER DIED AT ONCE."

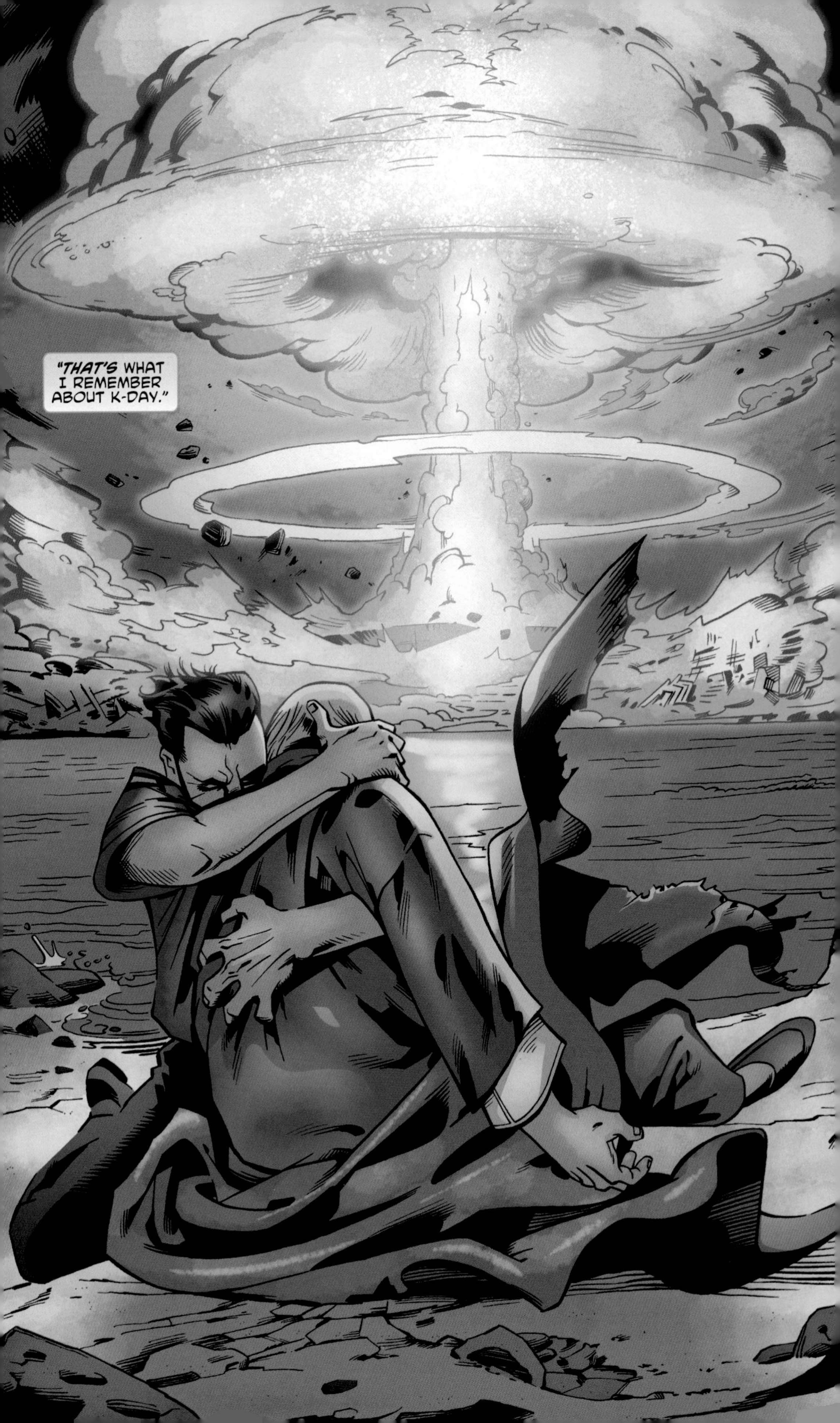
"THAT'S WHAT I REMEMBER ABOUT K-DAY."

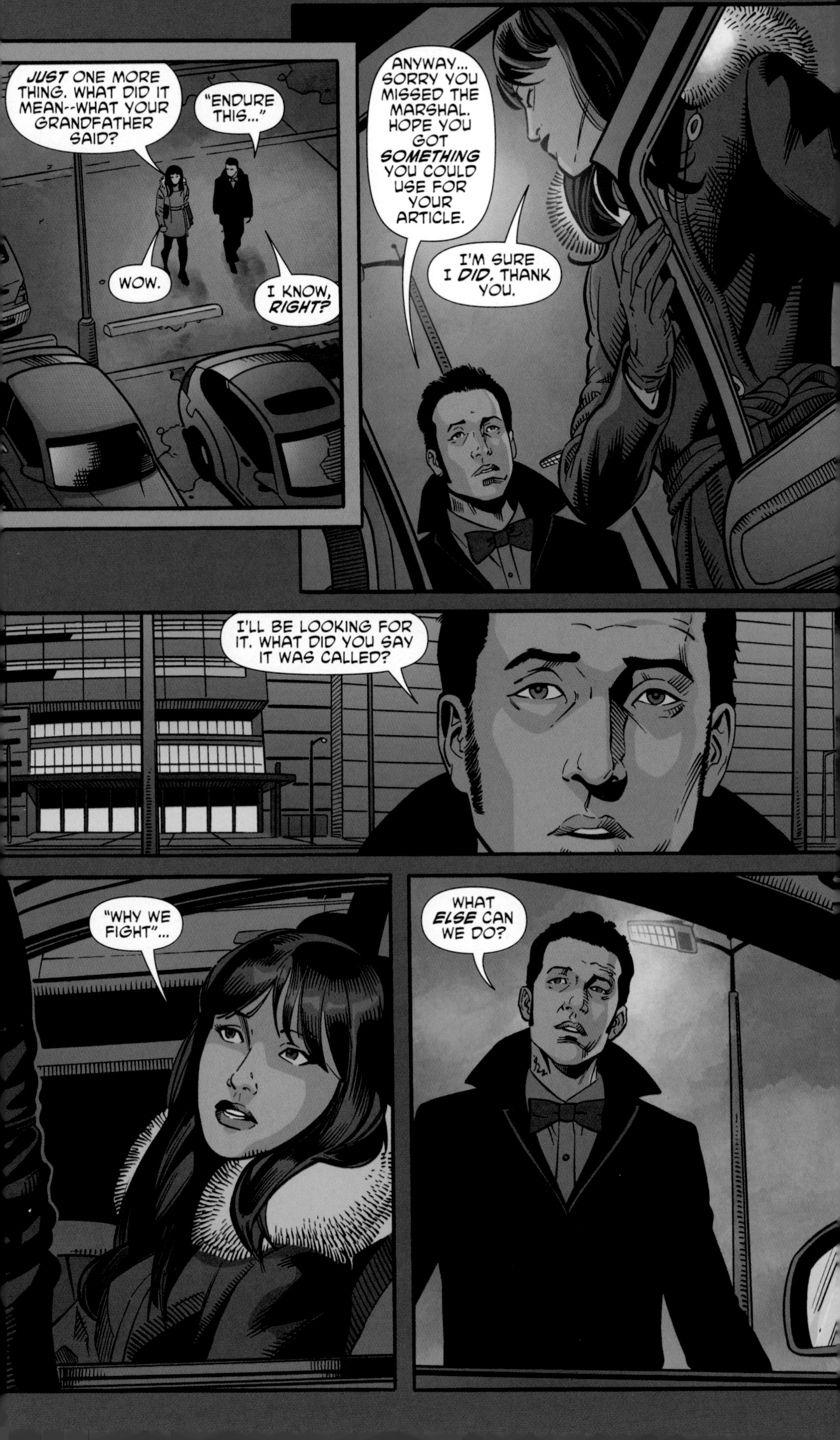
JUST ONE MORE THING. WHAT DID IT MEAN--WHAT YOUR GRANDFATHER SAID?
"ENDURE THIS..."
WOW.
I KNOW, RIGHT?
ANYWAY... SORRY YOU MISSED THE MARSHAL. HOPE YOU GOT SOMETHING YOU COULD USE FOR YOUR ARTICLE.
I'M SURE I DID. THANK YOU.
I'LL BE LOOKING FOR IT. WHAT DID YOU SAY IT WAS CALLED?
"WHY WE FIGHT"...
WHAT ELSE CAN WE DO?

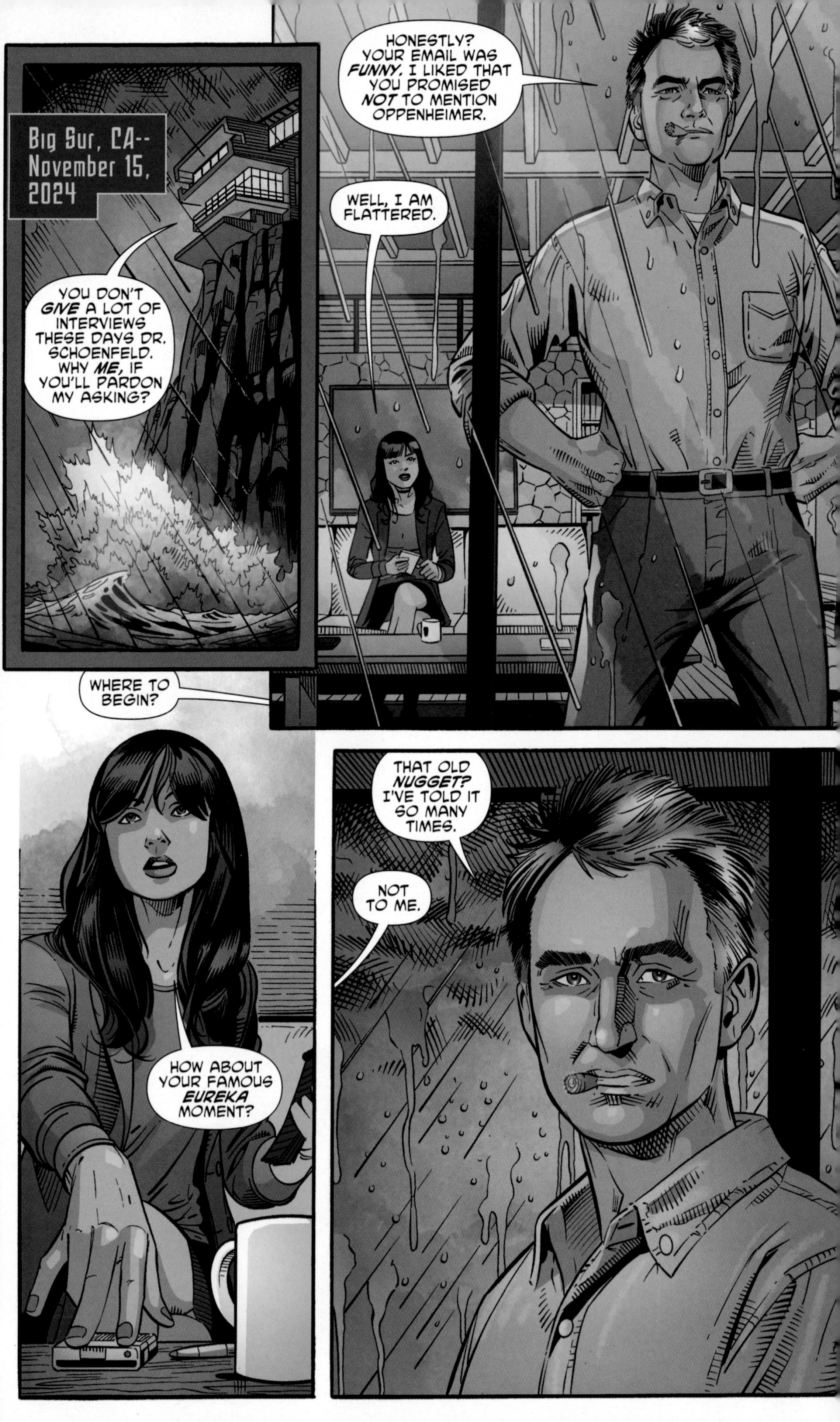
Big Sur, CA-- November 15, 2024
YOU DON'T GIVE A LOT OF INTERVIEWS THESE DAYS DR. SCHOENFELD. WHY ME, IF YOU'LL PARDON MY ASKING?
HONESTLY? YOUR EMAIL WAS FUNNY. I LIKED THAT YOU PROMISED NOT TO MENTION OPPENHEIMER.
WELL, I AM FLATTERED.
WHERE TO BEGIN?
HOW ABOUT YOUR FAMOUS EUREKA MOMENT?
THAT OLD NUGGET? I'VE TOLD IT SO MANY TIMES.
NOT TO ME.

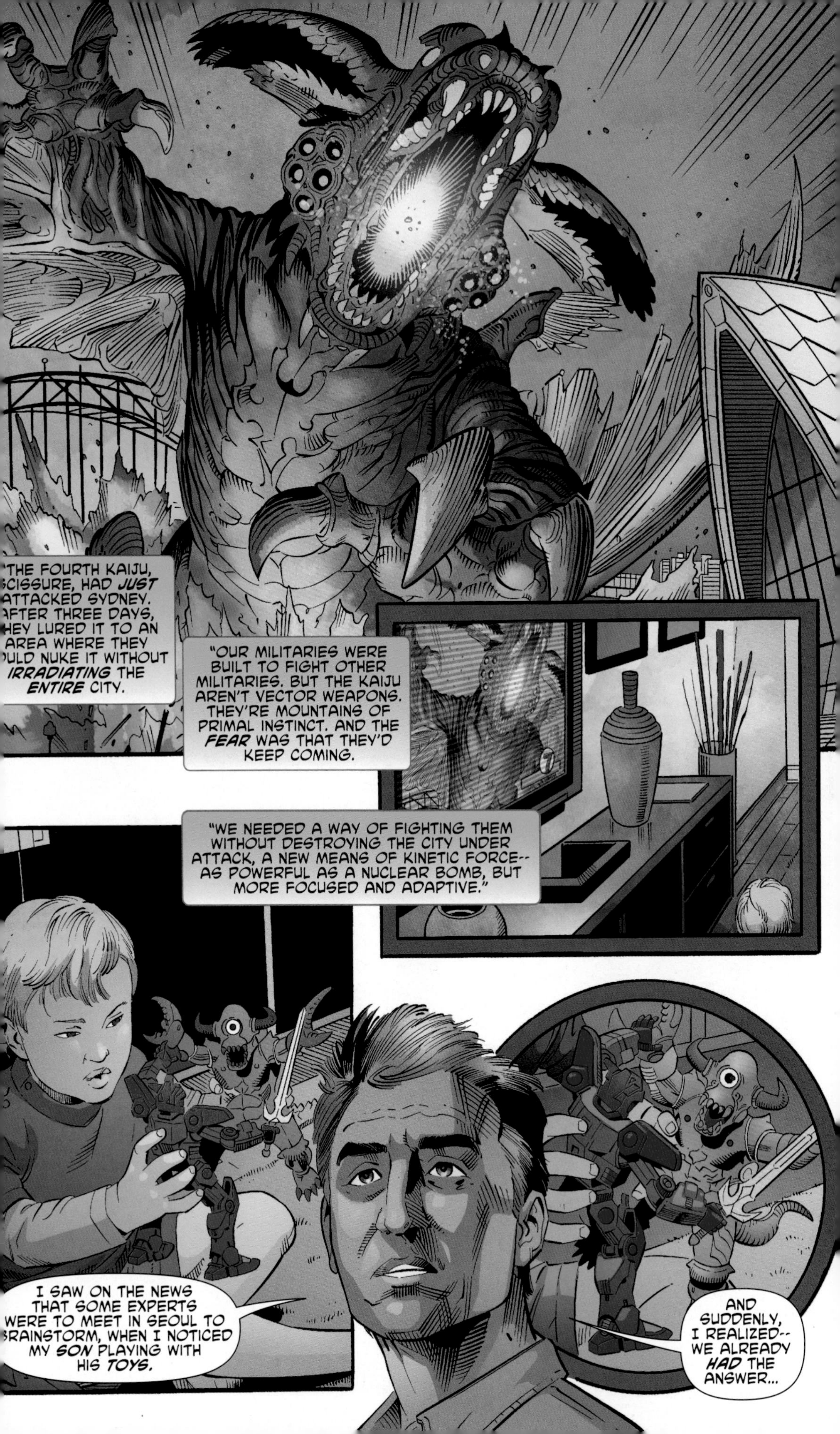
"THE FOURTH KAIJU, SCISSURE, HAD *JUST* ATTACKED SYDNEY. AFTER THREE DAYS, HEY LURED IT TO AN AREA WHERE THEY OULD NUKE IT WITHOUT *IRRADIATING* THE *ENTIRE* CITY.
"OUR MILITARIES WERE BUILT TO FIGHT OTHER MILITARIES. BUT THE KAIJU AREN'T VECTOR WEAPONS. THEY'RE MOUNTAINS OF PRIMAL INSTINCT. AND THE *FEAR* WAS THAT THEY'D KEEP COMING.
"WE NEEDED A WAY OF FIGHTING THEM WITHOUT DESTROYING THE CITY UNDER ATTACK, A NEW MEANS OF KINETIC FORCE--AS POWERFUL AS A NUCLEAR BOMB, BUT MORE FOCUSED AND ADAPTIVE."
I SAW ON THE NEWS THAT SOME EXPERTS WERE TO MEET IN SEOUL TO RAINSTORM, WHEN I NOTICED MY *SON* PLAYING WITH HIS *TOYS*.
AND SUDDENLY, I REALIZED--WE ALREADY *HAD* THE ANSWER...

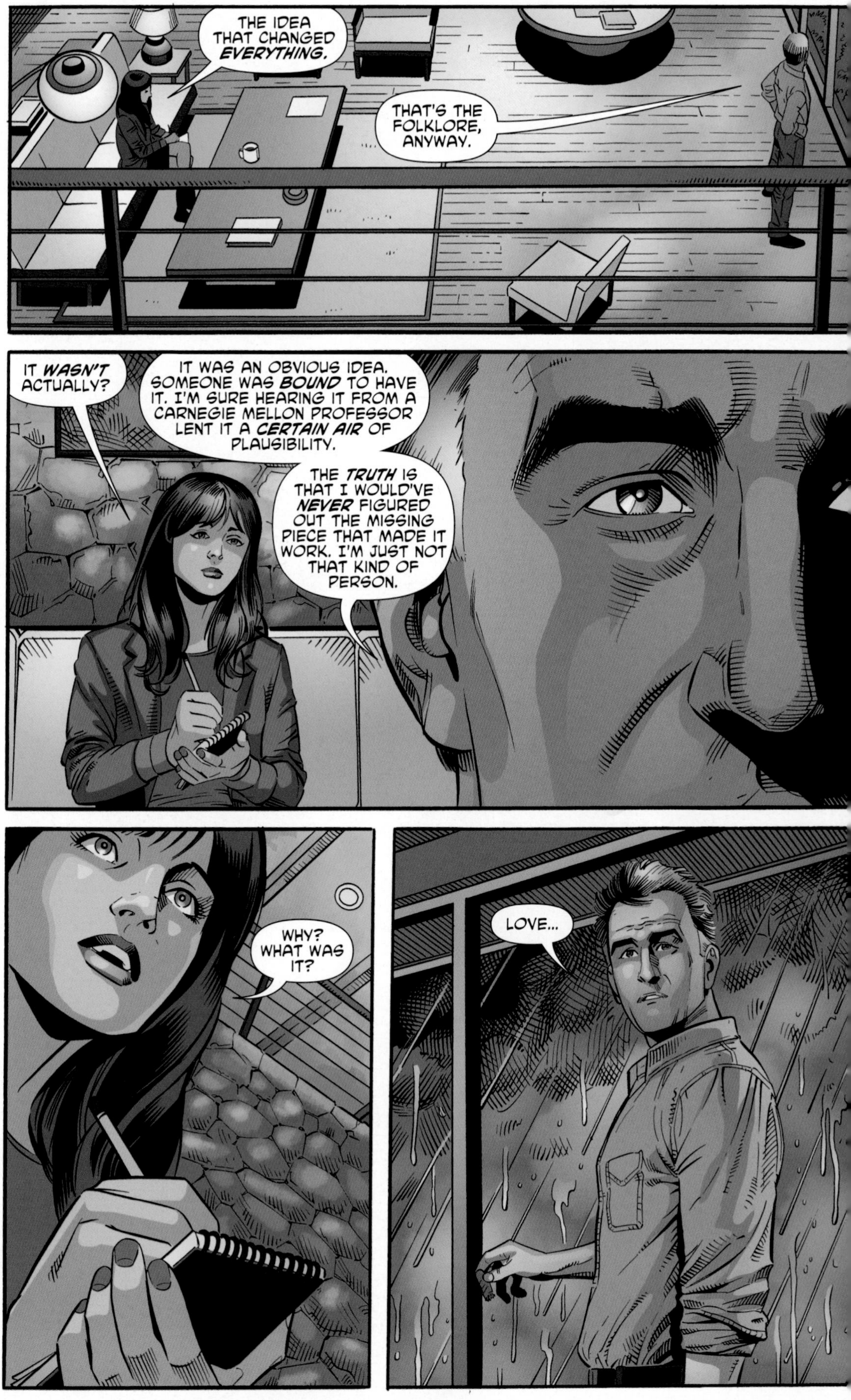
THE IDEA THAT CHANGED *EVERYTHING.*
THAT'S THE FOLKLORE, ANYWAY.
IT *WASN'T* ACTUALLY?
IT WAS AN OBVIOUS IDEA. SOMEONE WAS *BOUND* TO HAVE IT. I'M SURE HEARING IT FROM A CARNEGIE MELLON PROFESSOR LENT IT A *CERTAIN AIR* OF PLAUSIBILITY.
THE *TRUTH* IS THAT I WOULD'VE *NEVER* FIGURED OUT THE MISSING PIECE THAT MADE IT WORK. I'M JUST NOT THAT KIND OF PERSON.
WHY? WHAT WAS IT?
LOVE...

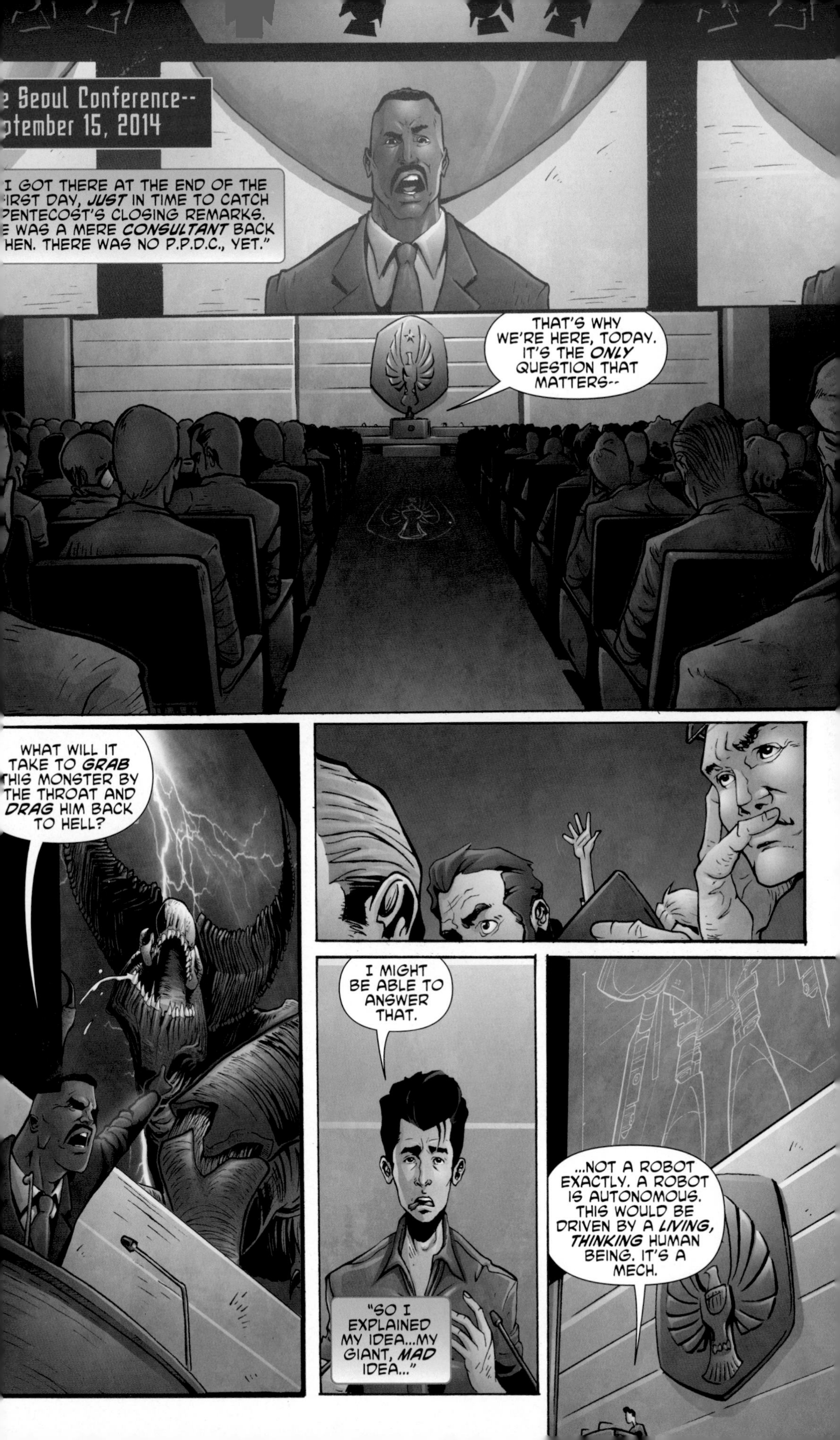
e Seoul Conference--
ptember 15, 2014
I GOT THERE AT THE END OF THE FIRST DAY, JUST IN TIME TO CATCH PENTECOST'S CLOSING REMARKS. E WAS A MERE CONSULTANT BACK HEN. THERE WAS NO P.P.D.C., YET."
THAT'S WHY WE'RE HERE, TODAY. IT'S THE ONLY QUESTION THAT MATTERS--
WHAT WILL IT TAKE TO GRAB THIS MONSTER BY THE THROAT AND DRAG HIM BACK TO HELL?
I MIGHT BE ABLE TO ANSWER THAT.
"SO I EXPLAINED MY IDEA...MY GIANT, MAD IDEA..."
...NOT A ROBOT EXACTLY. A ROBOT IS AUTONOMOUS. THIS WOULD BE DRIVEN BY A LIVING, THINKING HUMAN BEING. IT'S A MECH.

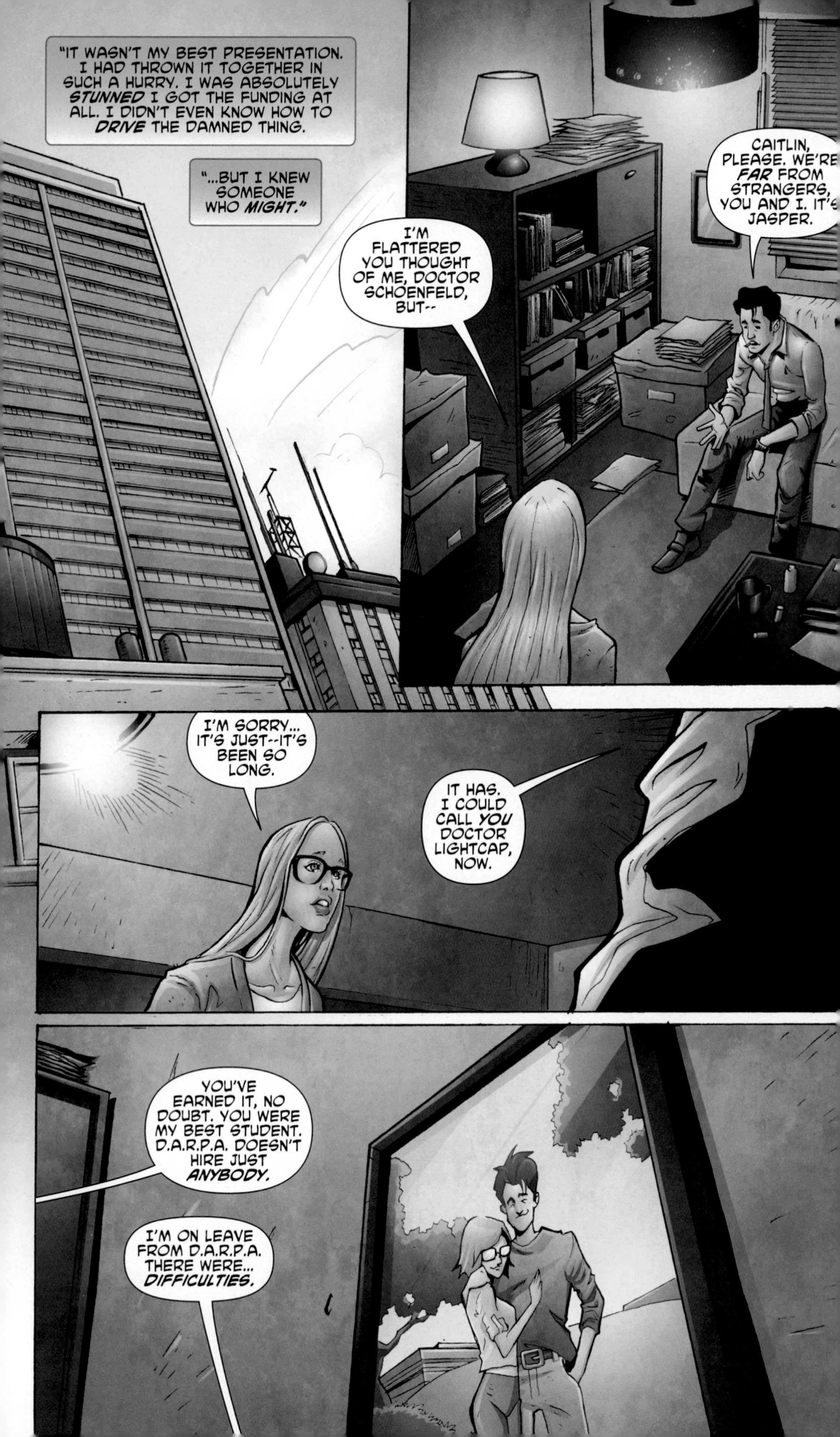
"IT WASN'T MY BEST PRESENTATION. I HAD THROWN IT TOGETHER IN SUCH A HURRY. I WAS ABSOLUTELY STUNNED I GOT THE FUNDING AT ALL. I DIDN'T EVEN KNOW HOW TO DRIVE THE DAMNED THING.
"...BUT I KNEW SOMEONE WHO MIGHT."
I'M FLATTERED YOU THOUGHT OF ME, DOCTOR SCHOENFELD, BUT--
CAITLIN, PLEASE. WE'RE FAR FROM STRANGERS, YOU AND I. IT'S JASPER.
I'M SORRY... IT'S JUST--IT'S BEEN SO LONG.
IT HAS. I COULD CALL YOU DOCTOR LIGHTCAP, NOW.
YOU'VE EARNED IT, NO DOUBT. YOU WERE MY BEST STUDENT. D.A.R.P.A. DOESN'T HIRE JUST ANYBODY.
I'M ON LEAVE FROM D.A.R.P.A. THERE WERE... DIFFICULTIES.

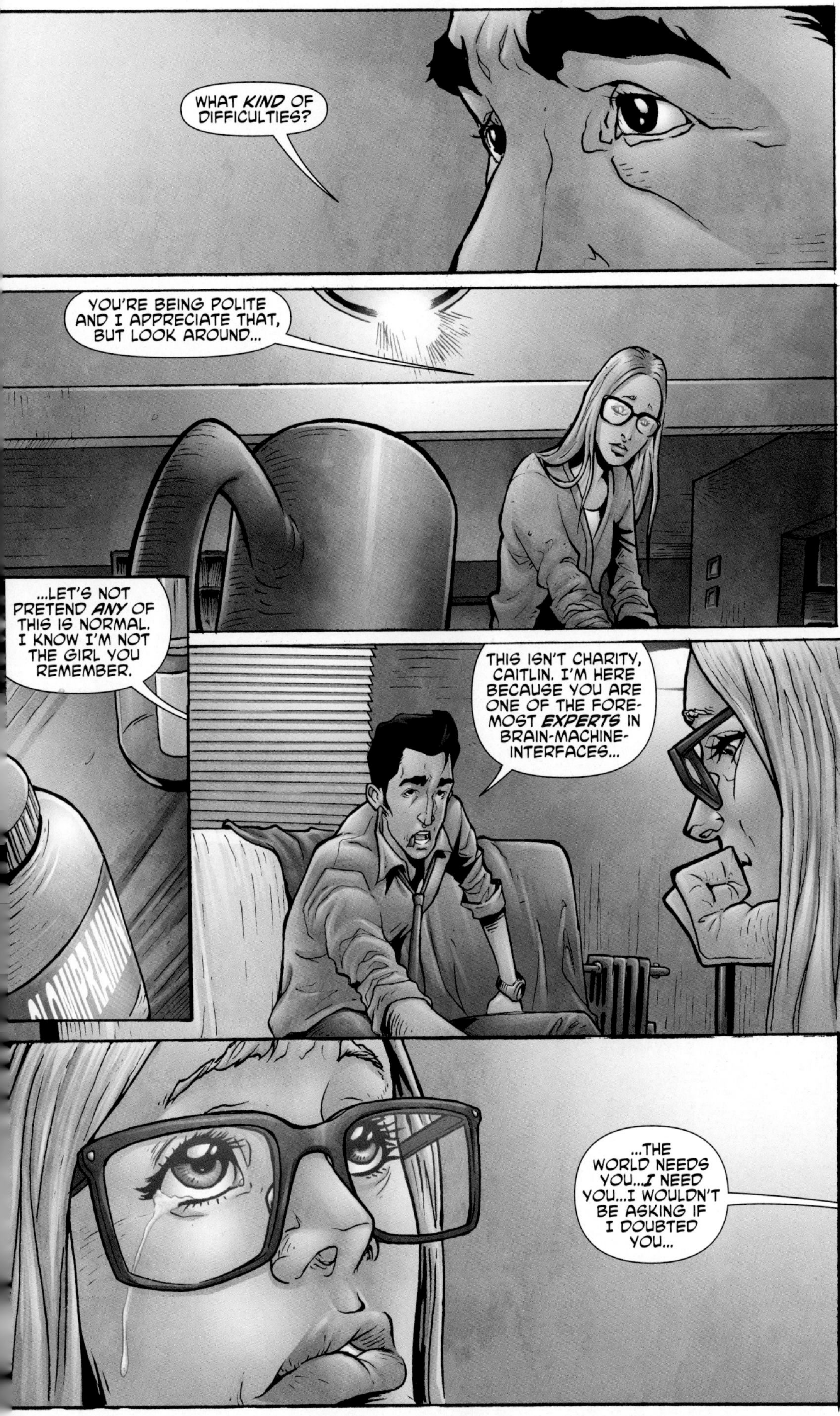
WHAT KIND OF DIFFICULTIES?
YOU'RE BEING POLITE AND I APPRECIATE THAT, BUT LOOK AROUND...
...LET'S NOT PRETEND ANY OF THIS IS NORMAL. I KNOW I'M NOT THE GIRL YOU REMEMBER.
THIS ISN'T CHARITY, CAITLIN. I'M HERE BECAUSE YOU ARE ONE OF THE FOREMOST EXPERTS IN BRAIN-MACHINE-INTERFACES...
...THE WORLD NEEDS YOU...I NEED YOU...I WOULDN'T BE ASKING IF I DOUBTED YOU...

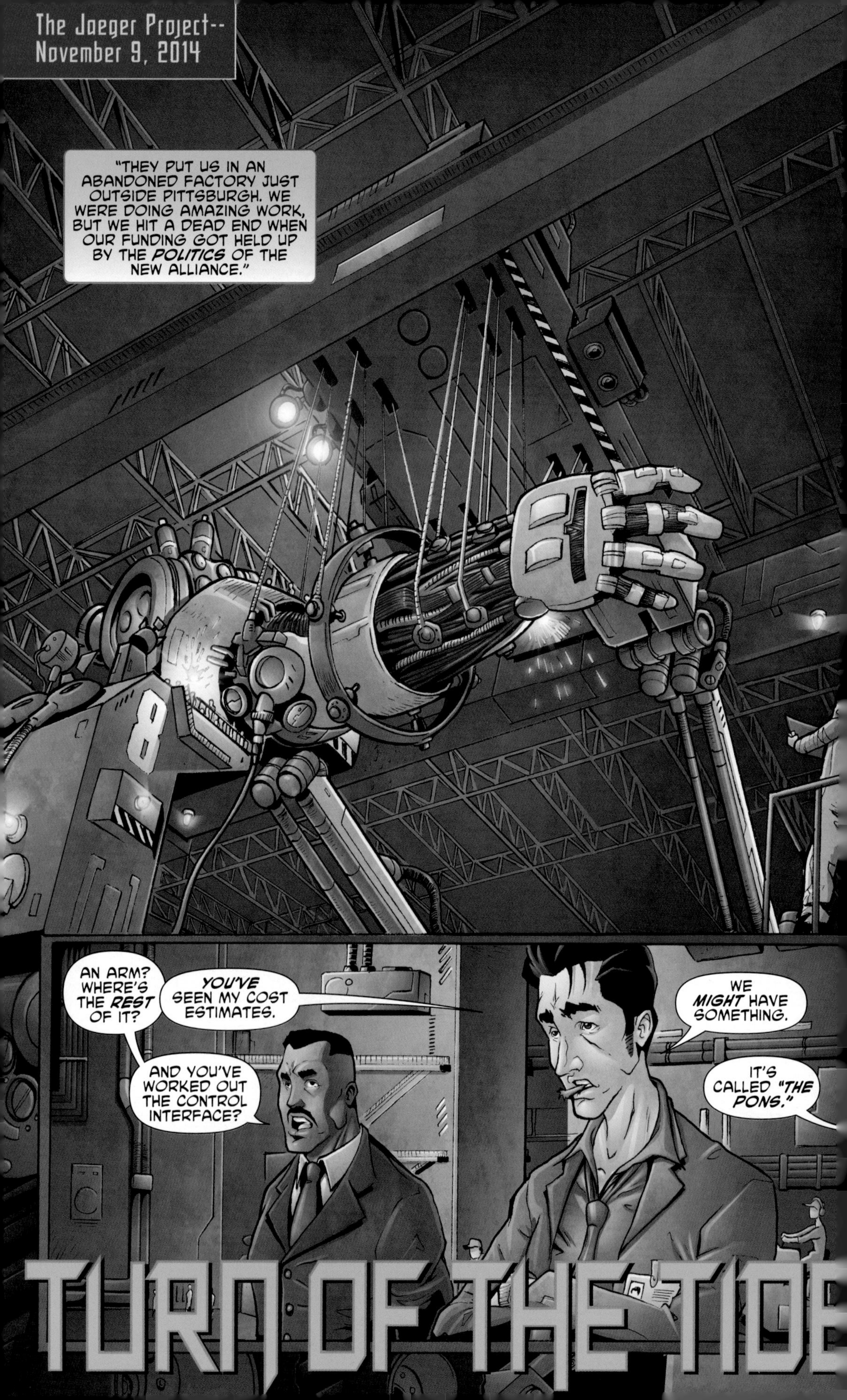

The Jaeger Project--
November 9, 2014
"THEY PUT US IN AN ABANDONED FACTORY JUST OUTSIDE PITTSBURGH. WE WERE DOING AMAZING WORK, BUT WE HIT A DEAD END WHEN OUR FUNDING GOT HELD UP BY THE *POLITICS* OF THE NEW ALLIANCE."
8
AN ARM? WHERE'S THE *REST* OF IT?
YOU'VE SEEN MY COST ESTIMATES.
AND YOU'VE WORKED OUT THE CONTROL INTERFACE?
WE *MIGHT* HAVE SOMETHING.
IT'S CALLED *"THE PONS."*
TURN OF THE TIDE

WHO'S THIS?

DOCTOR CAITLIN LIGHTCAP. *CAITLIN*, THIS IS STACKER PENTECOST.

SPECIAL LIAISON. I'M HERE TO EVALUATE YOUR PROGRESS. DID YOU SAY "PONG"?

IT'S LATIN FOR "BRIDGE."

I *KNOW* WHAT IT MEANS IN ROME, DOCTOR. WHAT DOES IT MEAN *HERE*?

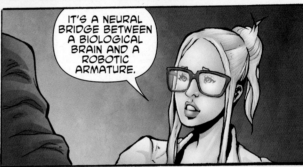

IT'S A NEURAL BRIDGE BETWEEN A BIOLOGICAL BRAIN AND A ROBOTIC ARMATURE.

SO YOU CAN MOVE THIS THING WITH JUST YOUR *THOUGHTS*?

IN *THEORY.* WE HAVEN'T TESTED THE UPLINK.

WHY NOT?

FUNDING. WE PUT IN A REQUEST TO RECRUIT PROPER TEST SUBJECTS. WE'RE *STILL* WAITING TO HEAR BACK.

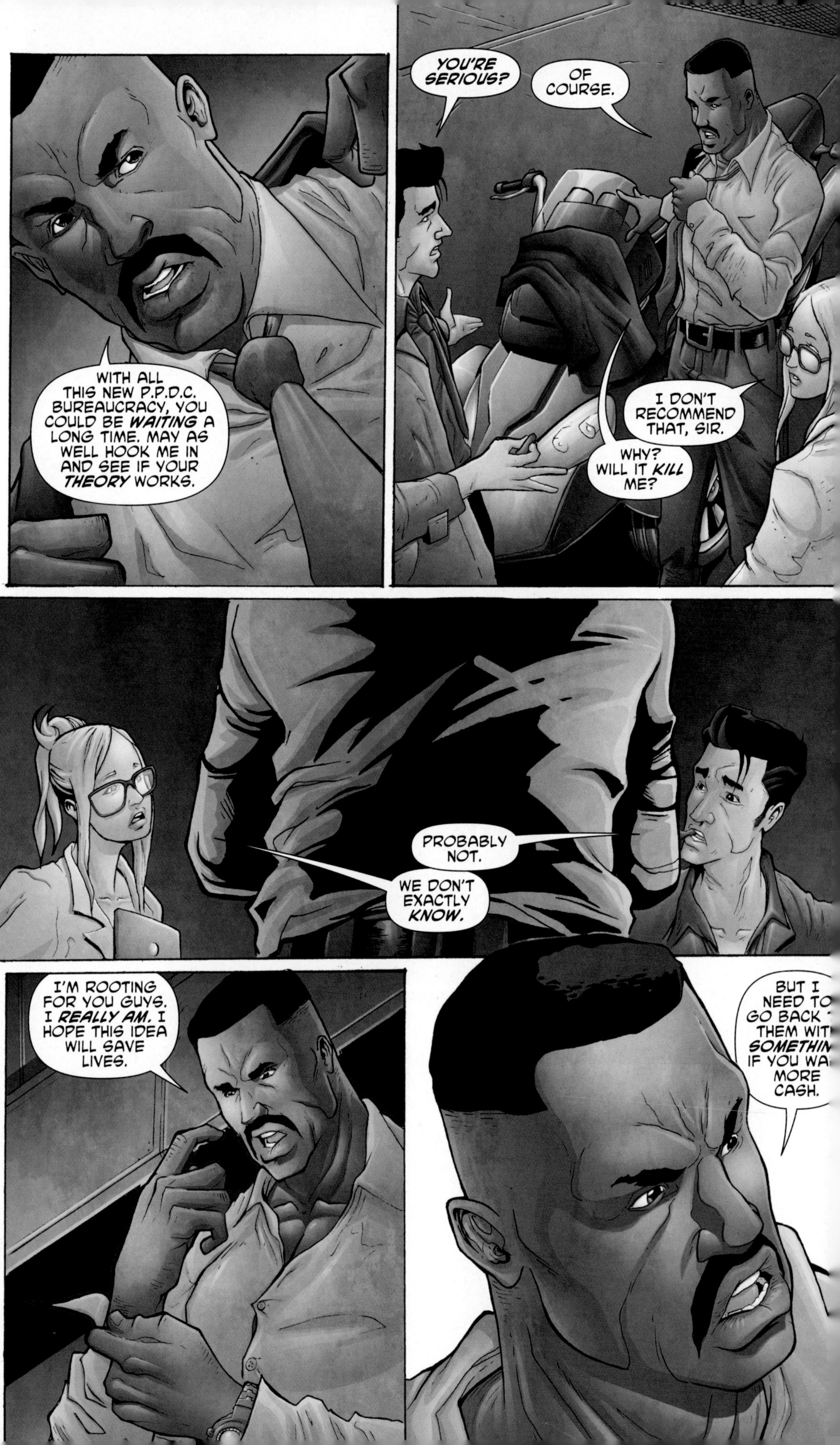
WITH ALL THIS NEW P.P.D.C. BUREAUCRACY, YOU COULD BE WAITING A LONG TIME. MAY AS WELL HOOK ME IN AND SEE IF YOUR THEORY WORKS.
YOU'RE SERIOUS?
OF COURSE.
I DON'T RECOMMEND THAT, SIR.
WHY? WILL IT KILL ME?
PROBABLY NOT.
WE DON'T EXACTLY KNOW.
I'M ROOTING FOR YOU GUYS. I REALLY AM. I HOPE THIS IDEA WILL SAVE LIVES.
BUT I NEED TO GO BACK T THEM WIT SOMETHIN IF YOU WA MORE CASH.

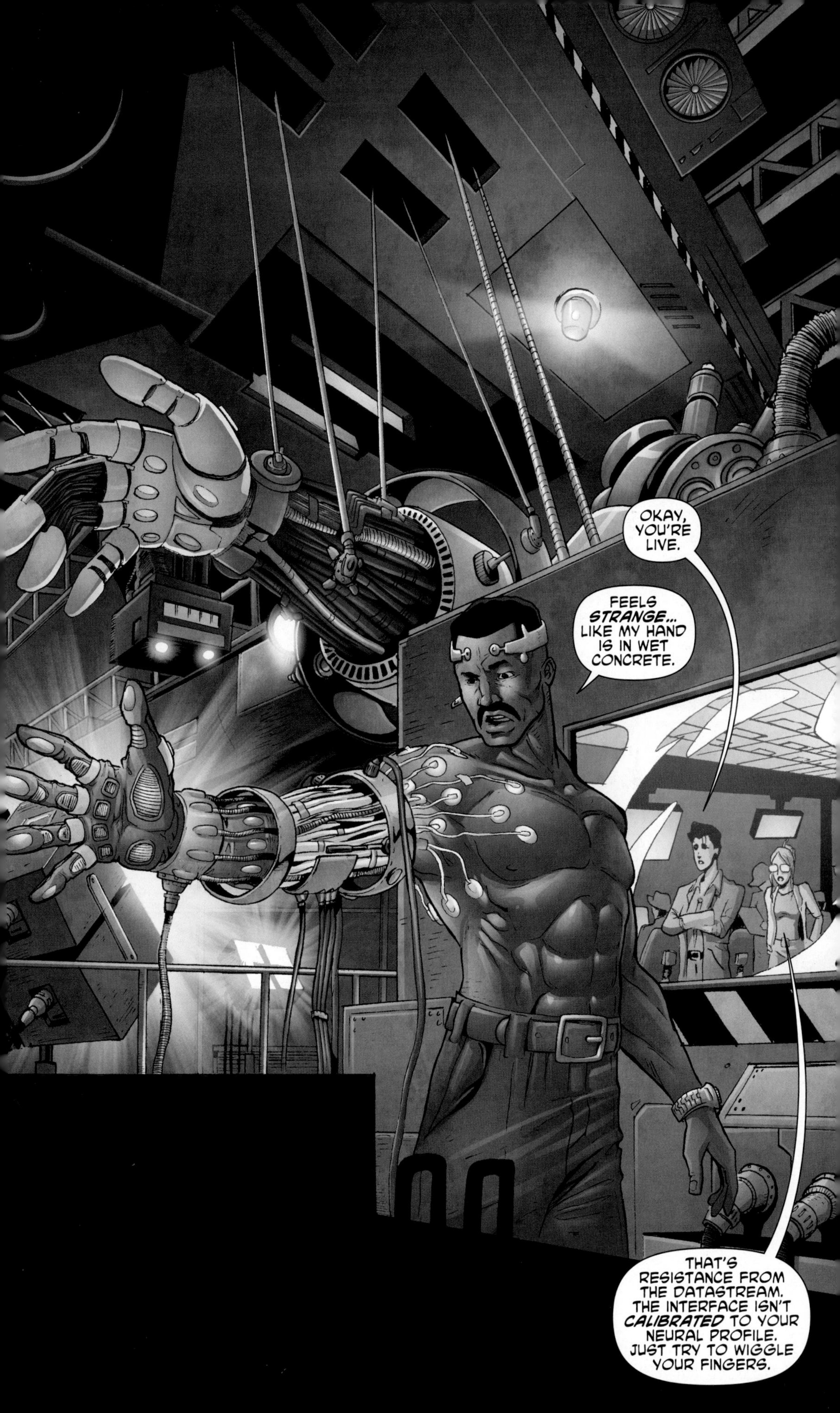
OKAY, YOU'RE LIVE.
FEELS *STRANGE*... LIKE MY HAND IS IN WET CONCRETE.
THAT'S RESISTANCE FROM THE DATASTREAM. THE INTERFACE ISN'T *CALIBRATED* TO YOUR NEURAL PROFILE. JUST TRY TO WIGGLE YOUR FINGERS.

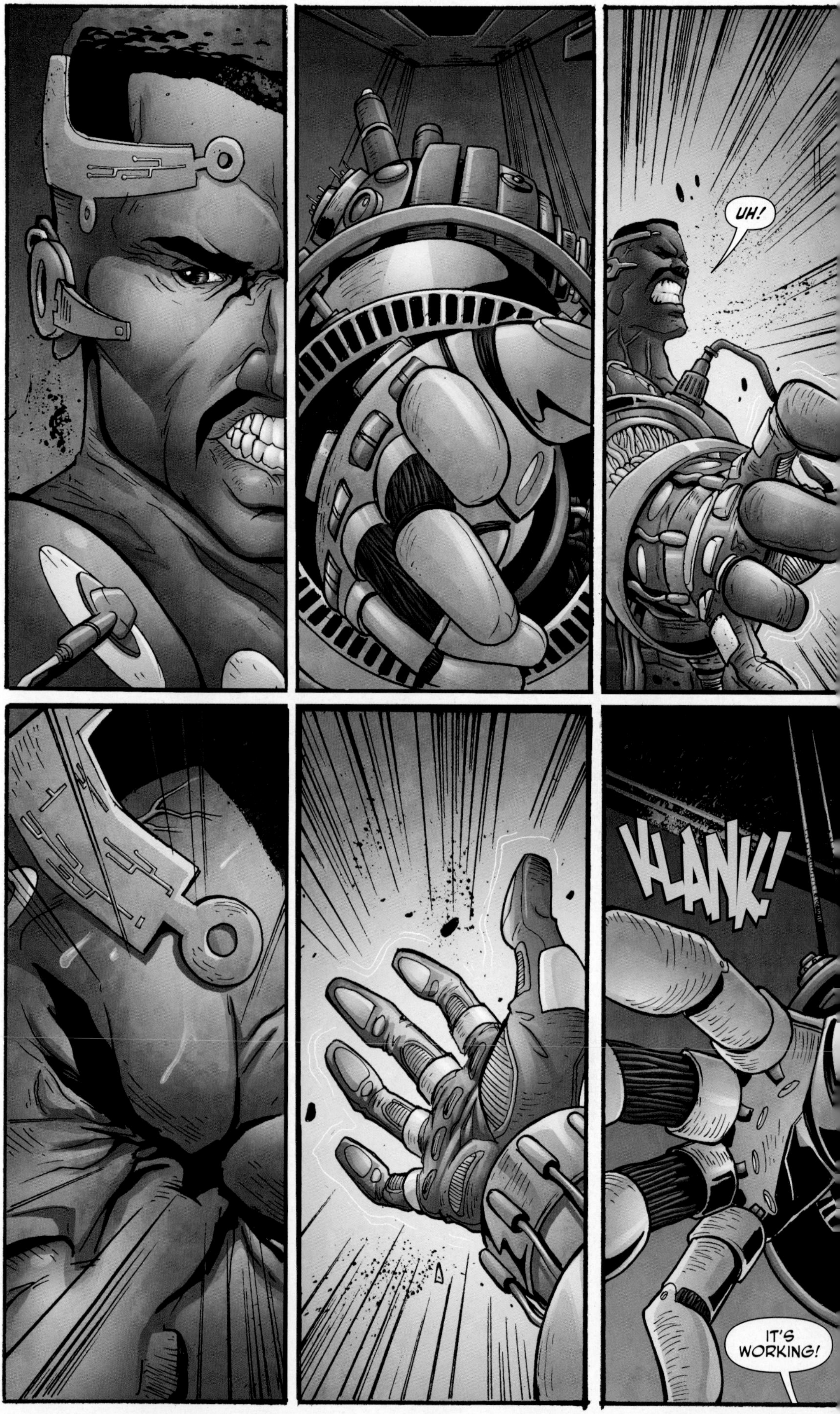
UH!
KLANK!
IT'S WORKING!

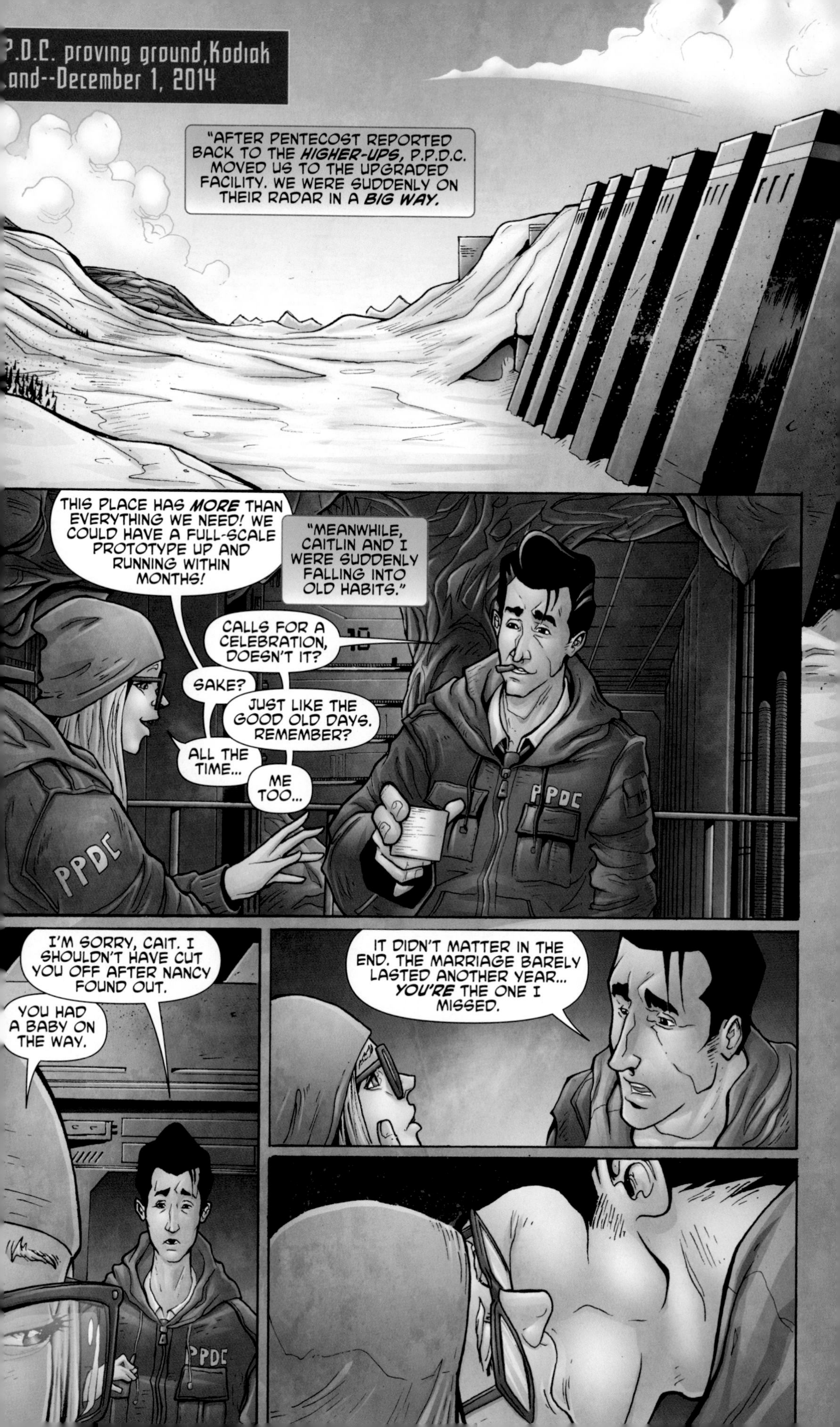

P.D.C. proving ground, Kodiak and--December 1, 2014
"AFTER PENTECOST REPORTED BACK TO THE HIGHER-UPS, P.P.D.C. MOVED US TO THE UPGRADED FACILITY. WE WERE SUDDENLY ON THEIR RADAR IN A BIG WAY.
THIS PLACE HAS MORE THAN EVERYTHING WE NEED! WE COULD HAVE A FULL-SCALE PROTOTYPE UP AND RUNNING WITHIN MONTHS!
"MEANWHILE, CAITLIN AND I WERE SUDDENLY FALLING INTO OLD HABITS."
CALLS FOR A CELEBRATION, DOESN'T IT?
SAKE?
JUST LIKE THE GOOD OLD DAYS. REMEMBER?
ALL THE TIME...
ME TOO...
PPDC
PPDC
I'M SORRY, CAIT. I SHOULDN'T HAVE CUT YOU OFF AFTER NANCY FOUND OUT.
YOU HAD A BABY ON THE WAY.
PPDC
IT DIDN'T MATTER IN THE END. THE MARRIAGE BARELY LASTED ANOTHER YEAR... YOU'RE THE ONE I MISSED.

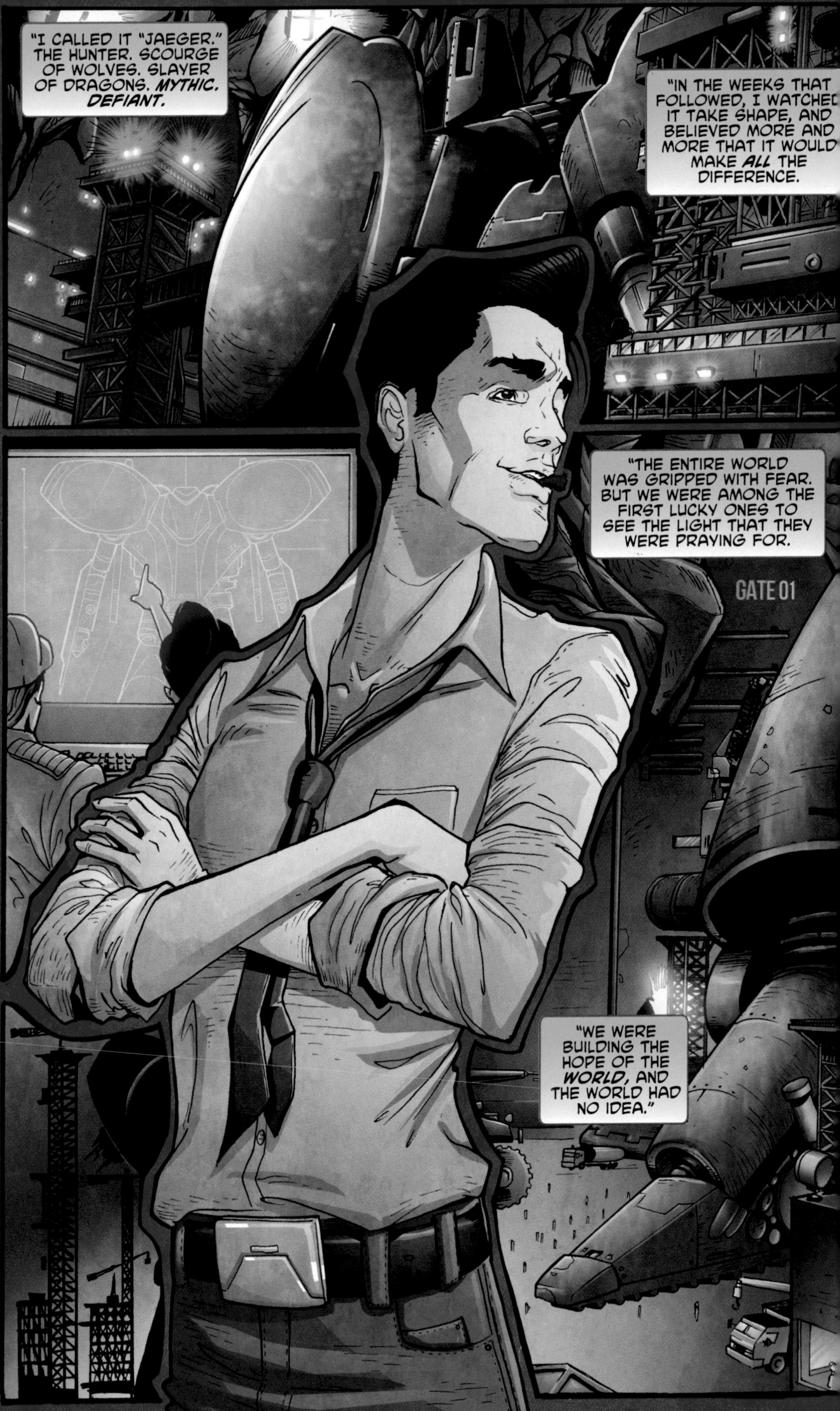
"I CALLED IT "JAEGER." THE HUNTER. SCOURGE OF WOLVES. SLAYER OF DRAGONS. *MYTHIC. DEFIANT.*
"IN THE WEEKS THAT FOLLOWED, I WATCHED IT TAKE SHAPE, AND BELIEVED MORE AND MORE THAT IT WOULD MAKE *ALL* THE DIFFERENCE.
"THE ENTIRE WORLD WAS GRIPPED WITH FEAR. BUT WE WERE AMONG THE FIRST LUCKY ONES TO SEE THE LIGHT THAT THEY WERE PRAYING FOR.
GATE 01
"WE WERE BUILDING THE HOPE OF THE *WORLD,* AND THE WORLD HAD NO IDEA."

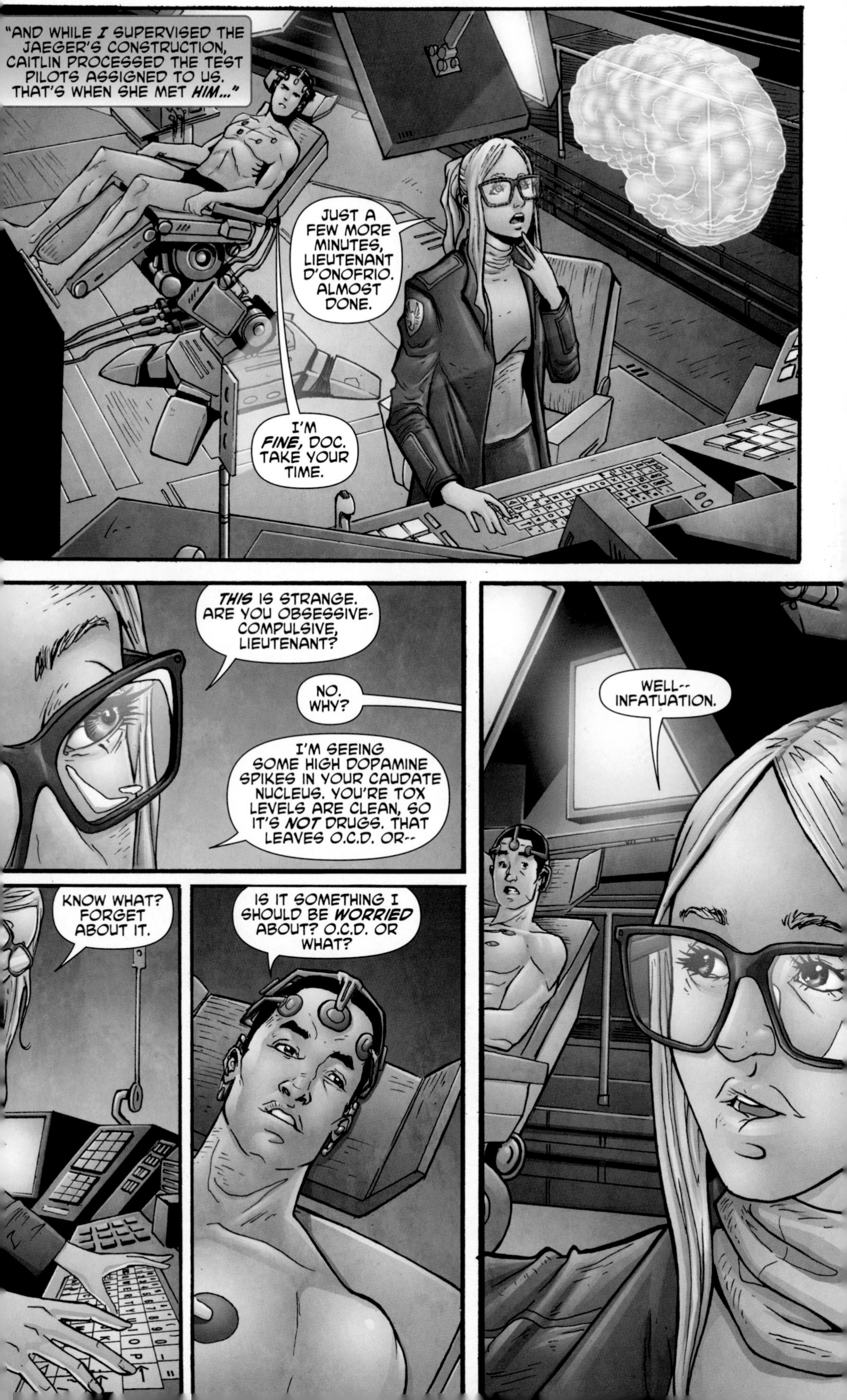
"AND WHILE *I* SUPERVISED THE JAEGER'S CONSTRUCTION, CAITLIN PROCESSED THE TEST PILOTS ASSIGNED TO US. THAT'S WHEN SHE MET *HIM*..."
JUST A FEW MORE MINUTES, LIEUTENANT D'ONOFRIO. ALMOST DONE.
I'M *FINE*, DOC. TAKE YOUR TIME.
THIS IS STRANGE. ARE YOU OBSESSIVE-COMPULSIVE, LIEUTENANT?
NO. WHY?
I'M SEEING SOME HIGH DOPAMINE SPIKES IN YOUR CAUDATE NUCLEUS. YOU'RE TOX LEVELS ARE CLEAN, SO IT'S *NOT* DRUGS. THAT LEAVES O.C.D. OR--
WELL-- INFATUATION.
KNOW WHAT? FORGET ABOUT IT.
IS IT SOMETHING I SHOULD BE *WORRIED* ABOUT? O.C.D. OR WHAT?

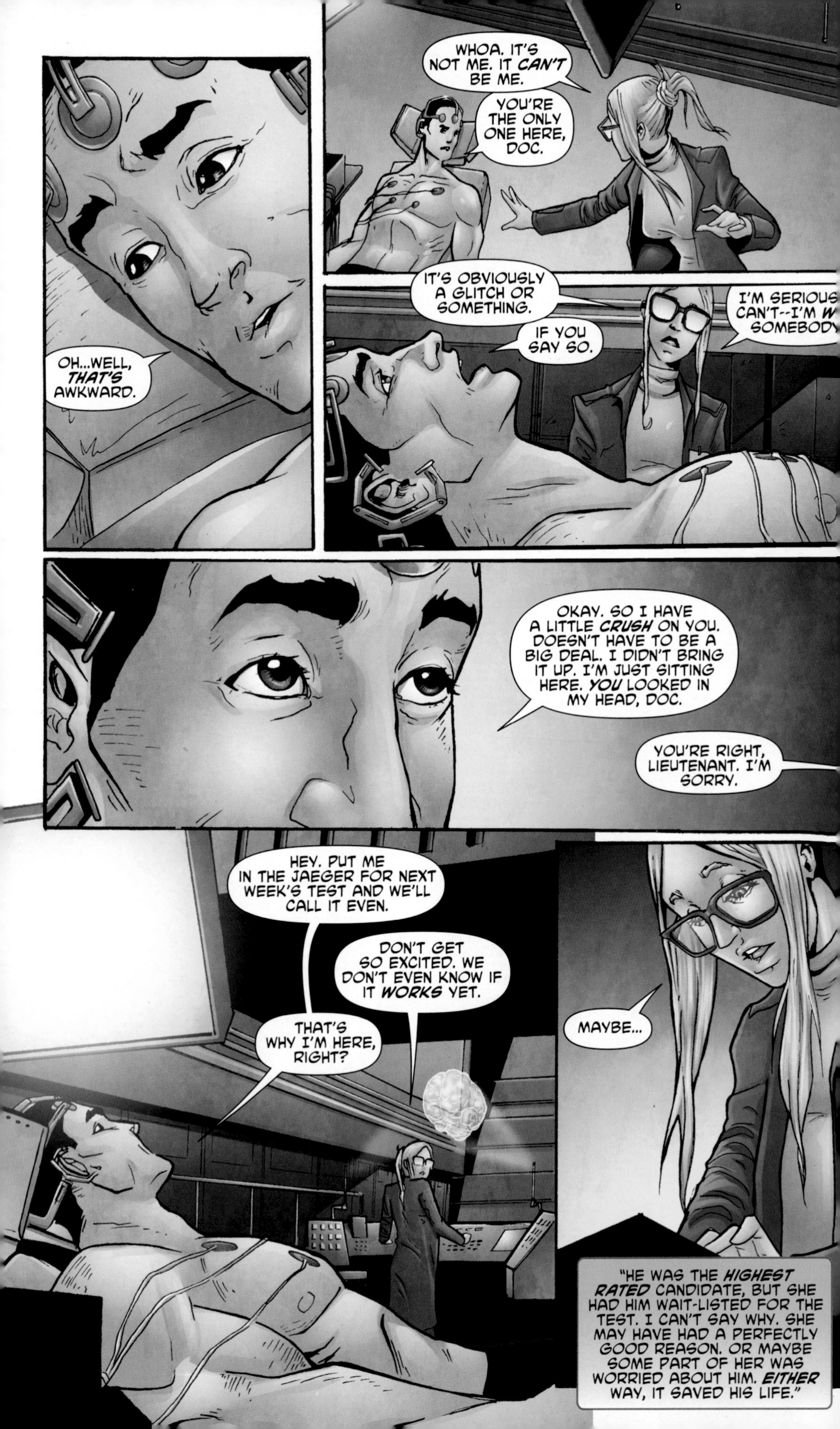
OH...WELL, THAT'S AWKWARD.
WHOA. IT'S NOT ME. IT CAN'T BE ME.
YOU'RE THE ONLY ONE HERE, DOC.
IT'S OBVIOUSLY A GLITCH OR SOMETHING.
IF YOU SAY SO.
I'M SERIOUS CAN'T--I'M
SOMEBODY
OKAY. SO I HAVE A LITTLE CRUSH ON YOU. DOESN'T HAVE TO BE A BIG DEAL. I DIDN'T BRING IT UP. I'M JUST SITTING HERE. YOU LOOKED IN MY HEAD, DOC.
YOU'RE RIGHT, LIEUTENANT. I'M SORRY.
HEY. PUT ME IN THE JAEGER FOR NEXT WEEK'S TEST AND WE'LL CALL IT EVEN.
DON'T GET SO EXCITED. WE DON'T EVEN KNOW IF IT WORKS YET.
THAT'S WHY I'M HERE, RIGHT?
MAYBE...
"HE WAS THE HIGHEST RATED CANDIDATE, BUT SHE HAD HIM WAIT-LISTED FOR THE TEST. I CAN'T SAY WHY. SHE MAY HAVE HAD A PERFECTLY GOOD REASON. OR MAYBE SOME PART OF HER WAS WORRIED ABOUT HIM. EITHER WAY, IT SAVED HIS LIFE."

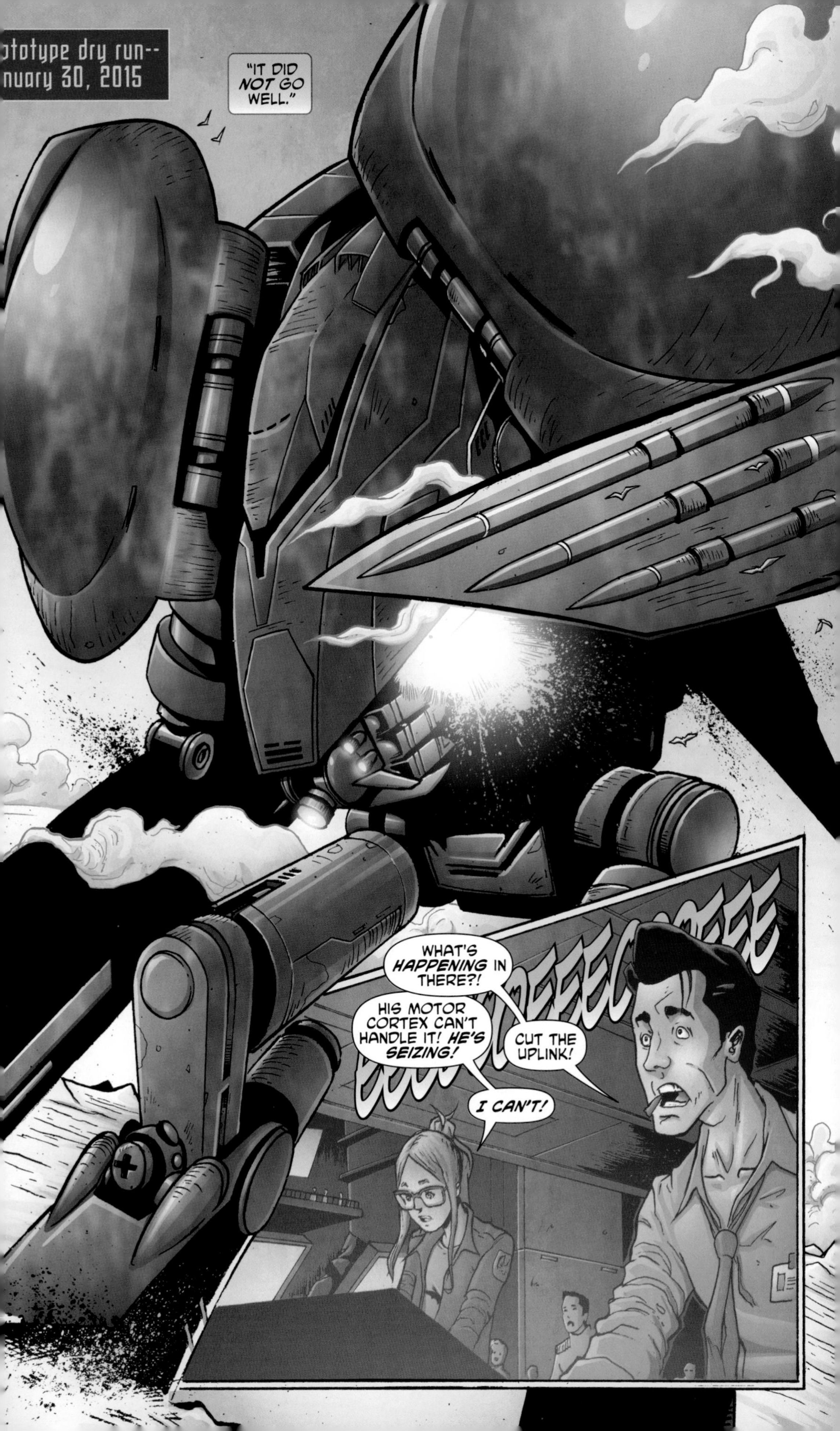

ototype dry run--
nuary 30, 2015
"IT DID NOT GO WELL."
WHAT'S HAPPENING IN THERE?!
CUT THE UPLINK!
HIS MOTOR CORTEX CAN'T HANDLE IT! HE'S SEIZING!
I CAN'T!

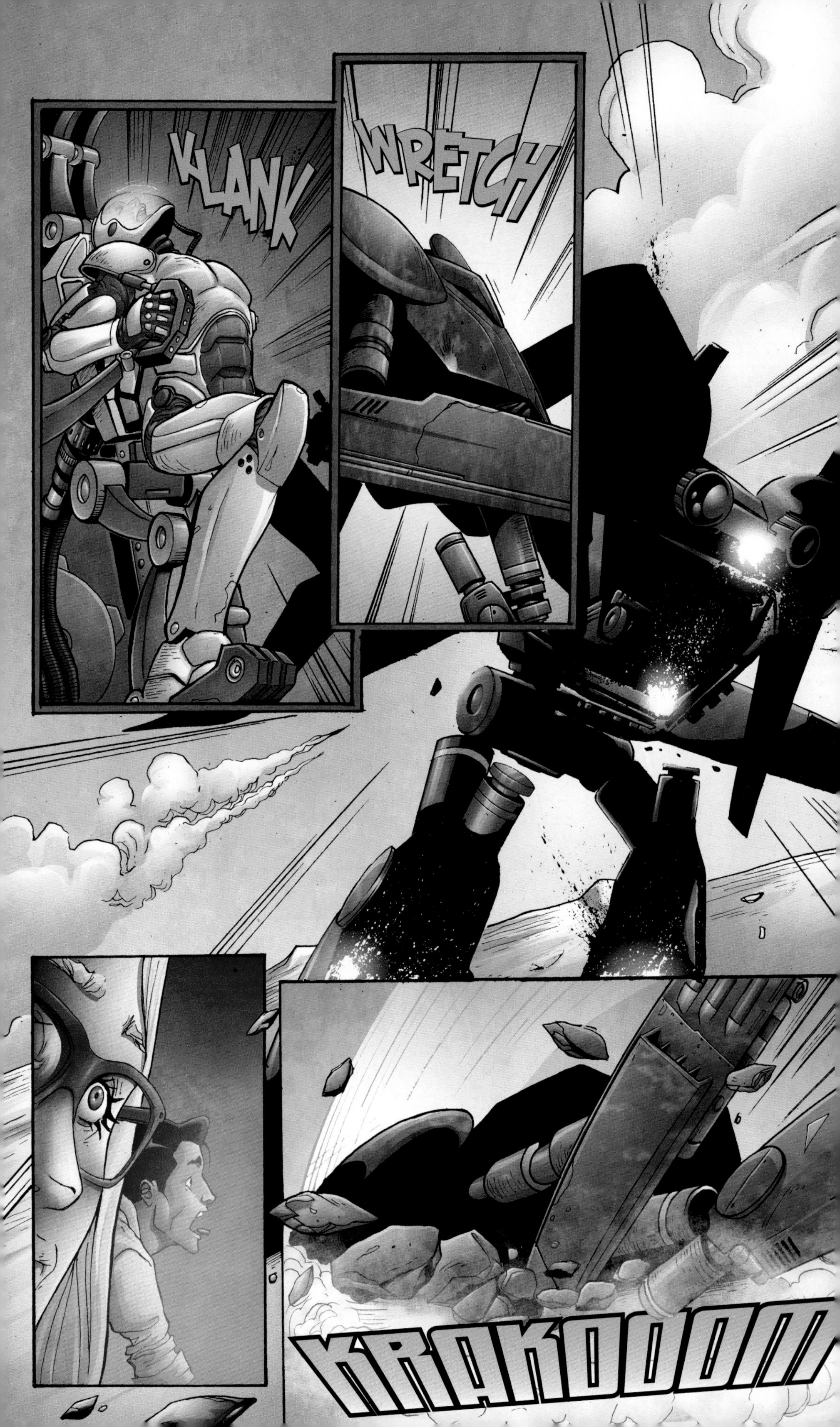
KLANK
WRETCH
KRAKOOOM

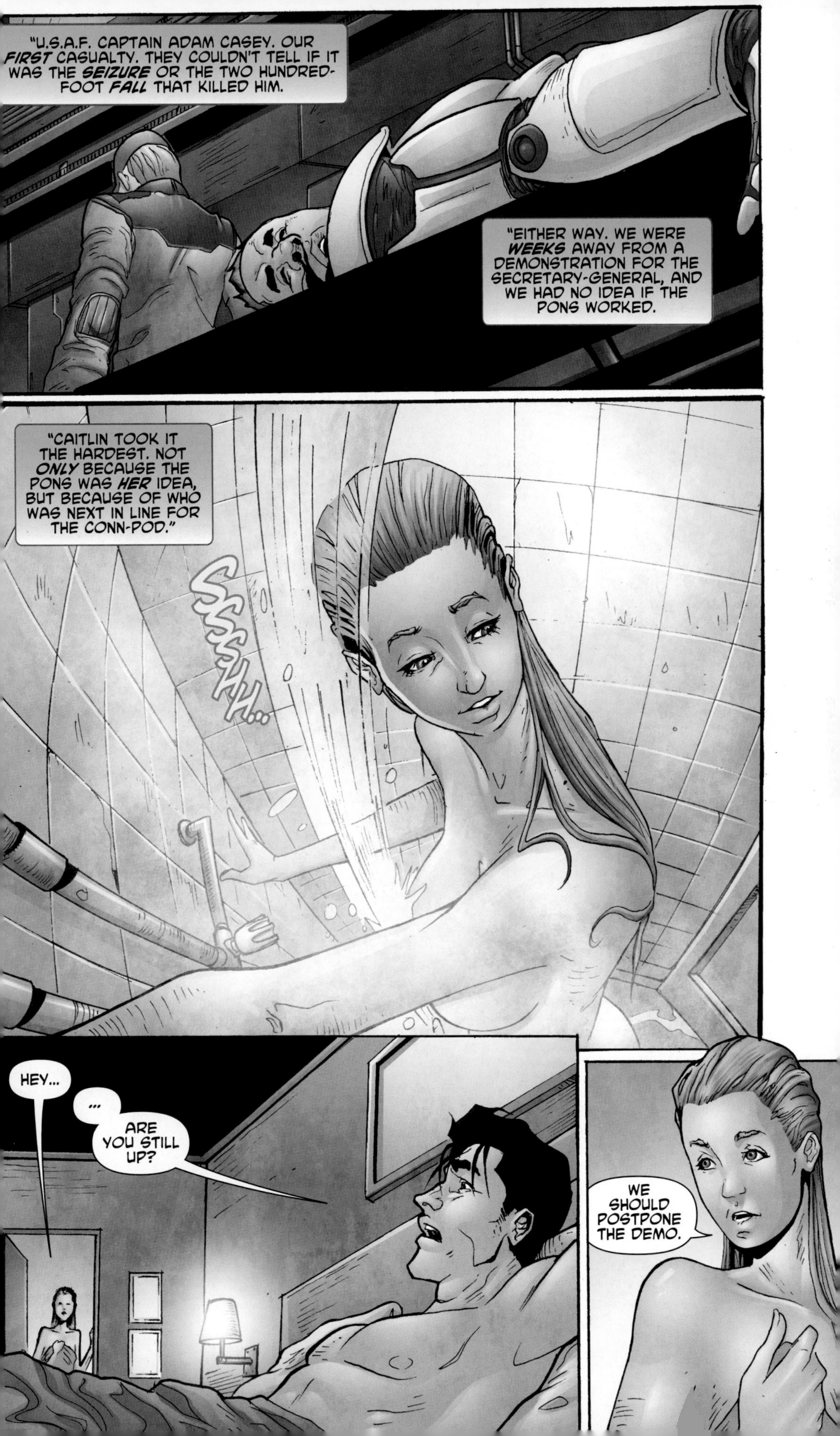
"U.S.A.F. CAPTAIN ADAM CASEY. OUR FIRST CASUALTY. THEY COULDN'T TELL IF IT WAS THE SEIZURE OR THE TWO HUNDRED-FOOT FALL THAT KILLED HIM.
"EITHER WAY. WE WERE WEEKS AWAY FROM A DEMONSTRATION FOR THE SECRETARY-GENERAL, AND WE HAD NO IDEA IF THE PONS WORKED.
"CAITLIN TOOK IT THE HARDEST. NOT ONLY BECAUSE THE PONS WAS HER IDEA, BUT BECAUSE OF WHO WAS NEXT IN LINE FOR THE CONN-POD."
SSSHHH...
HEY...
... ARE YOU STILL UP?
WE SHOULD POSTPONE THE DEMO.

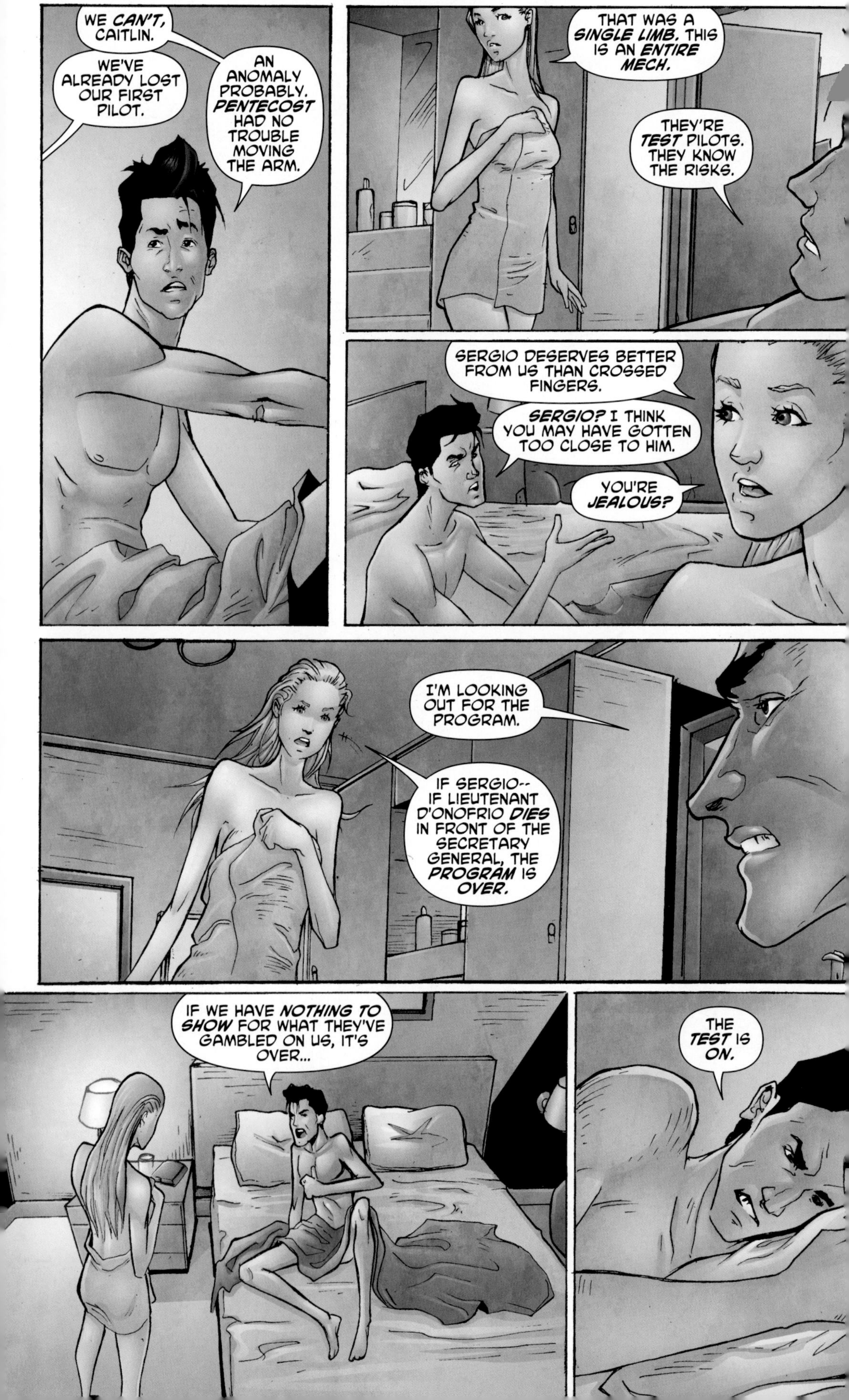

WE CAN'T, CAITLIN.
WE'VE ALREADY LOST OUR FIRST PILOT.
AN ANOMALY PROBABLY. PENTECOST HAD NO TROUBLE MOVING THE ARM.
THAT WAS A SINGLE LIMB. THIS IS AN ENTIRE MECH.
THEY'RE TEST PILOTS. THEY KNOW THE RISKS.
SERGIO DESERVES BETTER FROM US THAN CROSSED FINGERS.
SERGIO? I THINK YOU MAY HAVE GOTTEN TOO CLOSE TO HIM.
YOU'RE JEALOUS?
I'M LOOKING OUT FOR THE PROGRAM.
IF SERGIO-- IF LIEUTENANT D'ONOFRIO DIES IN FRONT OF THE SECRETARY GENERAL, THE PROGRAM IS OVER.
IF WE HAVE NOTHING TO SHOW FOR WHAT THEY'VE GAMBLED ON US, IT'S OVER...
THE TEST IS ON.

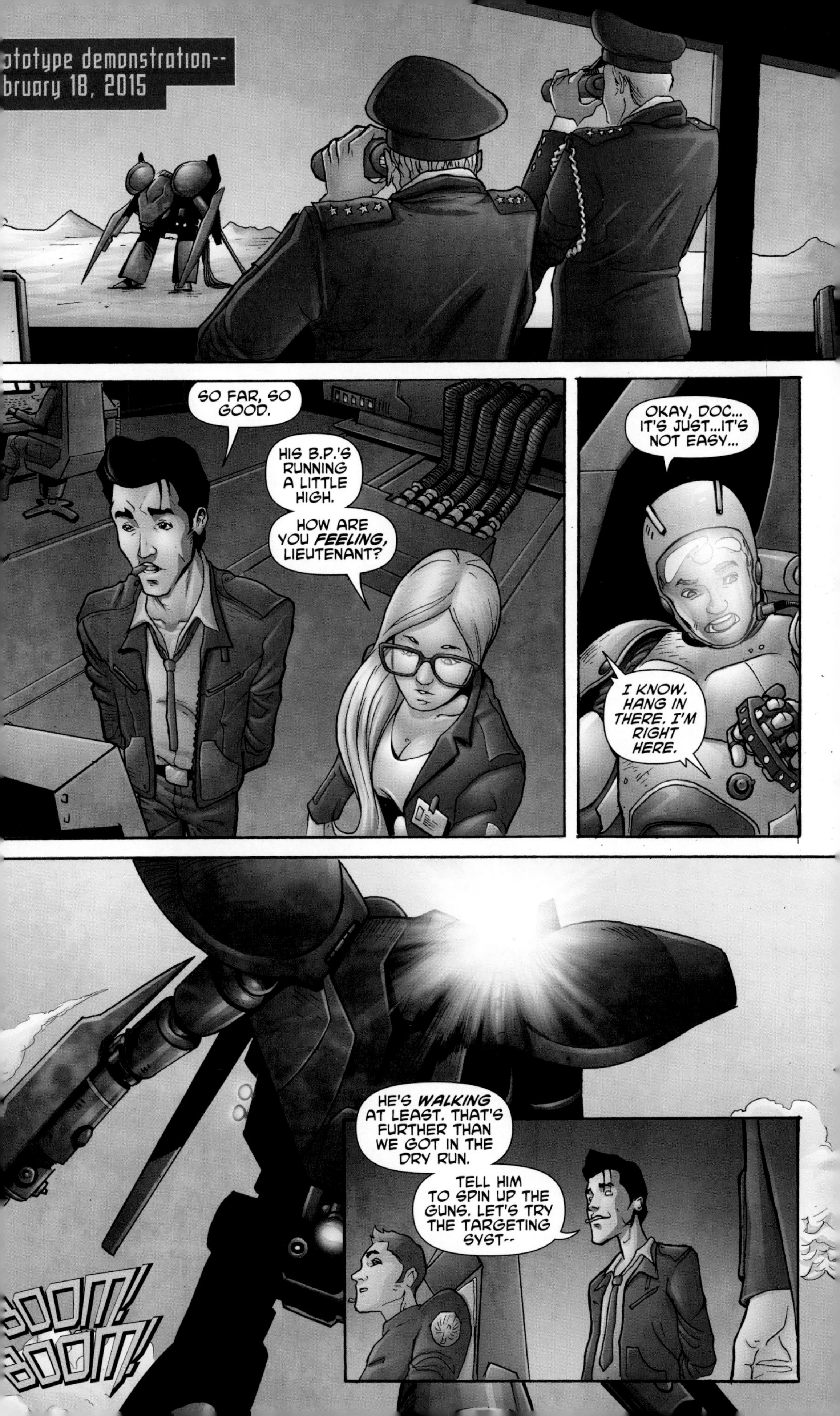
ototype demonstration--
bruary 18, 2015
SO FAR, SO GOOD.
HIS B.P.'S RUNNING A LITTLE HIGH.
HOW ARE YOU FEELING, LIEUTENANT?
OKAY, DOC... IT'S JUST...IT'S NOT EASY...
I KNOW. HANG IN THERE. I'M RIGHT HERE.
HE'S WALKING AT LEAST. THAT'S FURTHER THAN WE GOT IN THE DRY RUN.
TELL HIM TO SPIN UP THE GUNS. LET'S TRY THE TARGETING SYST--

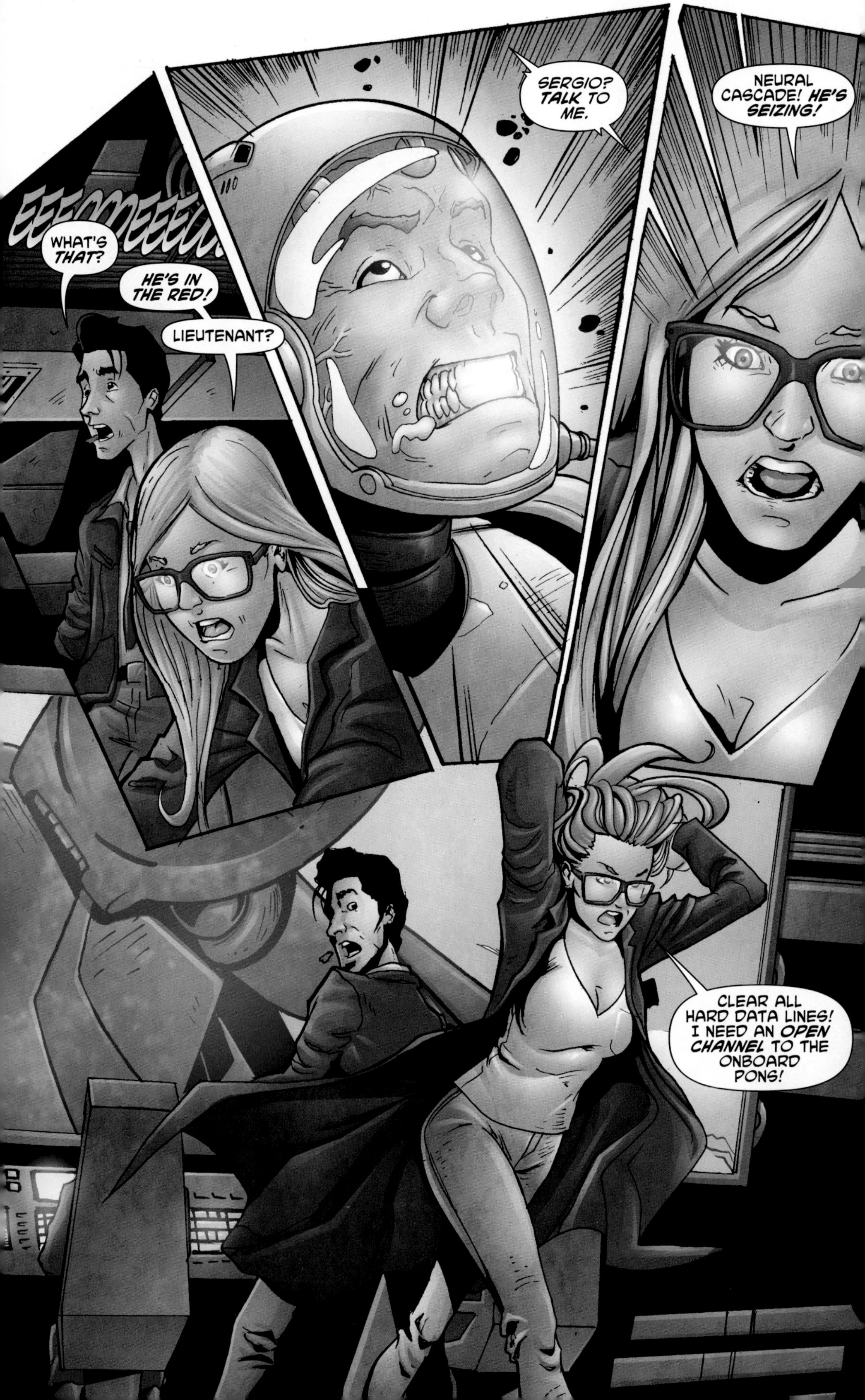
WHAT'S THAT?
HE'S IN THE RED!
LIEUTENANT?
SERGIO? TALK TO ME.
NEURAL CASCADE! HE'S SEIZING!
CLEAR ALL HARD DATA LINES! I NEED AN OPEN CHANNEL TO THE ONBOARD PONS!

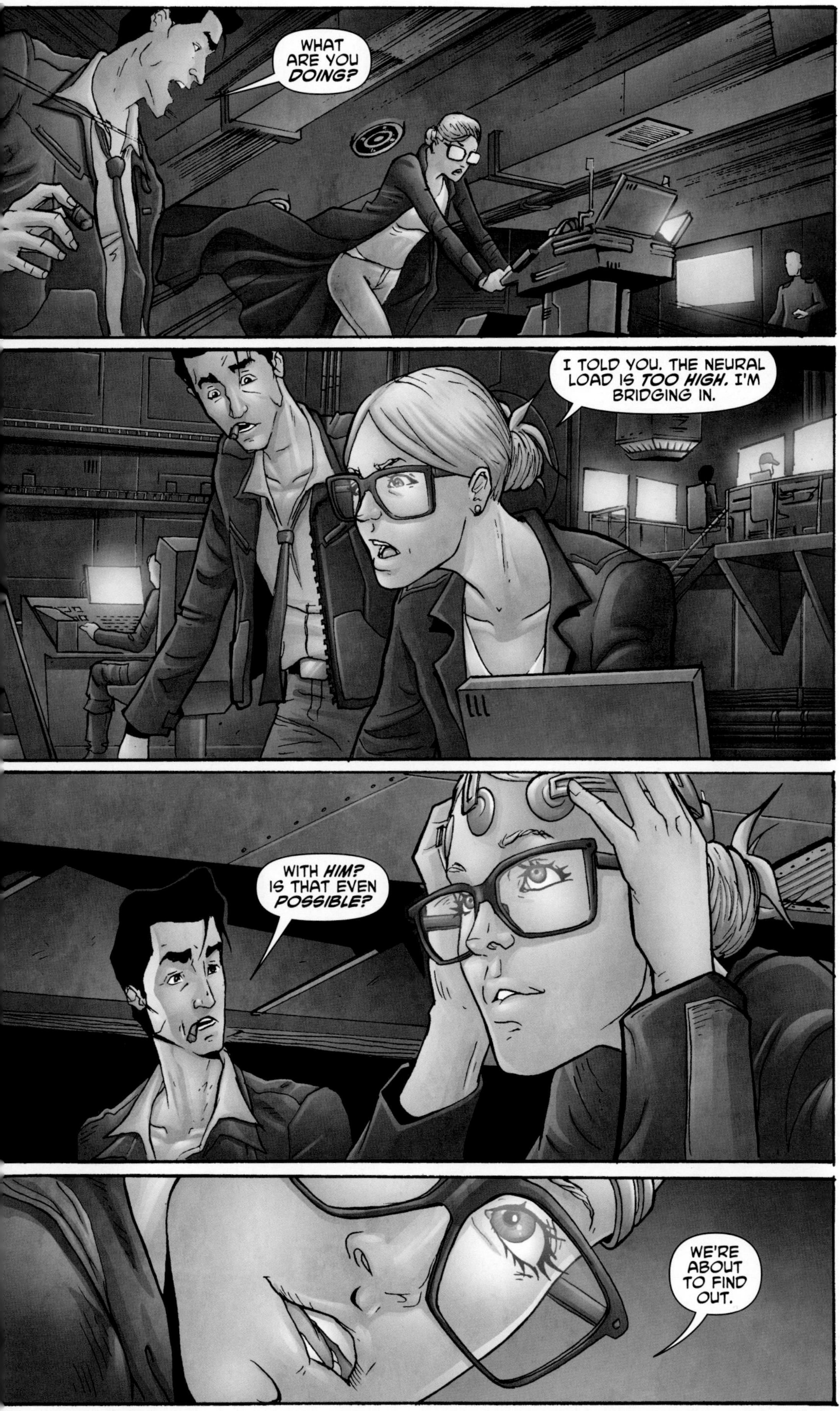
WHAT ARE YOU *DOING?*
I TOLD YOU. THE NEURAL LOAD IS *TOO HIGH.* I'M BRIDGING IN.
WITH *HIM?* IS THAT EVEN *POSSIBLE?*
WE'RE ABOUT TO FIND OUT.

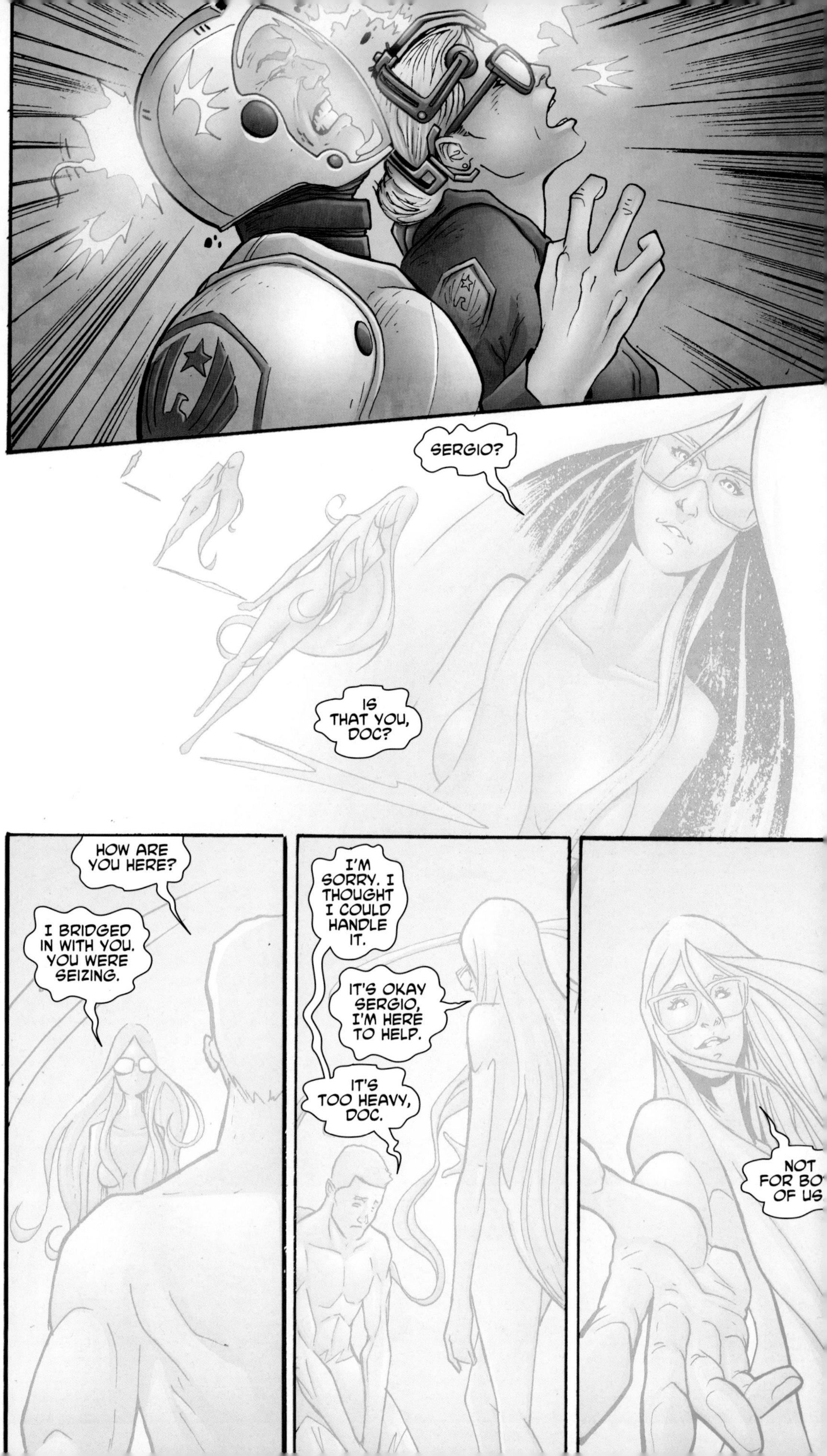
SERGIO?
IS THAT YOU, DOC?
HOW ARE YOU HERE?
I BRIDGED IN WITH YOU. YOU WERE SEIZING.
I'M SORRY. I THOUGHT I COULD HANDLE IT.
IT'S OKAY SERGIO, I'M HERE TO HELP.
IT'S TOO HEAVY, DOC.

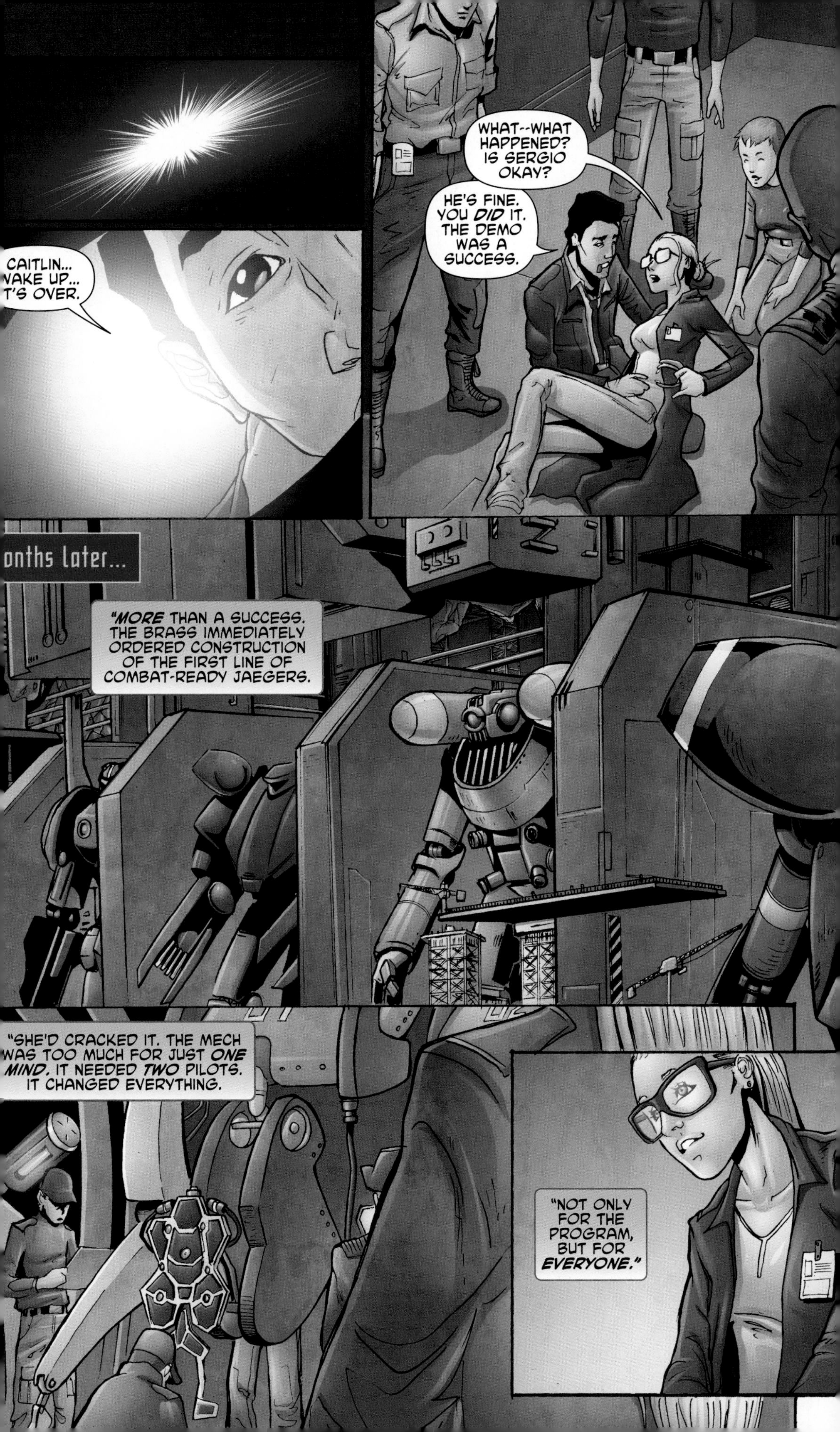

CAITLIN... WAKE UP... IT'S OVER.
WHAT--WHAT HAPPENED? IS SERGIO OKAY?
HE'S FINE. YOU *DID* IT. THE DEMO WAS A SUCCESS.
onths later...
"*MORE* THAN A SUCCESS. THE BRASS IMMEDIATELY ORDERED CONSTRUCTION OF THE FIRST LINE OF COMBAT-READY JAEGERS.
"SHE'D CRACKED IT. THE MECH WAS TOO MUCH FOR JUST *ONE MIND*. IT NEEDED *TWO* PILOTS. IT CHANGED EVERYTHING.
"NOT ONLY FOR THE PROGRAM, BUT FOR *EVERYONE*."

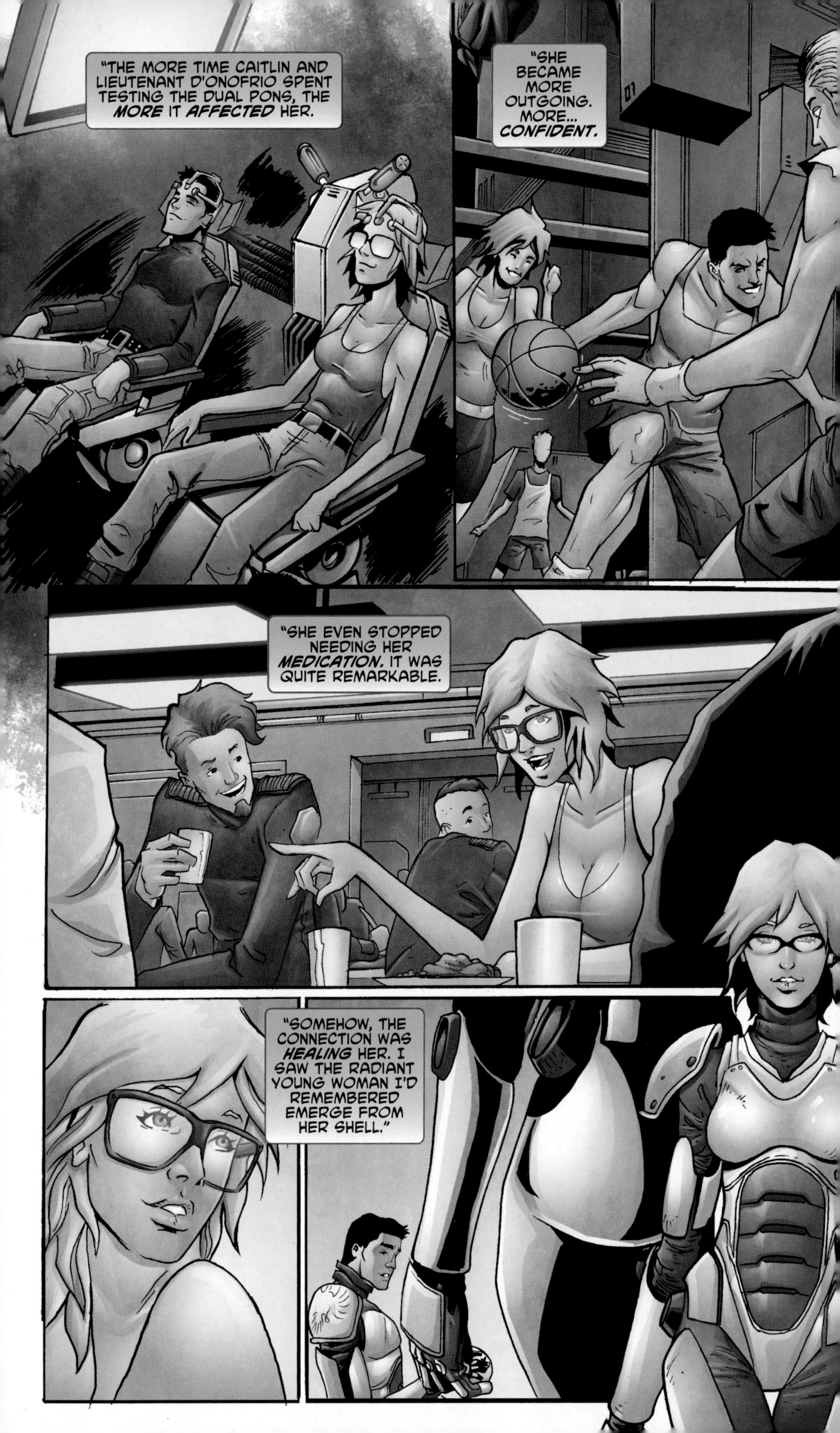
"THE MORE TIME CAITLIN AND LIEUTENANT D'ONOFRIO SPENT TESTING THE DUAL PONS, THE ***MORE*** IT ***AFFECTED*** HER.
"SHE BECAME MORE OUTGOING. MORE... ***CONFIDENT.***
"SHE EVEN STOPPED NEEDING HER ***MEDICATION.*** IT WAS QUITE REMARKABLE.
"SOMEHOW, THE CONNECTION WAS ***HEALING*** HER. I SAW THE RADIANT YOUNG WOMAN I'D REMEMBERED EMERGE FROM HER SHELL."

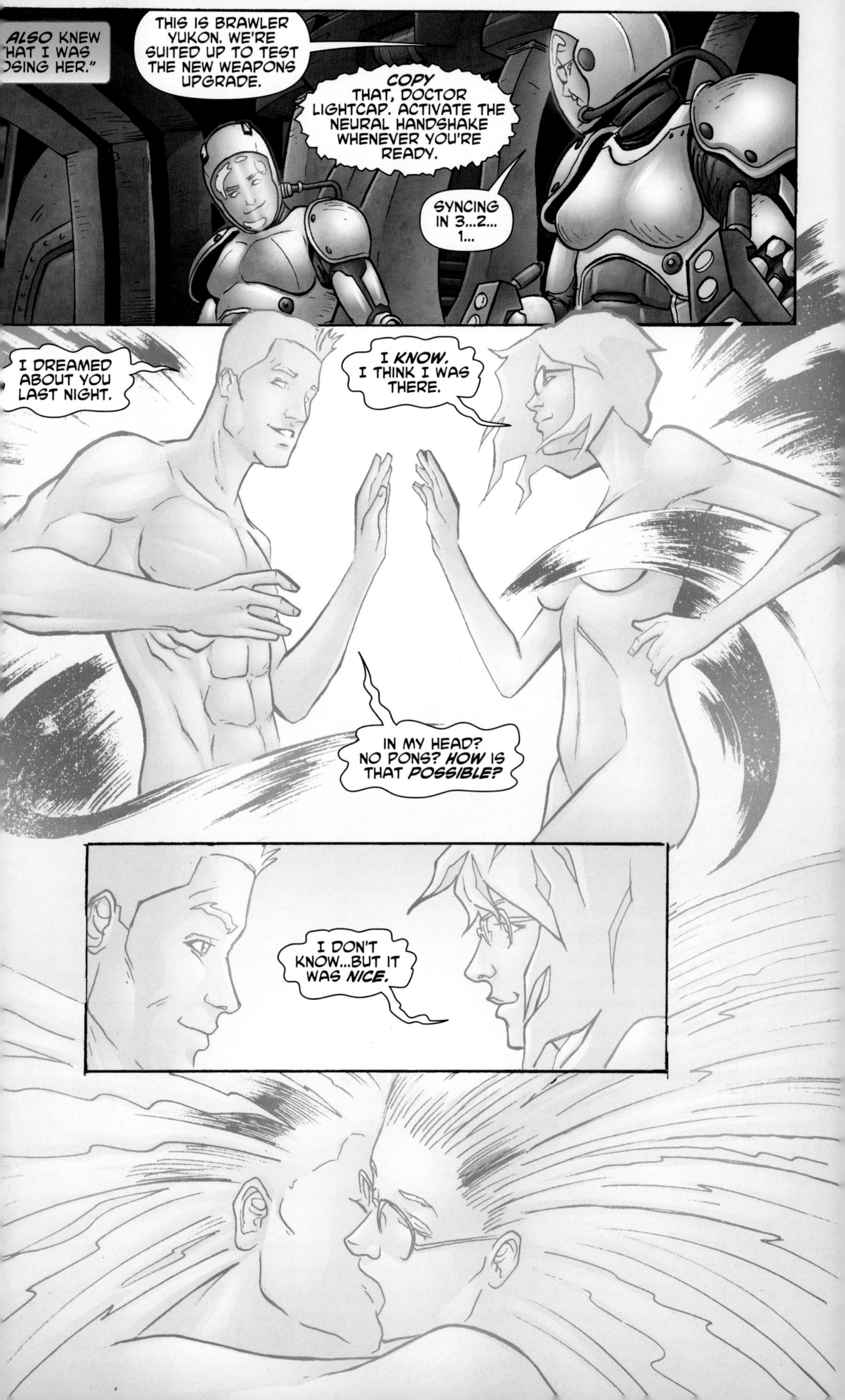
ALSO KNEW "HAT I WAS OSING HER."
THIS IS BRAWLER YUKON. WE'RE SUITED UP TO TEST THE NEW WEAPONS UPGRADE.
COPY THAT, DOCTOR LIGHTCAP. ACTIVATE THE NEURAL HANDSHAKE WHENEVER YOU'RE READY.
SYNCING IN 3...2... 1...
I DREAMED ABOUT YOU LAST NIGHT.
I KNOW. I THINK I WAS THERE.
IN MY HEAD? NO PONS? HOW IS THAT POSSIBLE?
I DON'T KNOW...BUT IT WAS NICE.

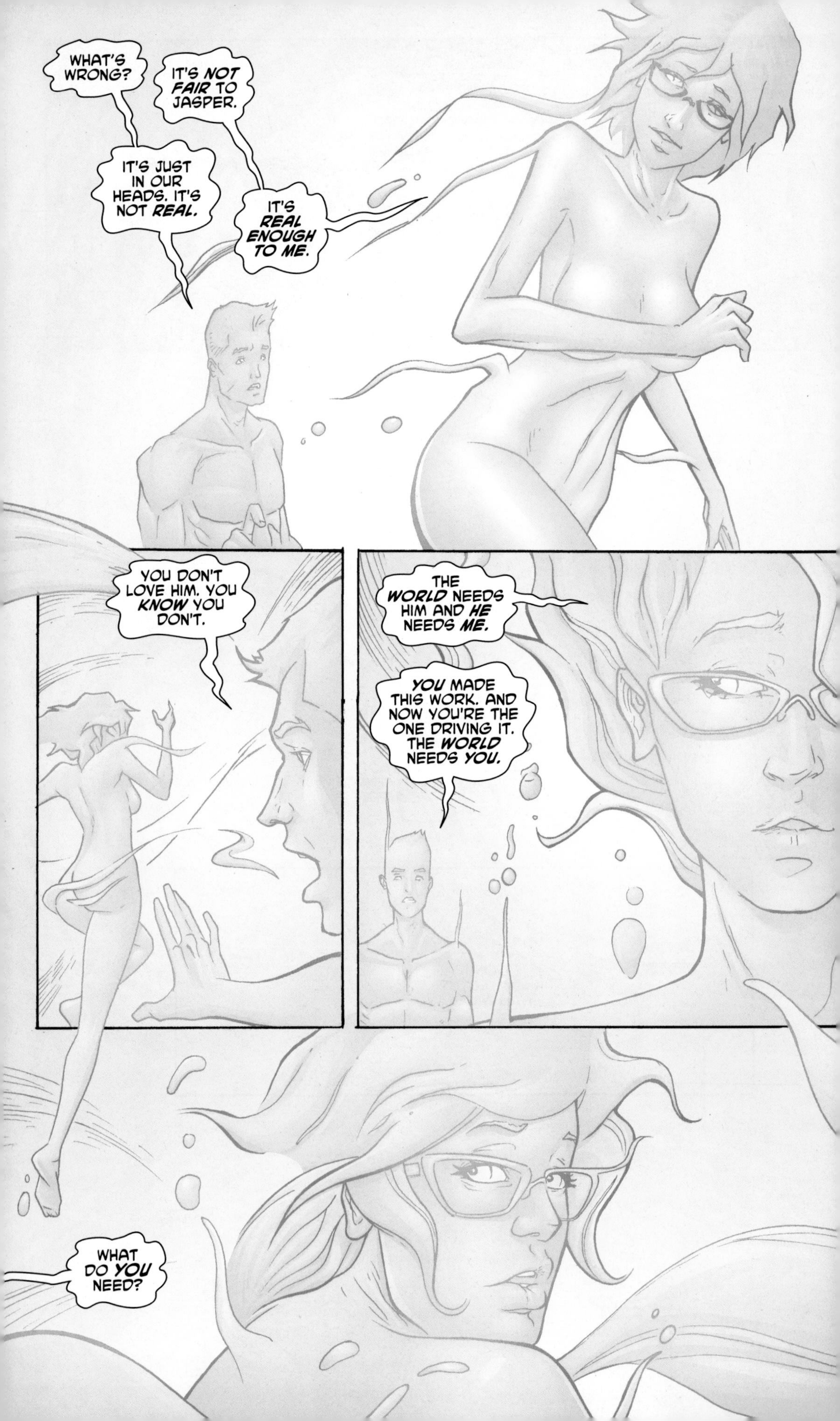
WHAT'S WRONG?
IT'S NOT FAIR TO JASPER.
IT'S JUST IN OUR HEADS. IT'S NOT REAL.
IT'S REAL ENOUGH TO ME.
YOU DON'T LOVE HIM. YOU KNOW YOU DON'T.
THE WORLD NEEDS HIM AND HE NEEDS ME.
YOU MADE THIS WORK. AND NOW YOU'RE THE ONE DRIVING IT. THE WORLD NEEDS YOU.
WHAT DO YOU NEED?

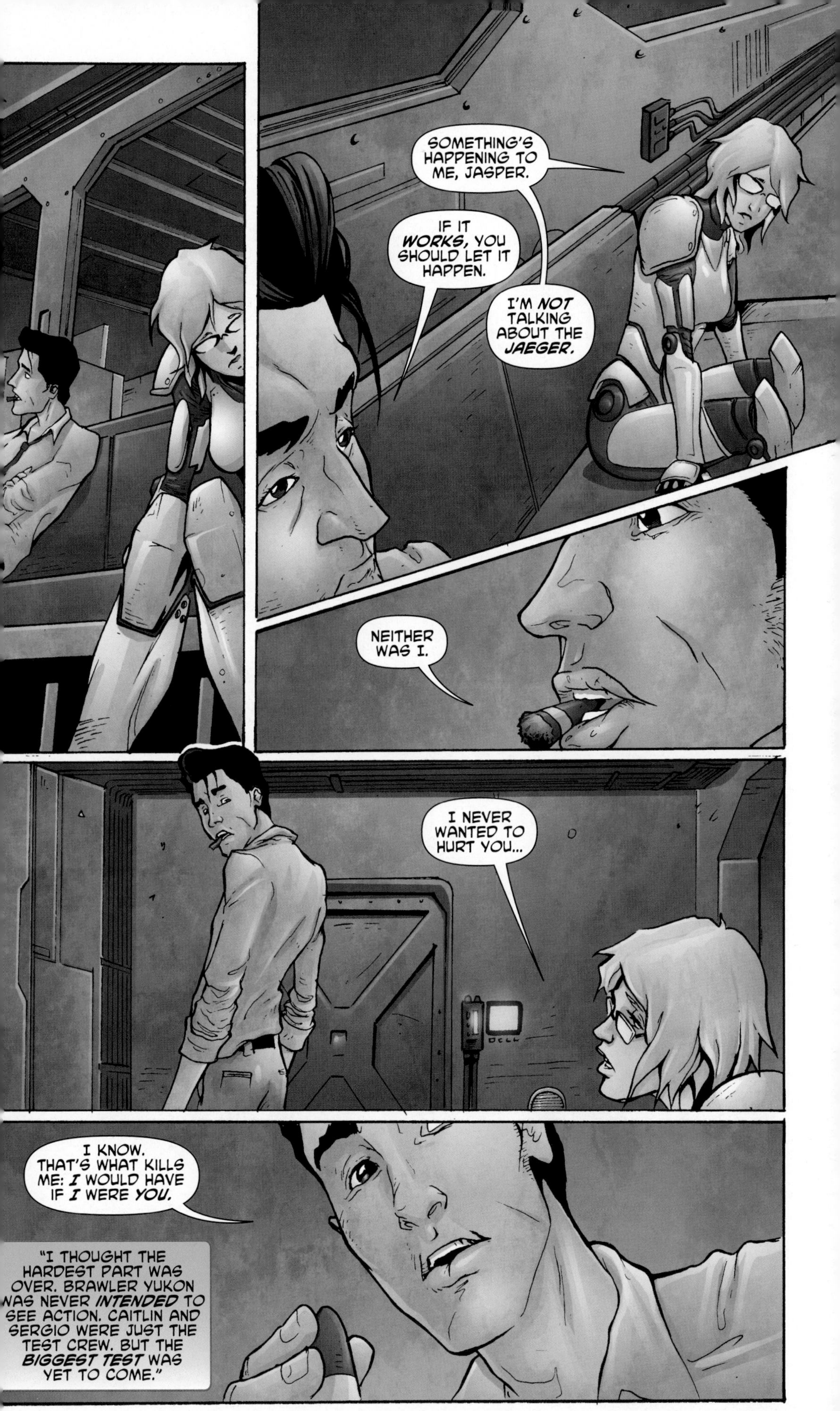
SOMETHING'S HAPPENING TO ME, JASPER.
IF IT *WORKS,* YOU SHOULD LET IT HAPPEN.
I'M *NOT* TALKING ABOUT THE *JAEGER.*
NEITHER WAS I.
I NEVER WANTED TO HURT YOU...
I KNOW. THAT'S WHAT KILLS ME: *I* WOULD HAVE IF *I* WERE *YOU.*
"I THOUGHT THE HARDEST PART WAS OVER. BRAWLER YUKON WAS NEVER *INTENDED* TO SEE ACTION. CAITLIN AND SERGIO WERE JUST THE TEST CREW. BUT THE *BIGGEST TEST* WAS YET TO COME."

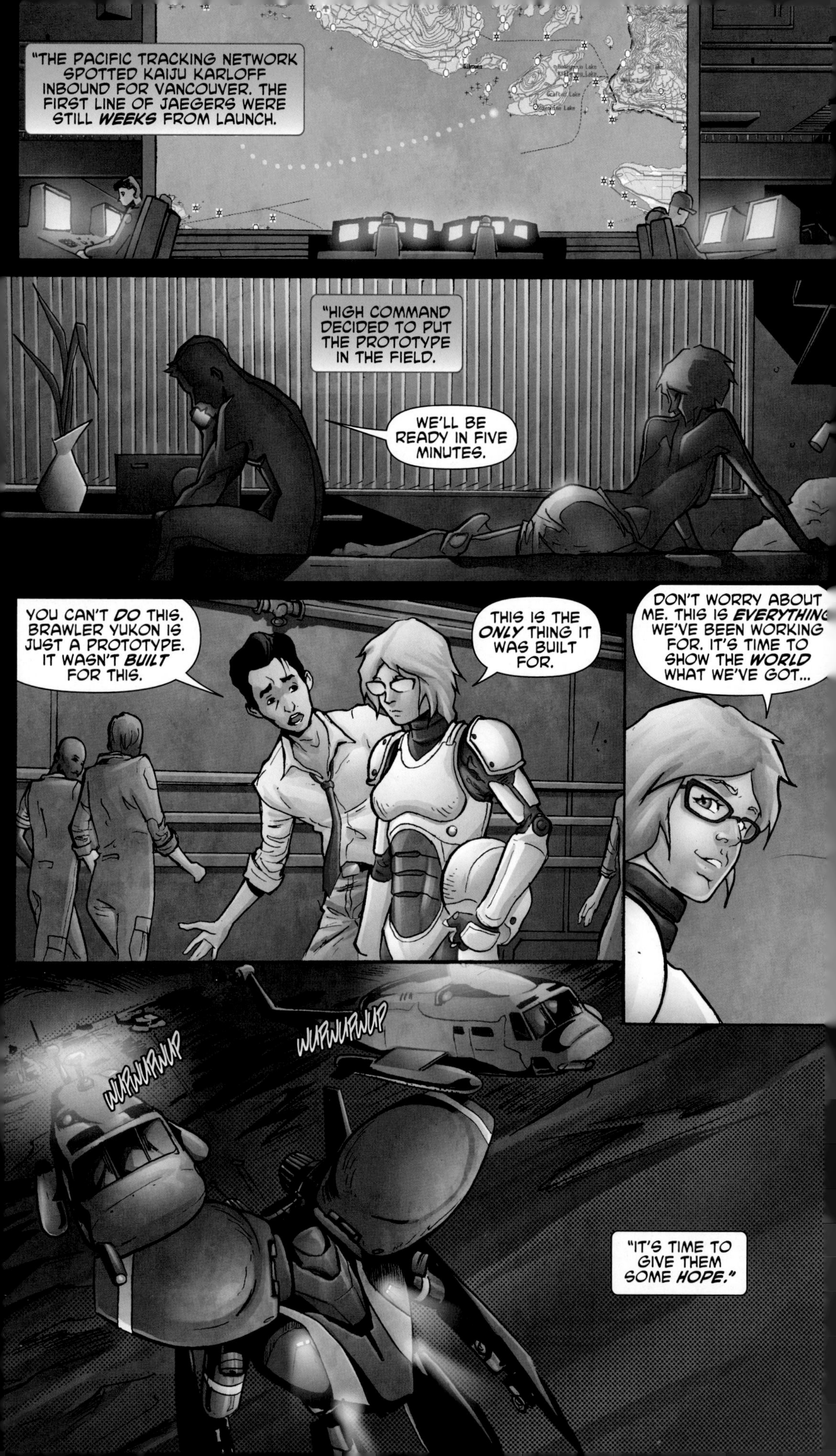
"THE PACIFIC TRACKING NETWORK SPOTTED KAIJU KARLOFF INBOUND FOR VANCOUVER. THE FIRST LINE OF JAEGERS WERE STILL *WEEKS* FROM LAUNCH.
"HIGH COMMAND DECIDED TO PUT THE PROTOTYPE IN THE FIELD.
WE'LL BE READY IN FIVE MINUTES.
YOU CAN'T *DO* THIS. BRAWLER YUKON IS JUST A PROTOTYPE. IT WASN'T *BUILT* FOR THIS.
THIS IS THE *ONLY* THING IT WAS BUILT FOR.
DON'T WORRY ABOUT ME. THIS IS *EVERYTHING* WE'VE BEEN WORKING FOR. IT'S TIME TO SHOW THE *WORLD* WHAT WE'VE GOT...
WUPWUPWUP
WUPWUPWUP
"IT'S TIME TO GIVE THEM SOME *HOPE.*"

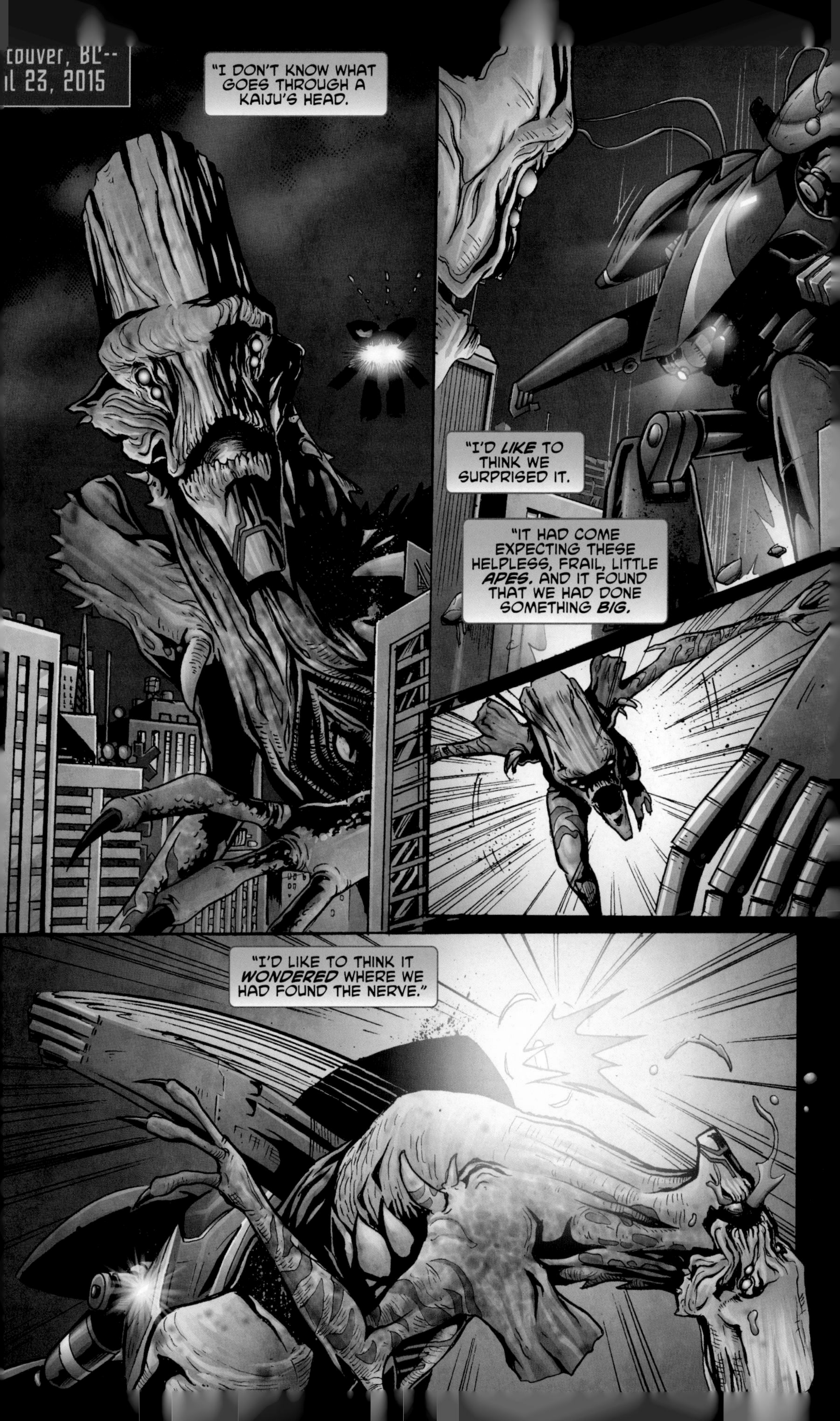

couver, BC--
il 23, 2015
"I DON'T KNOW WHAT GOES THROUGH A KAIJU'S HEAD.
"I'D LIKE TO THINK WE SURPRISED IT.
"IT HAD COME EXPECTING THESE HELPLESS, FRAIL, LITTLE APES. AND IT FOUND THAT WE HAD DONE SOMETHING BIG.
"I'D LIKE TO THINK IT WONDERED WHERE WE HAD FOUND THE NERVE."

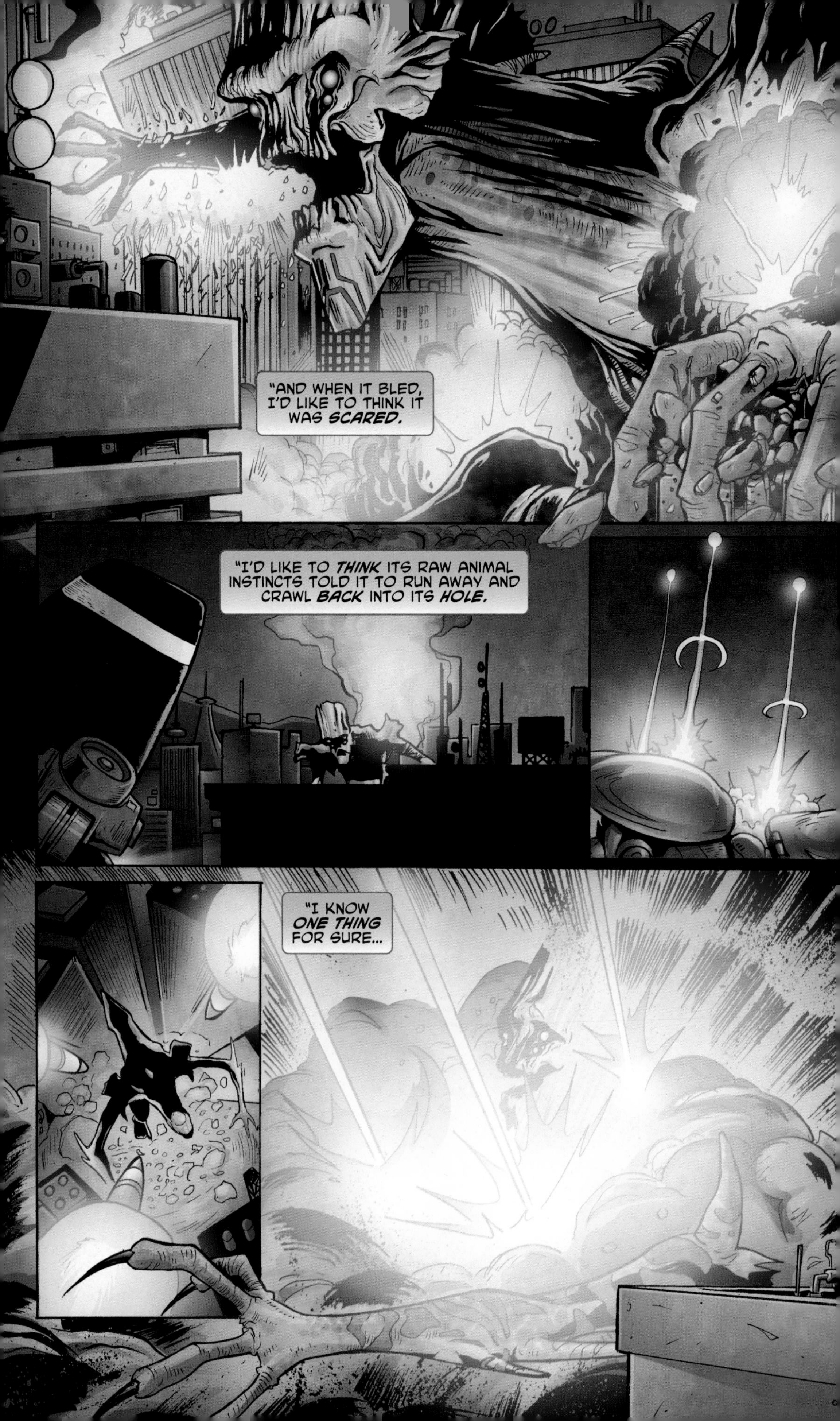
"AND WHEN IT BLED, I'D LIKE TO THINK IT WAS SCARED.
"I'D LIKE TO THINK ITS RAW ANIMAL INSTINCTS TOLD IT TO RUN AWAY AND CRAWL BACK INTO ITS HOLE.
"I KNOW ONE THING FOR SURE...

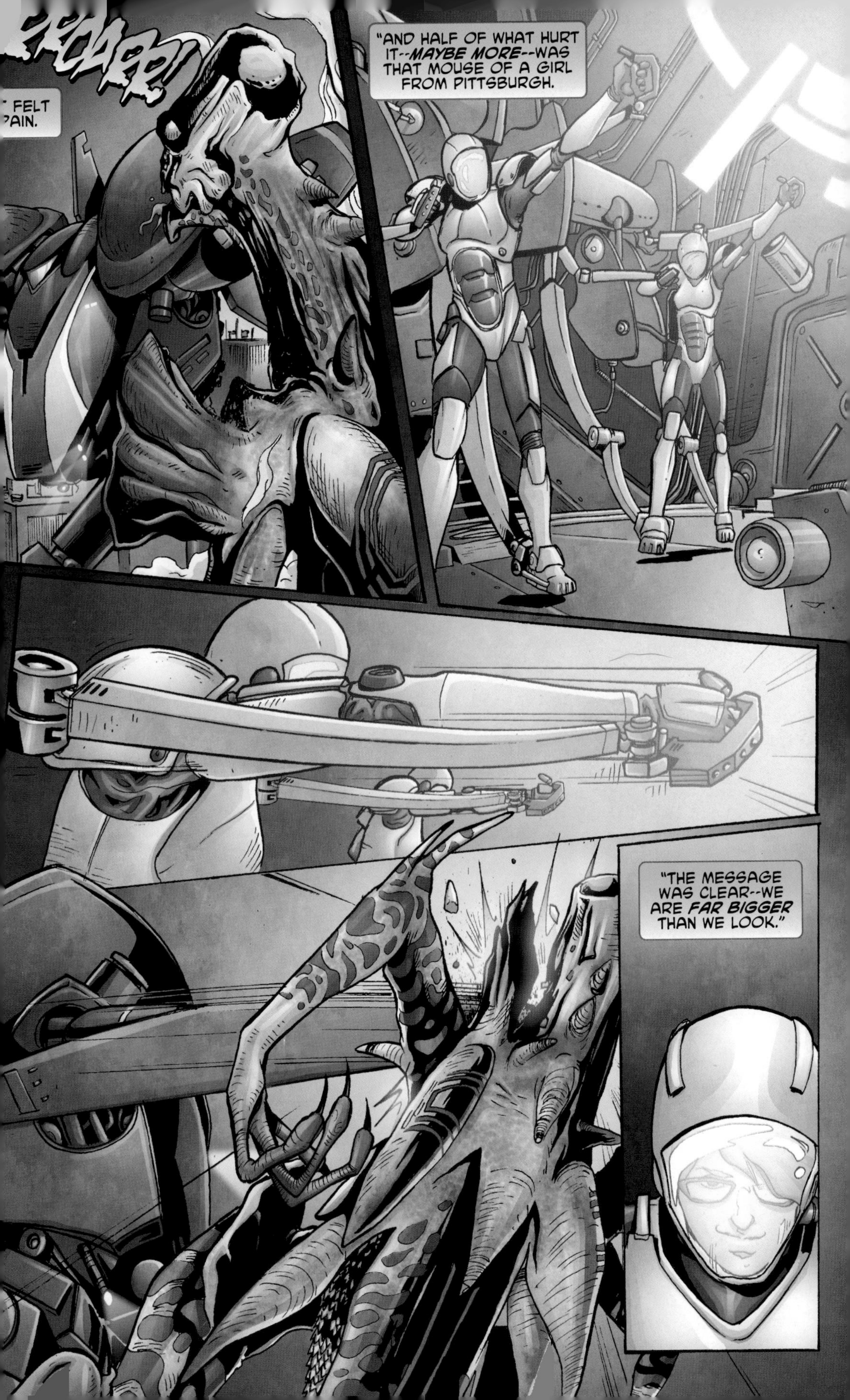
FELT
"AND HALF OF WHAT HURT IT--MAYBE MORE--WAS THAT MOUSE OF A GIRL FROM PITTSBURGH.
"THE MESSAGE WAS CLEAR--WE ARE FAR BIGGER THAN WE LOOK."

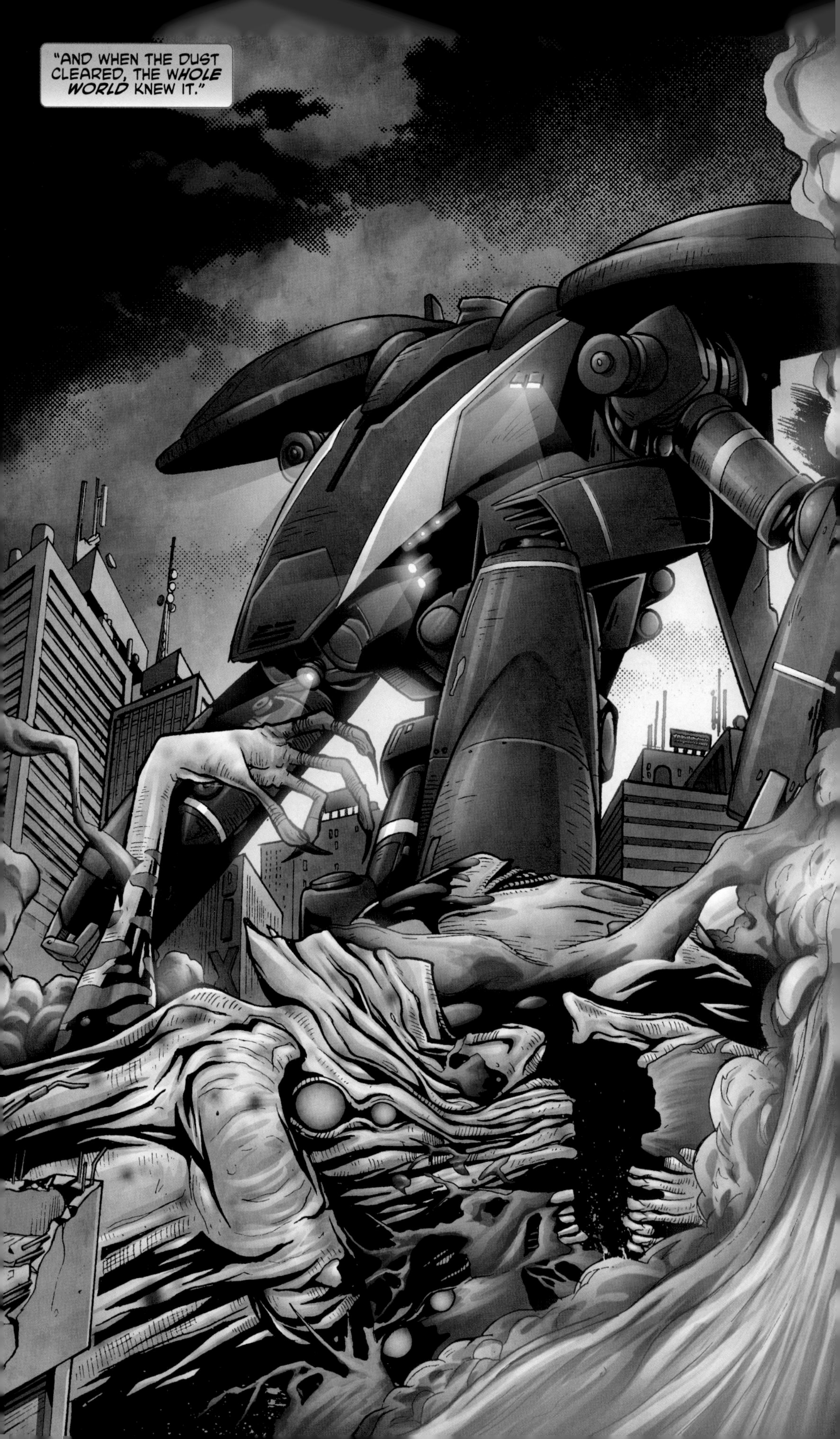
"AND WHEN THE DUST CLEARED, THE WHOLE WORLD KNEW IT."

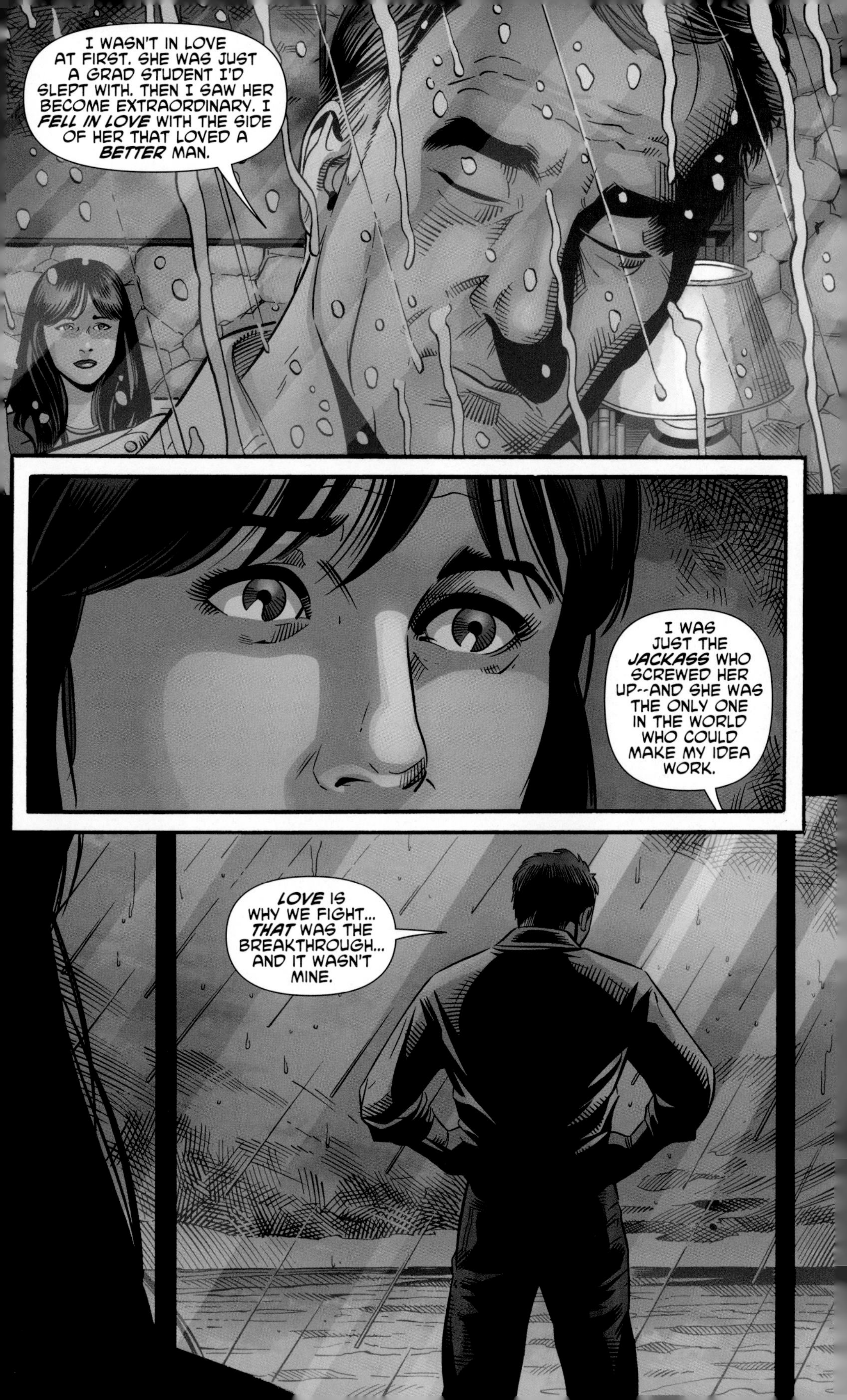
I WASN'T IN LOVE AT FIRST. SHE WAS JUST A GRAD STUDENT I'D SLEPT WITH. THEN I SAW HER BECOME EXTRAORDINARY. I *FELL IN LOVE* WITH THE SIDE OF HER THAT LOVED A *BETTER* MAN.
I WAS JUST THE *JACKASS* WHO SCREWED HER UP--AND SHE WAS THE ONLY ONE IN THE WORLD WHO COULD MAKE MY IDEA WORK.
LOVE IS WHY WE FIGHT... *THAT* WAS THE BREAKTHROUGH... AND IT WASN'T MINE.

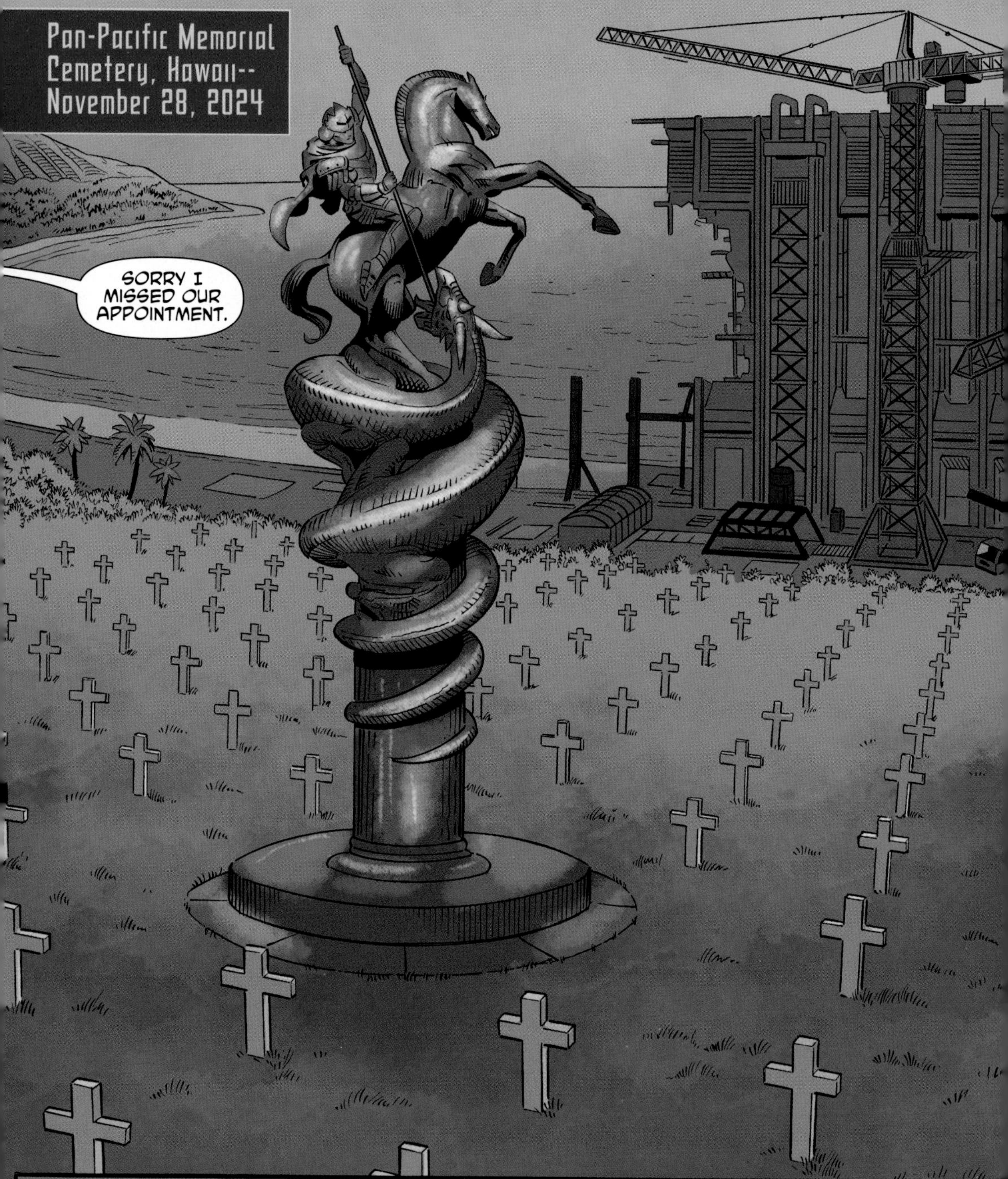
Pan-Pacific Memorial Cemetery, Hawaii-- November 28, 2024
SORRY I MISSED OUR APPOINTMENT.

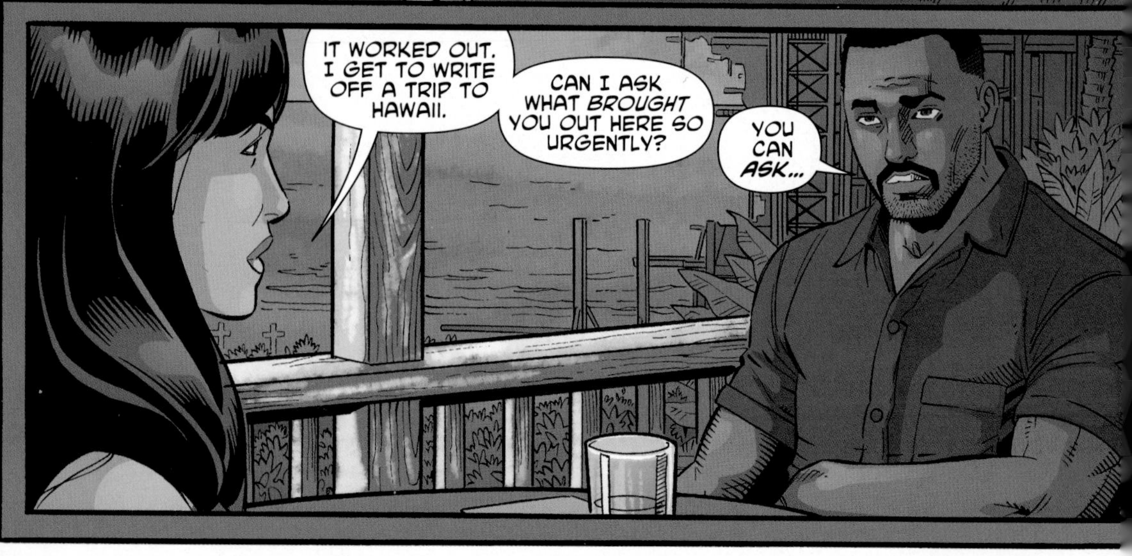
IT WORKED OUT. I GET TO WRITE OFF A TRIP TO HAWAII.
CAN I ASK WHAT *BROUGHT* YOU OUT HERE SO URGENTLY?
YOU CAN *ASK*...

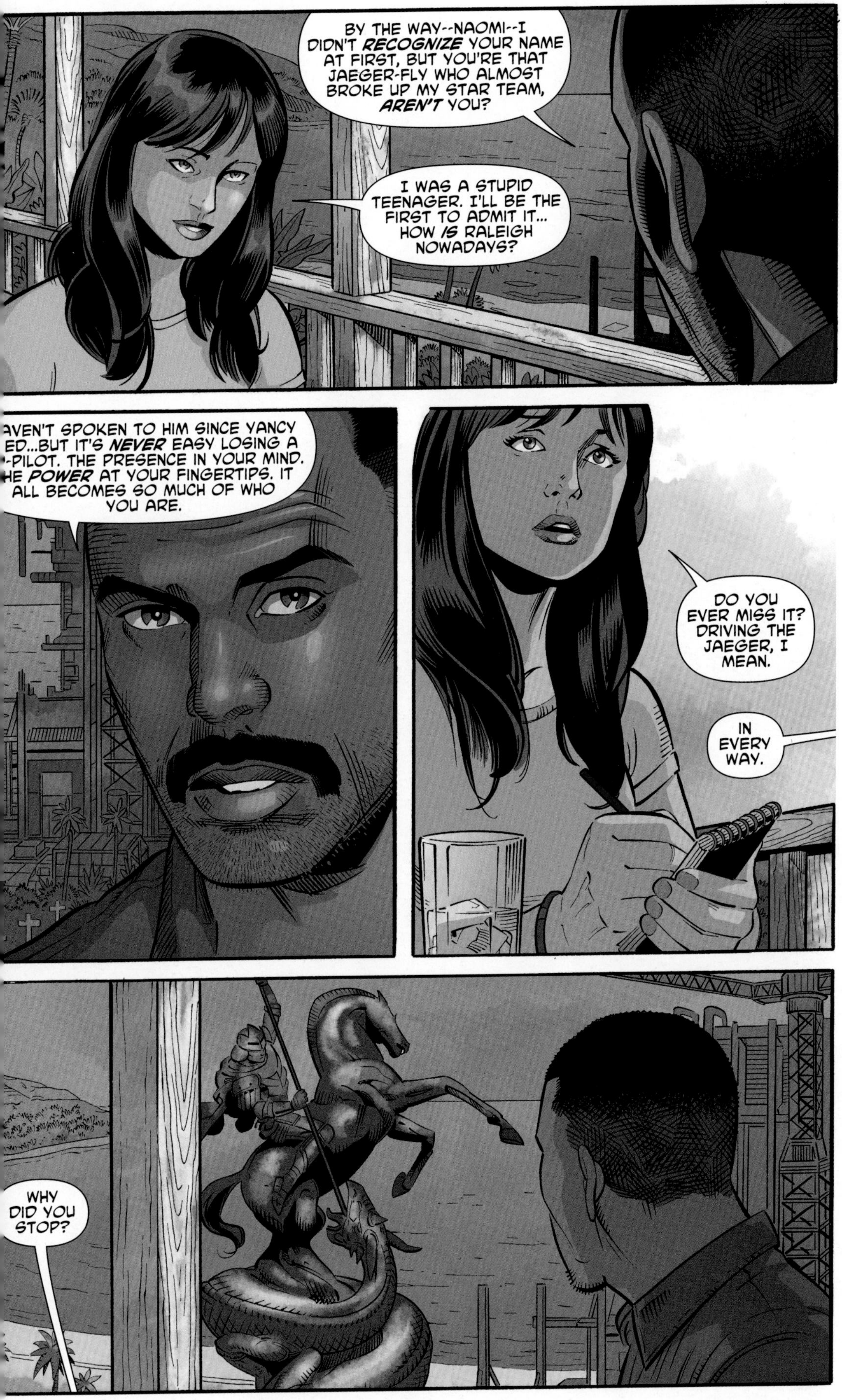
BY THE WAY--NAOMI--I DIDN'T RECOGNIZE YOUR NAME AT FIRST, BUT YOU'RE THAT JAEGER-FLY WHO ALMOST BROKE UP MY STAR TEAM, AREN'T YOU?
I WAS A STUPID TEENAGER. I'LL BE THE FIRST TO ADMIT IT... HOW IS RALEIGH NOWADAYS?
AVEN'T SPOKEN TO HIM SINCE YANCY ED...BUT IT'S NEVER EASY LOSING A -PILOT. THE PRESENCE IN YOUR MIND. HE POWER AT YOUR FINGERTIPS. IT ALL BECOMES SO MUCH OF WHO YOU ARE.
DO YOU EVER MISS IT? DRIVING THE JAEGER, I MEAN.
IN EVERY WAY.
WHY DID YOU STOP?

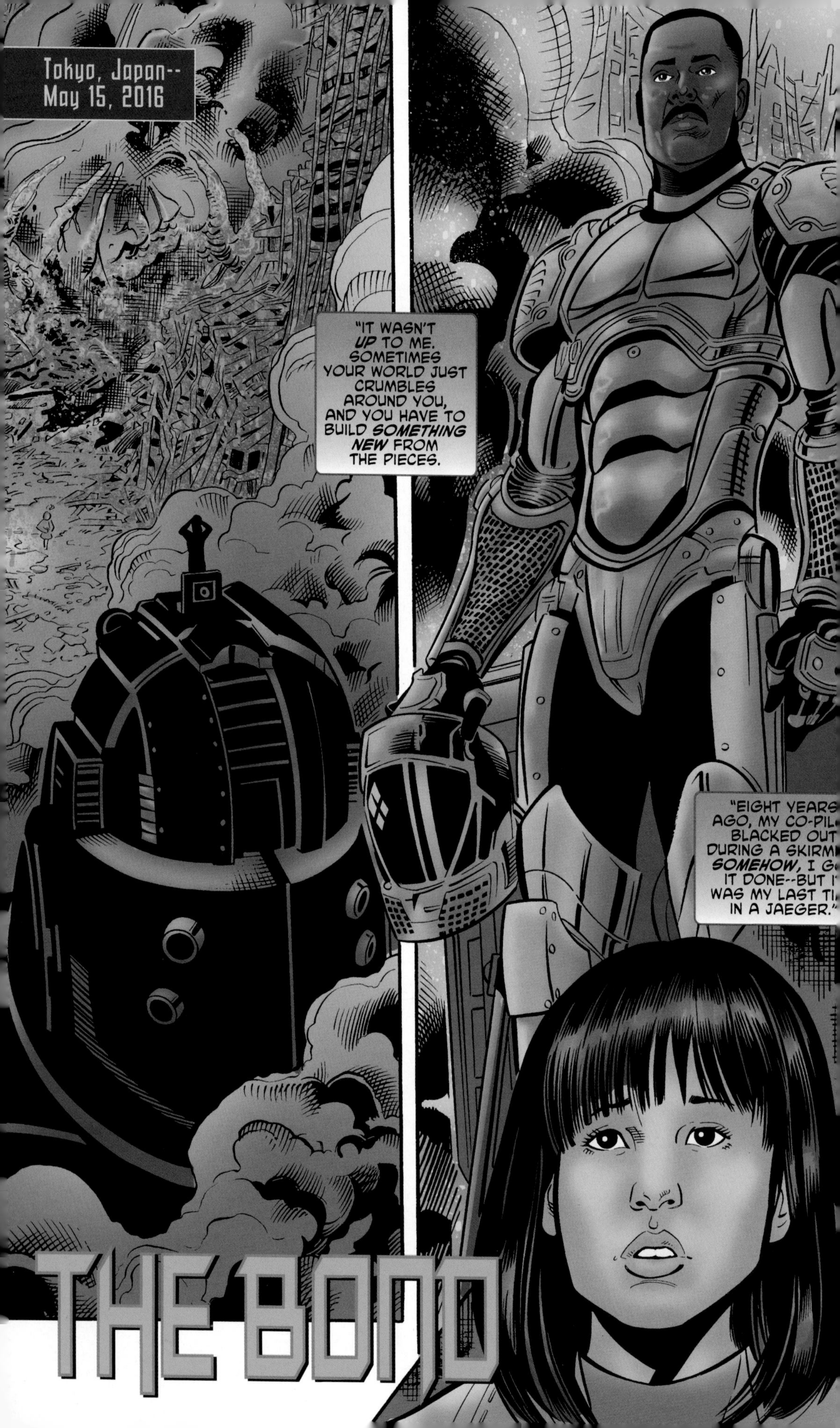
Tokyo, Japan--
May 15, 2016
"IT WASN'T UP TO ME. SOMETIMES YOUR WORLD JUST CRUMBLES AROUND YOU, AND YOU HAVE TO BUILD SOMETHING NEW FROM THE PIECES.
"EIGHT YEARS AGO, MY CO-PIL BLACKED OUT DURING A SKIRM SOMEHOW, I G IT DONE--BUT I WAS MY LAST TI IN A JAEGER."
THE BOND

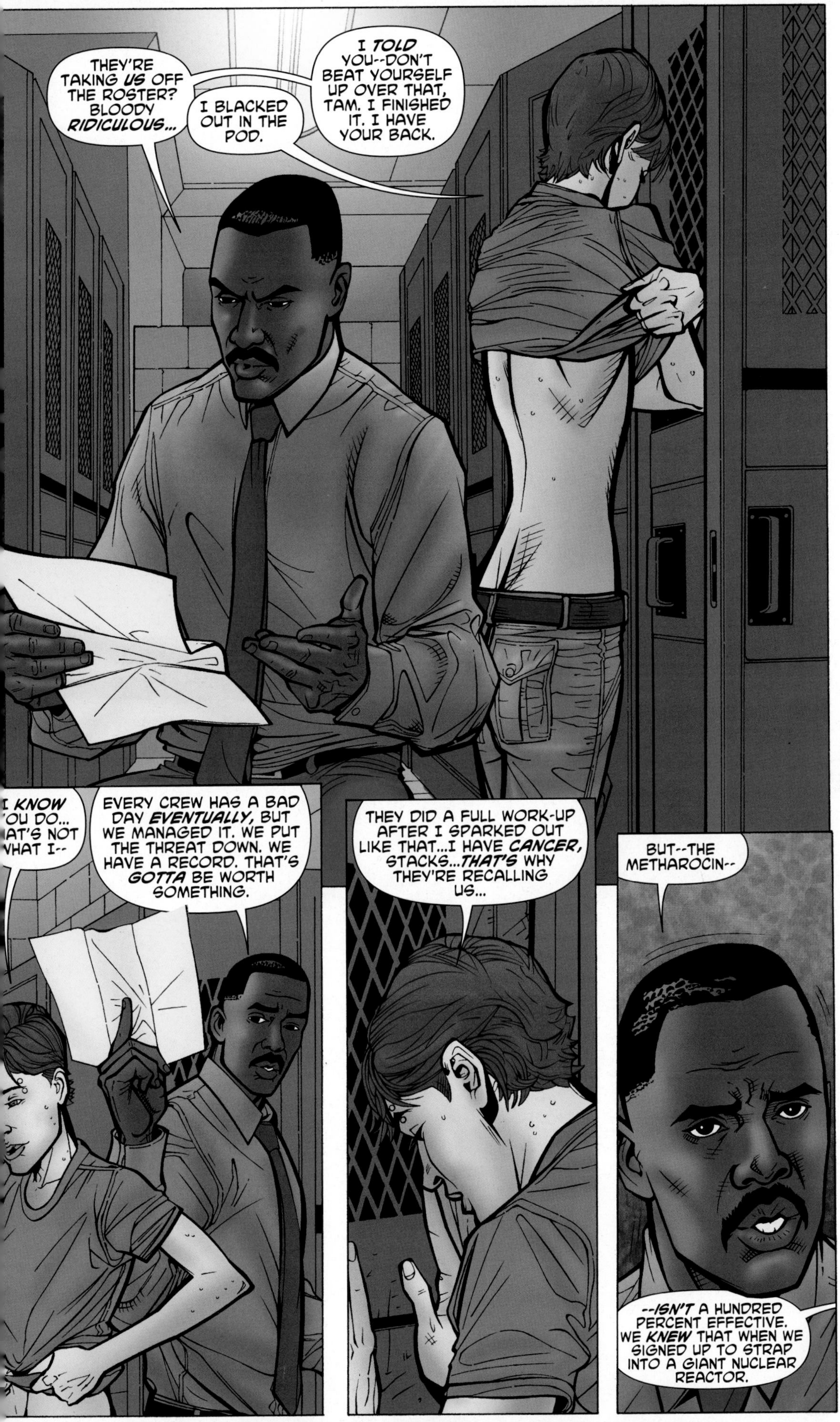
THEY'RE TAKING US OFF THE ROSTER? BLOODY RIDICULOUS...
I BLACKED OUT IN THE POD.
I TOLD YOU--DON'T BEAT YOURSELF UP OVER THAT, TAM. I FINISHED IT. I HAVE YOUR BACK.
I KNOW YOU DO... THAT'S NOT WHAT I--
EVERY CREW HAS A BAD DAY EVENTUALLY, BUT WE MANAGED IT. WE PUT THE THREAT DOWN. WE HAVE A RECORD. THAT'S GOTTA BE WORTH SOMETHING.
THEY DID A FULL WORK-UP AFTER I SPARKED OUT LIKE THAT...I HAVE CANCER, STACKS...THAT'S WHY THEY'RE RECALLING US...
BUT--THE METHAROCIN--
--ISN'T A HUNDRED PERCENT EFFECTIVE. WE KNEW THAT WHEN WE SIGNED UP TO STRAP INTO A GIANT NUCLEAR REACTOR.

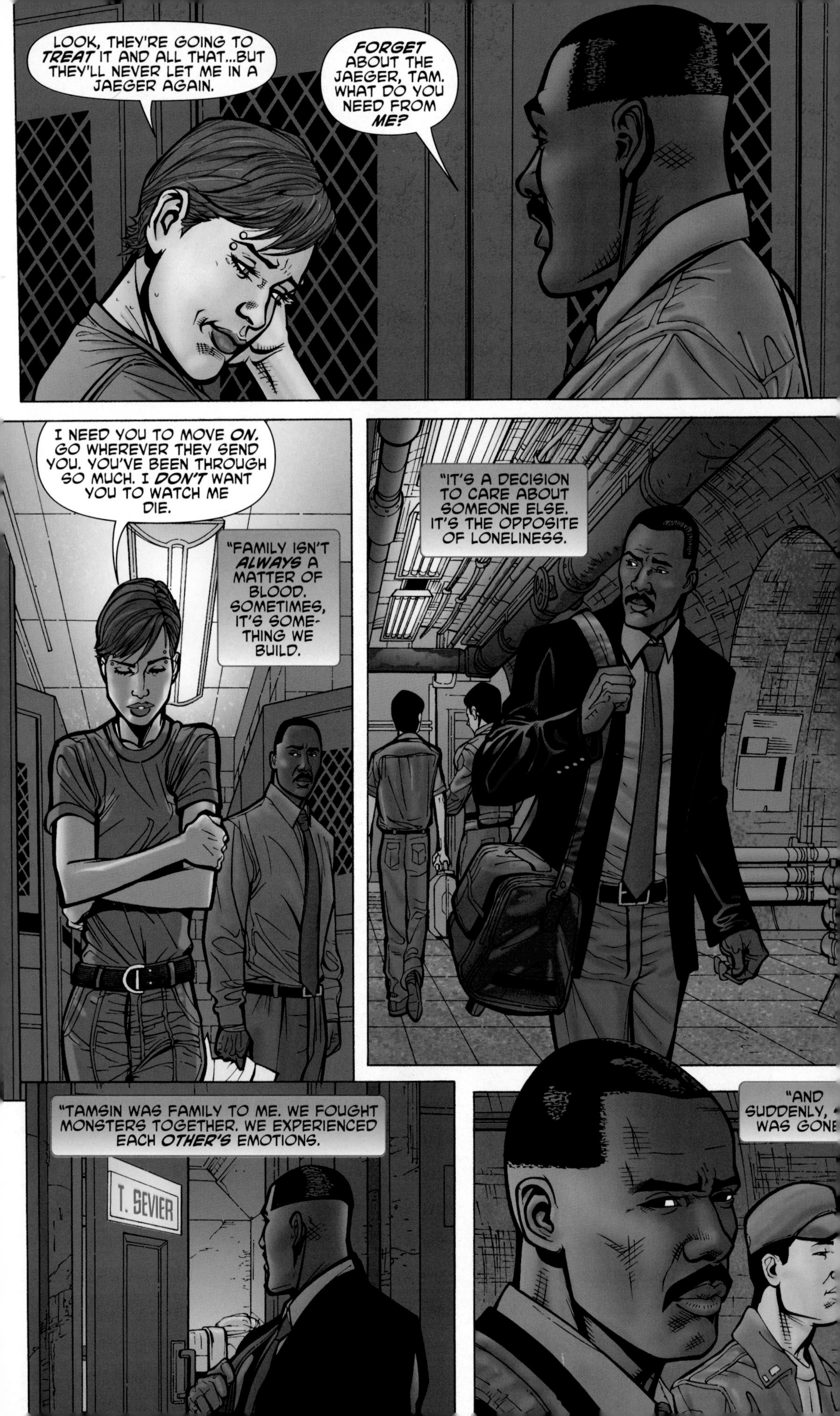
LOOK, THEY'RE GOING TO *TREAT* IT AND ALL THAT...BUT THEY'LL NEVER LET ME IN A JAEGER AGAIN.
FORGET ABOUT THE JAEGER, TAM. WHAT DO YOU NEED FROM *ME?*
I NEED YOU TO MOVE *ON.* GO WHEREVER THEY SEND YOU. YOU'VE BEEN THROUGH SO MUCH. I *DON'T* WANT YOU TO WATCH ME DIE.
"FAMILY ISN'T *ALWAYS* A MATTER OF BLOOD. SOMETIMES, IT'S SOMETHING WE BUILD.
"IT'S A DECISION TO CARE ABOUT SOMEONE ELSE. IT'S THE OPPOSITE OF LONELINESS.
"TAMSIN WAS FAMILY TO ME. WE FOUGHT MONSTERS TOGETHER. WE EXPERIENCED EACH *OTHER'S* EMOTIONS.
T. SEVIER
"AND SUDDENLY, WAS GONE

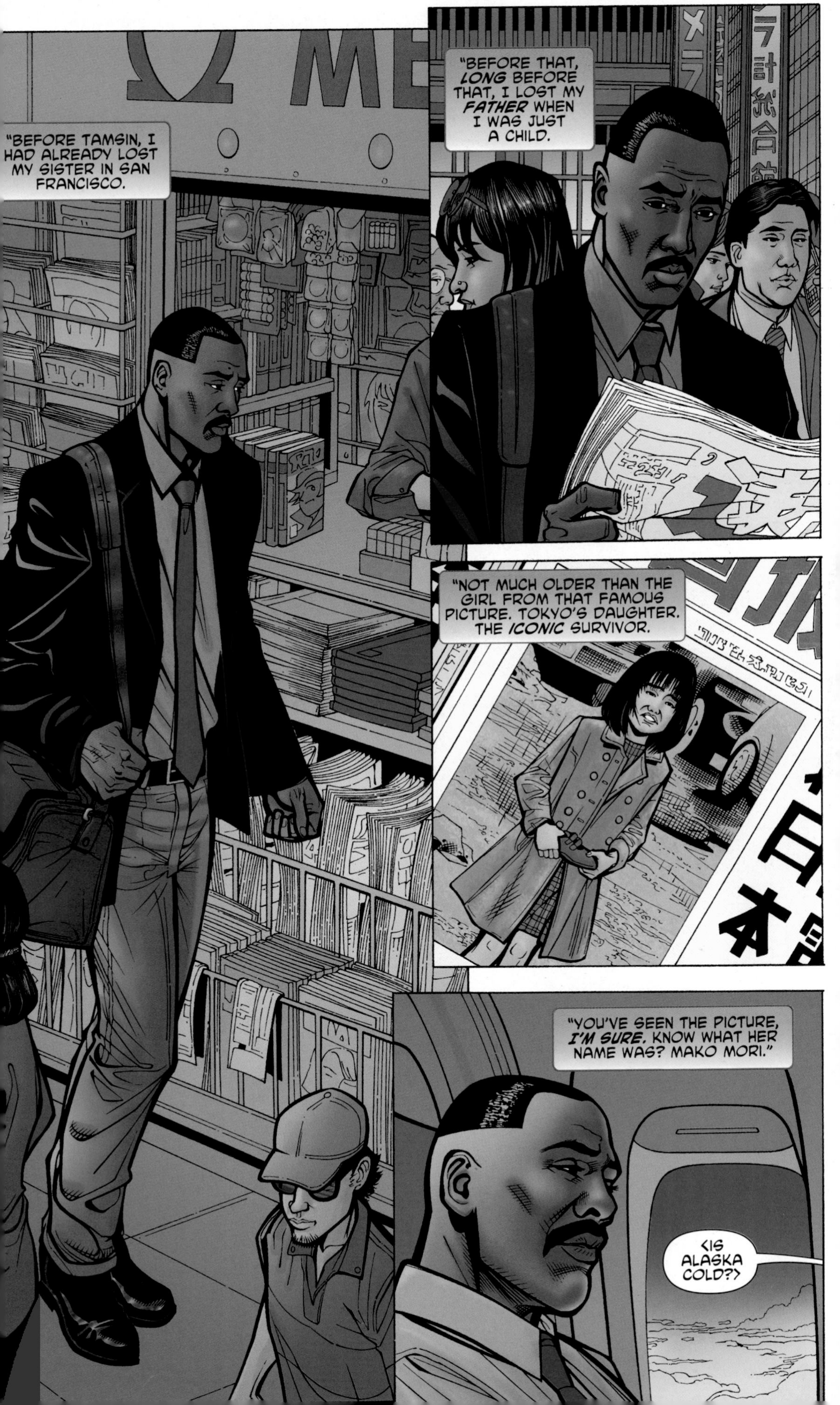
"BEFORE TAMSIN, I HAD ALREADY LOST MY SISTER IN SAN FRANCISCO.
"BEFORE THAT, *LONG* BEFORE THAT, I LOST MY *FATHER* WHEN I WAS JUST A CHILD.
"NOT MUCH OLDER THAN THE GIRL FROM THAT FAMOUS PICTURE. TOKYO'S DAUGHTER. THE *ICONIC* SURVIVOR.
"YOU'VE SEEN THE PICTURE, *I'M SURE.* KNOW WHAT HER NAME WAS? MAKO MORI."
<IS ALASKA COLD?>

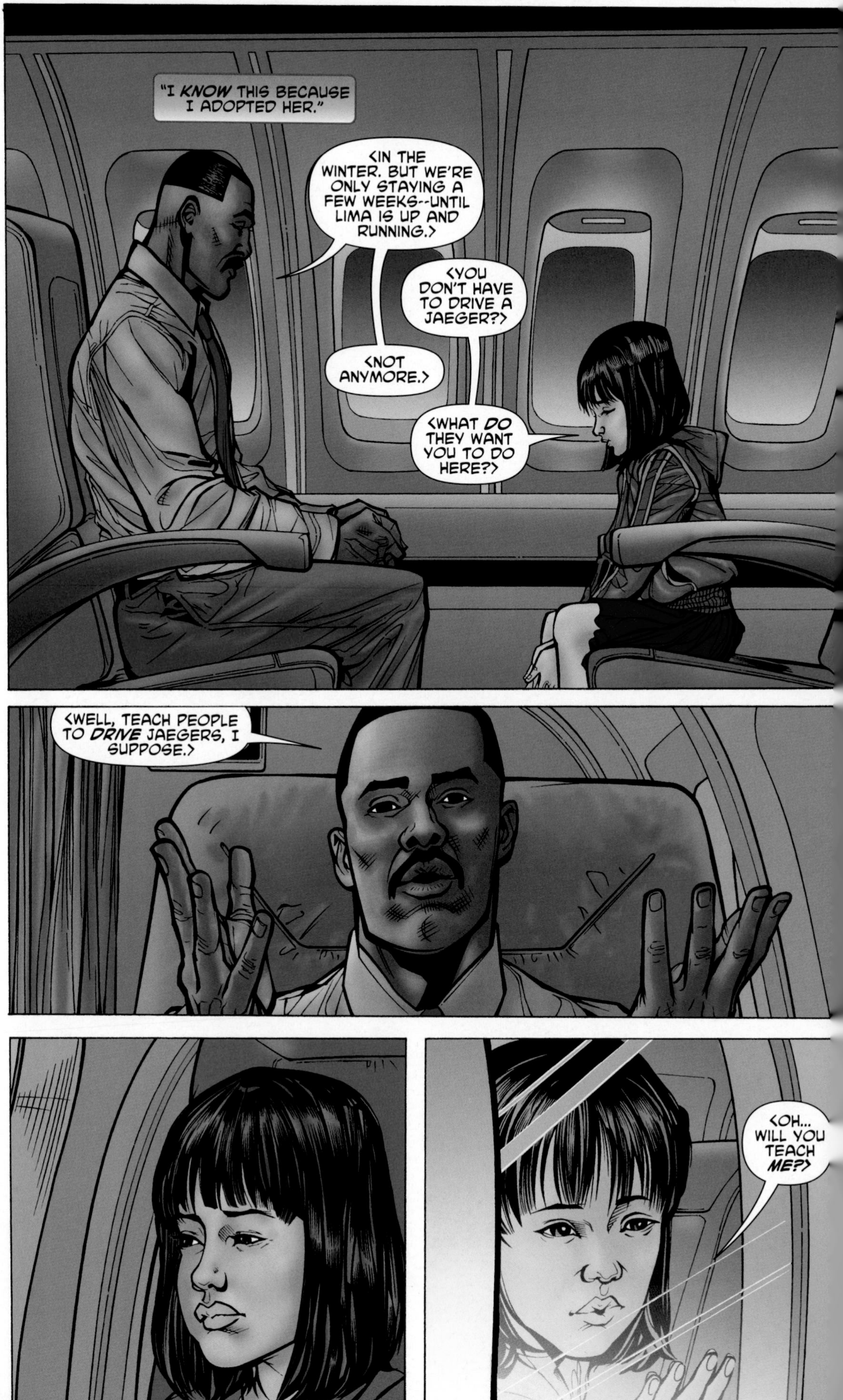
"I KNOW THIS BECAUSE I ADOPTED HER."
<IN THE WINTER. BUT WE'RE ONLY STAYING A FEW WEEKS--UNTIL LIMA IS UP AND RUNNING.>
<YOU DON'T HAVE TO DRIVE A JAEGER?>
<NOT ANYMORE.>
<WHAT DO THEY WANT YOU TO DO HERE?>
<WELL, TEACH PEOPLE TO DRIVE JAEGERS, I SUPPOSE.>
<OH... WILL YOU TEACH ME?>

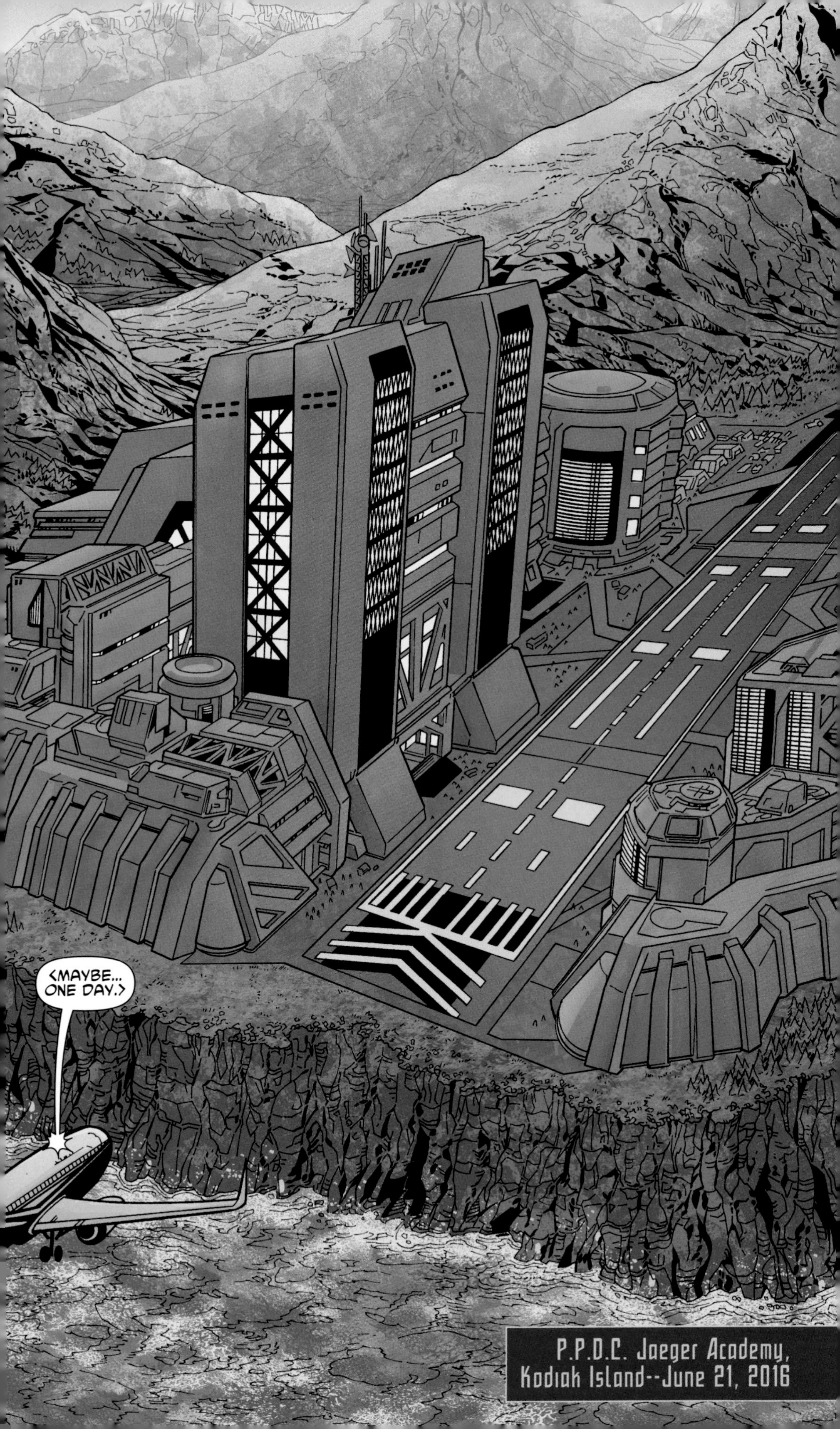
<MAYBE... ONE DAY.>
P.P.D.C. Jaeger Academy, Kodiak Island--June 21, 2016

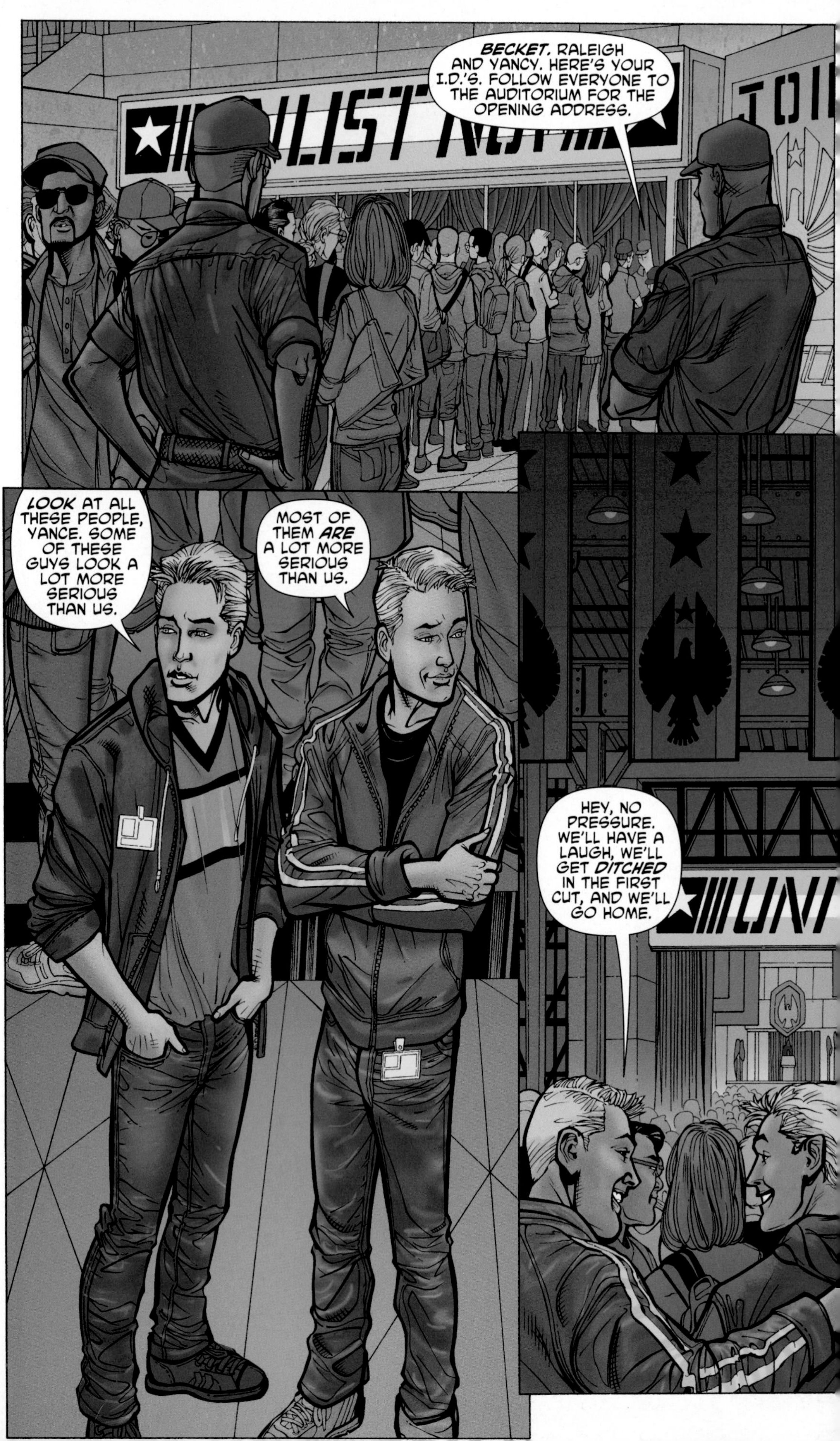
BECKET. RALEIGH AND YANCY. HERE'S YOUR I.D.'S. FOLLOW EVERYONE TO THE AUDITORIUM FOR THE OPENING ADDRESS.
LOOK AT ALL THESE PEOPLE, YANCE. SOME OF THESE GUYS LOOK A LOT MORE SERIOUS THAN US.
MOST OF THEM ARE A LOT MORE SERIOUS THAN US.
HEY, NO PRESSURE. WE'LL HAVE A LAUGH, WE'LL GET DITCHED IN THE FIRST CUT, AND WE'LL GO HOME.

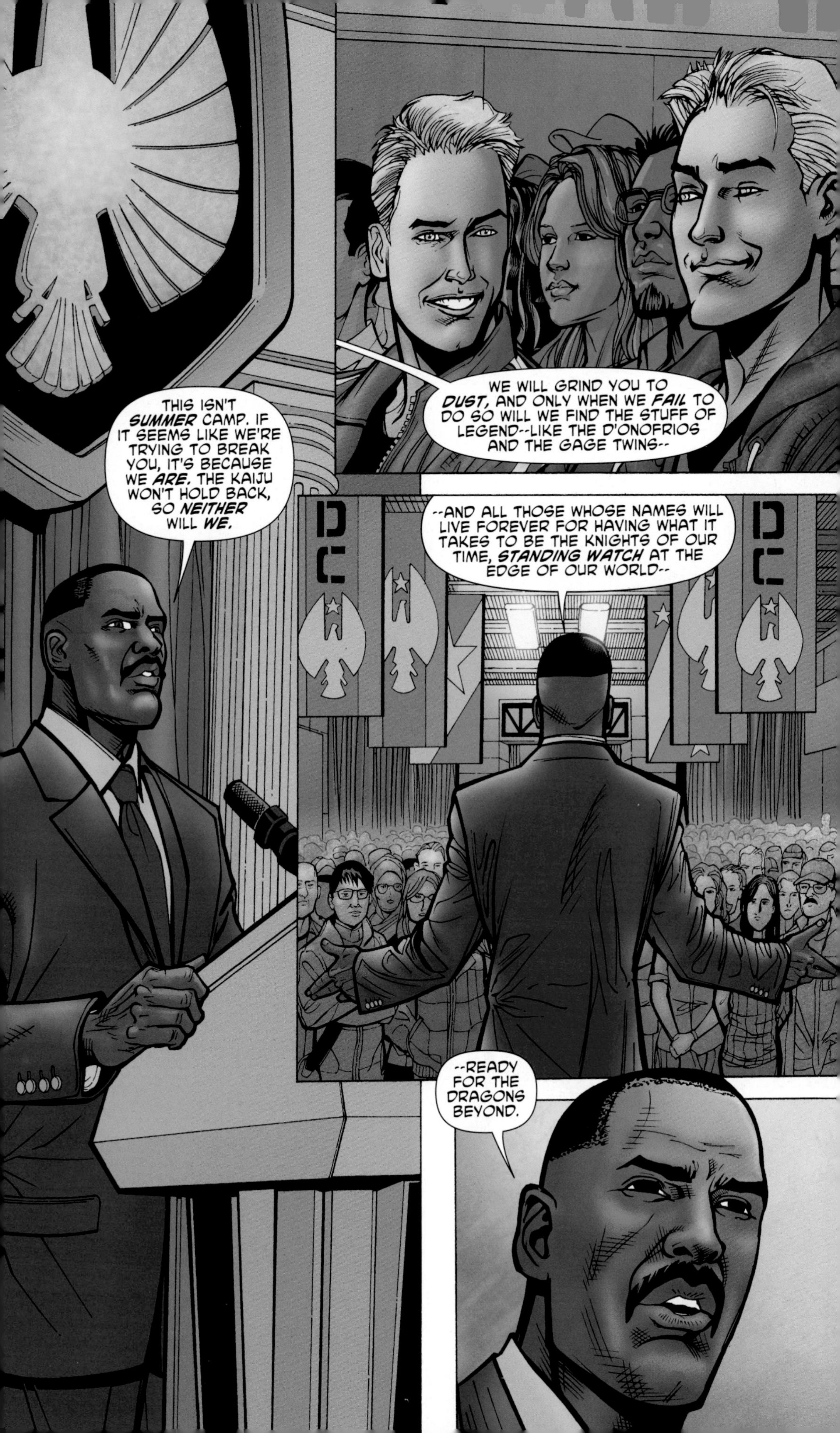

WE WILL GRIND YOU TO DUST, AND ONLY WHEN WE FAIL TO DO SO WILL WE FIND THE STUFF OF LEGEND--LIKE THE D'ONOFRIOS AND THE GAGE TWINS--
THIS ISN'T SUMMER CAMP. IF IT SEEMS LIKE WE'RE TRYING TO BREAK YOU, IT'S BECAUSE WE ARE. THE KAIJU WON'T HOLD BACK, SO NEITHER WILL WE.
--AND ALL THOSE WHOSE NAMES WILL LIVE FOREVER FOR HAVING WHAT IT TAKES TO BE THE KNIGHTS OF OUR TIME, STANDING WATCH AT THE EDGE OF OUR WORLD--
--READY FOR THE DRAGONS BEYOND.

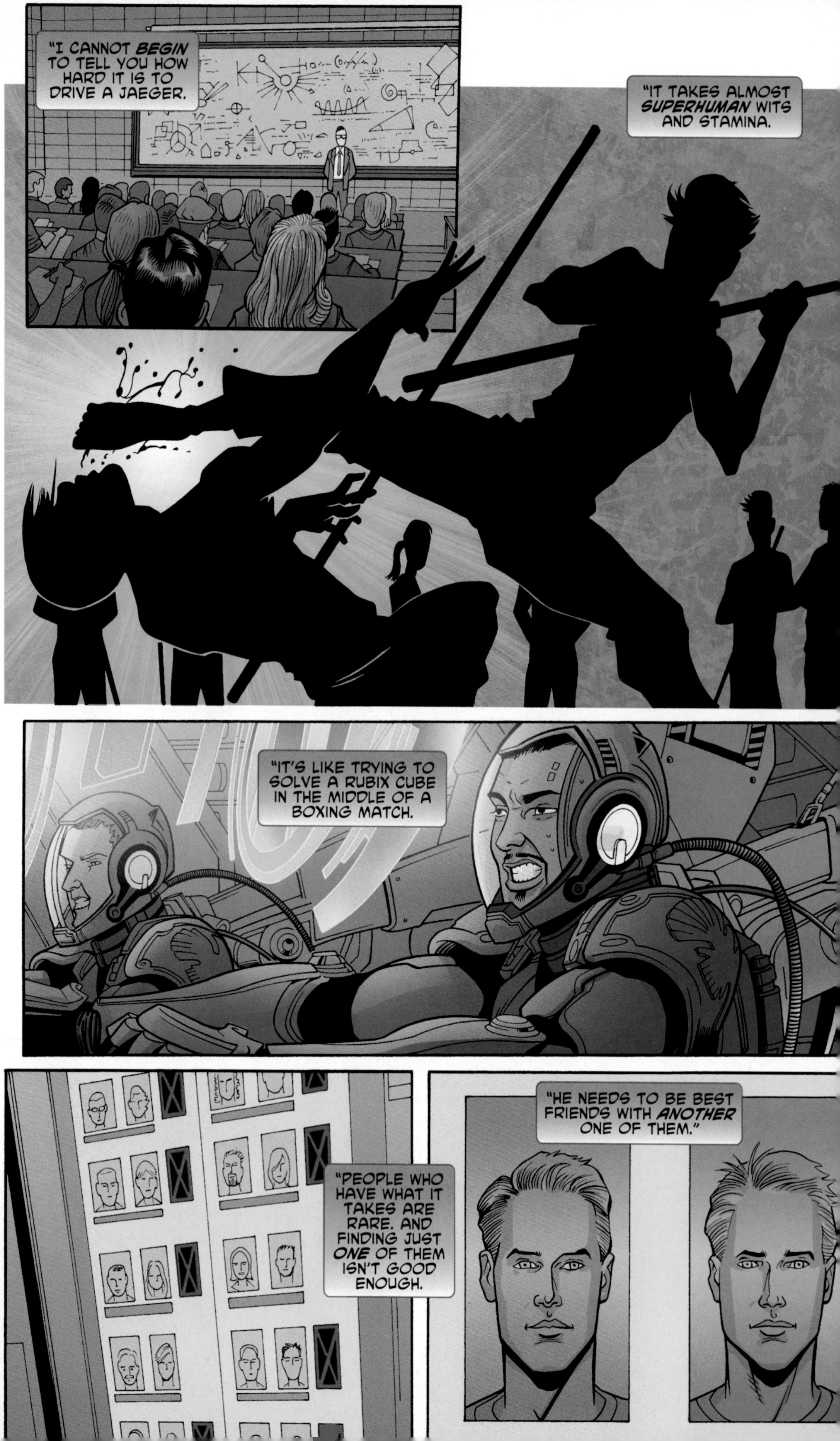
"I CANNOT BEGIN TO TELL YOU HOW HARD IT IS TO DRIVE A JAEGER.
"IT TAKES ALMOST SUPERHUMAN WITS AND STAMINA.
"IT'S LIKE TRYING TO SOLVE A RUBIX CUBE IN THE MIDDLE OF A BOXING MATCH.
"PEOPLE WHO HAVE WHAT IT TAKES ARE RARE. AND FINDING JUST ONE OF THEM ISN'T GOOD ENOUGH.
"HE NEEDS TO BE BEST FRIENDS WITH ANOTHER ONE OF THEM."

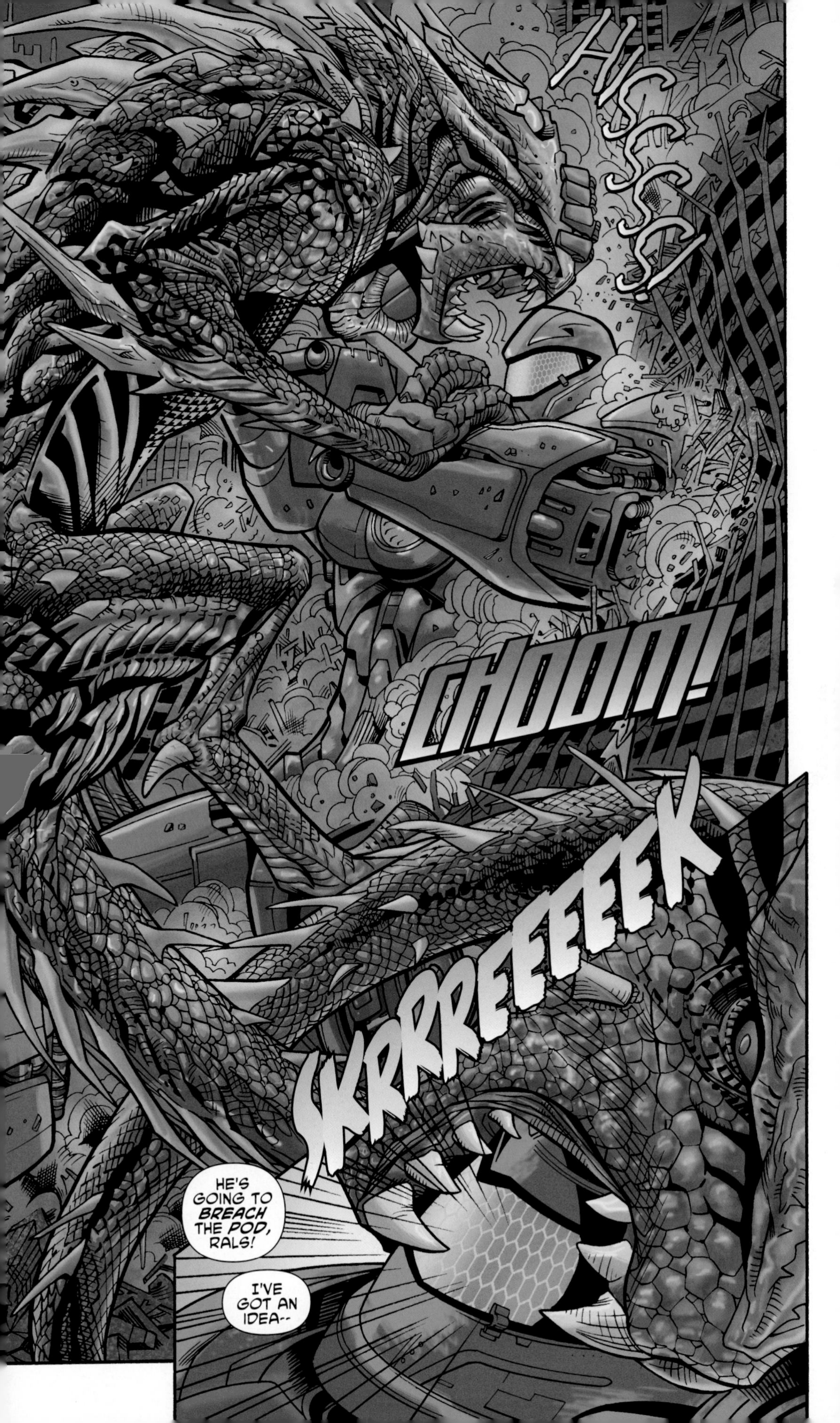
HISSSS!
CHOOM!
SKRRREEEEEK
HE'S GOING TO BREACH THE POD, RALS!
I'VE GOT AN IDEA--

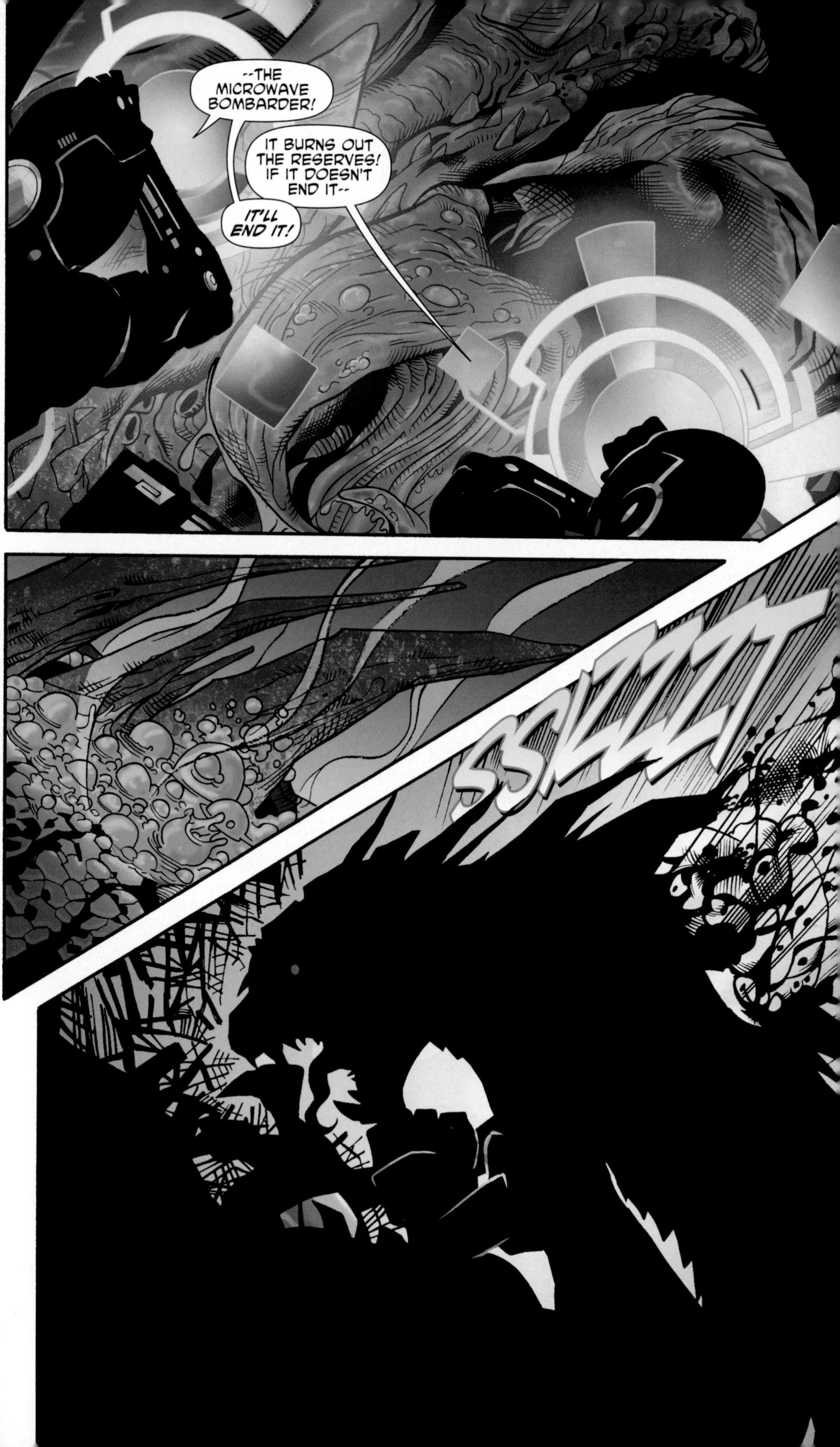
--THE MICROWAVE BOMBARDER!
IT BURNS OUT THE RESERVES! IF IT DOESN'T END IT--
IT'LL END IT!
SSSKZZZT

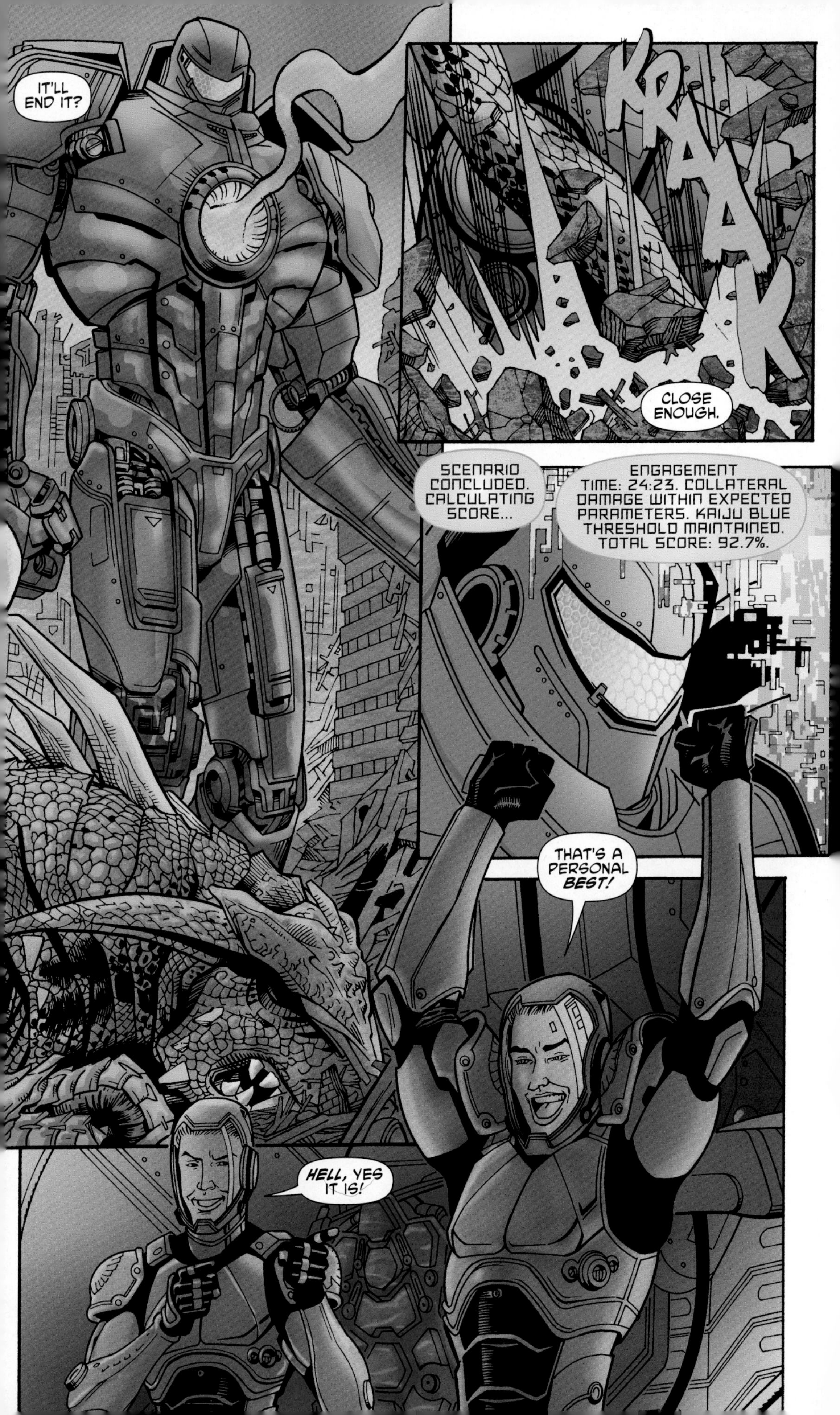
IT'LL END IT?
KRAAK
CLOSE ENOUGH.
SCENARIO CONCLUDED. CALCULATING SCORE...
ENGAGEMENT TIME: 24:23. COLLATERAL DAMAGE WITHIN EXPECTED PARAMETERS. KAIJU BLUE THRESHOLD MAINTAINED. TOTAL SCORE: 92.7%.
THAT'S A PERSONAL *BEST!*
HELL, YES IT IS!

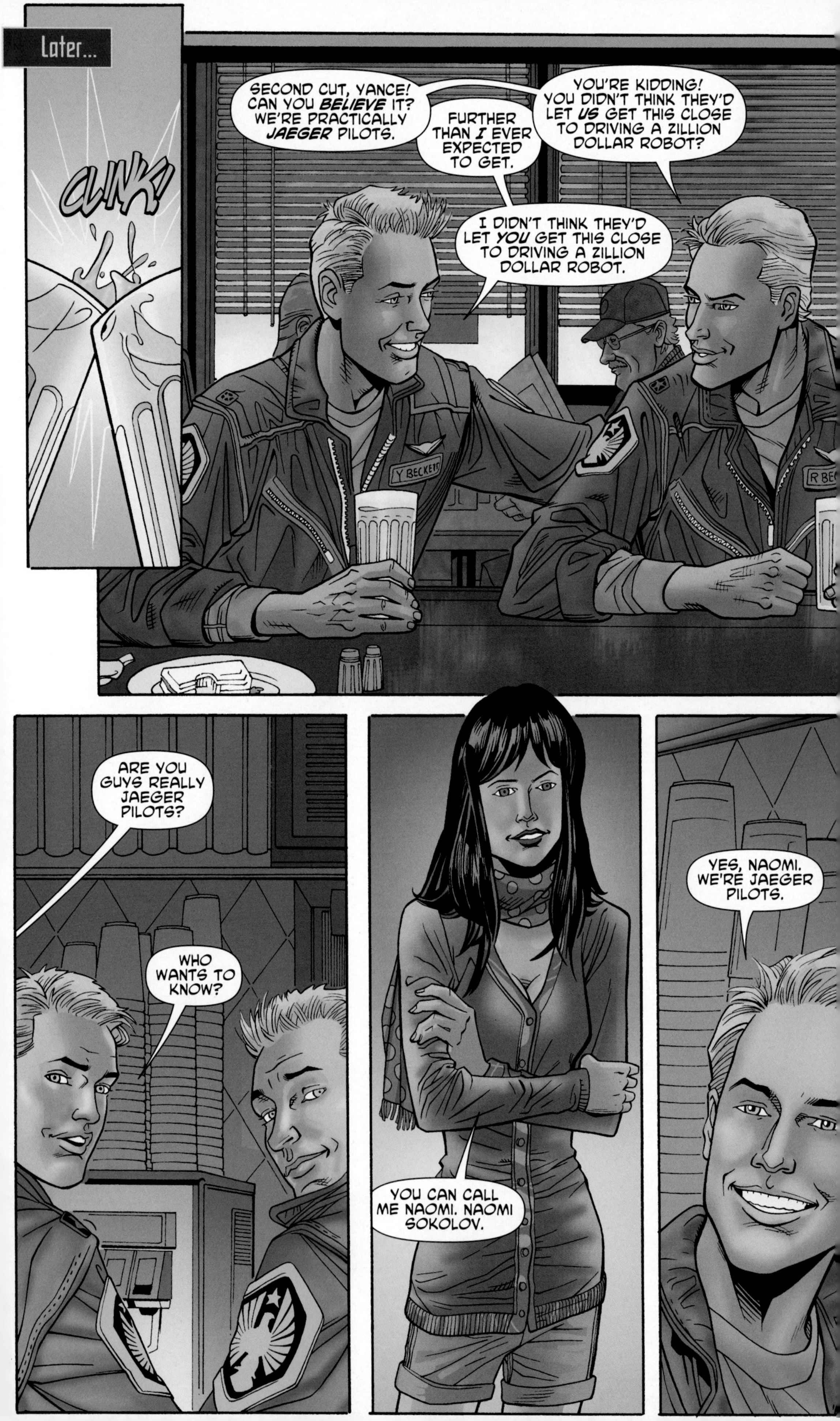
Later...
CLINK!
SECOND CUT, YANCE! CAN YOU BELIEVE IT? WE'RE PRACTICALLY JAEGER PILOTS.
FURTHER THAN I EVER EXPECTED TO GET.
YOU'RE KIDDING! YOU DIDN'T THINK THEY'D LET US GET THIS CLOSE TO DRIVING A ZILLION DOLLAR ROBOT?
I DIDN'T THINK THEY'D LET YOU GET THIS CLOSE TO DRIVING A ZILLION DOLLAR ROBOT.
Y BECKETT
R BEC
ARE YOU GUYS REALLY JAEGER PILOTS?
WHO WANTS TO KNOW?
YOU CAN CALL ME NAOMI. NAOMI SOKOLOV.
YES, NAOMI. WE'RE JAEGER PILOTS.

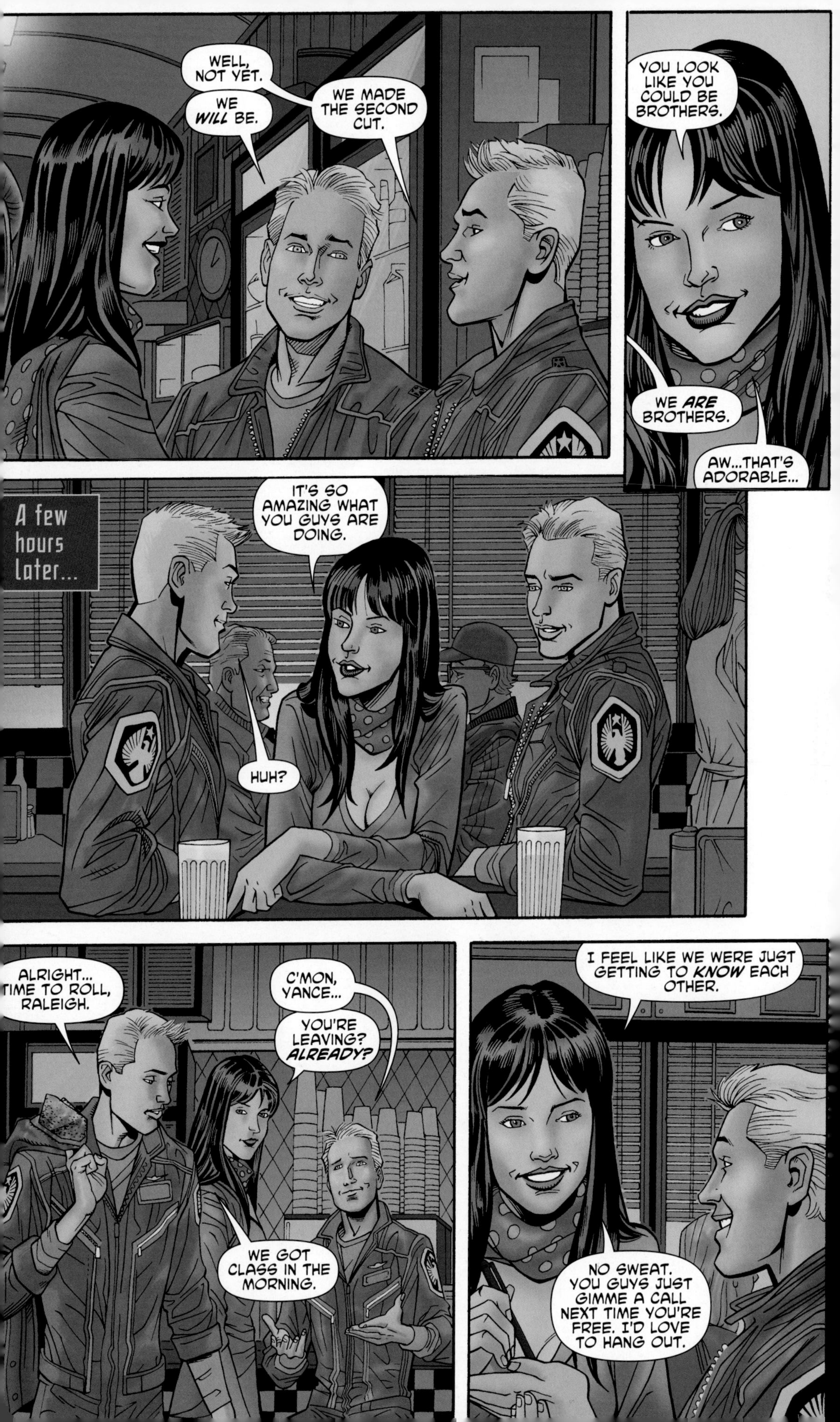
WELL, NOT YET.
WE *WILL* BE.
WE MADE THE SECOND CUT.
YOU LOOK LIKE YOU COULD BE BROTHERS.
WE *ARE* BROTHERS.
AW...THAT'S ADORABLE...
A few hours later...
IT'S SO AMAZING WHAT YOU GUYS ARE DOING.
HUH?
ALRIGHT... TIME TO ROLL, RALEIGH.
C'MON, YANCE...
YOU'RE LEAVING? *ALREADY?*
WE GOT CLASS IN THE MORNING.
I FEEL LIKE WE WERE JUST GETTING TO *KNOW* EACH OTHER.
NO SWEAT. YOU GUYS JUST GIMME A CALL NEXT TIME YOU'RE FREE. I'D LOVE TO HANG OUT.

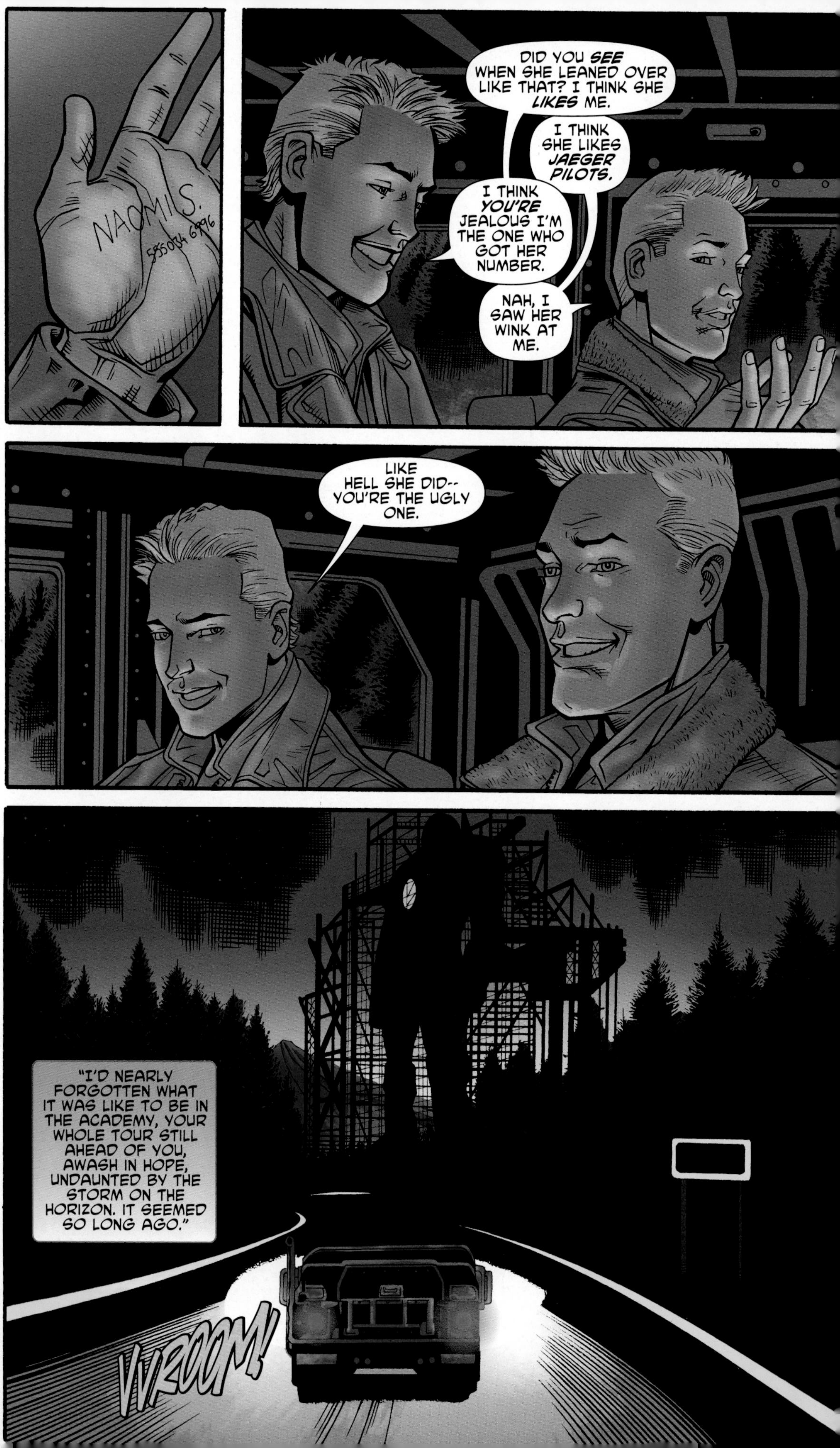
NAOMI S.
5550134 6996
DID YOU SEE WHEN SHE LEANED OVER LIKE THAT? I THINK SHE LIKES ME.
I THINK SHE LIKES JAEGER PILOTS.
I THINK YOU'RE JEALOUS I'M THE ONE WHO GOT HER NUMBER.
NAH, I SAW HER WINK AT ME.
LIKE HELL SHE DID-- YOU'RE THE UGLY ONE.
"I'D NEARLY FORGOTTEN WHAT IT WAS LIKE TO BE IN THE ACADEMY, YOUR WHOLE TOUR STILL AHEAD OF YOU, AWASH IN HOPE, UNDAUNTED BY THE STORM ON THE HORIZON. IT SEEMED SO LONG AGO."
VVROOM!

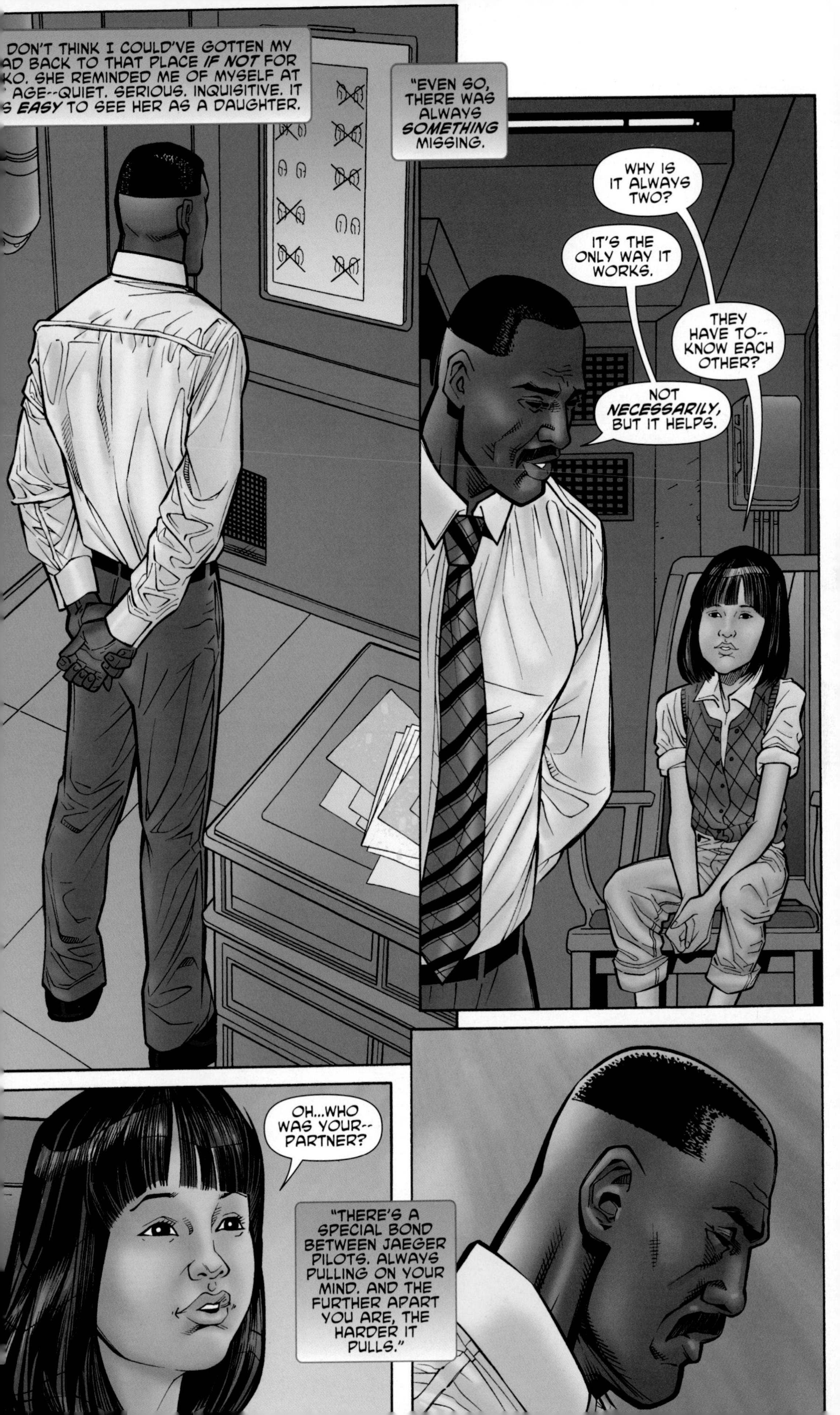
DON'T THINK I COULD'VE GOTTEN MY AD BACK TO THAT PLACE IF NOT FOR KO. SHE REMINDED ME OF MYSELF AT AGE--QUIET. SERIOUS. INQUISITIVE. IT S EASY TO SEE HER AS A DAUGHTER.
"EVEN SO, THERE WAS ALWAYS SOMETHING MISSING.
WHY IS IT ALWAYS TWO?
IT'S THE ONLY WAY IT WORKS.
THEY HAVE TO--KNOW EACH OTHER?
NOT NECESSARILY, BUT IT HELPS.
OH...WHO WAS YOUR--PARTNER?
"THERE'S A SPECIAL BOND BETWEEN JAEGER PILOTS. ALWAYS PULLING ON YOUR MIND. AND THE FURTHER APART YOU ARE, THE HARDER IT PULLS."

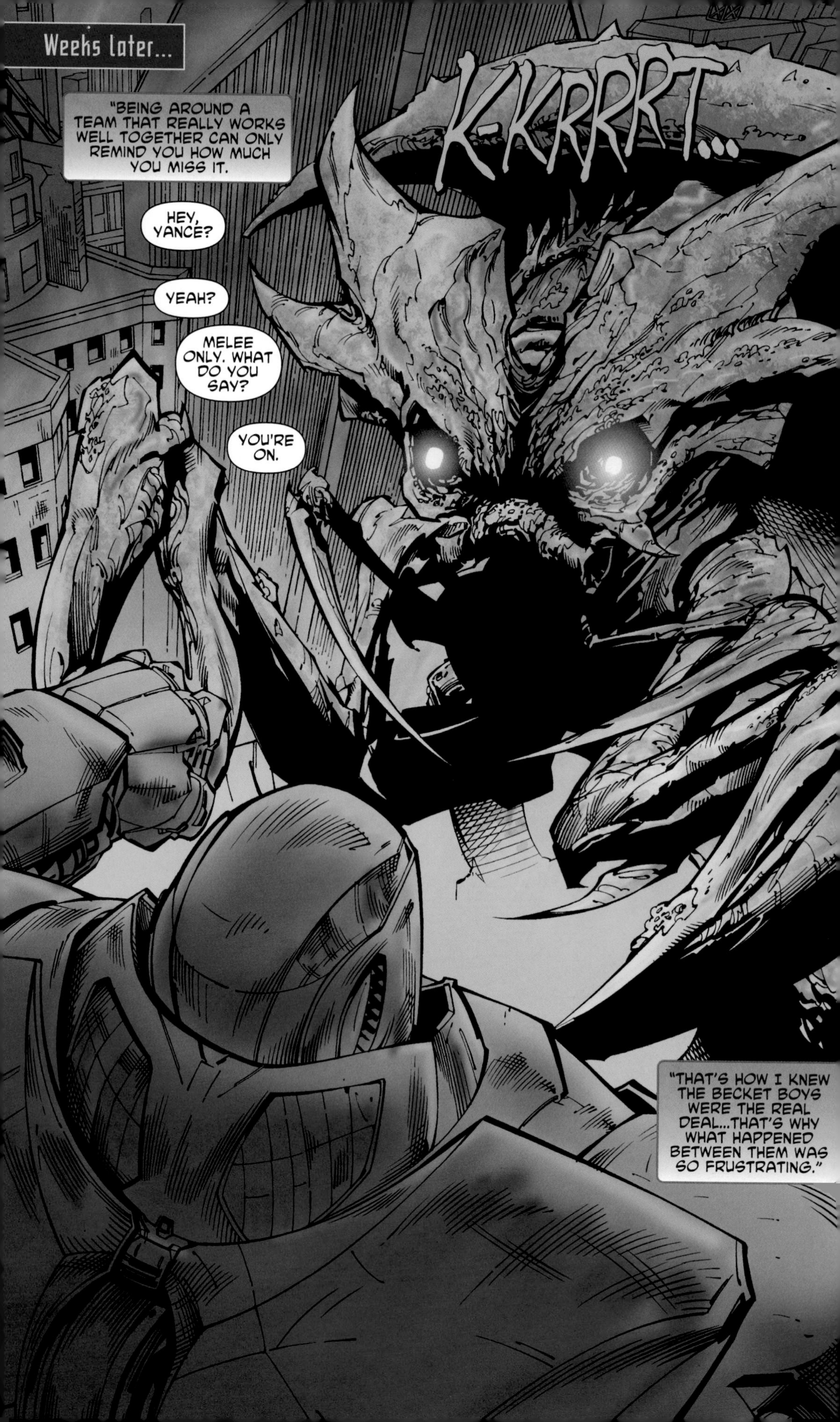
Weeks later...
"BEING AROUND A TEAM THAT REALLY WORKS WELL TOGETHER CAN ONLY REMIND YOU HOW MUCH YOU MISS IT.
K-KRRRRT...
HEY, YANCE?
YEAH?
MELEE ONLY. WHAT DO YOU SAY?
YOU'RE ON.
"THAT'S HOW I KNEW THE BECKET BOYS WERE THE REAL DEAL...THAT'S WHY WHAT HAPPENED BETWEEN THEM WAS SO FRUSTRATING."

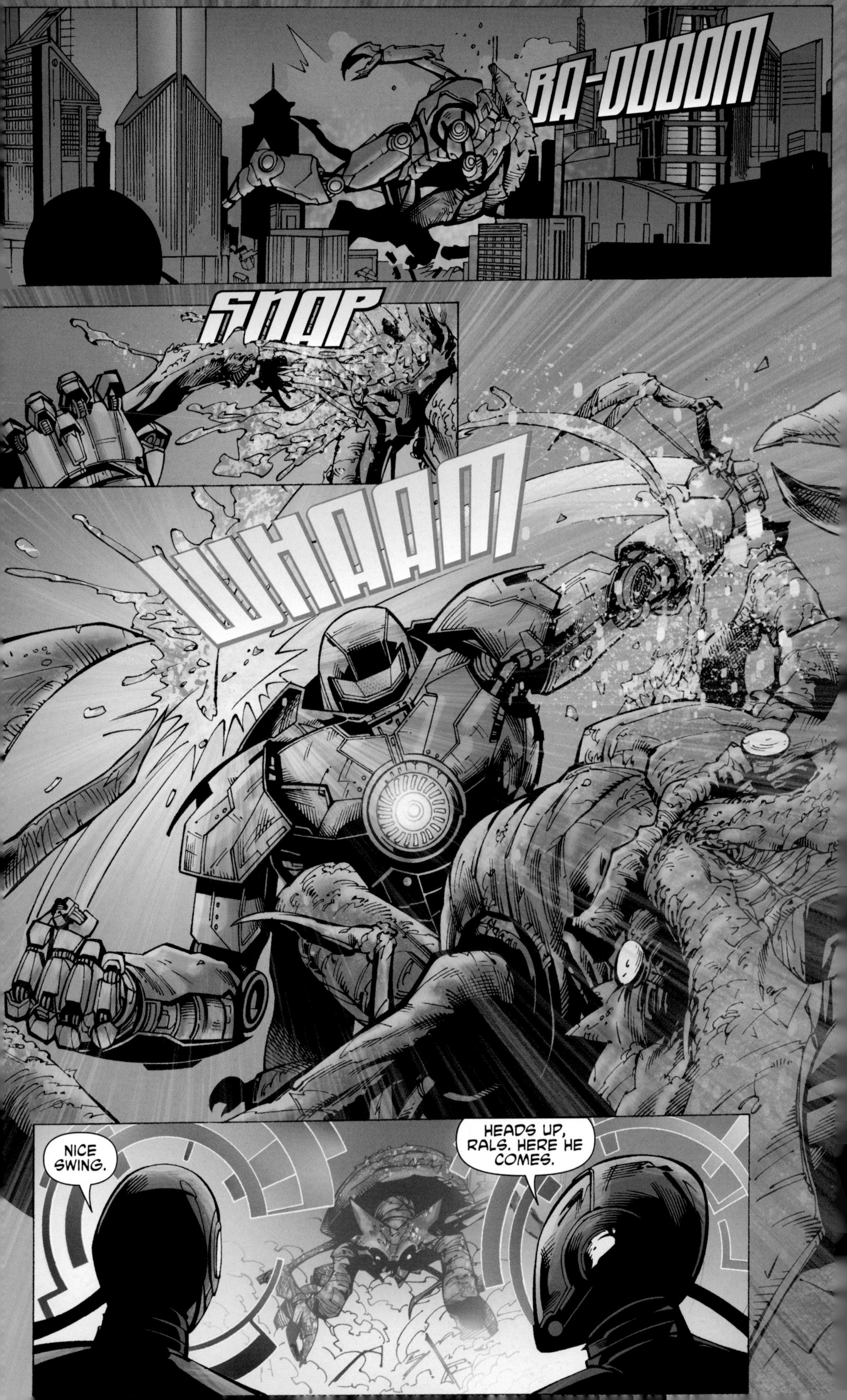
BA-DOOOM
SNAP
WHAAM
NICE SWING.
HEADS UP, RALS. HERE HE COMES.

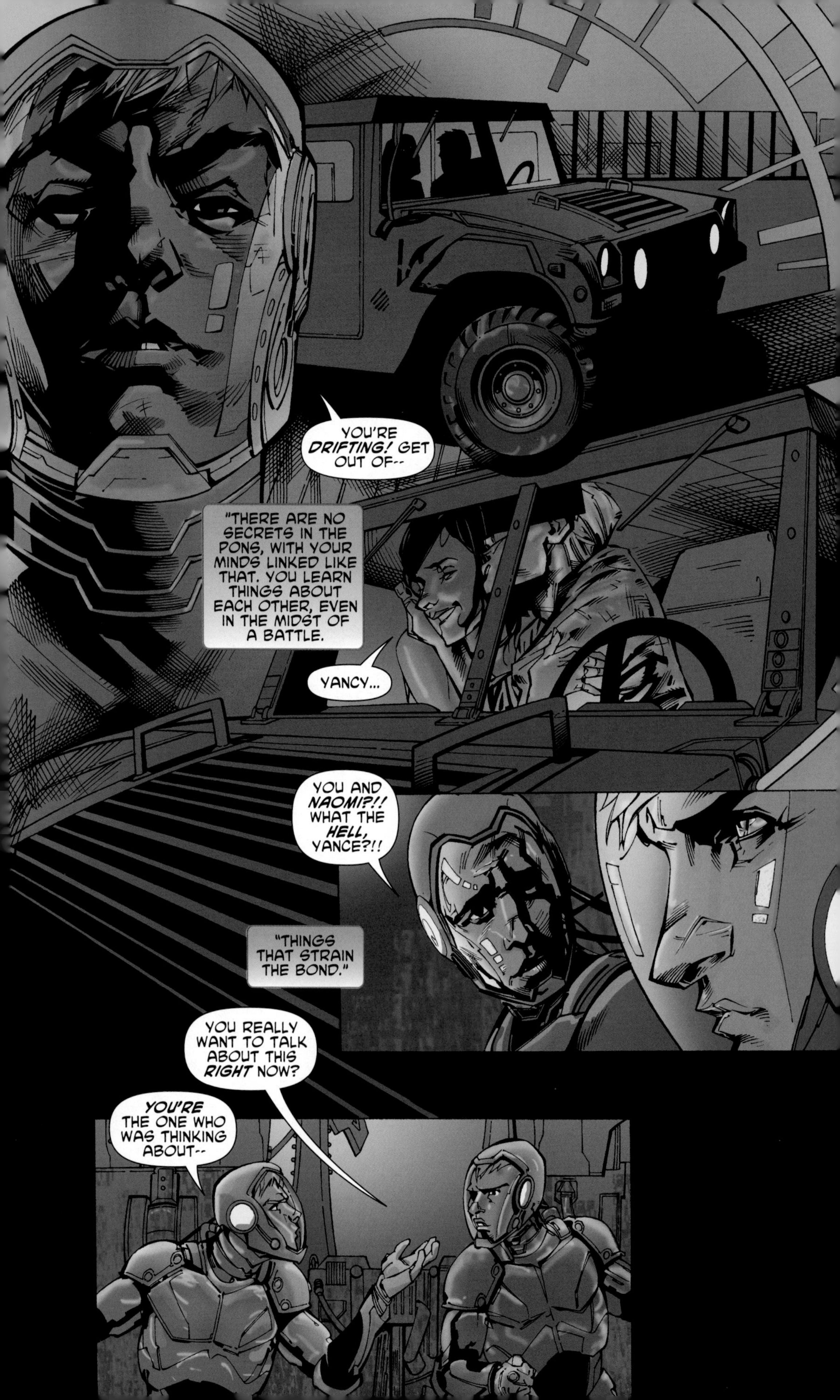
YOU'RE *DRIFTING!* GET OUT OF--
"THERE ARE NO SECRETS IN THE PONS, WITH YOUR MINDS LINKED LIKE THAT. YOU LEARN THINGS ABOUT EACH OTHER, EVEN IN THE MIDST OF A BATTLE.
YANCY...
YOU AND *NAOMI?!!* WHAT THE *HELL,* YANCE?!!
"THINGS THAT STRAIN THE BOND."
YOU REALLY WANT TO TALK ABOUT THIS *RIGHT* NOW?
YOU'RE THE ONE WHO WAS THINKING ABOUT--

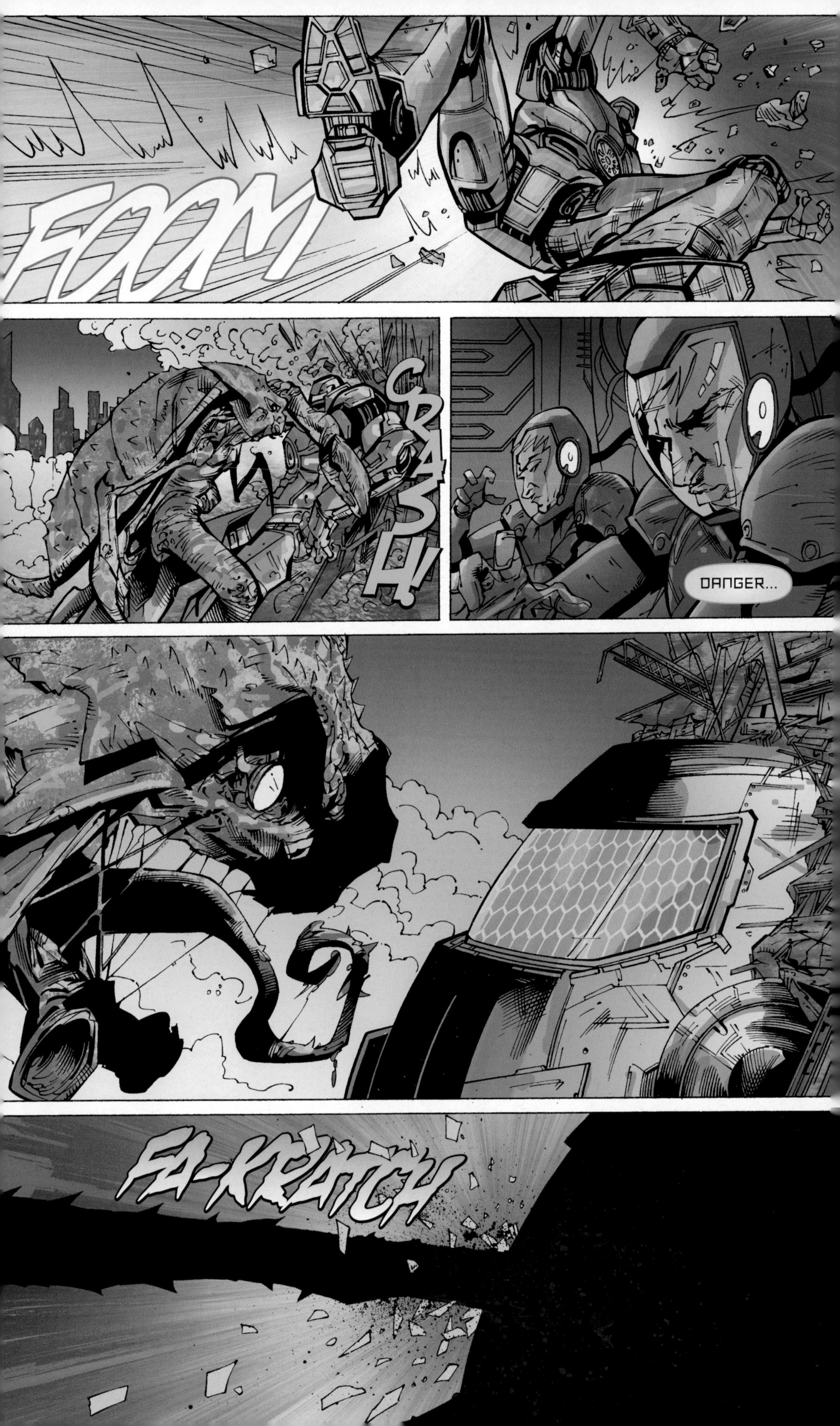
FOOM
CRASH!
DANGER...
FA-KRATCH

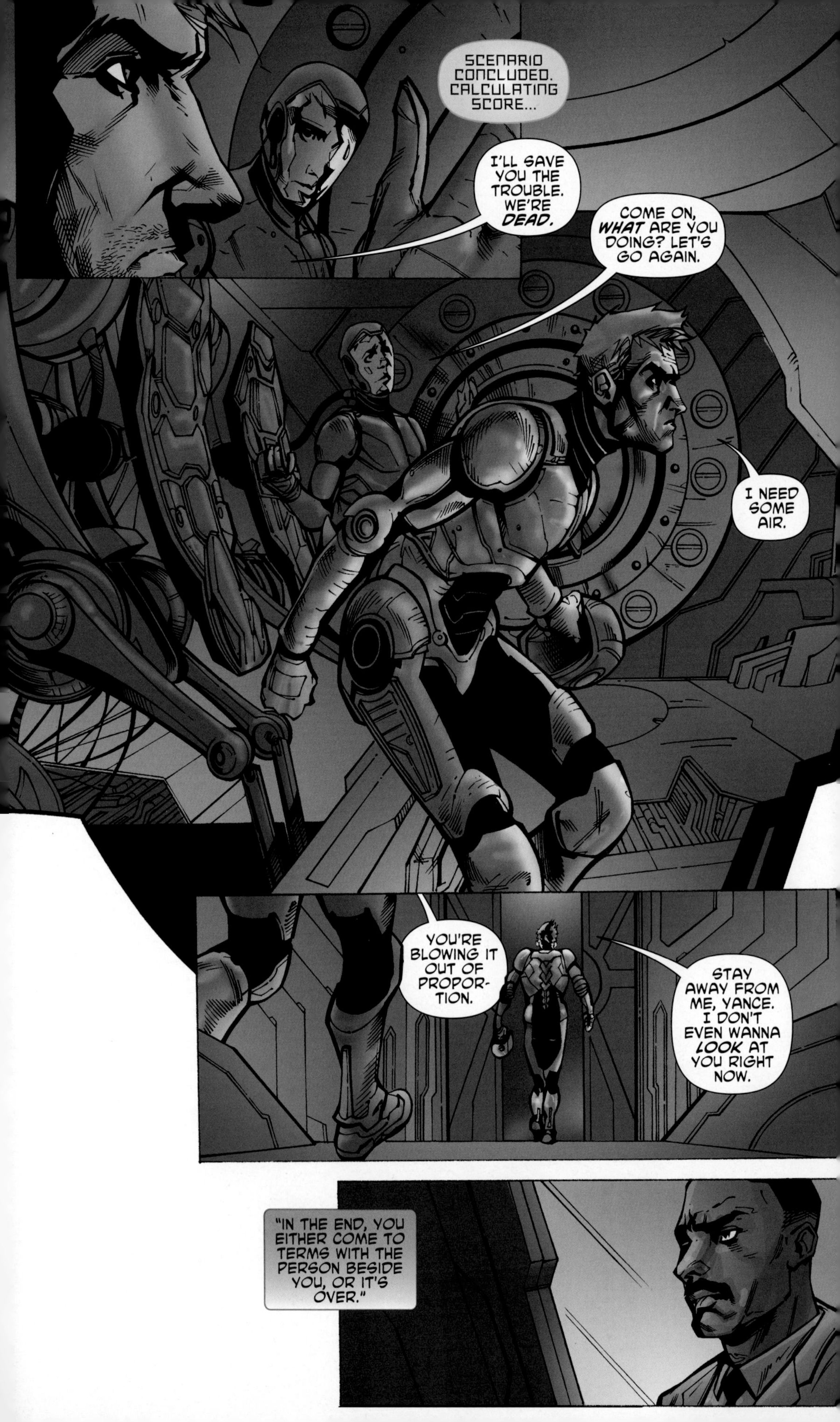
SCENARIO CONCLUDED. CALCULATING SCORE...
I'LL SAVE YOU THE TROUBLE. WE'RE *DEAD.*
COME ON, *WHAT* ARE YOU DOING? LET'S GO AGAIN.
I NEED SOME AIR.
YOU'RE BLOWING IT OUT OF PROPOR- TION.
STAY AWAY FROM ME, YANCE. I DON'T EVEN WANNA *LOOK* AT YOU RIGHT NOW.
"IN THE END, YOU EITHER COME TO TERMS WITH THE PERSON BESIDE YOU, OR IT'S OVER."

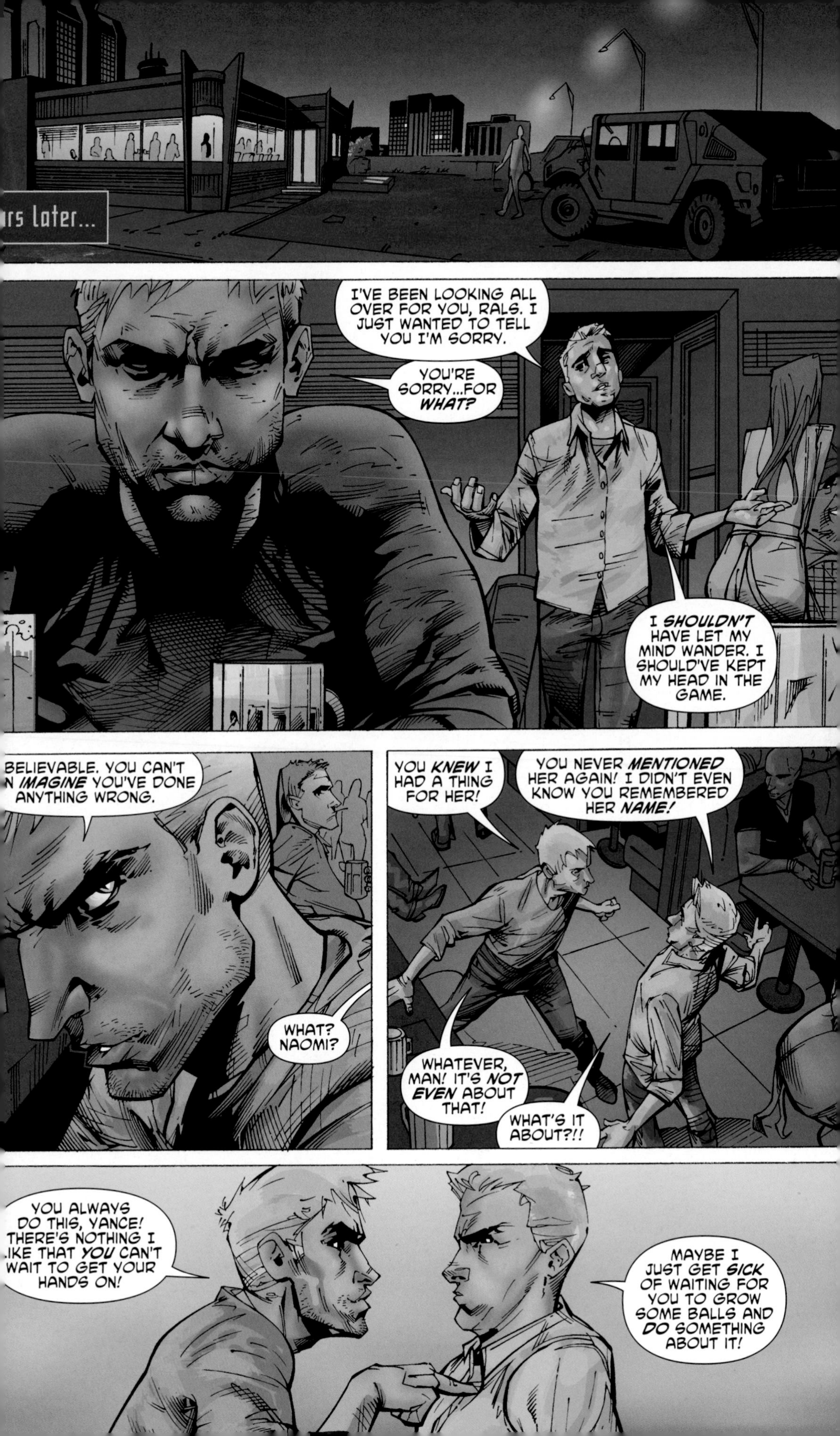
rs later...
I'VE BEEN LOOKING ALL OVER FOR YOU, RALS. I JUST WANTED TO TELL YOU I'M SORRY.
YOU'RE SORRY...FOR WHAT?
I SHOULDN'T HAVE LET MY MIND WANDER. I SHOULD'VE KEPT MY HEAD IN THE GAME.
BELIEVABLE. YOU CAN'T N IMAGINE YOU'VE DONE ANYTHING WRONG.
WHAT? NAOMI?
YOU KNEW I HAD A THING FOR HER!
YOU NEVER MENTIONED HER AGAIN! I DIDN'T EVEN KNOW YOU REMEMBERED HER NAME!
WHATEVER, MAN! IT'S NOT EVEN ABOUT THAT!
WHAT'S IT ABOUT?!!
YOU ALWAYS DO THIS, YANCE! THERE'S NOTHING I IKE THAT YOU CAN'T WAIT TO GET YOUR HANDS ON!
MAYBE I JUST GET SICK OF WAITING FOR YOU TO GROW SOME BALLS AND DO SOMETHING ABOUT IT!

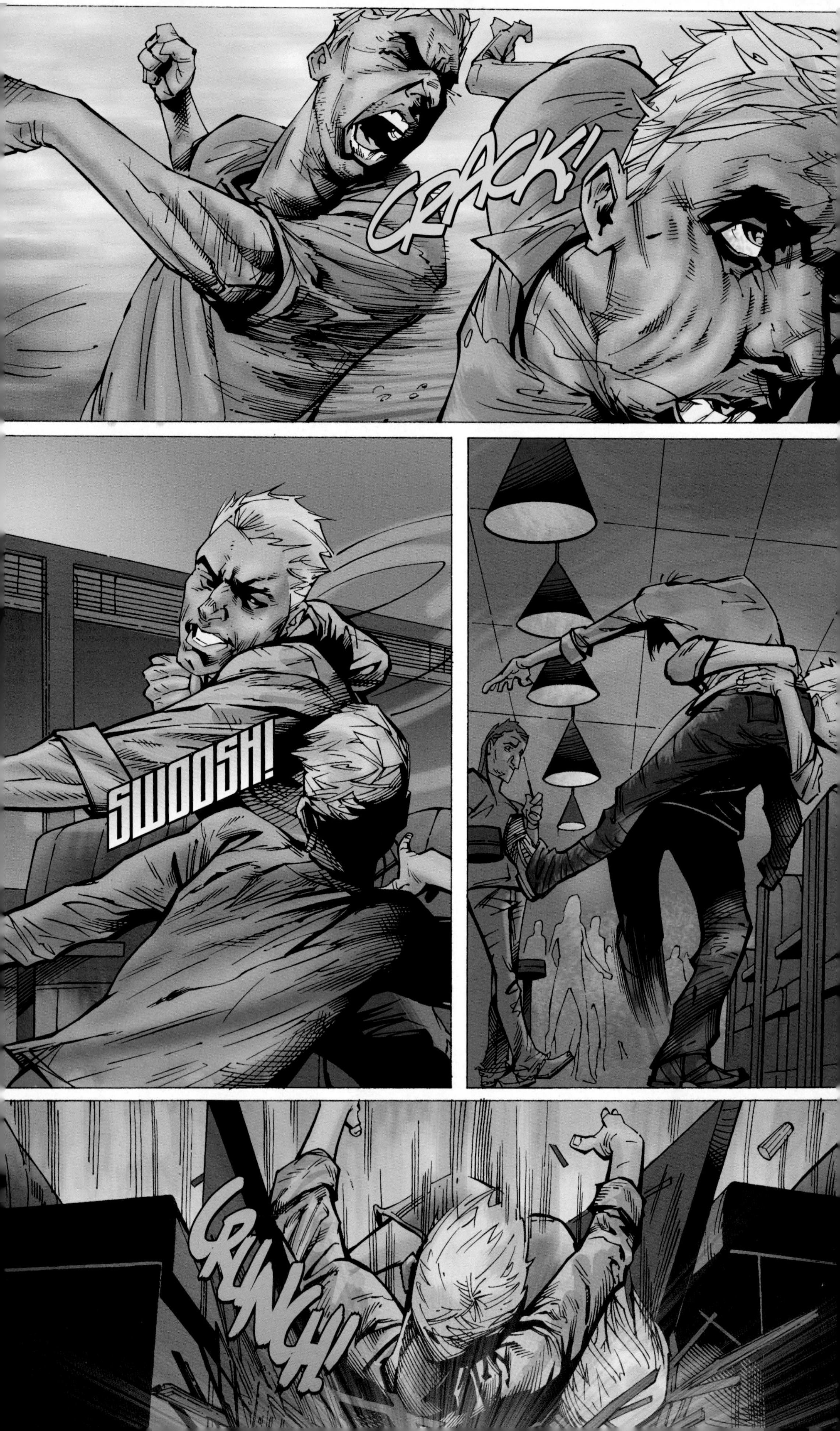
CRACK!
SWOOSH!
CRUNCH!

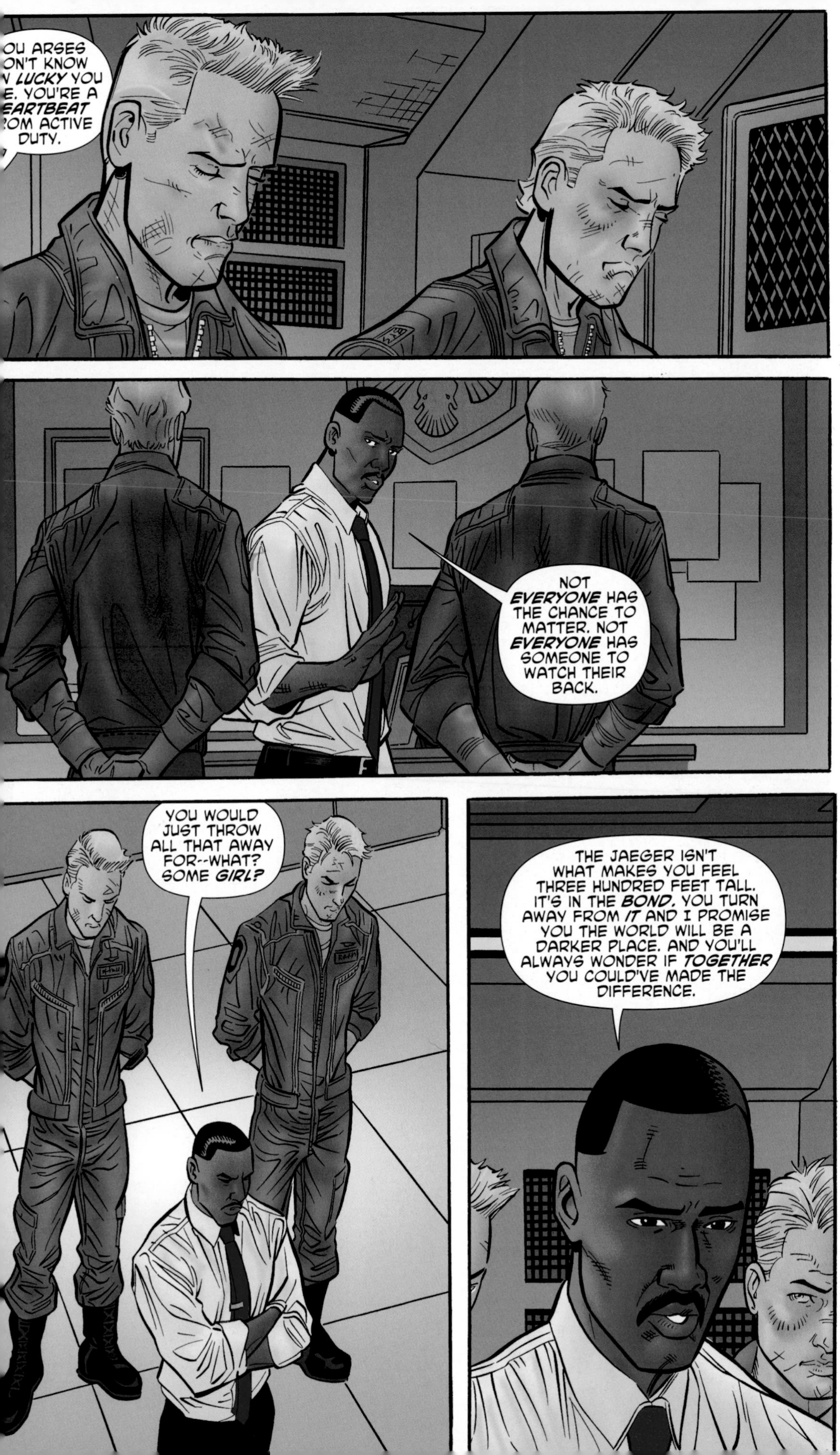
OU ARSES ON'T KNOW V LUCKY YOU E. YOU'RE A EARTBEAT ROM ACTIVE DUTY.
NOT EVERYONE HAS THE CHANCE TO MATTER. NOT EVERYONE HAS SOMEONE TO WATCH THEIR BACK.
YOU WOULD JUST THROW ALL THAT AWAY FOR--WHAT? SOME GIRL?
THE JAEGER ISN'T WHAT MAKES YOU FEEL THREE HUNDRED FEET TALL. IT'S IN THE BOND. YOU TURN AWAY FROM IT AND I PROMISE YOU THE WORLD WILL BE A DARKER PLACE. AND YOU'LL ALWAYS WONDER IF TOGETHER YOU COULD'VE MADE THE DIFFERENCE.

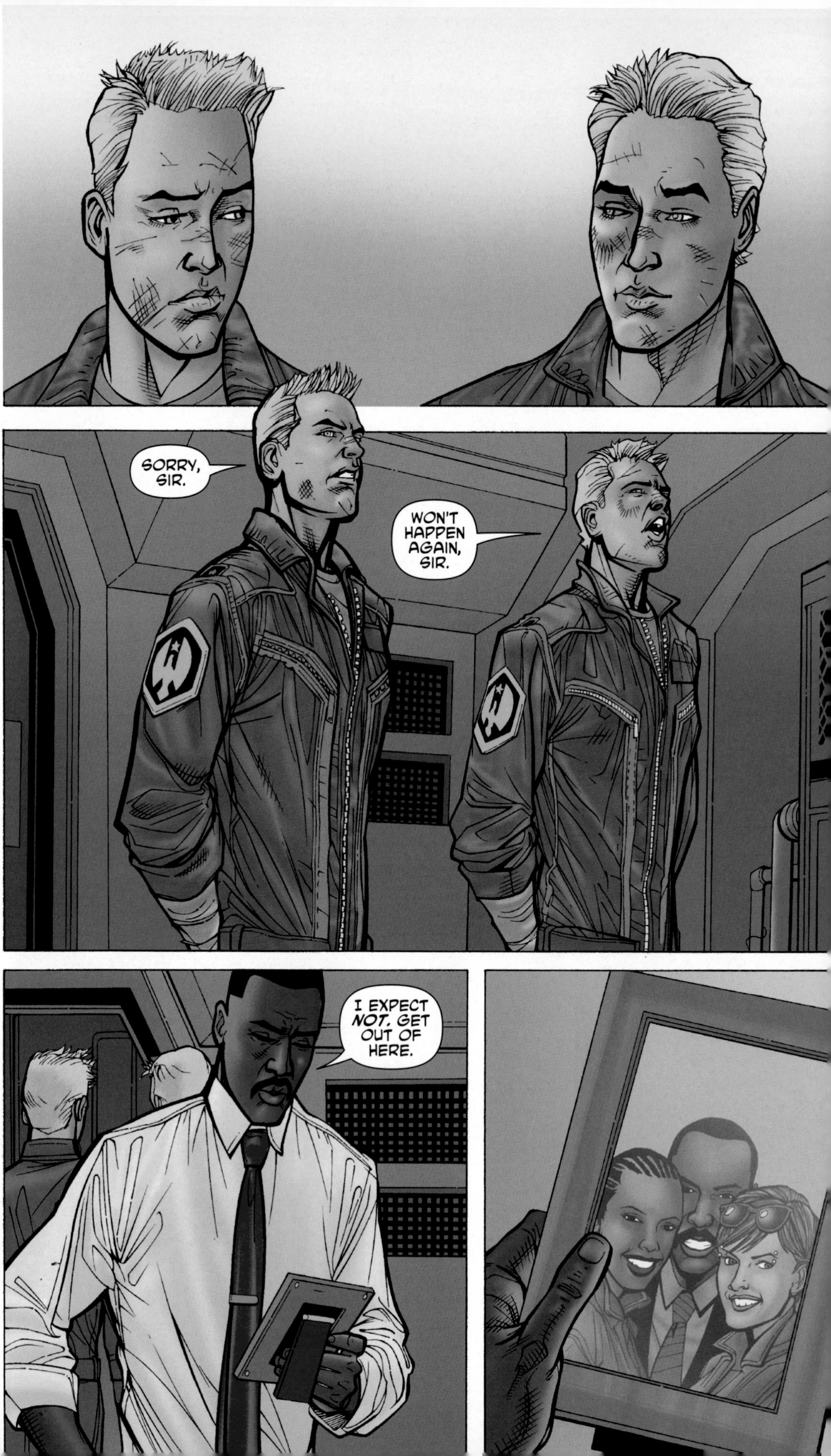
SORRY, SIR.
WON'T HAPPEN AGAIN, SIR.
I EXPECT *NOT.* GET OUT OF HERE.

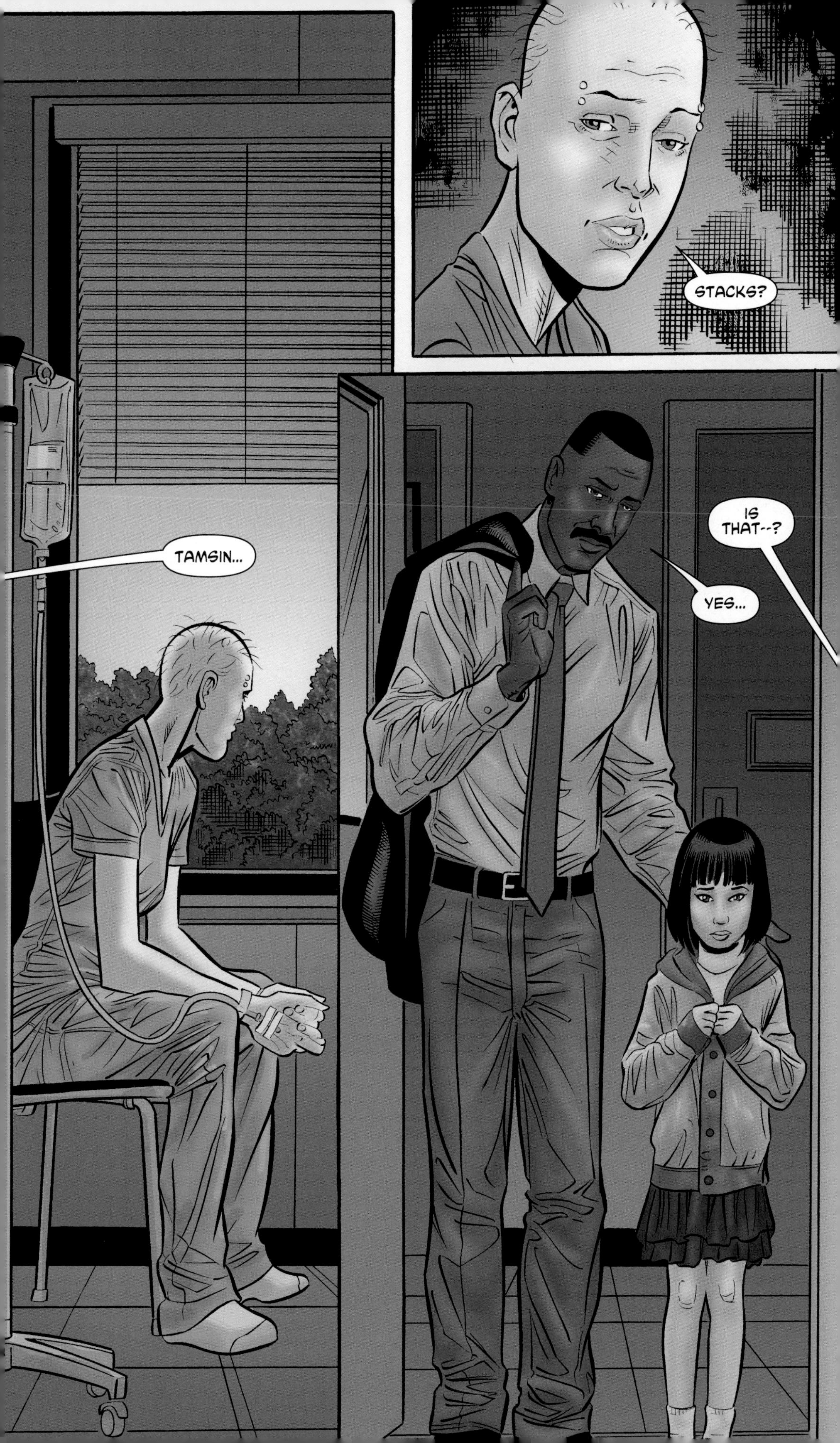
STACKS?
TAMSIN...
IS THAT--?
YES...

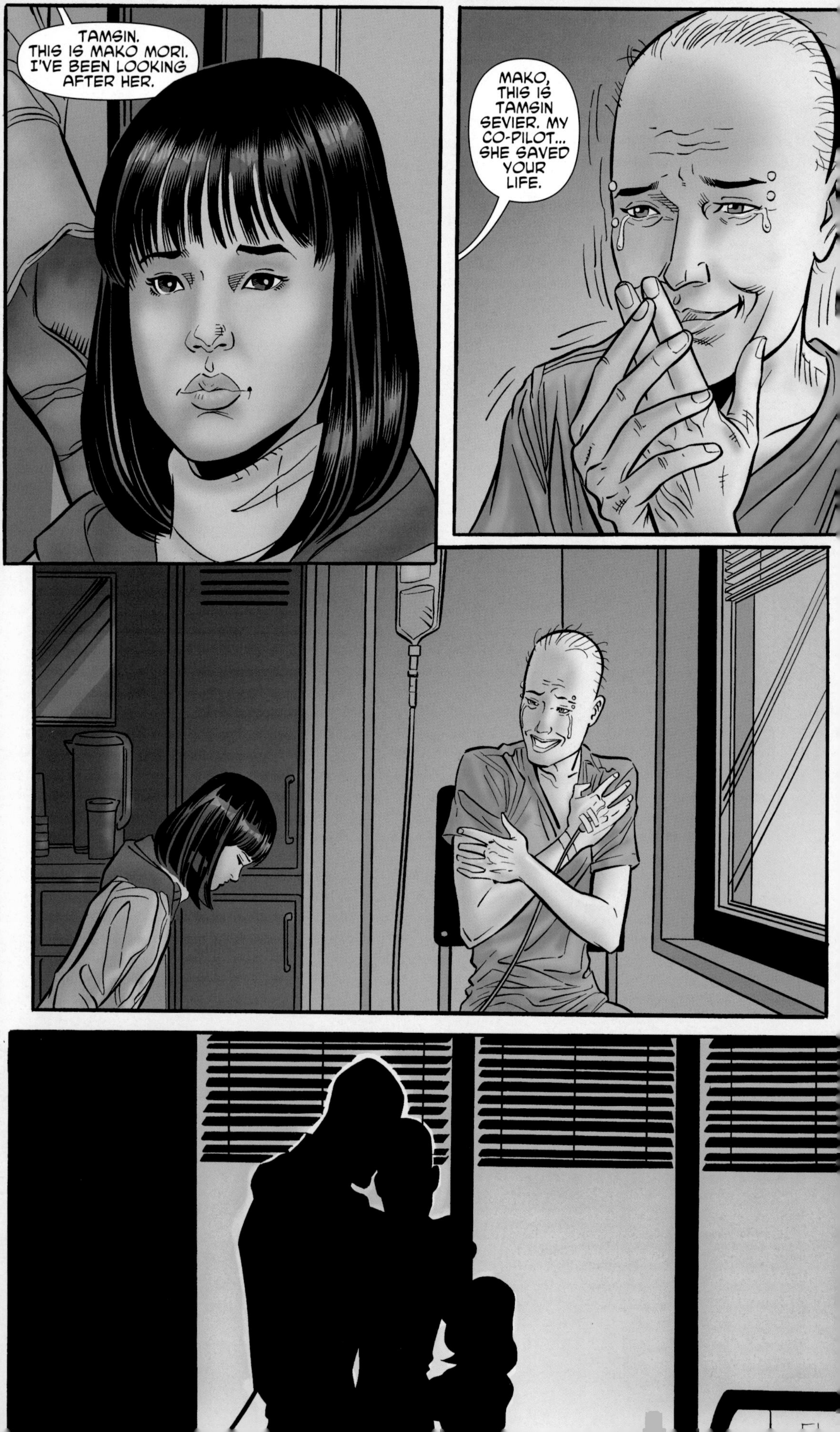
TAMSIN. THIS IS MAKO MORI. I'VE BEEN LOOKING AFTER HER.
MAKO, THIS IS TAMSIN SEVIER. MY CO-PILOT... SHE SAVED YOUR LIFE.

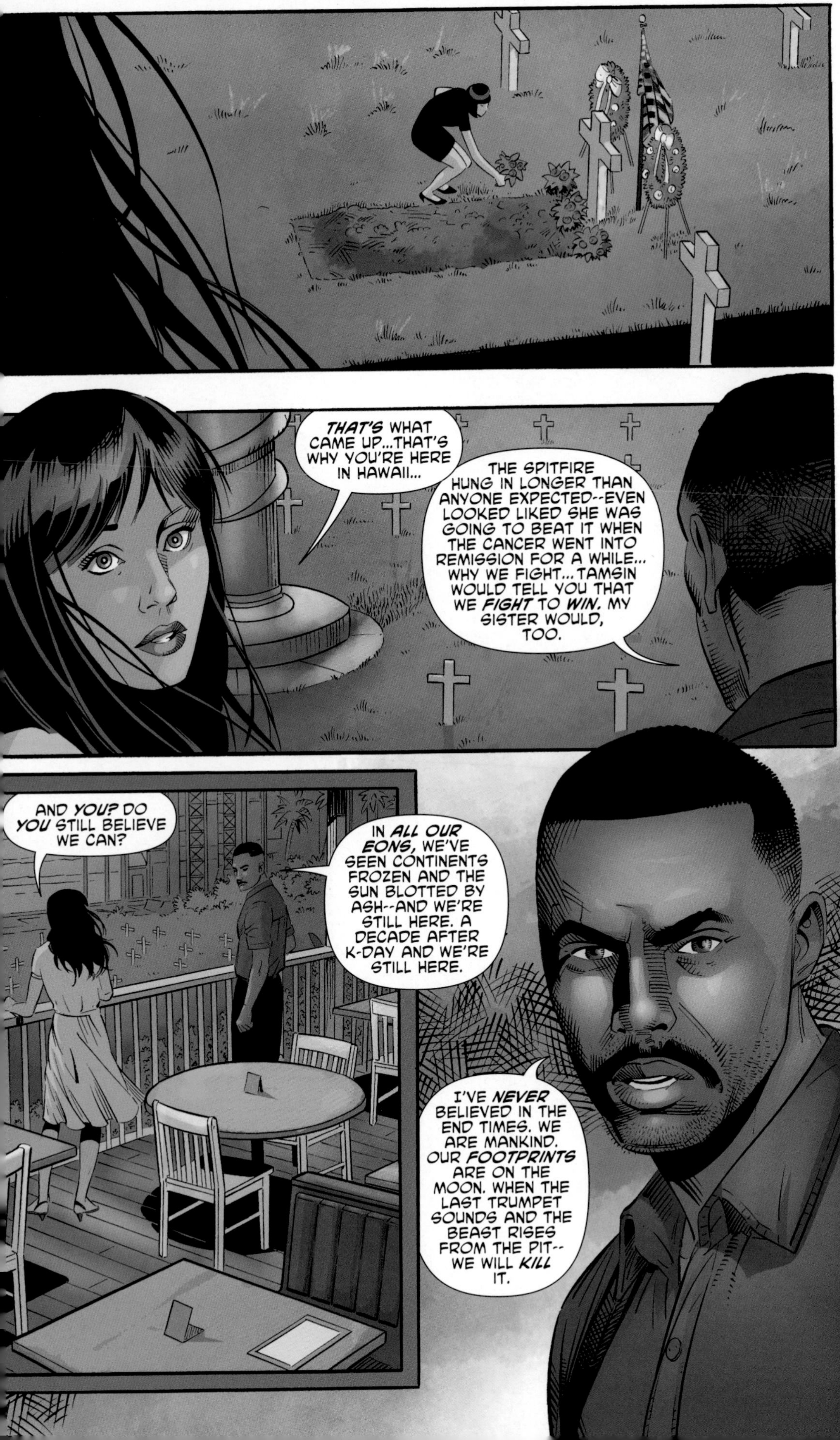
THAT'S WHAT CAME UP...THAT'S WHY YOU'RE HERE IN HAWAII...
THE SPITFIRE HUNG IN LONGER THAN ANYONE EXPECTED--EVEN LOOKED LIKED SHE WAS GOING TO BEAT IT WHEN THE CANCER WENT INTO REMISSION FOR A WHILE... WHY WE FIGHT...TAMSIN WOULD TELL YOU THAT WE FIGHT TO WIN. MY SISTER WOULD, TOO.
AND YOU? DO YOU STILL BELIEVE WE CAN?
IN ALL OUR EONS, WE'VE SEEN CONTINENTS FROZEN AND THE SUN BLOTTED BY ASH--AND WE'RE STILL HERE. A DECADE AFTER K-DAY AND WE'RE STILL HERE.
I'VE NEVER BELIEVED IN THE END TIMES. WE ARE MANKIND. OUR FOOTPRINTS ARE ON THE MOON. WHEN THE LAST TRUMPET SOUNDS AND THE BEAST RISES FROM THE PIT-- WE WILL KILL IT.

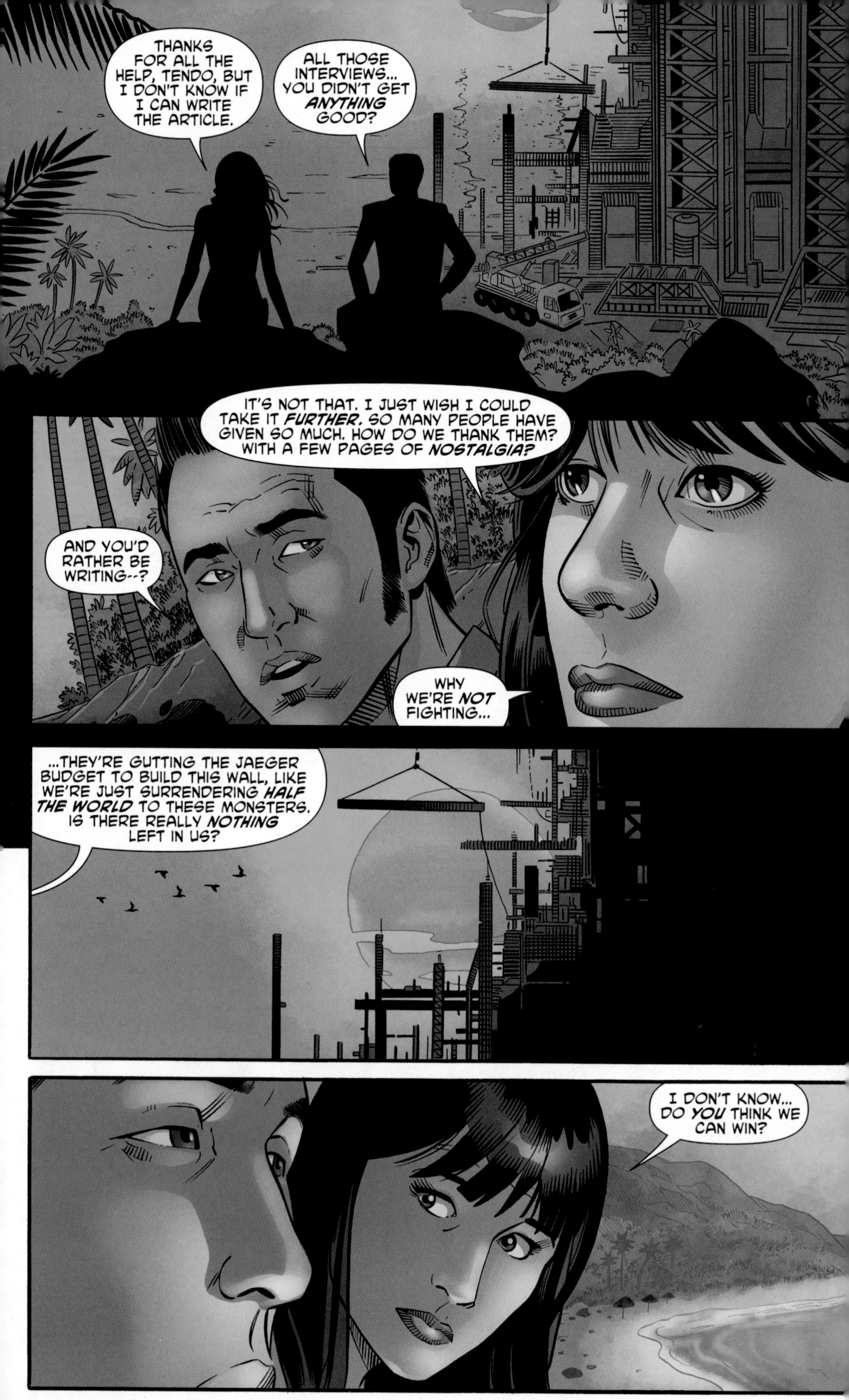
THANKS FOR ALL THE HELP, TENDO, BUT I DON'T KNOW IF I CAN WRITE THE ARTICLE.
ALL THOSE INTERVIEWS... YOU DIDN'T GET ANYTHING GOOD?
IT'S NOT THAT. I JUST WISH I COULD TAKE IT FURTHER. SO MANY PEOPLE HAVE GIVEN SO MUCH. HOW DO WE THANK THEM? WITH A FEW PAGES OF NOSTALGIA?
AND YOU'D RATHER BE WRITING--?
WHY WE'RE NOT FIGHTING...
...THEY'RE GUTTING THE JAEGER BUDGET TO BUILD THIS WALL, LIKE WE'RE JUST SURRENDERING HALF THE WORLD TO THESE MONSTERS. IS THERE REALLY NOTHING LEFT IN US?
I DON'T KNOW... DO YOU THINK WE CAN WIN?

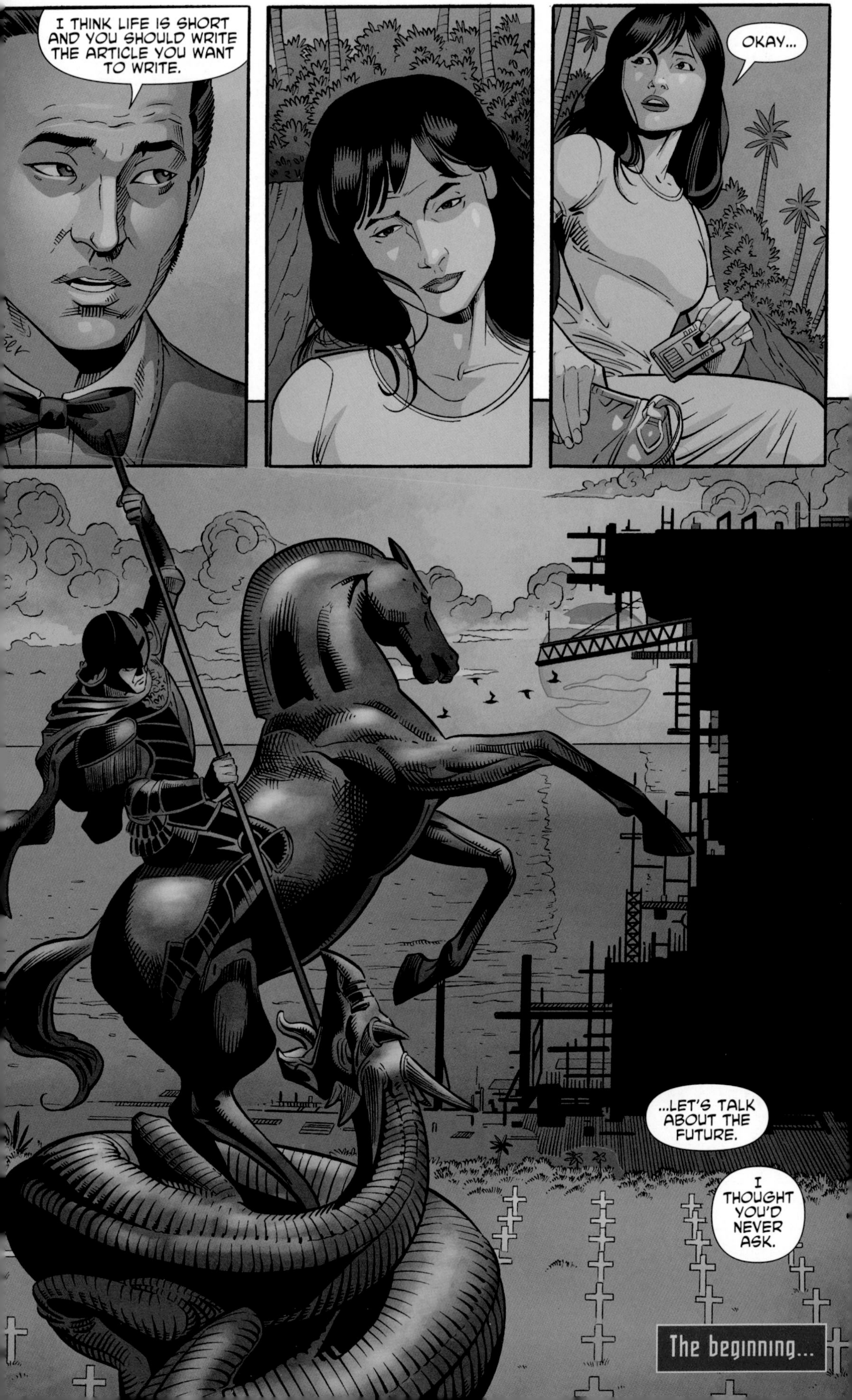
I THINK LIFE IS SHORT AND YOU SHOULD WRITE THE ARTICLE YOU WANT TO WRITE.
OKAY...
...LET'S TALK ABOUT THE FUTURE.
I THOUGHT YOU'D NEVER ASK.
The beginning...

FROM SCRIPT TO THE FINAL PAGE:
THE CREATIVE PROCESS

Both the editors and Guillermo del Toro review and approve the script and art at every stage. The following is a peek behind that creative process, giving you a glimpse into how a graphic novel of this size comes to life.

Once writer Travis Beacham has outlined the broad ideas of the story, he'll begin to script it page-by-page; adding panel descriptions and dialogue.

PAGE 21

1) FROM OVERHEAD -
- we see the squad flying in formation over the city.

2) ON LUNA -
- in her cockpit.

LUNA:
Target sighted.

TAMSIN (ON RADIO):
Jesus! Look at the size of him!

pg. 21

PAGE 20

1) THE EMBARCADERO
The docks are desolate and empty, except for two figures. Distant mountains of black smoke engulf the skyline behind them.

YEYE:
?

TENDO:
I don't know, Yeye.

2) CLOSER ON THE FIGURES
It's Tendo and his grandfather, waiting for a ferry that isn't there. Ashes and embers fall all around.

TENDO: (CONT'D)
We wait, I guess.

3) LOOKING DOWN -
- on Tendo as he looks up.

SFX: SHOOOO-

4) OPPOSITE ANGLE
A squad of fighter jets streak overhead.

SFX: -OOOOM

pg. 20

PAGE 22

SPLASH
The RAF squad approaches to join other squads weaving around the roaring monster, scarred and charred. Bitter. Angry. Mired in a frenzy of dust, smoke, fire, collapsing buildings, and tangled contrails.

LUNA (ON RADIO):
Focus, Tamsin! We'll take pictures when he's dead.

pg. 22

PAGE 23

1) TIGHT ON LUNA -
- in her cockpit.

LUNA:
Let's light him up.

2) LUNA'S JET -
- weaves between the creature's vast limbs, firing her guns.

SFX: TAKKATAKKA

3) ON LUNA'S CANOPY -
- as she looks up to take stock of the damage she's inflicted on the kaiju.

LUNA: (CONT'D)
Damn it! The tank buster rounds are just bouncing off his hide!

TAMSIN (ON RADIO):
AMRAAM's aren't doing much better.

pg. 23

PAGE 24

1) IN THE FOREGROUND -
- Luna's jet swings around for another pass at Trespasser, still wreaking havoc behind her.

TAMSIN (ON RADIO): (CONT'D)
I'll let you know when I find the ugly sod's ball-sack. We'll give it a proper kick.

2) IN FRONT OF THE NOSE -
- of the jet, looking straight through the glass at Luna inside, as she bears down on the monster.

LUNA:
Has anyone tried shoving a sidewinder down his throat?

pg. 24

PAGE 26

SPLASH
Trespasser rakes his huge talons across Luna's flight path, sweeping an arc of fire and debris from the explosion that used to be her jet.

TAMSIN (ON RADIO): (CONT'D)
Luna!!!

pg. 26

PAGE 25

1) TIGHT ON HER FACE
She glares dead ahead.

TAMSIN (ON RADIO):
Don't do anything stupid, Luna...

LUNA:
Who? Me?

2) LOOKING THROUGH -
- the targeting HUD at Trespasser, glaring hatefully right back at us.

TAMSIN (ON RADIO):
Luna...

3) LUNA'S EYES
Fiery and confident.

LUNA:
I've got him.

4) TRESPASSER'S JAWS -
- looms larger in the HUD, roaring as we rush towards his throat.

5) TIGHT ON -
- Luna's thumb, touching the red missile trigger.

TAMSIN (ON RADIO):
Watch your flank! He's --

pg. 25

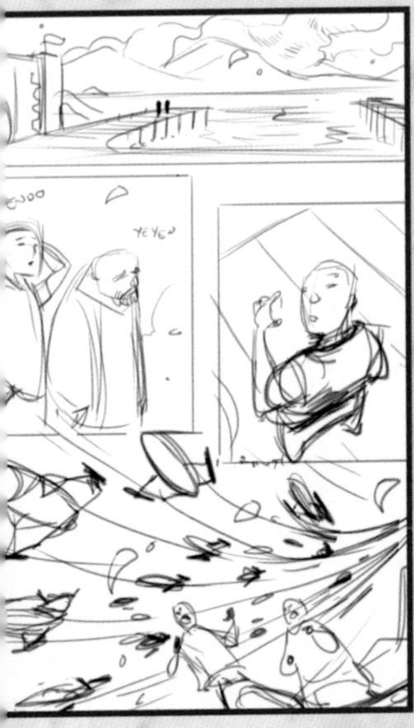

20

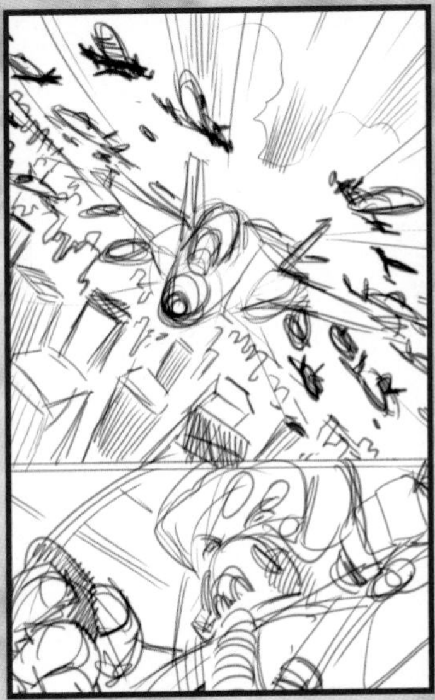

pg. 21

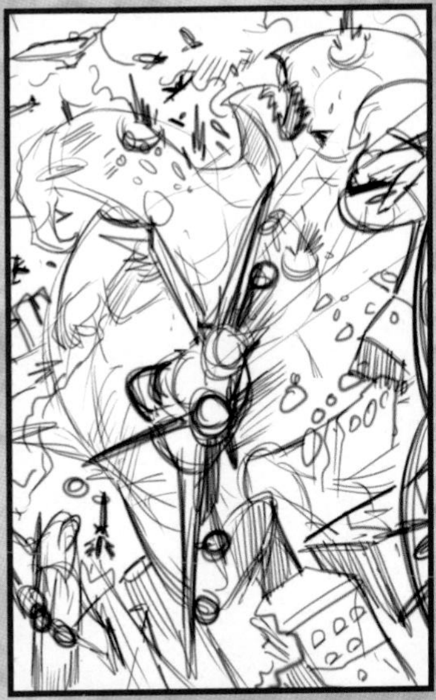

pg. 22

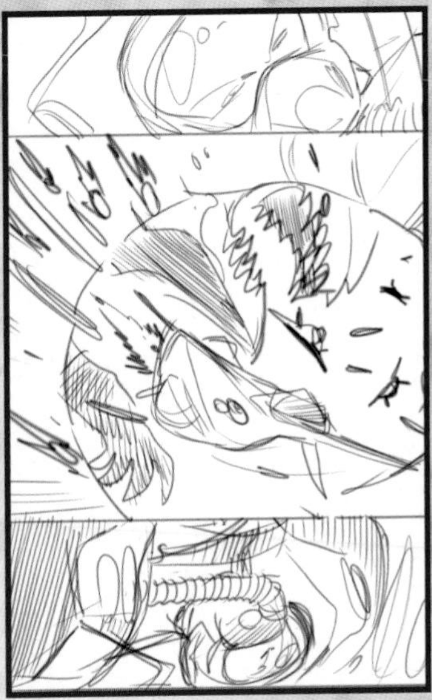

pg. 23

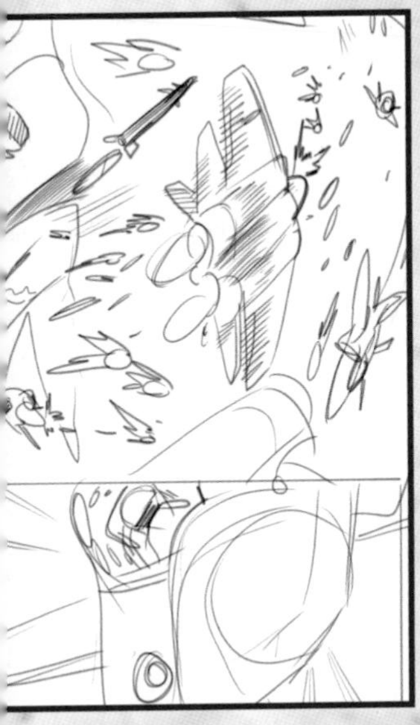

24

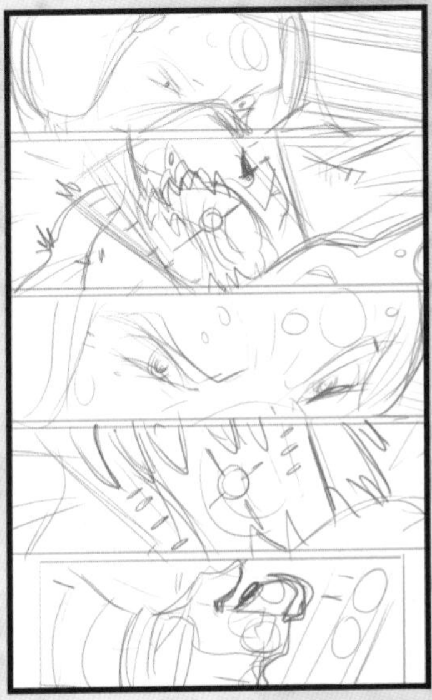

pg. 25

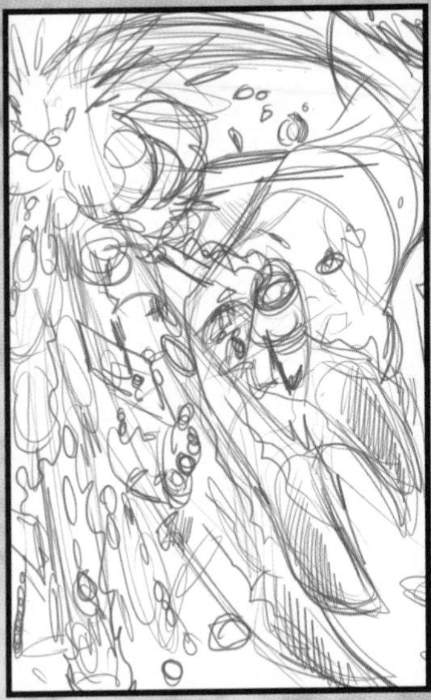

pg. 26

Once the script is finished, penciler Yvel Guichet will quickly sketch layouts incorporating the major shapes and figures on the page to determine the storytelling and placement of characters.

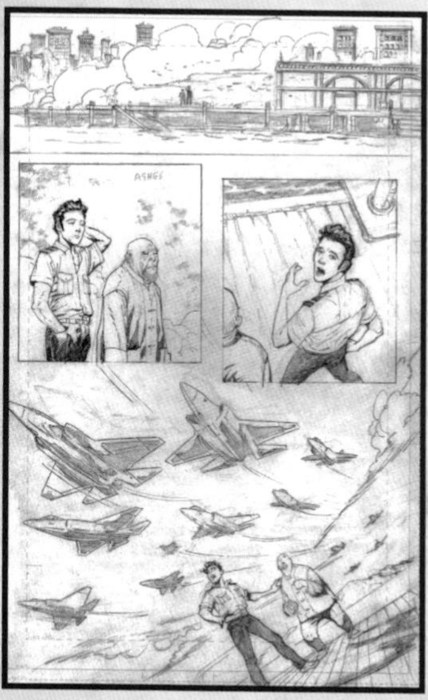
pg. 20

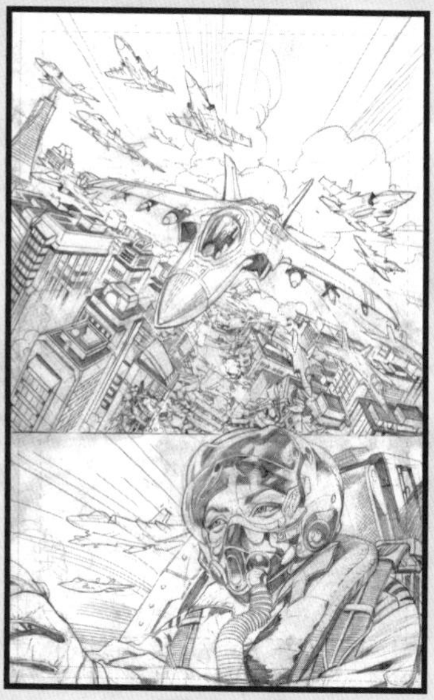
pg. 21

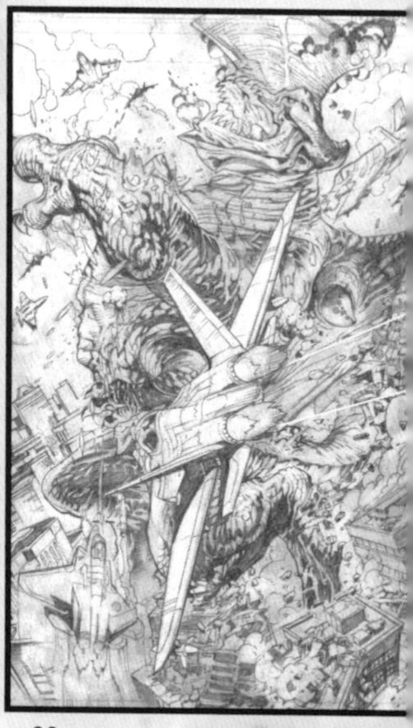
pg. 22

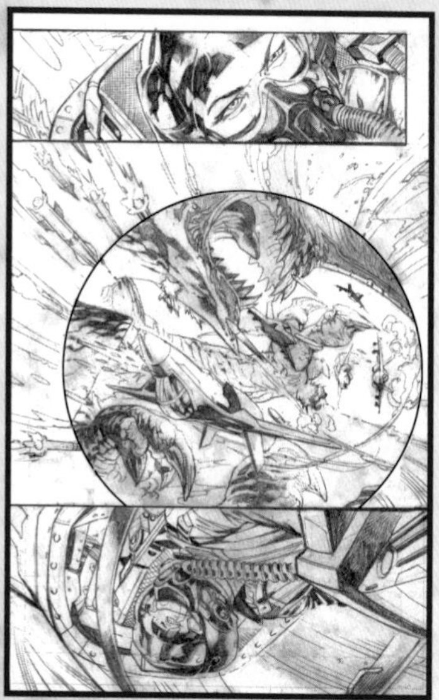
pg. 23

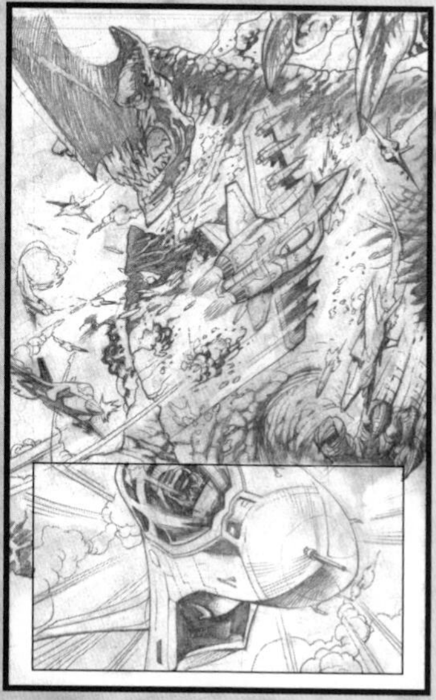
pg. 24

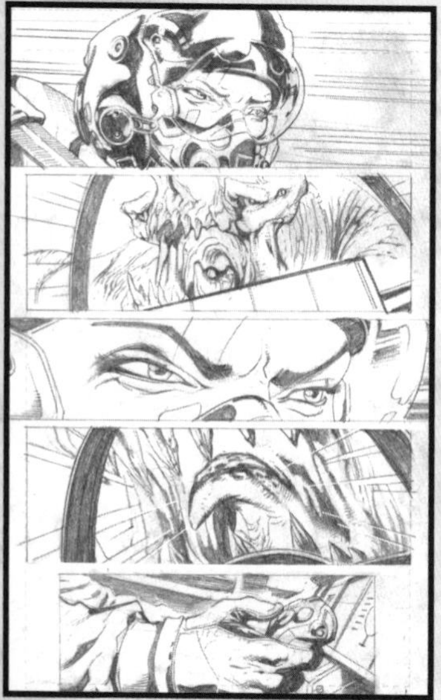
pg. 25

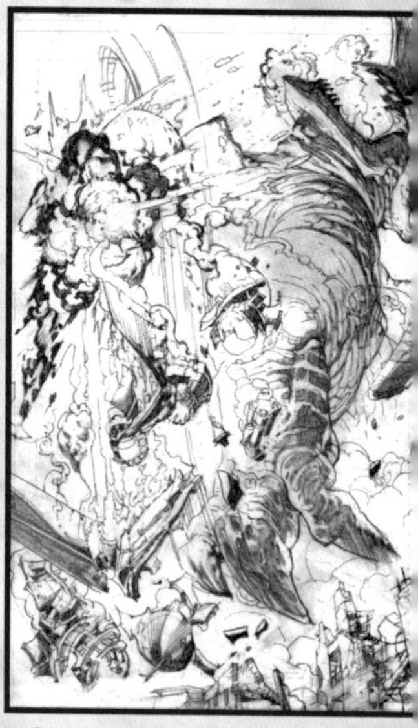
pg. 26

Once the layouts are approved, the penciler will begin fully rendering the page.

Once penciled, inker Steven Bird will use black india ink to enhance the penciler's linework so that it will properly reproduce for printing.

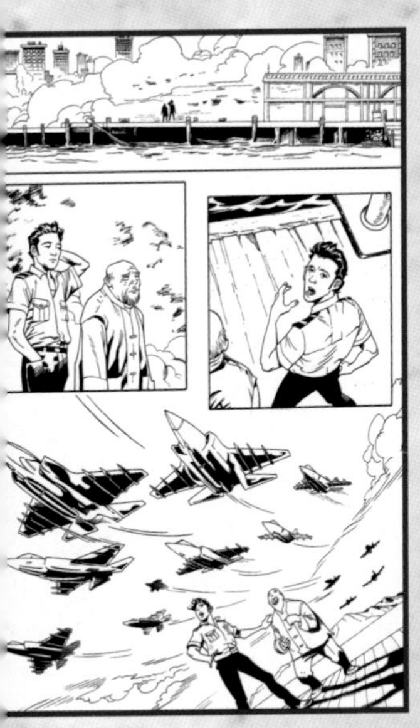

20

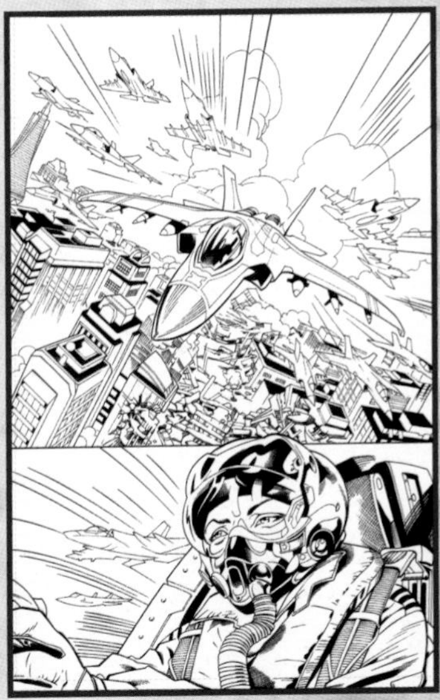

pg. 21

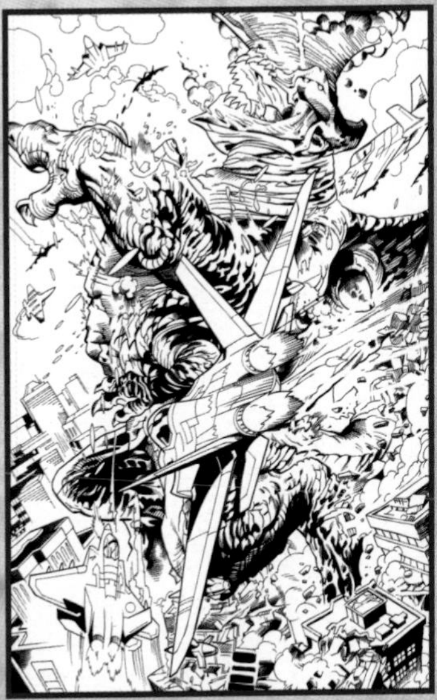

pg. 22

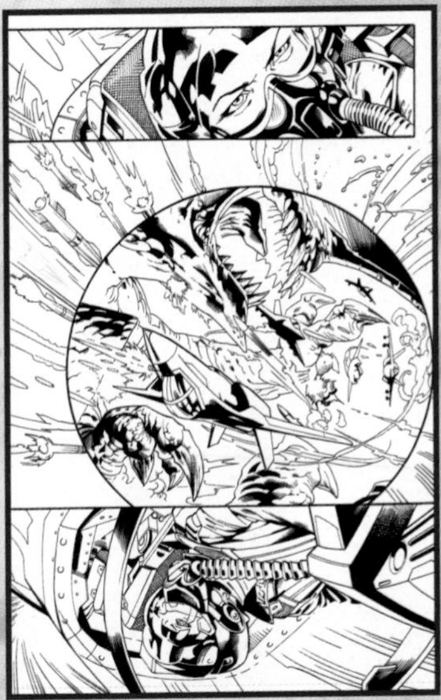

pg. 23

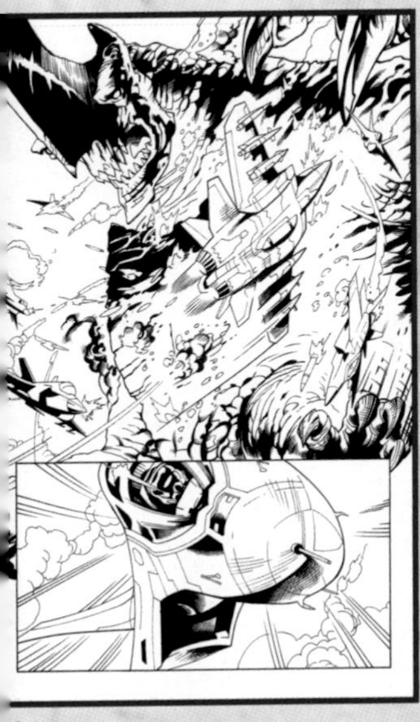

24

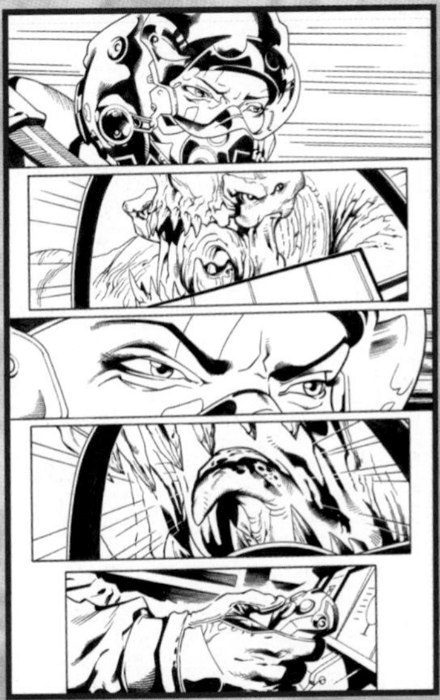

pg. 25

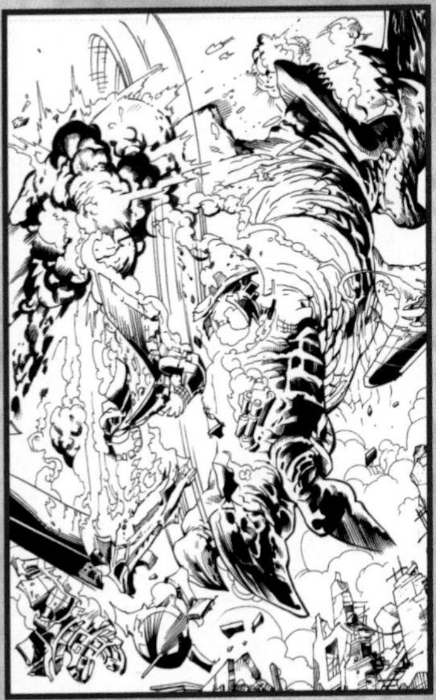

pg. 26

At this point, colorist Guy Major will receive a digital file of the page. Using Photoshop, he will begin adding layers of color to the work until finished.

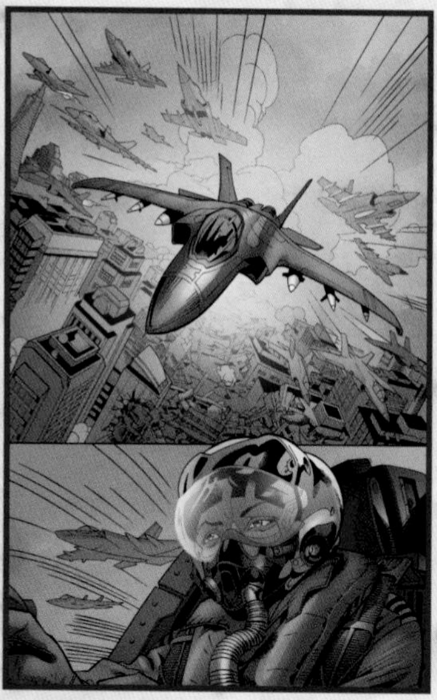

pg. 21

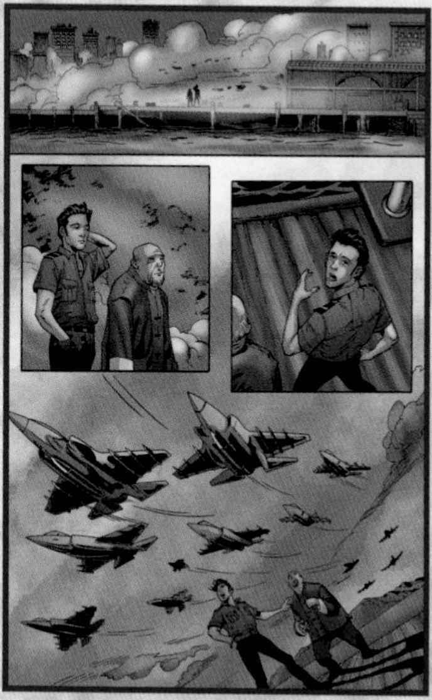

pg. 20

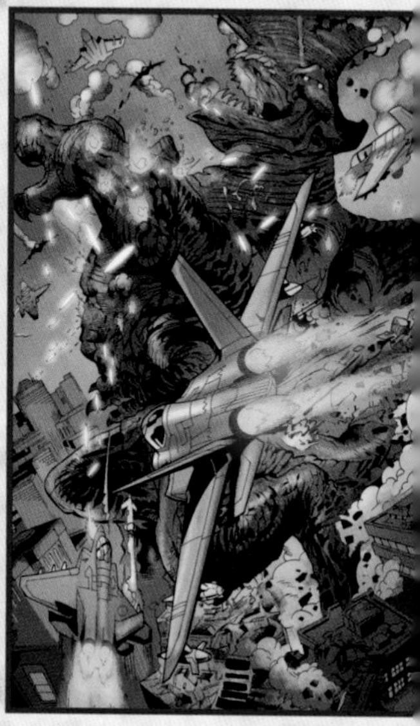

pg. 22

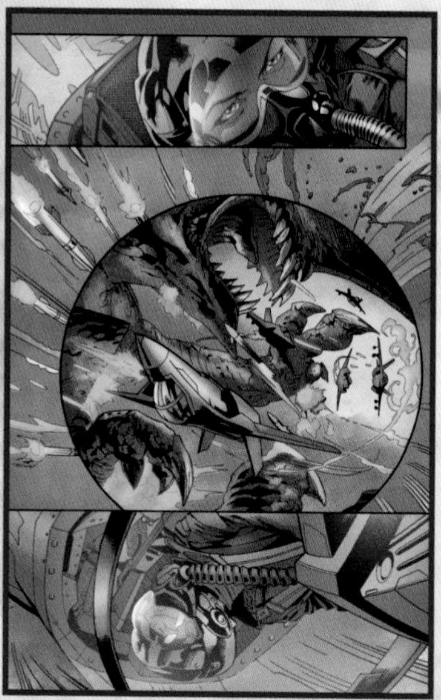

pg. 23

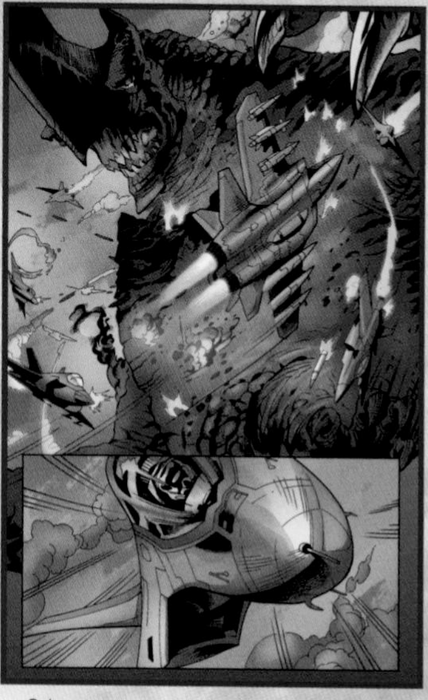

pg. 24

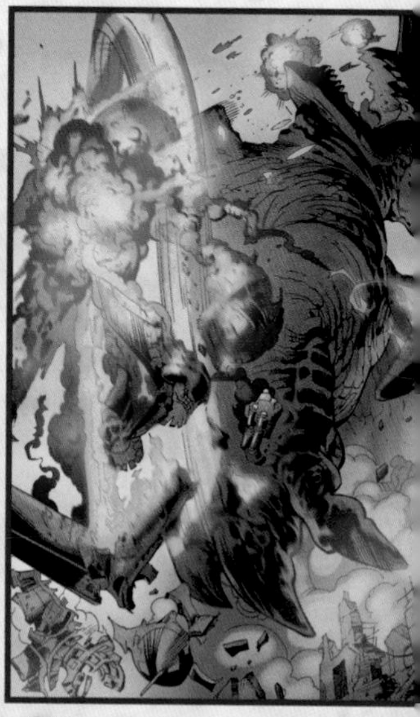

pg. 26

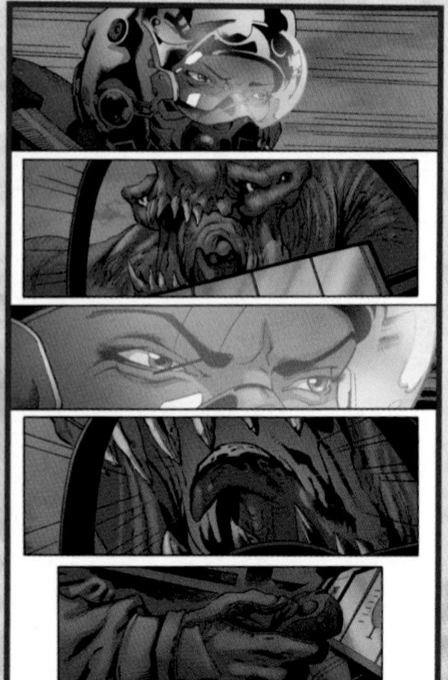

pg. 25

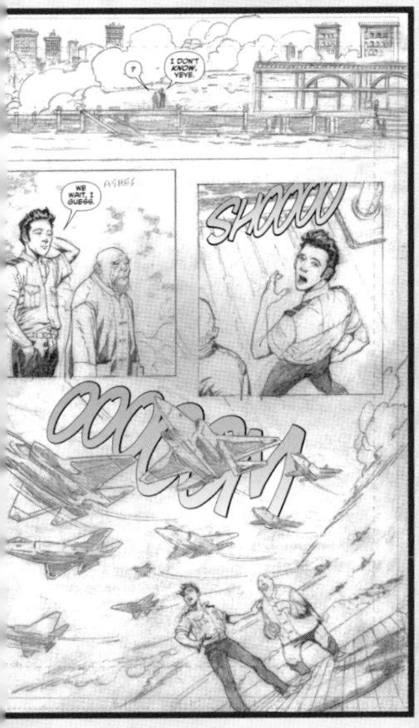
?
I DON'T KNOW, YEYE.
WE WAIT, I GUESS.

0

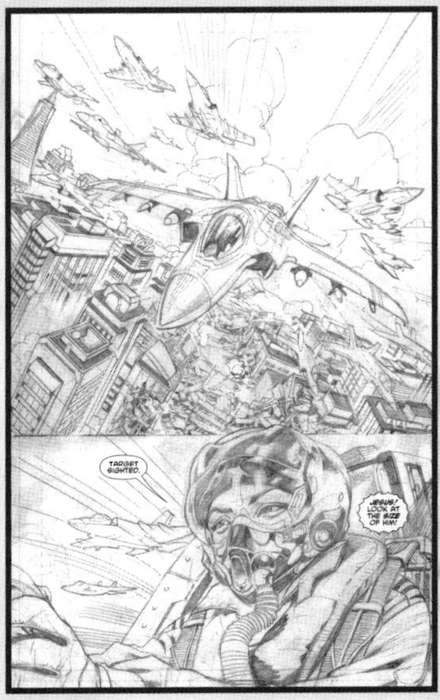
TARGET SIGHTED.
JESUS! LOOK AT THE SIZE OF HIM!

pg. 21

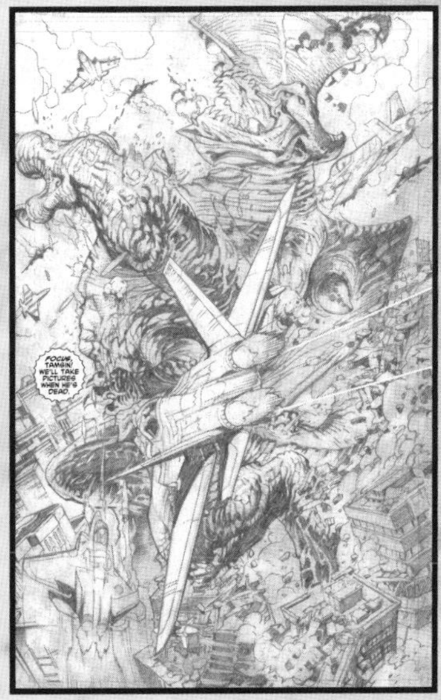
FOCUS, TAMSIN! WE'LL TAKE PICTURES WHEN HE'S DEAD.

pg. 22

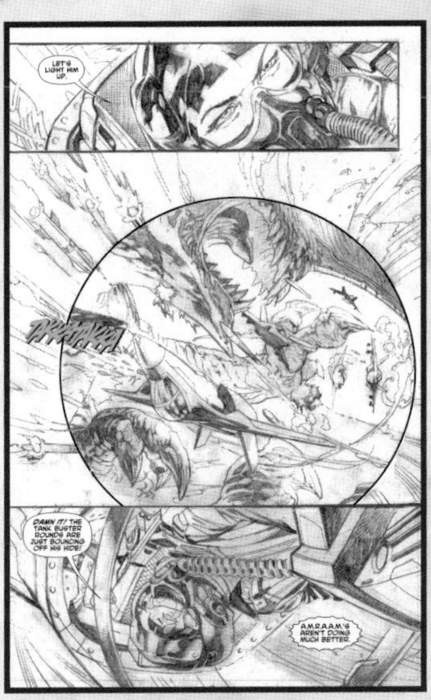
LET'S LIGHT HIM UP.
DAMN IT! THE TANK BUSTER ROUNDS ARE JUST BOUNCING OFF HIS HIDE!
A.M.R.A.A.M.'S AREN'T DOING MUCH BETTER.

pg. 23

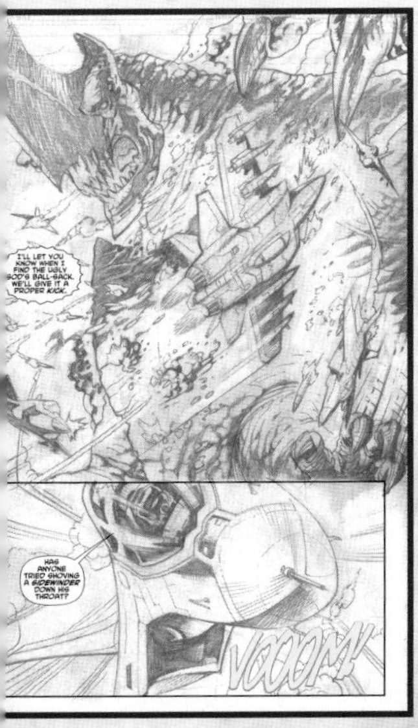
I'LL LET YOU KNOW WHEN I FIND THE UGLY SOD'S BALL-SACK. WE'LL GIVE IT A PROPER KICK.
HAS ANYONE TRIED SHOVING A SIDEWINDER DOWN HIS THROAT?
VOOOM!

4

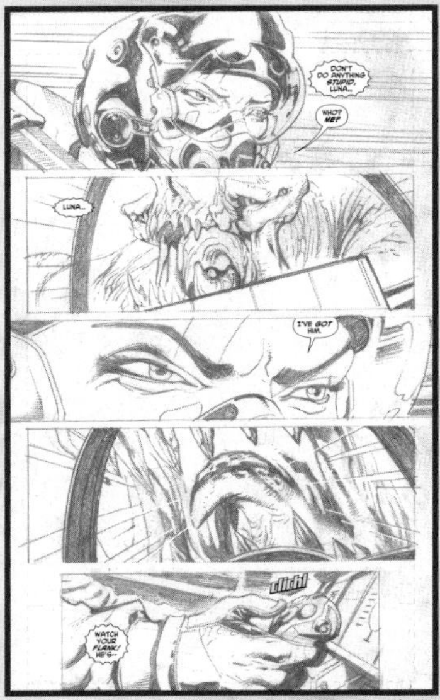
DON'T DO ANYTHING STUPID, LUNA...
WHOT ME?
LUNA...
I'VE GOT HIM.
click!
WATCH YOUR FLANK! HE'S--

pg. 25

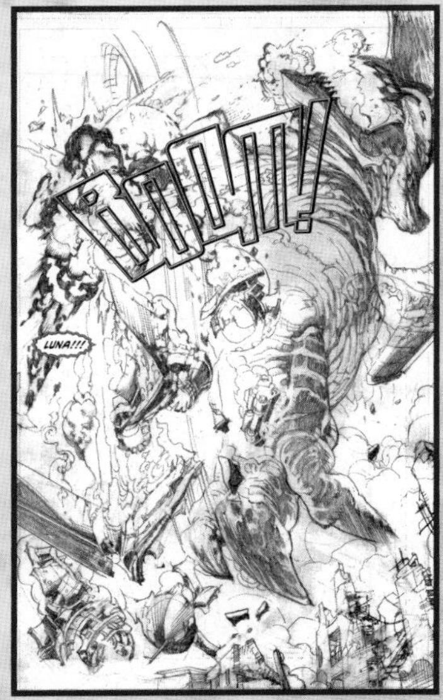
LUNA!!!

pg. 26

While the colorist is working on the page, letterer Patrick Brosseau is creating the balloons & captions and inserting the dialogue & text.

And there you have it!

KAIJU (ky-joo) ***n*** a Japanese word that literally translates to "Strange Beasts." However, the word *kaiju* has been universally translated and defined into English as "monsters" or "giant monsters" and refers to science fiction films from Japan featuring unnatural creatures of immense size.

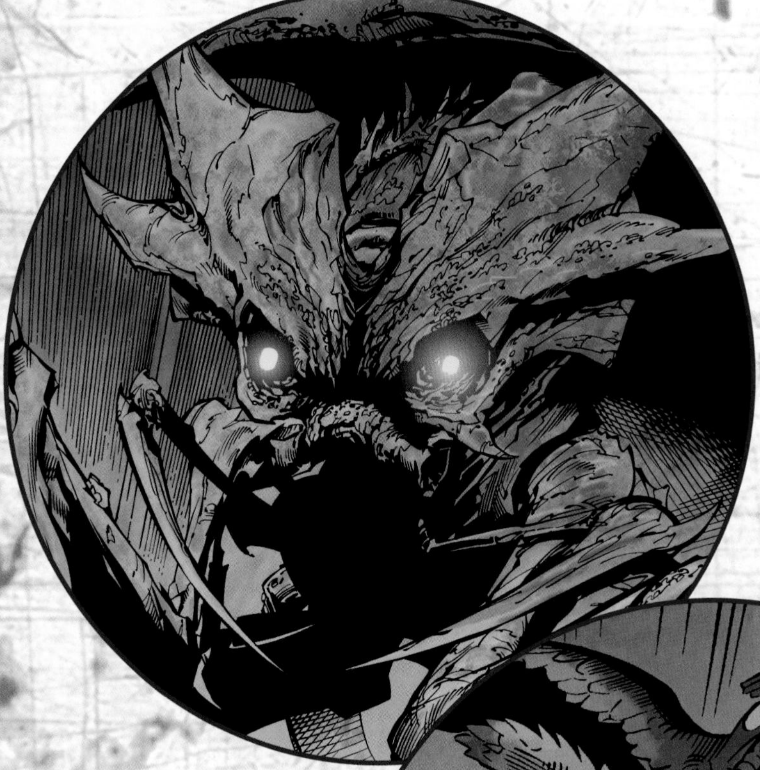

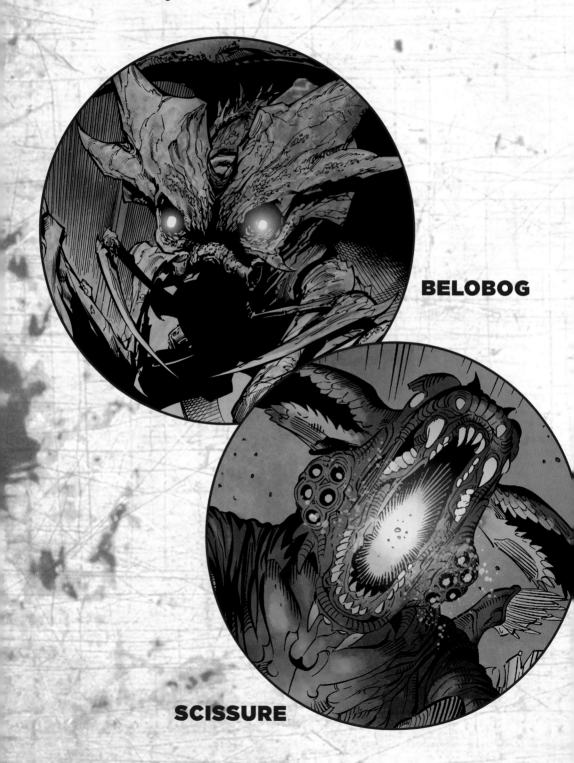

BELOBOG

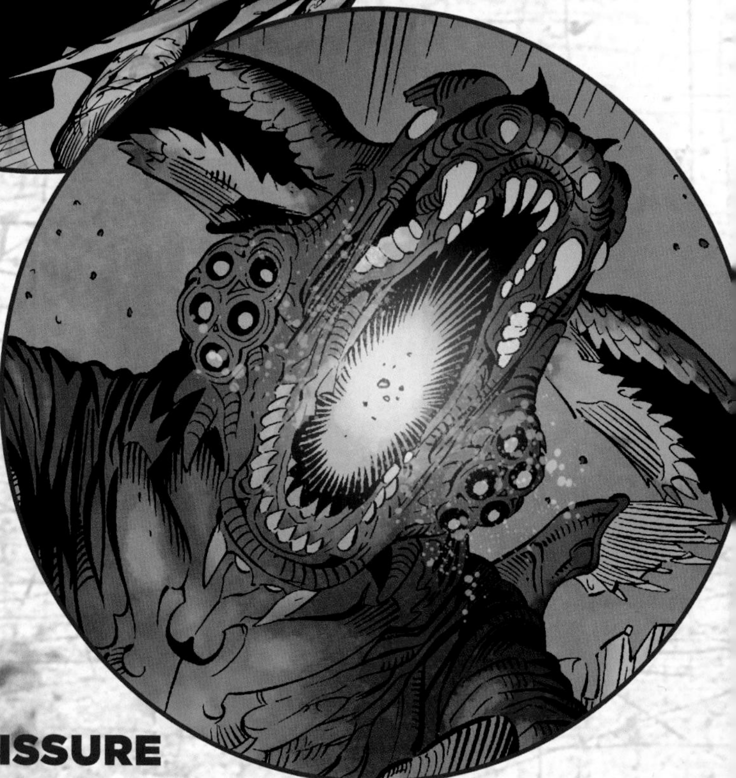

SCISSURE

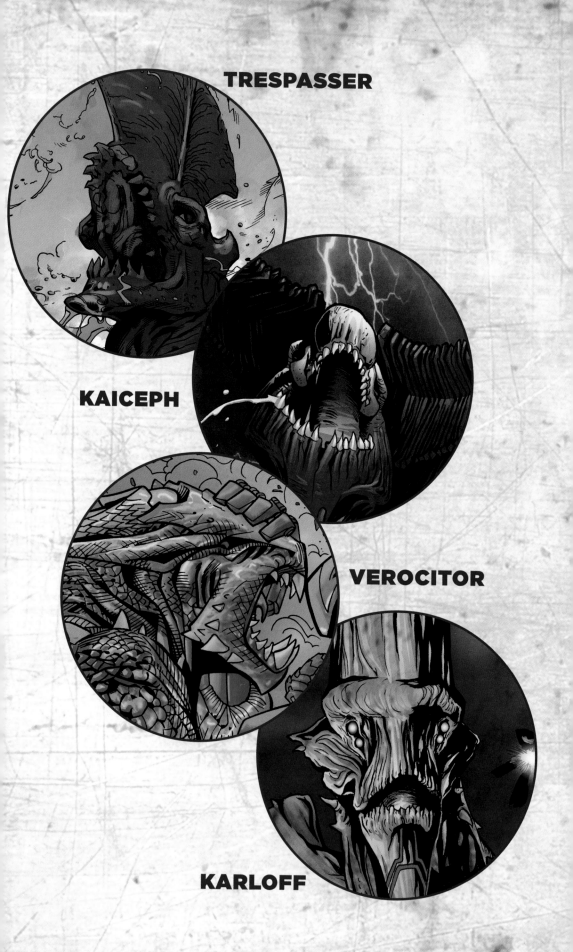

TRESPASSER

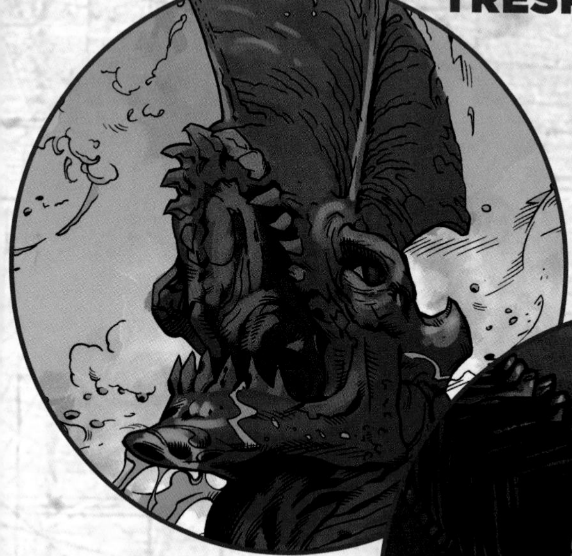

KAICEPH

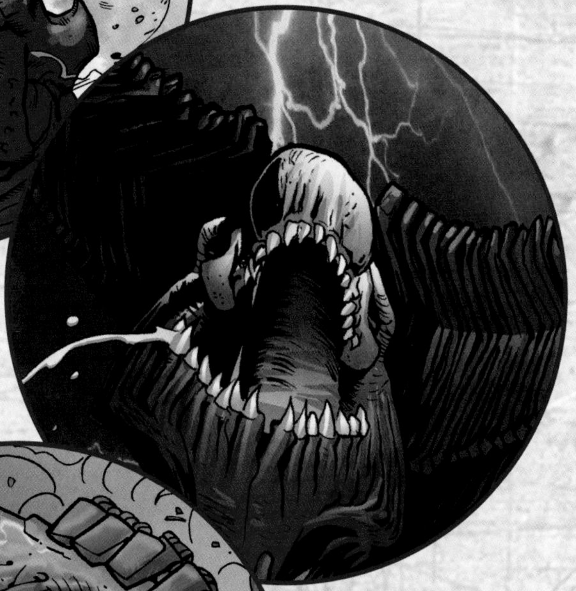

VEROCITOR

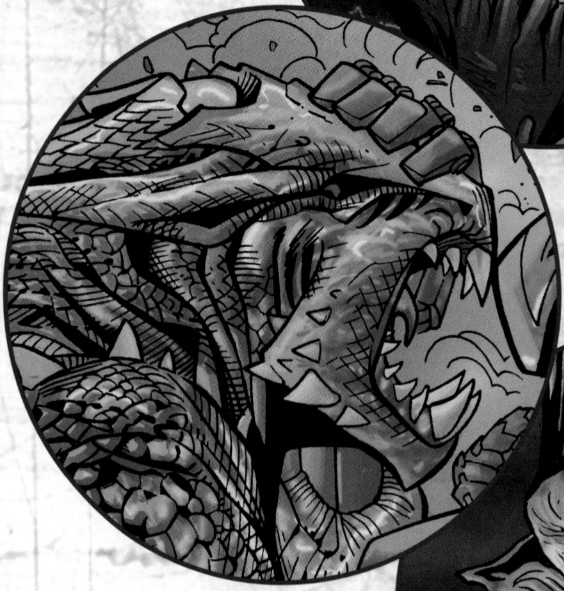

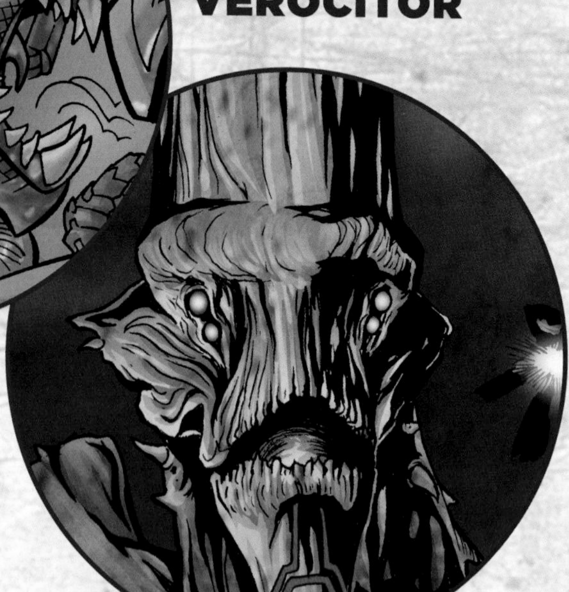

KARLOFF